W9-CDN-741

Beyond

By
John Galsworthy

"Che avo senza Euridice!"

London
William Heinemann

LONDON: WILLIAM HEINEMANN, 1917

PART I

I

At the door of St. George's registry office, Charles Clare Winton strolled forward in the wake of the taxi-cab that was bearing his daughter away with " the fiddler fellow " she had married. His sense of decorum forbade his walking with Nurse Betty—the only other witness of the wedding. A stout woman in a highly emotional condition would have been an incongruous companion to his slim, upright figure, moving with just that unexaggerated swing and balance becoming to a lancer of the old school, even if he has been on the retired list for sixteen years.

Poor Betty! He thought of her with irritated sympathy—she need not have given way to tears on the door-step. She might well feel lost now Gyp was gone, but not so lost as himself! His pale-gloved hand—the one real hand he had, for his right hand had been amputated at the wrist—twisted vexedly at the small, grizzling moustache lifting itself from the corners of his firm lips. On this grey February day he wore no overcoat; faithful to the absolute, almost shamefaced quietness of that wedding, he had not even donned black coat and silk hat, but wore a blue suit and a hard black felt. The instinct of a soldier and hunting man to exhibit no sign whatever of emotion did not desert him this dark day of his life;

but his grey-hazel eyes kept contracting, staring fiercely, contracting again; and, at moments, as if overpowered by some deep feeling, they darkened and seemed to draw back in his head. His face was narrow and weathered and thin-cheeked, with a clean-cut jaw, small ears, hair darker than the moustache, but touched at the side wings with grey—the face of a man of action, self-reliant, resourceful. And his bearing was that of one who has always been a bit of a dandy, and paid attention to " form," yet been conscious sometimes that there were things beyond. A man, who, preserving all the precision of a type, yet had in him a streak of something that was not typical. Such often have tragedy in their pasts.

Making his way towards the park, he turned into Mount Street. There was the house still, though the street had been very different then—the house he had passed, up and down, up and down in the fog, like a ghost, that November afternoon, like a cast-out dog, in such awful, unutterable agony of mind, twenty-three years ago, when Gyp was born. And then to be told at the door—he, with no right to enter, he, loving as he believed man never loved woman—to be told at the door that *she* was dead—dead in bearing what he and she alone knew was their child ! Up and down in the fog, hour after hour, knowing her time was upon her; and at last to be told that ! Of all fates that befall man, surely the most awful is to love too much.

Queer that his route should take him past the very house to-day, after this new bereavement ! Accursed luck—that gout which had sent him to Wiesbaden, last September ! Accursed luck that Gyp had ever set eyes on this fellow Fiorsen, with his fatal fiddle! Certainly not since Gyp had come to live with him, fifteen years ago, had he felt so forlorn and fit for nothing. To-morrow he would get back to Mildenham and see what hard riding would do. Without Gyp— to be without Gyp! A fiddler! A chap who had never been on a horse in his life! And with his crutch-handled cane he switched viciously at the air, as though carving a man in two.

His club, near Hyde Park Corner, had never seemed to him so desolate. From sheer force of habit he went into the card-room. The afternoon had so darkened that electric light already burned, and there were the usual dozen of players seated among the shaded gleams falling decorously on dark-wood tables, on the backs of chairs, on cards and tumblers, the little gilded coffee-cups, the polished nails of fingers holding cigars. A crony challenged him to piquet. He sat down listless. That three-legged whist—bridge—had always offended his fastidiousness—a mangled short cut of a game! Poker had something blatant in it. Piquet, though out of fashion, remained for him the only game worth playing—the only game which still had style. He held good cards, and rose the winner of five pounds that he would willingly have paid to escape the boredom of the bout. Where would they be by now? Past Newbury; Gyp sitting opposite that Swedish fellow with his greenish wildcat's eyes. Something furtive, and so foreign, about him! A mess—if he were any judge of horse or man! Thank God he had tied Gyp's money up—every farthing! And an emotion that was almost jealousy swept him at the thought of the fellow's arms round his soft-haired, dark-eyed daughter—that pretty, willowy creature, so like in face and limb to her whom he had loved so desperately.

Eyes followed him when he left the card-room, for he was one who inspired in other men a kind of admiration—none could say exactly why. Many quite as noted for general good sportsmanship attracted no such attention. Was it " style," or was it the streak of something not quite typical—the brand left on him by the past ?

Abandoning the club, he walked slowly along the railings of Piccadilly towards home, that house in Bury Street, St. James's, which had been his London abode since he was quite young—one of the few in the street that had been left untouched by the general passion for pulling down and building up, which had spoiled half London in his opinion.

A man, more silent than anything on earth, with the soft, quick, dark eyes of a woodcock and a long, greenish, knitted waistcoat, black cutaway, and tight trousers strapped over his boots, opened the door.

" I shan't go out again, Markey. Mrs. Markey must give me some dinner. Anything'll do."

Markey signalled that he had heard, and those brown eyes under eyebrows meeting and forming one long, dark line, took his master in from head to heel. He had already nodded last night, when his wife had said the gov'nor would take it hard. Retiring to the back premises, he jerked his head toward the street and made a motion upward with his hand, by which Mrs. Markey, an astute woman, understood that she had to go out and shop because the gov'nor was dining in. When she had gone, Markey sat down opposite Betty, Gyp's old nurse. The stout woman was still crying in a quiet way. It gave him the fair hump, for he felt inclined to howl like a dog himself. After watching her broad, rosy, tearful face in silence for some minutes, he shook his head, and, with a gulp and a tremor of her comfortable body, Betty desisted. One paid attention to Markey.

Winton went first into his daughter's bedroom, and gazed at its emptied silken order, its deserted silver mirror, twisting viciously at his little moustache. Then, in his sanctum, he sat down before the fire, without turning up the light. Anyone looking in, would have thought he was asleep; but the drowsy influence of that deep chair and cosy fire had drawn him back into the long-ago. What unhappy chance had made him pass *her* house to-day!

Some say there is no such thing as an affinity, no case —of a man, at least—made bankrupt of passion by a single love. In theory, it may be so; in fact, there are such men—neck-or-nothing men, quiet and self-contained, the last to expect that nature will play them such a trick, the last to desire such surrender of themselves, the last to know when their fate is on them. Who could have seemed to himself, and, indeed, to others, less likely than Charles Clare Winton to fall over head and ears in love when he stepped into the Belvoir Hunt ballroom at Grantham that December evening, twenty-four years ago? A keen soldier, a dandy, a first-rate man to hounds, already almost a proverb in his regiment for coolness and for a sort of courteous disregard of women as among the minor things of life—he had stood there by the door, in no hurry to dance, making survey with an air that just did not give an impression of " side " because it was not at all put on. And—behold !—*she* had walked past him, and his world was changed for ever. Was it an illusion of light that made her whole spirit seem to shine through a half-startled glance ? Or a little trick of gait, a swaying, seductive balance of body; was it the way her hair waved back, or a subtle scent, as of a flower ? What was it ? The wife of a squire of those parts, with a house in London. Her name ? It doesn't matter—she has been long enough dead. There was no excuse—not an ill-treated woman; an ordinary, humdrum marriage, of three years' standing; no children. An amiable good fellow of a husband, fifteen years older than herself, inclined already to be an invalid. No excuse ! Yet, in one month from that night, Winton and she were lovers, not only in thought but in deed. A thing so utterly beyond " good form " and his sense of what was honourable and becoming in an officer and gentleman that it was simply never a question of weighing pro and con, the cons had it so completely. And yet from that first evening, he was hers, she his. For each of them the one thought was how to be with the other. If so—why did they not at least go off together ? Not for want of his beseech-ing. And no doubt, if she had survived Gyp's birth, they would have gone. But to face the prospect of ruining two men, as it looked to her, had till then been too much for that soft-hearted creature. Death stilled her struggle before it was decided. There are women in whom utter devotion can still go hand in hand with a doubting soul. Such are generally the most fascinating; for the power of hard and prompt decision robs women of mystery, of the subtle atmo-sphere of change and chance. Though she had but one part in four of foreign blood, she was not at all English. But Winton was English to his back-bone,

English in his sense of form, and in that curious streak of whole-hearted desperation that will break form to smithereens in one department and leave it untouched in every other of its owner's life. To have called Winton a " crank " would never have occurred to anyone—his hair was always perfectly parted; his boots glowed; he was hard and reticent, accepting and observing every canon of well-bred existence. Yet, in that, his one infatuation, he was as lost to the world and its opinion as the longest-haired lentil-eater of us all. Though at any moment during that one year of their love he would have risked his life and sacrificed his career for a whole day in her company, he never, by word or look, compromised her. He had carried his punctilious observance of her " honour " to a point more bitter than death, consenting, even, to her covering up the tracks of their child's coming. Paying that gambler's debt was by far the bravest deed of his life, and even now its memory festered.

To this very room he had come back after hearing she was dead; this very room which he had refurnished to her taste, so that even now, with its satinwood chairs, little dainty Jacobean bureau, shaded old brass candelabra, divan, it still had an air exotic to bachelordom. There, on the table, had been a letter recalling him to his regiment, ordered on active service. If he had realized what he would go through before he had the chance of trying to lose his life out there, he would undoubtedly have taken that life, sitting in this very chair before the fire—the chair sacred to her and memory. He had not the luck he wished for in that little war—men who don't care whether they live or die seldom have. He secured nothing but distinction. When it was over, he went on, with a few more lines in his face, a few more wrinkles in his heart, soldiering, shooting tigers, pig-sticking, playing polo, riding to hounds harder than ever; giving nothing away to the world; winning steadily the curious, uneasy admiration that men feel for those who combine reckless daring with an ice-cool manner. Since he was less of a talker even than most of his kind, and had never in his life talked of women, he did not gain the reputation of a woman-hater, though he so manifestly avoided them. After six years' service in India and Egypt, he lost his right hand in a charge against dervishes, and had, perforce, to retire, with the rank of major, aged thirty-four. For a long time he had hated the very thought of the child—his child, in giving birth to whom the woman he loved had died. Then came a curious change of feeling; and for three years before his return to England, he had been in the habit of sending home odds and ends picked up in the bazaars, to serve as toys. In return, he had received, twice annually at least, a letter from the man who thought himself Gyp's father. These letters he read and answered. The squire was likable, and had been fond of *her ;* and though never once had it seemed possible to Winton to have acted otherwise than he did, he had all the time preserved a just and formal sense of the wrong he had done this man. He did not experience remorse, but he had always an irksome feeling as of a debt unpaid, mitigated by knowledge that no one had ever suspected, and discounted by memory of the awful torture he had endured to make sure against suspicion.

When, plus distinction and minus his hand, he was at last back in England, the squire had come to see him. The poor man was failing fast from Bright's disease. Winton entered again that house in Mount Street with an emotion, to stifle which required more courage than any cavalry charge. But one whose heart, as he would have put it, is " in the right place " does not indulge the quaverings of his nerves, and he faced those rooms where he had last seen her, faced that lonely little dinner with her husband, without sign of feeling. He did not see little Ghita, or Gyp, as she had nicknamed herself, for she was already in her bed; and it was a whole month before he brought himself to go there at an hour when he could see the child if he would. The fact is, he was afraid. What would the sight of this little creature stir in him ? When Betty, the nurse, brought her in to see the soldier gentleman with " the leather hand," who had sent her those funny toys, she stood calmly staring with her large, deep-brown eyes. Being seven, her little brown-velvet frock barely reached the knees of her thin, brown-stockinged legs planted one just in front of the other, as might be the legs of a small brown bird; the oval of her gravely wondering face was warm cream colour without red in it, except that of the lips, which were neither full nor thin, and had a little tuck, the tiniest possible dimple at one corner. Her hair of warm dark brown had been specially brushed and tied with a narrow red ribbon back from her forehead, which was broad and rather low, and this added to her gravity. Her eyebrows were thin and dark and perfectly arched; her little nose was perfectly straight, her little chin in perfect balance between round and point. She stood and stared till Winton smiled. Then the gravity of her face broke, her lips parted, her eyes seemed to fly a little. And Winton's heart turned over within him—she was the

very child of her that he had lost! And he said, in
a voice that seemed to him to tremble:

"Well, Gyp?"

"Thank you for my toys; I like them."

He held out his hand, and she gravely put her small
hand into it. A sense of solace, as if someone had
slipped a finger in and smoothed his heart, came over
Winton. Gently, so as not to startle her, he raised
her hand a little, bent, and kissed it. It may have
been from his instant recognition that here was one
as sensitive as child could be, or the way many soldiers
acquire from dealing with their men, those simple,
shrewd children—or some deeper instinctive sense of
ownership between them; whatever it was, from that
moment, Gyp conceived for him a rushing admiration,
one of those headlong affections children will sometimes
take for the most unlikely persons.

He used to go there at an hour when he knew the
squire would be asleep, between two and five. After
he had been with Gyp, walking in the park, riding with
her in the Row, or on wet days sitting in her lonely
nursery telling stories, while stout Betty looked on
half hypnotized, a rather queer and doubting look on
her comfortable face—after such hours, he found it
difficult to go to the squire's study and sit opposite
him, smoking. Those interviews reminded him too
much of past days, when he had kept such desperate
check on himself—too much of the old inward chafing
against the other man's legal ownership—too much
of the debt owing. But Winton was triple-proofed
against betrayal of feeling. The squire welcomed him
eagerly, saw nothing, felt nothing, was grateful for
his goodness to the child. Well, well! He had died
in the following spring. And Winton found that he

had been made Gyp's guardian and trustee. Since
his wife's death, the squire had muddled his affairs,
his estate was heavily mortgaged; but Winton accepted
the position with an almost savage satisfaction, and,
from that moment, schemed deeply to get Gyp all to
himself. The Mount Street house was sold; the
Lincolnshire place let. She and Nurse Betty were
installed at his own hunting-box, Mildenham. In
this effort to get her away from all the squire's relations,
he did not scruple to employ to the utmost the power
he undoubtedly had of making people feel him un-
approachable. He was never impolite to any of them;
he simply froze them out. Having plenty of money
himself, his motives could not be called in question.
In one year he had isolated her from all except stout
Betty. He had no qualms, for Gyp was no more
happy away from him than he from her. He had but
one bad half-hour. It came when he had at last
decided that she should be called by his name, if not
legally at least by custom, round Mildenham. It was
to Markey he had given the order that Gyp was to
be little Miss Winton for the future. When he came
in from hunting that day, Betty was waiting in his
study. She stood in the centre of the emptiest part
of that rather dingy room, as far as possible away
from any good or chattel. How long she had been
standing there, heaven only knew; but her round,
rosy face was confused between awe and resolution,
and she had made a sad mess of her white apron.
Her blue eyes met Winton's with a sort of desperation.

"About what Markey told me, sir. My old master
wouldn't have liked it, sir."

Touched on the raw by this reminder that before
the world he had been nothing to the loved one, that

before the world the squire, who had been nothing to her, had been everything, Winton said icily:

"Indeed! You will be good enough to comply with my wish, all the same."

The stout woman's face grew very red. She burst out, breathless:

"Yes, sir; but I've seen what I've seen. I never said anything, but I've got eyes. If Miss Gyp's to take your name, sir, then tongues'll wag, and my dear, dead mistress——"

But at the look on his face she stopped, with her mouth open.

"You will be kind enough to keep your thoughts to yourself. If any word or deed of yours gives the slightest excuse for talk—you go. Understand me, you go, and you never see Gyp again! In the meantime you will do what I ask. Gyp is my adopted daughter."

She had always been a little afraid of him, but she had never seen that look in his eyes or heard him speak in that voice. And she bent her full moon of a face and went, with her apron crumpled as apron had never been, and tears in her eyes. And Winton, at the window, watching the darkness gather, the leaves flying by on a sou'-westerly wind, drank to the dregs a cup of bitter triumph. He had never had the right to that dead, forever-loved mother of his child. He meant to have the child. If tongues must wag, let them! This was a defeat of all his previous precaution, a deep victory of natural instinct. And his eyes narrowed and stared into the darkness.

II

In spite of his victory over all human rivals in the heart of Gyp, Winton had a rival whose strength he fully realized perhaps for the first time now that she was gone, and he, before the fire, was brooding over her departure and the past. Not likely that one of his decisive type, whose life had so long been bound up with swords and horses, would grasp what music might mean to a little girl. Such ones, he knew, required to be taught scales, and " In a Cottage near a Wood " with other melodies. He took care not to go within sound of them, so that he had no conception of the avidity with which Gyp had mopped up all, and more than all, her governess could teach her. He was blind to the rapture with which she listened to any stray music that came its way to Mildenham—to carols in the Christmas dark, to certain hymns, and one special " Nunc Dimittis " in the village church, attended with a hopeless regularity; to the horn of the hunter far out in the quivering, dripping coverts; even to Markey's whistling, which was full and strangely sweet.

He could share her love of dogs and horses, take an anxious interest in her way of catching bumblebees in the hollow of her hand and putting them to her small, delicate ears to hear them buzz, sympathize with her continual ravages among the flower-beds, in the old-fashioned garden, full of lilacs and laburnums in spring, pinks, roses, cornflowers in summer, dahlias and sunflowers in autumn, and always a little neglected and overgrown, a little squeezed in, and elbowed by the more important surrounding paddocks. He could sympathize with her attempts to draw his attention to the song of birds; but it was simply not in him to understand how she loved and craved for music. She was a cloudy little creature, up and down in mood—rather like a brown lady spaniel that she had, now gay as a butterfly, now brooding as night. Any touch of harshness she took to heart fearfully. She was the strangest compound of pride and self-disparagement; the qualities seemed mixed in her so deeply that neither she nor anyone knew of which her cloudy fits were the result. Being so sensitive, she " fancied " things terribly. Things that others did to her, and thought nothing of, often seemed to her conclusive evidence that she was not loved by anybody, which was dreadfully unjust, because she wanted to love everyone—nearly. Then suddenly she would feel: " If they don't love me, I don't care. I don't want anything of anybody !" Presently, all would blow away just like a cloud, and she would love and be gay, until something fresh, perhaps not at all meant to hurt her, would again hurt her horribly. In reality, the whole household loved and admired her. But she was one of those delicate-treading beings, born with a skin too few, who—and especially in childhood—suffer from themselves in a world born with a skin too many.

To Winton's extreme delight, she took to riding as a duck to water, and knew no fear on horseback. She had the best governess he could get her, the daughter of an admiral, and, therefore, in distressed circumstances; and later on, a tutor for her music,

who came twice a week all the way from London—
a sardonic man who cherished for her even more
secret admiration than she for him. In fact, every
male thing fell in love with her at least a little. Unlike
most girls, she never had an epoch of awkward plainness, but grew like a flower, evenly, steadily. Winton
often gazed at her with a sort of intoxication; the turn
of her head, the way those perfectly shaped, wonderfully clear brown eyes would " fly," the set of her
straight, round neck, the very shaping of her limbs
were all such poignant reminders of what he had so
loved. And yet, for all that likeness to her mother,
there was a difference, both in form and character.
Gyp had, as it were, an extra touch of " breeding,"
more chiselling in body, more fastidiousness in soul,
a little more poise, a little more sheer grace; in mood,
more variance, in mind, more clarity and, mixed with
her sweetness, a distinct spice of scepticism which her
mother had lacked.

In modern times there are no longer " toasts," or
she would have been one with both the hunts. Though
delicate in build, she was not frail, and when her blood
was up would " go " all day, and come in so bone-
tired that she would drop on to the tiger skin before
the fire, rather than face the stairs. Life at Mildenham
was lonely, save for Winton's hunting cronies, and they
but few, for his spiritual dandyism did not gladly
suffer the average country gentleman and his frigid
courtesy frightened women.

Besides, as Betty had foreseen, tongues did wag—
those tongues of the countryside, avid of anything
that might spice the tedium of dull lives and brains.
And, though no breath of gossip came to Winton's
ears, no women visited at Mildenham. Save for the

friendly casual acquaintanceships of churchyard, hunting-field, and local race-meetings, Gyp grew up knowing hardly any of her own sex. This dearth developed her reserve, kept her backward in sex-perception, gave her a faint, unconscious contempt for men—creatures always at the beck and call of her smile, and so easily disquieted by a little frown—gave her also a secret yearning for companions of her own gender. Any girl or woman that she did chance to meet always took a fancy to her, because she was so nice to them, which made the transitory nature of these friendships tantalizing. She was incapable of jealousies or backbiting. Let men beware of such—there is coiled in their fibre a secret fascination !

Gyp's moral and spiritual growth was not the sort of subject that Winton could pay much attention to. It was pre-eminently a matter one did not talk about. Outward forms, such as going to church, should be preserved; manners should be taught her by his own example as much as possible; beyond this, nature must look after things. His view had much real wisdom. She was a quick and voracious reader, bad at remembering what she read; and though she had soon devoured all the books in Winton's meagre library, including Byron, Whyte-Melville, and Humboldt's " Cosmos," they had not left too much on her mind. The attempts of her little governess to impart religion were somewhat arid of result, and the interest of the vicar, Gyp, with her instinctive spice of scepticism, soon put into the same category as the interest of all the other males she knew. She felt that he enjoyed calling her " my dear " and patting her shoulder, and that this enjoyment was enough reward for his exertions.

Tucked away in that little old dark manor house, whose stables alone were up to date—three hours from London, and some thirty miles from The Wash, it must be confessed that herupbringing lacked modernity. About twice a year, Winton took her up to town to stay with his unmarried sister Rosamund in Curzon Street. Those weeks, if they did nothing else, increased her natural taste for charming clothes, fortified her teeth, and fostered her passion for music and the theatre. But the two main nourishments of the modern girl—discussion and games—she lacked utterly. Moreover, those years of her life from fifteen to nineteen were before the social resurrection of 1906, and the world still crawled like a winter fly on a window-pane. Winton was a Tory, Aunt Rosamund a Tory, everybody round her a Tory. The only spiritual development she underwent all those years of her girlhood was through her headlong love for her father. After all, was there any other way in which she could really have developed? Only love makes fruitful the soul. The sense of form that both had in such high degree prevented much demonstration; but to be with him, do things for him, to admire, and credit him with perfection; and, since she could not exactly wear the same clothes or speak in the same clipped, quiet, decisive voice, to dislike the clothes and voices of other men—all this was precious to her beyond everything. If she inherited from him that fastidious sense of form, she also inherited his capacity for putting all her eggs in one basket. And since her company alone gave him real happiness, the current of love flowed over her heart all the time. Though she never realized it, abundant love *for* somebody was as necessary to her as water running up the stems

of flowers, abundant love *from* somebody as needful
as sunshine on their petals. And Winton's somewhat
frequent little runs to town, to Newmarket, or where
not, were always marked in her by a fall of the
barometer, which recovered as his return grew near.

One part of her education, at all events, was not
neglected—cultivation of an habitual sympathy with
her poorer neighbours. Without concerning himself
in the least with problems or sociology, Winton had
by nature an open hand and heart for cottagers, and
abominated interference with their lives. And so it
came about that Gyp, who, by nature also never set
foot anywhere without invitation, was always hearing
the words: " Step in, Miss Gyp "; " Step in, and sit
down, lovey," and a good many words besides from
even the boldest and baddest characters. There is
nothing like a soft and pretty face and sympathetic
listening for seducing the hearts of " the people."

So passed the eleven years till she was nineteen and
Winton forty-six. Then, under the wing of her little
governess, she went to the hunt-ball. She had revolted against appearing a " fluffy miss," wanting to
be considered at once full-fledged; so that her dress,
perfect in fit, was not white but palest maize-colour,
as if she had already been to dances. She had all
Winton's dandyism, and just so much more as was
appropriate to her sex. With her dark hair, wonderfully fluffed and coiled, waving across her forehead,
her neck bare for the first time, her eyes really " flying,"
and a demeanour perfectly cool—as though she knew
that light and movement, covetous looks, soft speeches,
and admiration were her birthright—she was more
beautiful than even Winton had thought her. At her
breast she wore some sprigs of yellow jasmine procured

by him from town—a flower of whose scent she was very fond, and that he had never seen worn in ball-rooms. That swaying, delicate creature, warmed by excitement, reminded him, in every movement and by every glance of her eyes, of her whom he had first met at just such a ball as this. And by the carriage of his head, the twist of his little moustache, he conveyed to the world the pride he was feeling.

That evening held many sensations for Gyp—some delightful, one confused, one unpleasant. She revelled in her success. Admiration was very dear to her. She passionately enjoyed dancing, loved feeling that she was dancing well and giving pleasure. But, twice over, she sent away her partners, smitten with compassion for her little governess sitting there against the wall—all alone, with no one to take notice of her, because she was elderly, and roundabout, poor darling ! And, to that loyal person's horror, she insisted on sitting beside her all through two dances. Nor would she go into supper with anyone but Winton. Returning to the ballroom on his arm, she overheard an elderly woman say: " Oh, don't you know ? Of course he really *is* her father !" and an elderly man answer: " Ah, that accounts for it—quite so !" With those eyes at the back of the head which the very sensitive possess, she could see their inquisitive, cold, slightly malicious glances, and knew they were speaking of her. And just then her partner came for her.

" Really *is* her father !" The words meant *too* much to be grasped this evening of full sensations. They left a little bruise somewhere, but softened and anointed, just a sense of confusion at the back of her mind. And very soon came that other sensation, so disillusioning, that all else was crowded out. It was

after a dance—a splendid dance with a good-looking
man quite twice her age. They were sitting behind
some palms, he murmuring in his mellow, flown voice
admiration for her dress, when suddenly he bent his
flushed face and kissed her bare arm above the elbow.
If he had hit her he could not have astonished or hurt
her more. It seemed to her innocence that he would
never have done such a thing if she had not said something dreadful to encourage him. Without a word
she got up, gazed at him a moment with eyes dark
from pain, shivered, and slipped away. She went
straight to Winton. From her face, all closed up,
tightened lips, and the familiar little droop at their
corners, he knew something dire had happened, and
his eyes boded ill for the person who had hurt her; but
she would say nothing except that she was tired and
wanted to go home. And so, with the little faithful
governess, who, having been silent perforce nearly
all the evening, was now full of conversation, they
drove out into the frosty night. Winton sat beside
the chauffeur, smoking viciously, his fur collar turned
up over his ears, his eyes stabbing the darkness,
under his round, low-drawn fur cap. Who had dared
upset his darling? And, within the car, the little
governess chattered softly, and Gyp, shrouded in lace,
in her dark corner sat silent, seeing nothing but the
vision of that insult. Sad end to a lovely night!

She lay awake long hours in the darkness, while a
sort of coherence was forming in her mind. Those
words: " Really *is* her father!" and that man's kissing
of her bare arm were a sort of revelation of sex-mystery,
hardening the consciousness that there was something
at the back of her life. A child so sensitive had not
of course, quite failed to feel the spiritual draughts

around her; but instinctively she had recoiled from more definite perceptions. The time before Winton came was all so faint—Betty, toys, short glimpses of a kind, invalidish man called "Papa." As in that word there was no depth compared with the word "Dad" bestowed on Winton, so there had been no depth in her feelings towards the squire. When a girl has no memory of her mother, how dark are many things! None, except Betty, had ever talked of her mother. There was nothing sacred in Gyp's associations, no faiths to be broken by any knowledge that might come to her; isolated from other girls, she had little realization even of the conventions. Still, she suffered horribly, lying there in the dark—from bewilderment, from thorns dragged over her skin, rather than from a stab in the heart. The knowledge of something about her conspicuous, doubtful, provocative of insult, as she thought, grievously hurt her delicacy. Those few wakeful hours made a heavy mark. She fell asleep at last, still all in confusion, and woke up with a passionate desire to *know*. All that morning she sat at her piano, playing, refusing to go out, frigid to Betty and the little governess, till the former was reduced to tears and the latter to Wordsworth. After tea she went to Winton's study, that dingy little room where he never studied anything, with leather chairs and books which—except "Mr. Jorrocks," Byron, those on the care of horses, and the novels of Whyte-Melville—were never read; with prints of superequine celebrities, his sword, and photographs of Gyp and of brother officers on the walls. Two bright spots there were indeed—the fire, and the little bowl that Gyp always kept filled with flowers.

When she came gliding in like that, a slender,

rounded figure, her creamy, dark-eyed, oval face all cloudy, she seemed to Winton to have grown up of a sudden. He had known all day that something was coming, and had been cudgelling his brains finely. From the fervour of his love for her, he felt an anxiety that was almost fear. What could have happened last night—that first night of her entrance into society —meddlesome, gossiping society ! She slid down to the floor against his knee. He could not see her face, could not even touch her; for she had settled down on his right side. He mastered his tremors and said:

" Well, Gyp—tired ?"

" No."

" A little bit ?"

" No."

" Was it up to what you thought, last night ?"

" Yes."

The logs hissed and crackled; the long flames ruffled in the chimney-draft; the wind roared outside—then, so suddenly that it took his breath away:

" Dad, are you really and truly my father ?"

When that which one has always known might happen at last does happen, how little one is prepared ! In the few seconds before an answer that could in no way be evaded, Winton had time for a tumult of reflection. A less resolute character would have been caught by utter mental blankness, then flung itself in panic on " Yes " or " No." But Winton was incapable of losing his head; he would not answer without having faced the consequences of his reply. To be her father was the most warming thing in his life; but if he avowed it, how far would he injure her love for him ? What did a girl know ? How make her understand ? What would her feeling be about her

dead mother? How would that dead loved one feel?
What would she have wished?

It was a cruel moment. And the girl, pressed against
his knee, with face hidden, gave him no help. Impossible to keep it from her, now that her instinct was
roused! Silence, too, would answer for him. And
clenching his hand on the arm of his chair, he said:

"Yes, Gyp; your mother and I loved each other."

He felt a quiver go through her, would have given
much to see her face. What, even now, did she understand? Well, it must be gone through with, and he
said:

"What made you ask?"

She shook her head and murmured:

"I'm glad."

Grief, shock, even surprise would have roused all
his loyalty to the dead, all the old stubborn bitterness,
and he would have frozen up against her. But this
acquiescent murmur made him long to smooth it
down.

"Nobody has ever known. She died when you
were born. It was a fearful grief to me. If you've
heard anything, it's just gossip, because you go by
my name. Your mother was never talked about.
But it's best you should know, now you're grown up.
People don't often love as she and I loved. You
needn't be ashamed."

She had not moved, and her face was still turned
from him. She said quietly:

"I'm not ashamed. Am I very like her?"

"Yes; more than I could ever have hoped."

Very low she said:

"Then you don't love me for myself?"

Winton was but dimly conscious of how that question

revealed her nature, its power of piercing instinctively
to the heart of things, its sensitive pride, and demand
for utter and exclusive love. To things that go too
deep, one opposes the bulwark of obtuseness. And,
smiling, he simply said:

" What do you think ?"

Then, to his dismay, he perceived that she was
crying—struggling against it so that her shoulder
shook against his knee. He had hardly ever known
her cry, not in all the disasters of unstable youth, and
she had received her full meed of knocks and tumbles.
He could only stroke that shoulder, and say:

" Don't cry, Gyp; don't cry !"

She ceased as suddenly as she had begun, got up,
and, before he too could rise, was gone.

That evening, at dinner, she was just as usual.
He could not detect the slightest difference in her voice
or manner, or in her good-night kiss. And so a moment
that he had dreaded for years was over, leaving only
the faint shame which follows a breach of reticence on
the spirits of those who worship it. While the old
secret had been quite undisclosed, it had not troubled
him. Disclosed, it hurt him. But Gyp, in those
twenty-four hours, had left childhood behind for good;
her feeling toward men had hardened. If she did not
hurt them a little, they would hurt her ! The sex-
instinct had come to life. To Winton she gave as
much love as ever, even more, perhaps; but the dew
was off.

III

THE next two years were much less solitary, passed in more or less constant gaiety. His confession spurred Winton on to the fortification of his daughter's position. He would stand no nonsense, would not have her looked on askance. There is nothing like " style " for carrying the defences of society—only, it must be the genuine thing. Whether at Mildenham, or in London under the wing of his sister, there was no difficulty. Gyp was too pretty, Winton too cool, his quietness too formidable. She had every advantage. Society only troubles itself to make front against the visibly weak.

The happiest time of a girl's life is that when all appreciate and covet her, and she herself is free as air—a queen of hearts, for none of which she hankers; or, if not the happiest, at all events it is the gayest time. What did Gyp care whether hearts ached for her—she knew not love as yet, perhaps would never know the pains of unrequited love. Intoxicated with life, she led her many admirers a pretty dance, treating them with a sort of bravura. She did not want them to be unhappy, but she simply could not take them seriously. Never was any girl so heart-free. She was a queer mixture in those days, would give up any pleasure for Winton, and most for Betty or her aunt— her little governess was gone—but of nobody else did she seem to take account, accepting all that was laid at her feet as the due of her looks, her dainty frocks,

25

her music, her good riding and dancing, her talent for amateur theatricals and mimicry. Winton, whom at least she never failed, watched that glorious fluttering with quiet pride and satisfaction. He was getting to those years when a man of action dislikes interruption of the grooves into which his activity has fallen. He pursued his hunting, racing, card-playing, and his very stealthy alms and services to lame ducks of his old regiment, their families, and other unfortunates— happy in knowing that Gyp was always as glad to be with him as he to be with her. Hereditary gout, too, had begun to bother him.

The day that she came of age they were up in town, and he summoned her to the room, in which he now sat by the fire recalling all these things, to receive an account of his stewardship. He had nursed her greatly embarrassed inheritance very carefully till it amounted to some twenty thousand pounds. He had never told her of it—the subject was dangerous, and, since his own means were ample, she had not wanted for anything. When he had explained exactly what she owned, shown her how it was invested, and told her that she must now open her own banking account, she stood gazing at the sheets of paper, whose items she had been supposed to understand, and her face gathered the look which meant that she was troubled. Without lifting her eyes she asked:

"Does it all come from—him ?"

He had not expected that, and flushed under his tan.

"No; eight thousand of it was your mother's."

Gyp looked at him, and said:

"Then I won't take the rest—please, Dad."

Winton felt a sort of crabbed pleasure. What should be done with that money if she did not take it, he did not in the least know. But not to take it was like her, made her more than ever his daughter—a kind of final victory. He turned away to the window from which he had so often watched for her mother. There was the corner she used to turn ! In one minute, surely she would be standing there, colour glowing in her cheeks, her eyes soft behind her veil, her breast heaving a little with her haste, waiting for his embrace. There she would stand, drawing up her veil. He turned round. Difficult to believe it was not she ! And he said:

"Very well, my love. But you will take the equivalent from me instead. The other can be put by; someone will benefit some day !"

At those unaccustomed words, " My love " from his undemonstrative lips, the colour mounted in her cheeks and her eyes shone. She threw her arms round his neck.

She had her fill of music in those days, taking piano lessons from a Monsieur Harmost, a grey-haired native of Liége, with mahogany cheeks and the touch of an angel, who kept her hard at it and called her his " little friend." There was scarcely a concert of merit that she did not attend or a musician of mark whose playing she did not know, and, though fastidiousness saved her from squirming in adoration round the feet of those prodigious performers, she perched them all on pedestals, men and women alike, and now and then met them at her aunt's house in Curzon Street.

Aunt Rosamund, also musical, so far as breeding would allow, stood for a good deal to Gyp, who had built up about her a romantic story of love wrecked by pride from a few words she had once let drop. She was a tall and handsome woman, a year older than Winton, with a long, aristocratic face, deep-blue, rather shining eyes, a gentlemanly manner, warm heart, and one of those indescribable, not unmelodious drawls that one connects with an unshakable sense of privilege. She, in turn, was very fond of Gyp; and what passed within her mind, by no means devoid of shrewdness, as to their real relationship, remained ever discreetly hidden. She was, so far again as breeding would allow, something of a humanitarian and rebel, loving horses and dogs, and hating cats, except when they had four legs. The girl had just that softness which fascinates women who perhaps might have been happier if they had been born men. Not that Rosamund Winton was of an aggressive type —she merely had the resolute " catch hold of your tail, old fellow " spirit so often found in Englishwomen of the upper classes. A cheery soul, given to long coats and waistcoats, stocks, and a crutch-handled stick, she—like her brother—had " style," but more sense of humour—valuable in musical circles ! At her house, the girl was practically compelled to see fun as well as merit in all those prodigies, haloed with hair and filled to overflowing with music and themselves. And, since Gyp's natural sense of the ludicrous was extreme, she and her aunt could rarely talk about anything without going into fits of laughter.

Winton had his first really bad attack of gout when Gyp was twenty-two and, terrified lest he might not be able to sit a horse in time for the opening meets, he went off with her and Markey to Wiesbaden. They had rooms in the Wilhelmstrasse, overlooking the gardens, where leaves were already turning, that gorgeous September. The cure was long and obstinate, and Winton badly bored. Gyp fared much better.

Attended by the silent Markey, she rode daily on the Neroberg, chafing at regulations which reduced her to specified tracks in that majestic wood where the beeches glowed. Once or even twice a day she went to the concerts in the *Kurhaus*, either with her father or alone.

The first time she heard Fiorsen play she was alone. Unlike most violinists, he was tall and thin, with great pliancy of body and swift sway of movement. His face was pale, and went strangely with hair and moustache of a sort of dirt-gold colour, and his thin cheeks with very broad high cheek-bones had little narrow scraps of whisker. Those little whiskers seemed to Gyp awful—indeed, he seemed rather awful altogether —but his playing stirred and swept her in the most uncanny way. He had evidently remarkable technique; and the emotion, the intense wayward feeling of his playing was chiselled by that technique, as if a flame were being frozen in its swaying. When he stopped, she did not join in the tornado of applause, but sat motionless, looking up at him. Quite unconstrained by all those people, he passed the back of his hand across his hot brow, shoving up a wave or two of that queer-coloured hair; then, with a rather disagreeable smile, he made a short supple bow or two. And she thought, ' What strange eyes he has —like a great cat's !' Surely they were green; fierce, yet shy, almost furtive—mesmeric ! Certainly the strangest man she had ever seen, and the most frightening. He seemed looking straight at her; and, dropping her gaze, she clapped. When she looked again, his face had lost that smile for a kind of wistfulness. He made another of those little supple bows straight at her—it seemed to Gyp—and jerked his violin up

to his shoulder. 'He's going to play to me,' she
thought absurdly. He played without accompani-
ment a little tune that seemed to twitch the heart.
When he finished, this time she did not look up, but
was conscious that he gave one impatient bow and
walked off.

That evening at dinner she said to Winton:

" I heard a violinist to-day, Dad, the most wonderful
playing—Gustav Fiorsen. Is that Swedish, do you
think—or what ?"

Winton answered:

" Very likely. What sort of a bounder was he to
look at ? I used to know a Swede in the Turkish
army—nice fellow, too."

" Tall and thin and white-faced, with bumpy
cheek-bones, and hollows under them, and queer green
eyes. Oh, and little goldy side-whiskers."

" By Jove ! It sounds the limit."

Gyp murmured, with a smile:

" Yes; I think perhaps he is."

She saw him next day in the gardens. They were
sitting close to the Schiller statue, Winton reading
The Times, to whose advent he looked forward more
than he admitted, for he was loath by confessions of
boredom to disturb Gyp's manifest enjoyment of her
stay. While perusing the customary comforting anima-
diversions on the conduct of those " rascally Radicals "
who had just come into power, and the account of a
Newmarket meeting, he kept stealing sidelong glances
at his daughter.

Certainly she had never looked prettier, daintier,
shown more breeding than she did out here among
these Germans with their thick pasterns, and all the
cosmopolitan hairy-heeled crowd in this God-forsaken

place ! The girl, unconscious of his stealthy regale-
ment, was letting her clear eyes rest, in turn, on each
figure that passed, on the movements of birds and
dogs, watching the sunlight glisten on the grass,
burnish the copper beeches, the lime-trees, and those
tall poplars down there by the water. The doctor
at Mildenham, once consulted on a bout of headache,
had called her eyes " perfect organs," and certainly
no eyes could take things in more swiftly or completely.
She was attractive to dogs, and every now and then
one would stop, in two minds whether or no to put
his nose into this foreign girl's hand. From a flirtation
of eyes with a great Dane, she looked up and saw
Fiorsen passing, in company with a shorter, square
man, having very fashionable trousers and a corseted
waist. The violinist's tall, thin, loping figure was
tightly buttoned into a brownish-grey frock-coat suit;
he wore a rather broad-brimmed, grey, velvety hat;
in his buttonhole was a white flower; his cloth-topped
boots were of patent leather; his tie was bunched out
at the ends over a soft white-linen shirt—altogether
quite a dandy ! His most strange eyes suddenly
swept down on hers, and he made a movement as if
to put his hand to his hat.

' Why, he remembers me,' thought Gyp. That
thin-waisted figure with head set just a little forward
between rather high shoulders, and its long stride,
curiously suggested a leopard or some lithe creature.
He touched his short companion's arm, muttered
something, turned round, and came back. She could
see him staring her way, and knew he was coming
simply to look at her. She knew, too, that her father
was watching. And she felt that those greenish eyes
would waver before his stare—that stare of the

Englishman of a certain class, which never condescends
to be inquisitive. They passed; Gyp saw Fiorsen turn
to his companion, slightly tossing back his head in
their direction, and heard the companion laugh. A
little flame shot up in her.

Winton said:

" Rum-looking Johnnies one sees here !"

" That was the violinist I told you of—Fiorsen."

" Oh ! Ah !" But he had evidently forgotten.

The thought that Fiorsen should have picked her
out of all that audience for remembrance subtly
flattered her vanity. She lost her ruffled feeling.
Though her father thought his dress awful, it was
really rather becoming. He would not have looked
as well in proper English clothes. Once, at least,
during the next two days, she noticed the short, square
young man who had been walking with him, and was
conscious that he followed her with his eyes.

And then a certain Baroness von Maisen, a cosmopolitan friend of Aunt Rosamund's, German by
marriage, half-Dutch, half-French by birth, asked her
if she had heard the Swedish violinist, Fiorsen. He
would be, she said, the best violinist of the day, if—
and she shook her head. Finding that expressive
shake unquestioned, the baroness pursued her thoughts:

" Ah, these musicians ! He wants saving from himself. If he does not halt soon, he will be lost. Pity !
A great talent !"

Gyp looked at her steadily and asked:

" Does he drink, then ?"

" *Pas mal !* But there are things besides drink,
ma chère."

Instinct and so much life with Winton made the
girl regard it as beneath her to be shocked. She did

not seek knowledge of life, but refused to shy away from it or be discomfited; and the baroness, to whom innocence was piquant, went on:

"*Des femmes—toujours des femmes! C'est grand dommage.* It will spoil his spirit. His sole chance is to find one woman, but I pity her; *sapristi, quelle vie pour elle!*"

Gyp said calmly:

"Would a man like that ever love?"

The baroness goggled her eyes.

"I have known such a man become a slave. I have known him running after a woman like a lamb while she was deceiving him here and there. *On ne peut jamais dire. Ma belle, il y a des choses que vous ne savez pas encore.*" She took Gyp's hand. "And yet, one thing is certain. With those eyes and those lips and that figure, *you* have a time before you!"

Gyp withdrew her hand, smiled, and shook her head; she did not believe in love.

"Ah, but you will turn some heads! No fear! as you English say. There is fatality in those pretty brown eyes!"

A girl may be pardoned who takes as a compliment the saying that her eyes are fatal. The words warmed Gyp, uncontrollably light-hearted in these days, just as she was warmed when people turned to stare at her. The soft air, the mellowness of this gay place, much music, a sense of being a *rara avis* among people who, by their heavier type, enhanced her own, had produced in her a kind of intoxication, making her what the baroness called "*un peu folle.*" She was always breaking into laughter, having that precious feeling of twisting the world round her thumb, which does not come too often in the life of one who is sensi-

tive. Everything to her just then was either " funny "
or " lovely." And the baroness, conscious of the
girl's *chic*, genuinely attracted by one so pretty, took
care that she saw all the people, perhaps more than all,
that were desirable.

To women and artists, between whom there is ever
a certain kinship, curiosity is a vivid emotion. Besides, the more a man has conquered, the more precious
field he is for a woman's conquest. To attract a man
who has attracted many, what is it but a proof that
one's charm is superior to that of all those others ?
The words of the baroness deepened in Gyp the impression that Fiorsen was " impossible," but secretly
fortified the faint excitement she felt that he should
have remembered her out of all that audience. Later
on, they bore more fruit than that. But first came
that queer incident of the flowers.

Coming in from a ride, a week after she had sat with
Winton under the Schiller statue, Gyp found on her
dressing-table a bunch of Gloire de Dijon and La
France roses. Plunging her nose into them, she
thought : ' How lovely ! Who sent me these ? '
There was no card. All that the German maid could
say was that a boy had brought them from a flower
shop *" für Fräulein Vinton ";* it was surmised that
they came from the baroness. In her bodice at dinner,
and to the concert after, Gyp wore one La France and
one Gloire de Dijon—a daring mixture of pink and
orange against her oyster-coloured frock, which delighted her, who had a passion for experiments in
colour. They had bought no programme, all music
being the same to Winton, and Gyp not needing any.
When she saw Fiorsen come forward, her cheeks began
to colour from sheer anticipation.

He played first a minuet by Mozart; then the César Franck sonata; and when he came back to make his bow, he was holding in his hand a Gloire de Dijon and a La France rose. Involuntarily, Gyp raised her hand to her own roses. His eyes met hers; he bowed just a little lower. Then, quite naturally, put the roses to his lips as he was walking off the platform. Gyp dropped her hand, as if it had been stung. Then, with the swift thought: ' Oh ! that's schoolgirlish !' she contrived a little smile. But her cheeks were flushing. Should she take out those roses and let them fall ? Her father might see, might notice Fiorsen's— put two and two together ! He would consider she had been insulted. Had she ? She could not bring herself to think so. It was too pretty a compliment, as if he wished to tell her that he was playing to her alone. The baroness's words flashed through her mind: " He wants saving from himself. Pity ! A great talent !" It *was* a great talent. There must be something worth saving in one who could play like that ! They left after his last solo. Gyp put the two roses carefully back among the others.

Three days later, she went to an afternoon " at-home " at the Baroness von Maisen's. She saw him at once, over by the piano, with his short, square companion, listening to a voluble lady, and looking very bored and restless. All that overcast afternoon, still and with queer lights in the sky, as if rain were coming, Gyp had been feeling out of mood, a little homesick. Now she felt excited. She saw the short companion detach himself and go up to the baroness; a minute later, he was brought up to her and introduced —Count Rosek. Gyp did not like his face; there were dark rings under the eyes, and he was too perfectly self-possessed, with a kind of cold sweetness; but he was very agreeable and polite, and spoke English well. He was—it seemed—a Pole, who lived in London, and seemed to know all that was to be known about music. Miss Winton—he believed—had heard his friend Fiorsen play; but not in London? No? That was odd; he had been there some months last season. Faintly annoyed at her ignorance, Gyp answered:

"Yes; but I was in the country nearly all last summer."

"He had a great success. I shall take him back; it is best for his future. What do you think of his playing?"

In spite of herself, for she did not like expanding to this sphinxlike little man, Gyp murmured:

"Oh, simply wonderful, of course!"

He nodded, and then rather suddenly said, with a peculiar little smile:

"May I introduce him? Gustav—Miss Winton!"

Gyp turned. There he was, just behind her, bowing; and his eyes had a look of humble adoration which he made no attempt whatever to conceal. Gyp saw another smile slide over the Pole's lips; and she was alone in the bay window with Fiorsen. The moment might well have fluttered a girl's nerves after his recognition of her by the Schiller statue, after that episode of the flowers, and what she had heard of him. But life had not yet touched either her nerves or spirit; she only felt amused and a little excited. Close to, he had not so much that look of an animal behind bars, and he certainly was in his way a dandy, beautifully washed—always an important thing— and having some pleasant essence on his handkerchief or hair, of which Gyp would have disapproved if he had been English. He wore a diamond ring also, which did not somehow seem bad form on that particular little finger. His height, his broad cheekbones, thick but not long hair, the hungry vitality of his face, figure, movements, annulled those evidences of femininity. He was male enough, rather too male. Speaking with a queer, crisp accent, he said:

"Miss Winton, you are my audience here. I play to you—only to you."

Gyp laughed.

"You laugh at me; but you need not. I play for you because I admire you. I admire you terribly. If I sent you those flowers, it was not to be rude. It was my gratitude for the pleasure of your face." His voice actually trembled. And, looking down, Gyp answered:

"Thank you. It was very kind of you. I want to thank you for your playing. It is beautiful—really beautiful!"

He made her another little bow.

"When I go back to London, will you come and hear me?"

"I should think anyone would go to hear you, if they had the chance."

He gave a short laugh.

"Bah! Here, I do it for money; I hate this place. It bores me—bores me! Was that your father sitting with you under the statue?"

Gyp nodded, suddenly grave. She had not forgotten the slighting turn of his head.

He passed his hand over his face, as if to wipe off its expression.

"He is very English. But you—of no country—you belong to all!"

Gyp made him an ironical little bow.

"No; I should not know your country—you are neither of the North nor of the South. You are just Woman, made to be adored. I came here hoping to meet you; I am extremely happy. Miss Winton, I am your very devoted servant."

He was speaking very fast, very low, with an agitated earnestness that surely could not be put on. But suddenly muttering: "These people!" he made her another of his little bows and abruptly slipped away. The baroness was bringing up another man. The chief thought left by that meeting was: "Is that how he begins to everyone?" She could not quite believe it. The stammering earnestness of his voice, those humbly adoring looks! Then she remembered the smile on the lips of the little Pole, and thought: ' But he must know I'm not silly enough just to be taken in by vulgar flattery!'

Too sensitive to confide in anyone, she had no chance to ventilate the curious sensations of attraction and repulsion that began fermenting in her, feelings defying analysis, mingling and quarrelling deep down in her heart. It was certainly not love, not even the beginning of that; but it was the kind of dangerous interest children feel in things mysterious, out of reach, yet within reach, if only they dared! And the tug of music was there, and the tug of those words of the baroness about salvation—the thought of achieving the impossible, reserved only for the woman of supreme charm, for the true victress. But all these thoughts and feelings were as yet in embryo. She might never see him again! And she certainly did not know whether she even wanted to.

IV

GYP was in the habit of walking with Winton to the Kochbrunnen, where, with other patient-folk, he was required to drink slowly for twenty minutes every morning. While he was imbibing she would sit in a remote corner of the garden, and read a novel in the *Reclam* edition, as a daily German lesson.

She was sitting there, the morning after the " at-home " at the Baroness von Maisen's, reading Turgenev's " Torrents of Spring," when she saw Count Rosek sauntering down the path with a glass of the waters in his hand. Instant memory of the smile with which he had introduced Fiorsen made her take cover beneath her sunshade. She could see his patent-leathered feet, and well-turned, peg-top-trousered legs go by with the gait of a man whose waist is corseted. The certainty that he wore those prerogatives of womanhood increased her dislike. How dare men be so effeminate ? Yet someone had told her that he was a good rider, a good fencer, and very strong. She drew a breath of relief when he was past, and, for fear he might turn and come back, closed her little book and slipped away. But her figure and her springing step were more unmistakable than she knew.

Next morning on the same bench, she was reading breathlessly the scene between Gemma and Sanin at the window, when she heard Fiorsen's voice, behind her, say:

" Miss Winton !"

He, too, held a glass of the waters in one hand, and his hat in the other.

"I have just made your father's acquaintance. May I sit down a minute?"

Gyp drew to one side on the bench, and he sat down.

"What are you reading?"

"A story called 'Torrents of Spring.'"

"Ah, the finest ever written! Where are you?"

"Gemma and Sanin in the thunderstorm."

"Wait! You have Madame Polozov to come! What a creation! How old are you, Miss Winton?"

"Twenty-two."

"You would be too young to appreciate that story if you were not *you*. But you know much—by instinct. What is your Christian name—forgive me!"

"Ghita."

"Ghita? Not soft enough."

"I am always called Gyp."

"Gyp—ah, Gyp! Yes; Gyp!"

He repeated her name so impersonally that she could not be angry.

"I told your father I have had the pleasure of meeting you. He was very polite."

Gyp said coldly:

"My father is always polite."

"Like the ice in which they put champagne."

Gyp smiled; she could not help it.

And suddenly he said:

"I suppose they have told you that I am a *mauvais sujet*." Gyp inclined her head. He looked at her steadily, and said: "It is true. But I could be better —much."

She wanted to look at him, but could not. A queer

sort of exultation had seized on her. This man had power; yet she had power over him. If she wished she could make him her slave, her dog, chain him to her. She had but to hold out her hand, and he would go on his knees to kiss it. She had but to say, "Come," and he would come from wherever he might be. She had but to say "Be good," and he would be good. It was her first experience of power; and it was intoxicating. But—but! Gyp could never be self-confident for long; over her most victorious moments brooded the shadow of distrust. As if he read her thought, Fiorsen said:

"Tell me to do something—anything; I will do it, Miss Winton."

"Then—go back to London at once. You are wasting yourself here, you know. You said so!"

He looked at her, bewildered and upset, and muttered:

"You have asked me the one thing I can't do, Miss—Miss Gyp!"

"Please—not that; it's like a servant!"

"I *am* your servant!"

"Is that why you won't do what I ask you?"

"You are cruel."

Gyp laughed.

He got up and said, with sudden fierceness:

"I am not going away from you; do not think it." Bending with the utmost swiftness, he took her hand, put his lips to it, and turned on his heel.

Gyp, uneasy and astonished, stared at her hand, still tingling from the pressure of his bristly moustache. Then she laughed again—it was just "foreign" to have your hand kissed—and went back to her book, without taking in the words.

Was ever courtship more strange than that which followed ? It is said that the cat fascinates the bird it desires to eat; here the bird fascinated the cat, but the bird too was fascinated. Gyp never lost the sense of having the whip-hand, always felt like one giving alms, or extending favour, yet had a feeling of being unable to get away, which seemed to come from the very strength of the spell she laid on him. The magnetism with which she held him reacted on herself. Thoroughly sceptical at first, she could not remain so. He was too utterly morose and unhappy if she did not smile on him, too alive and excited and grateful if she did. The change in his eyes from their ordinary restless, fierce, and furtive expression to humble adoration or wistful hunger when they looked at her could never have been simulated. And she had no lack of chance to see that metamorphosis. Wherever she went, there he was. If to a concert, he would be a few paces from the door, waiting for her entrance. If to a confectioner's for tea, as likely as not he would come in. Every afternoon he walked where she must pass, riding to the Neroberg.

Except in the gardens of the Kochbrunnen, when he would come up humbly and ask to sit with her five minutes, he never forced his company, or tried in any way to compromise her. Experience, no doubt, served him there; but he must have had an instinct that it was dangerous with one so sensitive. There were other moths, too, round that bright candle, and they served to keep his attentions from being too conspicuous. Did she comprehend what was going on, understand how her defences were being sapped, grasp the danger to retreat that lay in permitting him to hover round her ? Not really. It all served to swell the triumphant intoxication of days when she was ever more and more in love with living, more and more conscious that the world appreciated and admired her, that she had power to do what others couldn't.

Was not Fiorsen, with his great talent, and his dubious reputation, proof of that ? And he excited her. Whatever else one might be in his moody, vivid company, one would not be dull. One morning, he told her something of his life. His father had been a small Swedish landowner, a very strong man and a very hard drinker; his mother, the daughter of a painter. She had taught him the violin, but died while he was still a boy. When he was seventeen he had quarrelled with his father, and had to play his violin for a living in the streets of Stockholm. A well-known violinist, hearing him one day, took him in hand. Then his father had drunk himself to death, and he had inherited the little estate. He had sold it at once— " for follies," as he put it crudely. " Yes, Miss Winton; I have committed many follies, but they are nothing to those I shall commit the day I do not see you any more !" And, with that disturbing remark, he got up and left her. She had smiled at his words, but within herself, she felt excitement, scepticism, compassion, and something she did not understand at all. In those days, she understood herself very little.

But how far did Winton understand, how far see what was going on ? He was a stoic; but that did not prevent jealousy from taking alarm, and causing him twinges more acute than those he still felt in his left foot. He was afraid of showing disquiet by any dramatic change, or he would have carried her off a fortnight at least before his cure was over. He knew too well the signs of passion. That long, loping, wolfish fiddling fellow with the broad cheek-bones and little side-whiskers (Good God !) and greenish eyes whose looks at Gyp he secretly marked down, roused his complete distrust. Perhaps his inbred English contempt for foreigners and artists kept him from direct action. He *could* not take it quite seriously. Gyp, his fastidious perfect Gyp, succumbing, even a little to a fellow like that ! Never ! His jealous affection, too, could not admit that she would neglect to consult him in any doubt or difficulty. He forgot the sensitive secrecy of girls, forgot that his love for her had ever shunned words, her love for him never indulged in confidences. Nor did he see more than a little of what there was to see, and that little was doctored by Fiorsen for his eyes, shrewd though they were. Nor was there in all so very much, except one episode the day before they left, and of that he knew nothing.

That last afternoon was very still, a little mournful. It had rained the night before, and the soaked tree-trunks, the soaked fallen leaves gave off a faint liquorice-like perfume. In Gyp there was a feeling, as if her spirit had been suddenly emptied of excitement and delight. Was it the day, or the thought of leaving this place where she had so enjoyed herself ? After lunch, when Winton was settling his accounts, she wandered out through the long park stretching up the valley. The sky was brooding-grey, the trees were still and melancholy. It was all a little melancholy, and she went on and on, across the stream, round into a muddy lane that led up through the outskirts of a village, on to the higher ground whence she could return by the main road. Why must things come to an end ? For the first time in her life, she thought of Mildenham and hunting without enthusiasm. She would rather stay in London. There she would not be cut off from music, from dancing, from people, and all the exhilaration of being appreciated. On the air came the shrilly, hollow droning of a thresher, and the sound seemed exactly to express her feelings. A pigeon flew over, white against the leaden sky; some birch-trees that had gone golden shivered and let fall a shower of drops. It was lonely here! And, suddenly, two little boys bolted out of the hedge, nearly upsetting her, and scurried down the road. Something had startled them. Gyp, putting up her face to see, felt on it soft pin-points of rain. Her frock would be spoiled, and it was one she was fond of—dove-coloured, velvety, not meant for weather. She turned for refuge to the birch-trees. It would be over directly, perhaps. Muffled in distance, the whining drone of that thresher still came travelling, deepening her discomfort. Then in the hedge, whence the boys had bolted down, a man reared himself above the lane, and came striding along toward her. He jumped down the bank, among the birch-trees. And she saw it was Fiorsen—panting, dishevelled, pale with heat. He must have followed her, and climbed straight up the hillside from the path she had come along in the bottom, before crossing the stream. His artistic dandyism had been harshly treated by that scramble. She might have laughed; but, instead, she felt excited, a little scared by the look on his hot, pale face. He said, breathlessly:

" I have caught you. So you are going to-morrow, and never told me! You thought you would slip away—not a word for me! Are you always so cruel? Well, I will not spare you, either!"

Crouching suddenly, he took hold of her broad

ribbon sash, and buried his face in it. Gyp stood
trembling—the action had not stirred her sense of
the ridiculous. He circled her knees with his arms.

"Oh, Gyp, I love you—I love you—don't send me
away—let me be with you! I am your dog—your
slave. Oh, Gyp, I love you!"

His voice moved and terrified her. Men had said
"I love you," several times during those last two
years, but never with that lost-soul ring of passion,
never with that look in the eyes at once fiercely hungry
and so supplicating, never with that restless, eager,
timid touch of hands. She could only murmur:

"Please get up!"

But he went on:

"Love me a little, only a little—love me! Oh,
Gyp!"

The thought flashed through Gyp: 'To how many
has he knelt, I wonder?' His face had a kind of
beauty in its abandonment—the beauty that comes
from yearning—and she lost her frightened feeling.
He went on, with his stammering murmur: "I am a
prodigal, I know; but if you love me, I will no longer
be. I will do great things for you. Oh, Gyp, if you
will some day marry me! Not now. When I have
proved. Oh, Gyp, you are so sweet—so wonderful!"

His arms crept up till he had buried his face against
her waist. Without quite knowing what she did,
Gyp touched his hair, and said again:

"No; please get up."

He got up then, and standing near, with his hands
hard clenched at his sides, whispered:

"Have mercy! Speak to me!"

She could not. All was strange and mazed and
quivering in her, her spirit straining away, drawn to

him, fantastically confused. She could only look into
his face with her troubled, dark eyes. And suddenly
she was seized and crushed to him. She shrank away,
pushing him back with all her strength. He hung his
head, abashed, suffering, with eyes shut, lips trembling;
and her heart felt again that quiver of compassion.
She murmured:

"I don't know. I will tell you later—later—in
England."

He bowed, folding his arms, as if to make her feel
safe from him. And when, regardless of the rain,
she began to move on, he walked beside her, a yard or
so away, humbly, as though he had never poured out
those words or hurt her lips with the violence of his
kiss.

Back in her room, taking off her wet dress, Gyp tried
to remember what he had said and what she had
answered. She had not promised anything. But she
had given him her address, both in London and the
country. Unless she resolutely thought of other
things, she still felt the restless touch of his hands,
the grip of his arms, and saw his eyes as they were
when he was kissing her; and once more she felt
frightened and excited.

He was playing at the concert that evening—her
last concert. And surely he had never played like
that—with a despairing beauty, a sort of frenzied
rapture. Listening, there came to her a feeling—a
feeling of fatality—that, whether she would or no,
she could not free herself from him.

V

ONCE back in England, Gyp lost that feeling, or very
nearly. Her scepticism told her that Fiorsen would
soon see someone else who seemed all he had said she
was ! How ridiculous to suppose that he would stop
his follies for her, that she had any real power over
him ! But, deep down, she did not quite believe this.
It would have wounded her belief in herself too much—
a belief so subtle and intimate that she was not conscious
of it; belief in that something about her which had
inspired the baroness to use the word " fatality."

Winton, who breathed again, hurried her off to
Mildenham. He had bought her a new horse. They
were in time for the last of the cubbing. And, for a
week at least, the passion for riding and the sight
of hounds carried all before it. Then, just as the real
business of the season was beginning, she began to feel
dull and restless. Mildenham was dark; the autumn
winds made dreary noises. Her little brown spaniel,
very old, who seemed only to have held on to life
just for her return, died. She accused herself terribly
for having left it so long when it was failing. Thinking of all the days Lass had been watching for her to
come home—as Betty, with that love of woeful recital
so dear to simple hearts, took good care to make plain
—she felt as if she had been cruel. For events such
as these, Gyp was both too tender-hearted and too
hard on herself. She was quite ill for several days.
The moment she was better, Winton, in dismay,

whisked her back to Aunt Rosamund, in town. He
would lose her company, but if it did her good, took
her out of herself, he would be content. Running up
for the week-end, three days later, he was relieved to
find her decidedly perked-up, and left her again with
the easier heart.

It was on the day after he went back to Mildenham
that she received a letter from Fiorsen, forwarded from
Bury Street. He was—it said—just returning to
London; he had not forgotten any look she had ever
given him, or any word she had spoken. He should
not rest till he could see her again. " For a long
time," the letter ended, " before I first saw you, I
was like the dead—lost. All was bitter apples to me.
Now I am a ship that comes from the whirlpools to
a warm blue sea; now I see again the evening star.
I kiss your hands, and am your faithful slave,—Gustav
Fiorsen." These words, which from any other man
would have excited her derision, renewed in Gyp that
fluttered feeling, the pleasurable, frightened sense
that she could not get away from his pursuit.

She wrote in answer to the address he gave her
in London, to say that she was staying for a few days
in Curzon Street with her aunt, who would be glad
to see him if he cared to come in any afternoon between
five and six, and signed herself " Ghita Winton."
She was long over that little note. Its curt formality
gave her satisfaction. Was she really mistress of
herself—and him; able to dispose as she wished ?
Yes; and surely the note showed it.

It was never easy to tell Gyp's feelings from her
face; even Winton was often baffled. Her preparation
of Aunt Rosamund for the reception of Fiorsen was
a masterpiece of casualness. When he duly came,

4

he, too, seemed doubly alive to the need for caution, only gazing at Gyp when he could not be seen doing so. But, going out, he whispered: " Not like this— not like this; I must see you alone—I must !" She smiled and shook her head. But bubbles had come back to the wine in her cup.

That evening she said quietly to Aunt Rosamund:

" Dad doesn't like Mr. Fiorsen—can't appreciate his playing, of course."

And this most discreet remark caused Aunt Rosamund, avid—in a well-bred way—of music, to omit mention of the intruder when writing to her brother. The next two weeks he came almost every day, always bringing his violin, Gyp playing his accompaniments, and though his hungry stare sometimes made her feel hot, she would have missed it.

But when Winton next came up to Bury Street, she was in a quandary. To confess that Fiorsen was here, having omitted to speak of him in her letters ? Not to confess, and leave him to find it out from Aunt Rosamund ? Which was worse ? Seized with panic, she did neither, but told her father she was dying for a gallop. Hailing that as the best of signs, he took her forthwith back to Mildenham. And curious were her feelings—light-hearted, compunctious, as of one who escapes yet knows she will soon be seeking to return. The meet was rather far next day, but she insisted on riding to it, since old Pettance, the super-annuated jockey, charitably employed as extra stable help at Mildenham, was to bring on her second horse. There was a good scenting-wind, with rain in the offing, and outside the covert they had a corner to themselves —Winton knowing a trick worth two of the field's at-large. They had slipped there, luckily unseen, for the knowing were given to following the one-handed horseman in faded pink, who, on his bang-tailed black mare, had a knack of getting so well away. One of the whips, a little dark fellow with smouldery eyes and sucked-in weathered cheeks, dashed out of covert, rode past, saluting, and dashed in again. A jay came out with a screech, dived, and doubled back; a hare made off across the fallow—the light-brown lopping creature was barely visible against the brownish soil. Pigeons, very high up, flew over and away to the next wood. The shrilling voices of the whips rose from the covert-depths, and just a whimper now and then from the hounds, swiftly wheeling their noses among the fern and briers.

Gyp, crisping her fingers on the reins, drew-in deep breaths. It smelled so sweet and soft and fresh under that sky, pied of blue, and of white and light-grey swift-moving clouds—not half the wind down here that there was up there, just enough to be carrying off the beech and oak leaves, loosened by frost two days before. If only a fox would break this side, and they could have the first fields to themselves! It was so lovely to be alone with hounds! One of these came trotting out, a pretty young creature, busy and unconcerned, raising its tan-and-white head, its mild reproachful deep-brown eyes, at Winton's, " Loo-in Trix !" What a darling! A burst of music from the covert, and the darling vanished among the briers.

Gyp's new brown horse pricked its ears. A young man in a grey cutaway, buff cords, and jack-boots, on a low chestnut mare, came slipping round the covert. Oh—did that mean they were all coming? Impatiently she glanced at this intruder, who raised his hat a little and smiled. That smile, faintly impudent, was so infectious, that Gyp was melted to a slight response. Then she frowned. He had spoiled their lovely loneliness. Who was he? He looked unpardonably serene and happy sitting there. She did not remember his face at all, yet there was something familiar about it. He had taken his hat off—a broad face, very well cut, and clean-shaved, with dark curly hair, extraordinary clear eyes, a bold, cool, merry look. Where had she seen somebody like him?

A tiny sound from Winton made her turn her head. The fox—stealing out beyond those further bushes! Breathless, she fixed her eyes on her father's face. It was hard as steel, watching. Not a sound, not a quiver, as if horse and man had turned to metal. Was he never going to give the view-halloo? Then his lips writhed, and out it came. Gyp cast a swift smile of gratitude at the young man for having had taste and sense to leave that to her father, and again he smiled at her. There were the first hounds streaming out—one on the other—music and feather! Why didn't Dad go? They would all be round this way in a minute!

Then the black mare slid past her, and, with a bound, her horse followed. The young man on the chestnut was away on the left. Only the huntsman and one whip—beside their three selves! Glorious! The brown horse went too fast at that first fence and Winton called back: "Steady, Gyp! Steady him!" But she couldn't; and it didn't matter. Grass, three fields of grass! Oh, what a lovely fox—going so straight! And each time the brown horse rose, she thought: 'Perfect! I *can* ride! Oh, I am happy!' And she hoped her father and the young man were looking. There was no feeling in the world like this, with a leader like Dad, hounds moving free, good going, and the field distanced. Better than dancing; better —yes, better than listening to music. If one could spend one's life galloping, sailing over fences; if it would never stop ! The new horse was a darling, though he *did* pull.

She crossed the next fence level with the young man, whose low chestnut mare moved with a stealthy action. His hat was crammed down now, and his face very determined, but his lips still had something of that smile. Gyp thought: ' He's got a good seat— very strong, only he looks like " thrusting." Nobody rides like Dad—so beautifully quiet !' Indeed, Winton's seat on a horse was perfection, all done with such a minimum expenditure. The hounds swung round in a curve. Now she was with them, really with them ! What a pace—cracking ! No fox could stand this long !

And suddenly she caught sight of him, barely a field ahead, scurrying desperately, brush down; and the thought flashed through her: ' Oh ! don't let's catch you. Go on, fox; go on ! Get away !' Were they really all after that little hunted red thing—a hundred great creatures, horses and men and women and dogs, and only that one little fox ! But then came another fence, and quickly another, and she lost feelings of shame and pity in the exultation of flying over them. A minute later the fox went to earth within a few hundred yards of the leading hound, and she was glad. She had been in at deaths before—horrid ! But it had been a lovely gallop. And, breathless, smiling rapturously, she wondered whether she could mop her face before the field came up, without that young man noticing.

She could see him talking to her father, and taking out a wisp of a handkerchief that smelled of cyclamen, she had a good scrub round. When she rode up, the young man raised his hat, and looking full at her said: "You did go!" His voice, rather high-pitched, had in it a spice of pleasant laziness. Gyp made him an ironical little bow, and murmured: "My new horse, you mean." He broke again into that irrepressible smile, but, all the same, she knew that he admired her. And she kept thinking: 'Where *have* I seen someone like him?'

They had two more runs, but nothing like that first gallop. Nor did she again see the young man, whose name—it seemed—was Summerhay, son of a certain Lady Summerhay at Widrington, ten miles from Mildenham.

All that long, silent jog home with Winton in fading daylight, she felt very happy—saturated with air and elation. The trees and fields, the hay-stacks, gates, and ponds beside the lanes grew dim; lights came up in the cottage windows; the air smelled sweet of wood smoke. And, for the first time all day, she thought of Fiorsen, thought of him almost longingly. If he could be there in the cosy old drawing-room, to play to her while she lay back—drowsing, dreaming by the fire in the scent of burning cedar logs—the Mozart minuet, or that little heart-catching tune of Poise, played the first time she heard him, or a dozen other of the things he played unaccompanied! That would be the most lovely ending to this lovely day. Just the glow and warmth wanting, to make all perfect—the glow and warmth of music and adoration!

And touching the mare with her heel, she sighed. To indulge fancies about music and Fiorsen was safe

here, far away from him; she even thought she would
not mind if he were to behave again as he had under
the birch-trees in the rain at Wiesbaden. It was so
good to be adored. Her old mare, ridden now six
years, began the series of contented snuffles that
signified she smelt home. Here was the last turn,
and the loom of the short beech-tree avenue to the
house—the old manor-house, comfortable, roomy,
rather dark, with wide shallow stairs. Ah, she was
tired; and it was drizzling now. She would be nicely
stiff to-morrow. In the light coming from the open
door she saw Markey standing; and while fishing from
her pocket the usual lumps of sugar, heard him say :
" Mr. Fiorsen, sir—gentleman from Wiesbaden—to
see you."

Her heart thumped. What did this mean ? Why
had he come ? How had he dared ? How could he
have been so treacherous to her ? Ah, but he was
ignorant, of course, that she had not told her father.
A veritable judgment on her ! She ran straight in
and up the stairs. The voice of Betty: " Your bath's
ready, Miss Gyp," roused her. And crying, " Oh,
Betty darling, bring me up my tea !" she ran into the
bathroom. She was safe there; and in the delicious
heat of the bath faced the situation better.

There could be only one meaning. He had come to
ask for her. And, suddenly, she took comfort. Better
so; there would be no more secrecy from Dad ! And he
would stand between her and Fiorsen if—if she decided
not to marry him. The thought staggered her. Had
she, without knowing it, got so far as this ? Yes,
and further. It was all no good; Fiorsen would never
accept refusal, even if she gave it ! But, did she want
to refuse ?

She loved hot baths, but had never stayed in one so long. Life was so easy there, and so difficult outside. Betty's knock forced her to get out at last, and let her in with tea and the message. Would Miss Gyp please to go down when she was ready?

VI

WINTON was staggered. With a glance at Gyp's vanishing figure, he said curtly to Markey, "Where have you put this gentleman?" But the use of the word "this" was the only trace he showed of his emotions. In that little journey across the hall he entertained many extravagant thoughts. Arrived at the study, he inclined his head courteously enough, waiting for Fiorsen to speak. The "fiddler," still in his fur-lined coat, was twisting a squash hat in his hands. In his own peculiar style he was impressive. But why couldn't he look you in the face; or, if he did, why did he seem about to eat you?

"You knew I was returned to London, Major Winton?"

Then Gyp had been seeing the fellow without letting him know! The thought was chill and bitter to Winton. He must not give her away, however, and he simply bowed. He felt that his visitor was afraid of his frigid courtesy; and he did not mean to help him over that fear. He could not, of course, realize that this ascendancy would not prevent Fiorsen from laughing at him behind his back and acting as if he did not exist. No real contest, in fact, was possible between men moving on such different planes, neither having the slightest respect for the other's standards or beliefs.

Fiorsen, who had begun to pace the room, stopped, and said with agitation:

57

"Major Winton, your daughter is the most beautiful thing on earth. I love her desperately. I am a man with a future, though you may not think it. I have what future I like in my art if only I can marry her. I have a little money, too—not much; but in my violin there is all the fortune she can want."

Winton's face expressed nothing but cold contempt. That this fellow should take him for one who would consider money in connection with his daughter simply affronted him.

Fiorsen went on:

"You do not like me—that is clear. I saw it the first moment. You are an English gentleman "—he pronounced the words with a sort of irony—" I am nothing to you. Yet, in *my* world, I am something. I am not an adventurer. Will you permit me to beg your daughter to be my wife?" He raised his hands that still held the hat; involuntarily they had assumed the attitude of prayer.

For a second, Winton realized that he was suffering. That weakness went in a flash, and he said frigidly:

"I am obliged to you, sir, for coming to me first. You are in my house, and I don't want to be discourteous, but I should be glad if you would be good enough to withdraw and take it that I shall certainly oppose your wish as best I can."

The almost childish disappointment and trouble in Fiorsen's face changed quickly to an expression fierce, furtive, mocking; and then shifted to despair.

"Major Winton, you have loved; you must have loved her mother. I suffer!"

Winton, who had turned abruptly to the fire, faced round again.

"I don't control my daughter's affections, sir; she

will do as she wishes. I merely say it will be against my hopes and judgment if she marries you. I imagine you've not altogether waited for my leave. I was not blind to the way you hung about her at Wiesbaden, Mr. Fiorsen."

Fiorsen answered with a twisted, miserable smile:

" Poor wretches do what they can. May I see her ? Let me just see her."

Was it any good to refuse ? She had been seeing the fellow already without his knowledge, keeping from him—*him*—all her feelings, whatever they were. And he said:

" I'll send for her. In the meantime, perhaps you'll have some refreshment ?"

Fiorsen shook his head, and there followed half an hour of acute discomfort. Winton, in his mud-stained clothes before the fire, supported it better than his visitor. That child of nature, after endeavouring to emulate his host's quietude, renounced all such efforts with an expressive gesture, fidgeted here, fidgeted there, tramped the room, went to the window, drew aside the curtains and stared out into the dark; came back as if resolved again to confront Winton; then, baffled by that figure so motionless before the fire, flung himself down in an armchair, and turned his face to the wall. Winton was not cruel by nature, but he enjoyed the writhings of this fellow who was endangering Gyp's happiness. Endangering ? Surely not possible that she would accept him ! Yet, if not, why had she not told him ? And he, too, suffered.

Then she came. He had expected her to be pale and nervous; but Gyp never admitted being naughty till she had been forgiven. Her smiling face had in it a kind of warning closeness. She went up to Fiorsen, and holding out her hand, said calmly:

" How nice of you to come !"

Winton had the bitter feeling that he—he—was the outsider. Well, he would speak plainly; there had been too much underhand doing.

" Mr. Fiorsen has done us the honour to wish to marry you. I've told him that you decide such things for yourself. If you accept him, it will be against my wish, naturally."

While he was speaking, the glow in her cheeks deepened; she looked neither at him nor at Fiorsen. Winton noted the rise and fall of the lace on her breast. She was smiling, and gave the tiniest shrug of her shoulders. And, suddenly smitten to the heart, he walked stiffly to the door. It was evident that she had no use for his guidance. If her love for him was not worth to her more than this fellow ! But there his resentment stopped. He knew that he could not afford wounded feelings; could not get on without her. Married to the greatest rascal on earth, he would still be standing by her, wanting her companionship and love. She represented too much in the present and—the past. With sore heart, indeed, he went down to dinner.

Fiorsen was gone when he came down again. What the fellow had said, or she had answered, he would not for the world have asked. Gulfs between the proud are not lightly bridged. And when she came up to say good-night, both their faces were as though coated with wax.

In the days that followed, she gave no sign, uttered no word in any way suggesting that she meant to go against his wishes. Fiorsen might not have existed,

for any mention made of him. But Winton knew well
that she was moping, and cherishing some feeling
against himself. And this he could not bear. So,
one evening, after dinner, he said quietly:

"Tell me frankly, Gyp; do you care for that chap?"

She answered as quietly:

"In a way—yes."

"Is that enough?"

"I don't know, Dad."

Her lips had quivered; and Winton's heart softened,
as it always did when he saw her moved. He put
his hand out, covered one of hers, and said:

"I shall never stand in the way of your happiness,
Gyp. But it must *be* happiness. Can it possibly be
that? I don't think so. You know what they said
of him out there?"

"Yes."

He had not thought she knew. And his heart sank.

"That's pretty bad, you know. And is he of our
world at all?"

Gyp looked up.

"Do you think *I* belong to 'our world,' Dad?"

Winton turned away. She followed, slipping her
hand under his arm.

"I didn't mean to hurt. But it's true, isn't it?
I don't belong among society people. They wouldn't
have me, you know—if they knew about what you told
me. Ever since that I've felt I don't belong to them.
I'm nearer him. Music means more to me than
anything!"

Winton gave her hand a convulsive grip. A sense
of coming defeat and bereavement was on him.

"If your happiness went wrong, Gyp, I should be
most awfully cut up."

"But why shouldn't I be happy, Dad?"

"If you were, I could put up with anyone. But, I tell you, I can't believe you would be. I beg you, my dear—for God's sake, make sure. I'll put a bullet into the man who treats you badly."

Gyp laughed, then kissed him. But they were silent. At bedtime he said:

"We'll go up to town to-morrow."

Whether from a feeling of the inevitable, or from the forlorn hope that seeing more of the fellow might be the only chance of curing her—he put no more obstacles in the way.

And the queer courtship began again. By Christmas she had consented, still under the impression that she was the mistress, not the slave—the cat, not the bird. Once or twice, when Fiorsen let passion out of hand and his overbold caresses affronted her, she recoiled almost with dread from what she was going toward. But, in general, she lived elated, intoxicated by music and his adoration, withal remorseful that she was making her father sad. She was but little at Mildenham, and he, in his unhappiness, was there nearly all the time, riding extra hard, and leaving Gyp with his sister. Aunt Rosamund, though under the spell of Fiorsen's music, had agreed with her brother that Fiorsen was "impossible." But nothing she said made any effect on Gyp. It was new and startling to discover in this soft, sensitive girl such a vein of stubbornness. Opposition seemed to harden her resolution. And the good lady's natural optimism began to persuade her that Gyp would make a silk purse out of that sow's ear yet. After all, the man was a celebrity in his way!

It was settled for February. A house with a garden was taken in St. John's Wood. The last month went, as all such last months go, in those intoxicating pastimes, the buying of furniture and clothes. If it were not for that, who knows how many engagement knots would slip!

And to-day they had been married. To the last, Winton had hardly believed it would come to that. He had shaken the hand of her husband and kept pain and disappointment out of his face, knowing well that he deceived no one. Thank heaven, there had been no church, no wedding-cake, invitations, congratulations, fal-lals of any kind—he could never have stood them. Not even Rosamund—who had influenza —to put up with!

Lying back in the recesses of that old chair, he stared into the fire.

They would be just about at Torquay by now—just about. Music! Who would have thought noises made out of string and wood could have stolen her away from him? Yes, they would be at Torquay by now, at their hotel. And the first prayer Winton had uttered for years escaped his lips:

" Let her be happy! Let her be happy!"

Then, hearing Markey open the door, he closed his eyes and feigned sleep.

PART II

I

WHEN a girl first sits opposite the man she has married, of what does she think? Not of the issues and emotions that lie in wait. They are too overwhelming; she would avoid them while she can. Gyp thought of her frock, a mushroom-coloured velvet cord. Few girls of her class are married without "fal-lals," as Winton had called them. Few girls sit in the corner of their reserved first-class compartments without the excitement of having been supreme centre of the world for some flattering hours to buoy them up on that train journey, with no memories of friends' behaviour, speech, appearance, to chat of with her husband, so as to keep thought away. For Gyp, her dress, first worn that day, Betty's breakdown, the faces, blank as hats, of the registrar and clerk, were about all she had to distract her. She stole a look at her husband, clothed in blue serge, just opposite. Her husband! Mrs. Gustav Fiorsen! No! People might call her that; to herself, she was Ghita Winton. Ghita Fiorsen would never seem right. And, not confessing that she was afraid to meet his eyes, but afraid all the same, she looked out of the window. A dull, bleak, dismal day; no warmth, no sun, no music in it—the Thames as grey as lead, the willows on its banks forlorn.

Suddenly she felt his hand on hers. She had not seen his face like that before—yes; once or twice when he was playing—a spirit shining through. She felt suddenly secure. If it stayed like that, then !—His hand rested on her knee; his face changed just a little; the spirit seemed to waver, to be fading; his lips grew fuller. He crossed over and sat beside her. Instantly she began to talk about their house, where they were going to put certain things—presents and all that. He, too, talked of the house; but every now and then he glanced at the corridor, and muttered. It was pleasant to feel that the thought of her possessed him through and through, but she was tremulously glad of that corridor. Life is mercifully made up of little things ! And Gyp was always able to live in the moment. In the hours they had spent together, up to now, he had been like a starved man snatching hasty meals; now that he had her to himself for good, he was another creature altogether—like a boy out of school, and kept her laughing nearly all the time.

Presently he got down his practice violin, and putting on the mute, played, looking at her over his shoulder with a droll smile. She felt happy, much warmer at heart, now. And when his face was turned away, she looked at him. He was so much better looking now than when he had those little whiskers. One day she had touched one of them and said: "Ah ! if only these wings could fly !" Next morning they had flown. His face was not one to be easily got used to; she was not used to it yet, any more than she was used to his touch. When it grew dark, and he wanted to draw down the blinds, she caught him by the sleeve, and said:

"No, no; they'll know we're honeymooners !"

" Well, my Gyp, and are we not ?"

But he obeyed; only, as the hours went on, his eyes seemed never to let her alone.

At Torquay, the sky was clear and starry; the wind brought whiffs of sea-scent into their cab; lights winked far out on a headland; and in the little harbour, all bluish dark, many little boats floated like tame birds. He had put his arm round her, and she could feel his hand resting on her heart. She was grateful that he kept so still. When the cab stopped and they entered the hall of the hotel, she whispered:

" Don't let's let them see !"

Still, mercifully, little things ! Inspecting the three rooms, getting the luggage divided between dressing-room and bedroom, unpacking, wondering which dress to put on for dinner, stopping to look out over the dark rocks and the sea, where the moon was coming up, wondering if she dared lock the door while she was dressing, deciding that it would be silly; dressing so quickly, fluttering when she found him suddenly there close behind her, beginning to do up her hooks. Those fingers were too skilful ! It was the first time she had thought of his past with a sort of hurt pride and fastidiousness. When he had finished, he twisted her round, held her away, looked at her from head to foot, and said below his breath:

" Mine !"

Her heart beat fast then; but suddenly he laughed, slipped his arm about her, and danced her twice round the room. He let her go demurely down the stairs in front of him, saying:

" They shan't see—my Gyp. Oh, they shan't see ! We are old married people, tired of each other— very !"

At dinner it amused him at first—her too, a little—
to keep up this farce of indifference. But every now
and then he turned and stared at some inoffensive
visitor who was taking interest in them, with such
fierce and genuine contempt that Gyp took alarm;
whereon he laughed. When she had drunk a little
wine and he had drunk a good deal, the farce of indifference came to its end. He talked at a great rate
now, slyly nicknaming the waiters and mimicking
the people around—happy thrusts that made her
smile but shiver a little, lest they should be heard or
seen. Their heads were close together across the little
table. They went out into the lounge. Coffee came,
and he wanted her to smoke with him. She had never
smoked in a public room. But it seemed stiff and
" missish " to refuse—she must do now as his world
did. And it was another little thing; she wanted
little things, all the time wanted them. She drew back
a window-curtain, and they stood there side by side.
The sea was deep blue beneath bright stars, and the
moon shone through a ragged pine-tree on a little
headland. Though she stood five feet six in her
shoes, she was only up to his mouth. He sighed and
said: " Beautiful night, my Gyp !" And suddenly
it struck her that she knew nothing of what was in
him, and yet he was her husband ! " Husband "—
funny word, not pretty ! She felt as a child opening
the door of a dark room, and, clutching his arm, said:
" Look ! There's a sailing-boat. What's it doing
out there at night ?" Another little thing ! Any
little thing !

Presently he said:

" Come up-stairs ! I'll play to you."

Up in their sitting-room was a piano, but—not
possible; to-morrow they would have to get another.

To-morrow! The fire was hot, and he took off his
coat to play. In one of his shirt-sleeves there was a
rent. She thought, with a sort of triumph: ' I shall
mend that !' It was something definite, actual—a
little thing. There were lilies in the room that gave
a strong, sweet scent. He brought them up to her
to sniff, and, while she was sniffing, stooped suddenly
and kissed her neck. She shut her eyes with a shiver.
He took the flowers away at once, and when she opened
her eyes again, his violin was at his shoulder. For
a whole hour he played, and Gyp, in her cream-coloured
frock, lay back, listening. She was tired, not sleepy.
It would have been nice to have been sleepy. Her
mouth had its little sad tuck or dimple at the corner;
her eyes were deep and dark—a cloudy child. His
gaze never left her face; he played and played, and his
own fitful face grew clouded. At last he put away the
violin, and said:

" Go to bed, Gyp; you're tired."

Obediently she got up and went into the bedroom.
With a sick feeling in her heart, and as near the fire
as she could get, she undressed with desperate haste,
and got to bed. An age—it seemed—she lay there
shivering in her flimsy lawn against the cold sheets,
her eyes not quite closed, watching the flicker of the
firelight. She did not think—could not—just lay
stiller than the dead. The door creaked. She shut
her eyes. Had she a heart at all? It did not seem
to beat. She lay thus, with eyes shut, till she could
bear it no longer. By the firelight she saw him crouching at the foot of the bed; could just see his face—like
a face—a face—where seen? Ah yes !—a picture—
of a wild man crouching at the feet of Iphigenia—so
humble, so hungry—so lost in gazing. She gave a
little smothered sob and held out her hand.

II

GYP was too proud to give by halves. And in those early days she gave Fiorsen everything except—her heart. She earnestly desired to give that too; but hearts only give themselves. Perhaps if the wild man in him, maddened by beauty in its power, had not so ousted the spirit man, her heart might have gone with her lips and the rest of her. He knew he was not getting her heart, and it made him, in the wildness of his nature and the perversity of a man, go just the wrong way to work, trying to conquer her by the senses, not the soul.

Yet she was not unhappy—it cannot be said she was unhappy, except for a sort of lost feeling sometimes, as if she were trying to grasp something that kept slipping, slipping away. She was glad to give him pleasure. She felt no repulsion—this was man's nature. Only there was always that feeling that she was not close. When he was playing to her, with the spirit-look on his face, she would feel: ' Now, surely I shall get close to him !' But the look would go; how to keep it there she did not know, and when it went, her hope went too.

Their little suite of rooms was at the very end of the hotel, so that he might play as much as he wished. While he practised in the mornings she would go into the garden, which sloped in rock-terraces down to the sea. Wrapped in fur, she would sit there with a book. She soon knew each evergreen, or flower that was coming out—aubretia, and laurustinus, a little white flower whose name was uncertain, and one star-periwinkle. The air was often soft; the birds sang already and were busy with their weddings, and twice, at least, spring came in her heart—that wonderful feeling when first the whole being scents new life preparing in the earth and the wind—the feeling that only comes when spring is not yet, and one aches and rejoices all at once. Seagulls often came over her, craning down their greedy bills and uttering cries like a kitten's mewing.

Out here she had feelings, that she did not get with him, of being at one with everything. She did not realize how tremendously she had grown up in these few days, how the ground bass had already come into the light music of her life. Living with Fiorsen was opening her eyes to much beside mere knowledge of "man's nature"; with her perhaps fatal receptivity, she was already soaking up the atmosphere of his philosophy. He was always in revolt against accepting things because he was expected to; but, like most executant artists, he was no reasoner, just a mere instinctive kicker against the pricks. He would lose himself in delight with a sunset, a scent, a tune, a new caress, in a rush of pity for a beggar or a blind man, a rush of aversion from a man with large feet or a long nose, of hatred for a woman with a flat chest or an expression of sanctimony. He would swing along when he was walking, or dawdle, dawdle; he would sing and laugh, and make her laugh too till she ached, and half an hour later would sit staring into some pit of darkness in a sort of powerful brooding of his whole being. Insensibly she shared in this deep drinking of sensation, but always gracefully, fastidiously, never losing sense of other people's feelings.

In his love-raptures, he just avoided setting her nerves on edge, because he never failed to make her feel his enjoyment of her beauty; that perpetual consciousness, too, of not belonging to the proper and respectable, which she had tried to explain to her father, made her set her teeth against feeling shocked. But in other ways he did shock her. She could not get used to his utter oblivion of people's feelings, to the ferocious contempt with which he would look at those who got on his nerves, and make half-audible comments, just as he had commented on her own father when he and Count Rosek passed them, by the Schiller statue. She would visibly shrink at those remarks, though they were sometimes so excruciatingly funny that she had to laugh, and feel dreadful immediately after. She saw that he resented her shrinking; it seemed to excite him to run amuck the more. But she could not help it. Once she got up and walked away. He followed her, sat on the floor beside her knees, and thrust his head, like a great cat, under her hand.

"Forgive me, my Gyp; but they are such brutes. Who could help it? Now tell me—who could, except my Gyp?" And she had to forgive him. But, one evening, when he had been really outrageous during dinner, she answered:

"No; I can't. It's you that are the brute. You *were* a brute to them!"

He leaped up with a face of furious gloom and went out of the room. It was the first time he had given way to anger with her. Gyp sat by the fire, very disturbed; chiefly because she was not really upset at having hurt him. Surely she ought to be feeling miserable at that!

But when, at ten o'clock, he had not come back, she began to flutter in earnest. She had said a dreadful thing ! And yet, in her heart, she did not take back her judgment. He really *had* been a brute. She would have liked to soothe herself by playing, but it was too late to disturb people, and going to the window, she looked out over the sea, feeling beaten and confused. This was the first time she had given free rein to her feeling against what Winton would have called his " bounderism." If he had been English, she would never have been attracted by one who could trample so on other people's feelings. What, then, had attracted her ? His strangeness, wildness, the mesmeric pull of his passion for her, his music ! Nothing could spoil that in him. The sweep, the surge, and sigh in his playing was like the sea out there, dark, and surf-edged, beating on the rocks; or the sea deep-coloured in daylight, with white gulls over it; or the sea with those sinuous paths made by the wandering currents, the subtle, smiling, silent sea, holding in suspense its unfathomable restlessness, waiting to surge and spring again. That was what she wanted from him—not his embraces, not even his adoration, his wit, or his queer, lithe comeliness touched with felinity; no, only that in his soul which escaped through his fingers into the air and dragged at her soul. If, when he came in, she were to run to him, throw her arms round his neck, make herself feel close, lose herself in him ! Why not ? It was her duty; why not her delight, too ? But she shivered. Some instinct too deep for analysis, something in the very heart of her nerves made her recoil, as if she were afraid, literally scared of letting herself sink into love— the subtlest instinct of self-preservation against some-

thing fatal; against being led on beyond—yes, it was
like that curious, instinctive shrinking which some feel
at the mere sight of a precipice, a dread of going
near, lest they should be drawn on and over by
resistless attraction.

She passed into their bedroom and began slowly to
undress. To go to bed without knowing where he was,
what doing, thinking, seemed already a little odd; and
she sat brushing her hair slowly with the silver-backed
brushes, staring at her own pale face, whose eyes
looked so very large and dark. At last there came to
her the feeling: 'I can't help it! I don't care!'
And, getting into bed, she turned out the light. It
seemed queer and lonely; there was no fire. And then,
without more ado, she slept.

She had a dream of being between Fiorsen and her
father in a railway-carriage out at sea, with the water
rising higher and higher, swishing and sighing.
Awakening always, like a dog, to perfect presence of
mind, she knew that he was playing in the sitting-room,
playing—at that time of night? She lay listening
to a quivering, gibbering tune that she did not know.
Should she be first to make it up, or should she wait
for him? Twice she half slipped out of bed, but both
times, as if fate meant her not to move, he chose that
moment to swell out the sound, and each time she
thought: 'No, I can't. It's just the same now; he
doesn't care how many people he wakes up. He does
just what he likes, and cares nothing for anyone.'
And covering her ears with her hands, she continued
to lie motionless.

When she withdrew her hands at last, he had stopped.
Then she heard him coming, and feigned sleep. But
he did not spare even sleep. She submitted to his

kisses without a word, her heart hardening within her—surely he smelled of brandy! Next morning he seemed to have forgotten it all. But Gyp had not. She wanted badly to know what he had felt, where he had gone, but was too proud to ask.

She wrote twice to her father in the first week, but afterwards, except for a postcard now and then, she never could. Why tell him what she was doing, in company of one whom he could not bear to think of? Had he been right? To confess that would hurt her pride too much. But she began to long for London. The thought of her little house was a green spot to dwell on. When they were settled in, and could do what they liked without anxiety about people's feelings, it would be all right perhaps. When he could start again really working, and she helping him, all would be different. Her new house, and so much to do; her new garden, and fruit-trees coming into blossom! She would have dogs and cats, would ride when Dad was in town. Aunt Rosamund would come, friends, evenings of music, dances still, perhaps—he danced beautifully, and loved it, as she did. And his concerts —the elation of being identified with his success! But, above all, the excitement of making her home as dainty as she could, with daring experiments in form and colour. And yet, at heart she knew that to be already looking forward, banning the present, was a bad sign.

One thing, at all events, she enjoyed—sailing. They had blue days when even the March sun was warm, and there was just breeze enough. He got on excellently with the old salt whose boat they used, for he was at his best with simple folk, whose lingo he could understand about as much as they could understand his.

In those hours, Gyp had some real sensations of
romance. The sea was so blue, the rocks and wooded
spurs of that Southern coast so dreamy in the bright
land-haze. Oblivious of "the old salt," he would
put his arm round her; out there, she could swallow
down her sense of form, and be grateful for feeling
nearer to him in spirit. She made loyal efforts to
understand him in these weeks that were bringing a
certain disillusionment. The elemental part of marriage was not the trouble; if she did not herself feel
passion, she did not resent his. When, after one of
those embraces, his mouth curled with a little bitter
smile, as if to say, " Yes, much you care for me,"
she would feel compunctious and yet aggrieved. But
the trouble lay deeper—the sense of an insuperable
barrier; and always that deep, instinctive recoil from
letting herself go. She could not let herself be known,
and she could not know him. Why did his eyes often
fix her with a stare that did not seem to see her ?
What made him, in the midst of serious playing, break
into some furious or desolate little tune, or drop his
violin ? What gave him those long hours of dejection, following the maddest gaiety ? Above all, what
dreams had he in those rare moments when music
transformed his strange pale face ? Or was it a mere
physical illusion—had he any dreams ? " The heart
of another is a dark forest "—to all but the one who
loves.

One morning, he held up a letter.

" Ah ! ha ! Paul Rosek went to see our house. ' A
pretty dove's nest !' he calls it."

The memory of the Pole's sphinxlike, sweetish face,
and eyes that seemed to know so many secrets, always
affected Gyp unpleasantly. She said quietly:

" Why do you like him, Gustav ?"

" Like him ? Oh, he is useful. A good judge of music, and—many things."

" I think he is hateful."

Fiorsen laughed.

" Hateful ? Why hateful, my Gyp ? He is a good friend. And he admires you—oh, he admires you very much ! He has success with women. He always says, ' *J'ai une technique merveilleuse pour séduire une femme.*' "

Gyp laughed.

" Ugh ! He's like a toad, I think."

" Ah, I shall tell him that ! He will be flattered."

" If you do; if you give me away—I——"

He jumped up and caught her in his arms; his face was so comically compunctious that she calmed down at once. She thought over her words afterwards and regretted them. All the same, Rosek was a sneak and a cold sensualist, she was sure. And the thought that he had been spying at their little house tarnished her anticipations of home-coming.

They went to Town three days later. While the taxi was skirting Lord's Cricket-ground, Gyp slipped her hand into Fiorsen's. She was brimful of excitement. The trees were budding in the gardens that they passed; the almond-blossom coming—yes, really coming ! They were in the road now. Five, seven, nine—thirteen ! Two more ! There it was, nineteen, in white figures on the leaf-green railings, under the small green lilac buds; yes, and their almond-blossom was out, too ! She could just catch a glimpse over those tall railings of the low white house with its green outside shutters. She jumped out almost into the arms of Betty, who stood smiling all over her broad, flushed face, while from under each arm peered forth the head of a black devil, with pricked ears and eyes as bright as diamonds.

" Betty ! What darlings !"

" Major Winton's present, my dear—ma'am !"

Giving the stout shoulders a hug, Gyp seized the black devils, and ran up the path under the trellis, while the Scotch-terrier pups, squeezed against her breast, made confused small noises and licked her nose and ears. Through the square hall she ran into the drawing-room, which opened out on to the lawn; and there, in the French window, stood spying back at the spick-and-span room, where everything was, of course, placed just wrong. The colouring, white, ebony, and satinwood, looked nicer even than she had hoped. Out in the garden—her own garden—the pear trees were thickening, but not in blossom yet; a few daffodils were in bloom along the walls, and a magnolia had one bud opened. And all the time she kept squeezing the puppies to her, enjoying their young, warm, fluffy savour, and letting them kiss her. She ran out of the drawing-room, up the stairs. Her bedroom, the dressing-room, the spare room, the bathroom—she dashed into them all. Oh, it was nice to be in your own place, to be—— Suddenly she felt herself lifted off the ground from behind, and in that undignified position, her eyes flying, she turned her face till he could reach her lips.

III

To wake, and hear the birds at early practice, and feel that winter is over—is there any pleasanter moment?

That first morning in her new house, Gyp woke with the sparrow, or whatever the bird which utters the first cheeps and twitters, soon eclipsed by so much that is more important in bird-song. It seemed as if all the feathered creatures in London must be assembled in her garden; and the old verse came into her head:

> " All dear Nature's children sweet
> Lie at bride and bridegroom's feet,
> Blessing their sense.
> Not a creature of the air,
> Bird melodious or bird fair
> Be absent hence !"

She turned and looked at her husband. He lay with his head snoozled down into the pillow, so that she could only see his thick, rumpled hair. And a shiver went through her, exactly as if a strange man were lying there. Did he really belong to her, and she to him—for good? And was this their house— together? It all seemed somehow different, more serious and troubling, in this strange bed, of this strange room, that was to be so permanent. Careful not to wake him, she slipped out and stood between the curtains and the window. Light was all in confusion yet; away low down behind the trees, the rose of dawn still clung. One might almost have been in the country, but for the faint, rumorous noises of the town beginning to wake, and that film of ground-mist which veils the feet of London mornings. She thought: " I am mistress in this house, have to direct it all— see to everything ! And my pups ! Oh, what do they eat ?"

That was the first of many hours of anxiety, for she was very conscientious. Her fastidiousness desired perfection, but her sensitiveness refused to demand it of others—especially servants. Why should she harry them ?

Fiorsen had not the faintest notion of regularity. She found that he could not even begin to appreciate her struggles in housekeeping. And she was much too proud to ask his help, or perhaps too wise, since he was obviously unfit to give it. To live like the birds of the air was his motto. Gyp would have liked nothing better; but, for that, one must not have a house with three servants, several meals, two puppy-dogs, and no great experience of how to deal with any of them.

She spoke of her difficulties to no one and suffered the more. With Betty—who, bone-conservative, ad-mitted Fiorsen as hardly as she had once admitted Winton—she had to be very careful. But her great trouble was with her father. Though she longed to see him, she literally dreaded their meeting. He first came—as he had been wont to come when she was a tiny girl—at the hour when he thought the fellow to whom she now belonged would most likely be out. Her heart beat, when she saw him under the trellis. She opened the door herself, and hung about him so that his shrewd eyes should not see her face. And she began at once to talk of the puppies, whom she had named Don and Doff. They were perfect darlings;

nothing was safe from them; her slippers were completely done for; they had already got into her china-
cabinet and gone to sleep there! He must come and
see all over.

Hooking her arm into his, and talking all the time,
she took him up-stairs and down, and out into the
garden, to the studio, or music-room, at the end,
which had an entrance to itself on to a back lane.
This room had been the great attraction. Fiorsen
could practise there in peace. Winton went along
with her very quietly, making a shrewd comment now
and then. At the far end of the garden, looking over
the wall, down into that narrow passage which lay
between it and the back of another garden, he squeezed
her arm suddenly and said:

" Well, Gyp, what sort of a time ?"

The question had come at last.

" Oh, rather lovely—in some ways." But she did
not look at him, nor he at her. " See, Dad! The
cats have made quite a path there !"

Winton bit his lips and turned from the wall. The
thought of that fellow was bitter within him. She
meant to tell him nothing, meant to keep up that
lighthearted look—which didn't deceive him a bit !

" Look at my crocuses! It's really spring to-
day !'

It was. Even a bee or two had come. The tiny
leaves had a transparent look, too thin as yet to keep
the sunlight from passing through them. The purple,
delicate-veined crocuses, with little flames of orange
blowing from their centres, seemed to hold the light
as in cups. A wind, without harshness, swung the
boughs; a dry leaf or two still rustled round here and
there. And on the grass, and in the blue sky, and on

6

the almond-blossom was the first spring brilliance.
Gyp clasped her hands behind her head.

"Lovely—to feel the spring!"

And Winton thought: 'She's changed!' She had
softened, quickened—more depth of colour in her,
more gravity, more sway in her body, more sweetness
in her smile. But—was she happy?

A voice said:

"Ah, what a pleasure!"

The fellow had slunk up like the great cat he was.
And it seemed to Winton that Gyp had winced.

"Dad thinks we ought to have dark curtains in the
music-room, Gustav."

Fiorsen made a bow.

"Yes, yes—like a London club."

Winton, watching, was sure of supplication in her
face. And, forcing a smile, he said:

"You seem very snug here. Glad to see you again.
Gyp looks splendid."

Another of those bows he so detested! Mounte-
bank! Never, never would he be able to stand the
fellow! But he must not, would not, show it. And,
as soon as he decently could, he went, taking his
lonely way back through this region, of which his
knowledge was almost limited to Lord's Cricket-ground,
with a sense of doubt and desolation, an irritation
more than ever mixed with the resolve to be always at
hand if the child wanted him.

He had not been gone ten minutes before Aunt
Rosamund appeared, with a crutch-handled stick and
a gentlemanly limp, for she, too, indulged her ancestors
in gout. A desire for exclusive possession of their
friends is natural to some people, and the good lady
had not known how fond she was of her niece till the

girl had slipped off into this marriage. She wanted her back, to go about with and make much of, as before. And her well-bred drawl did not quite disguise this feeling.

Gyp could detect Fiorsen subtly mimicking that drawl; and her ears began to burn. The puppies afforded a diversion—their points, noses, boldness, and food, held the danger in abeyance for some minutes. Then the mimicry began again. When Aunt Rosamund had taken a somewhat sudden leave, Gyp stood at the window of her drawing-room with the mask off her face. Fiorsen came up, put his arm round her from behind, and said with a fierce sigh:

" Are they coming often—these excellent people ?"

Gyp drew back from him against the wall.

" If you love me, why do you try to hurt the people who love me too ?"

" Because I am jealous. I am jealous even of those puppies."

" And shall you try to hurt them ?"

" If I see them too much near you, perhaps I shall."

" Do you think I can be happy if you hurt things because they love me ?"

He sat down and drew her on to his knee. She did not resist, but made not the faintest return to his caresses. The first time—the very first friend to come into her own new home ! It was too much !

Fiorsen said hoarsely:

" You do not love me. If you loved me, I should feel it through your lips. I should see it in your eyes. Oh, love me, Gyp ! You shall !"

But to say to Love: " Stand and deliver !" was not the way to touch Gyp. It seemed to her mere ill-bred

stupidity. She froze against him in soul, all the more
that she yielded her body. When a woman refuses
nothing to one whom she does not really love, shadows
are already falling on the bride-house. And Fiorsen
knew it; but his self-control about equalled that of
the two puppies.

Yet, on the whole, these first weeks in her new
home were happy, too busy to allow much room for
doubting or regret. Several important concerts were
fixed for May. She looked forward to these with
intense eagerness, and pushed everything that inter-
fered with preparation into the background. As
though to make up for that instinctive recoil from
giving her heart, of which she was always subconscious,
she gave him all her activities, without calculation or
reserve. She was ready to play for him all day and
every day, just as from the first she had held herself
at the disposal of his passion. To fail him in these
ways would have tarnished her opinion of herself.
But she had some free hours in the morning, for he
had the habit of lying in bed till eleven, and was
never ready for practice before twelve. In those early
hours she got through her orders and her shopping—
that pursuit which to so many women is the only real
" sport "—a chase of the ideal; a pitting of one's
taste and knowledge against that of the world at
large; a secret passion, even in the beautiful, for
making oneself and one's house more beautiful. Gyp
never went shopping without that faint thrill running
up and down her nerves. She hated to be touched
by strange fingers, but not even that stopped her
pleasure in turning and turning before long mirrors,
while the saleswoman or man, with admiration at
first crocodilic and then genuine, ran the tips of fingers

over those curves, smoothing and pinning, and uttering the word, " moddam."

On other mornings, she would ride with Winton, who would come for her, leaving her again at her door after their outings. One day, after a ride in Richmond Park, where the horse-chestnuts were just coming into flower, they had late breakfast on the verandah of a hotel before starting for home. Some fruit-trees were still in blossom just below them, and the sunlight showering down from a blue sky brightened to silver the windings of the river, and to gold the budding leaves of the oak trees. Winton, smoking his after-breakfast cigar, stared down across the tops of those trees toward the river and the wooded fields beyond. Stealing a glance at him, Gyp said very softly:

" Did you ever ride with my mother, Dad ?"

" Only once—the very ride we've been to-day. She was on a black mare; I had a chestnut——" Yes, in that grove on the little hill, which they had ridden through that morning, he had dismounted and stood beside her.

Gyp stretched her hand across the table and laid it on his.

" Tell me about her, dear. Was she beautiful ?"

" Yes."

" Dark ? Tall ?"

" Very like you, Gyp. A little—a little "—he did not know how to describe that difference—" a little more foreign-looking perhaps. One of her grand-mothers was Italian, you know."

" How did you come to love her ? Suddenly ?"

" As suddenly as "—he drew his hand away and laid it on the verandah rail—" as that sun came on my hand."

Gyp said quietly, as if to herself:

"Yes; I don't think I understand that—yet."

Winton drew breath through his teeth with a subdued hiss. Whether to be glad or sorry, he by no means knew.

"Did she love you at first sight, too?"

"One easily believes what one wants to—but I think she did. She used to say so."

"And how long?"

"Only a year."

Gyp said very softly:

"Poor darling Dad." And suddenly she added: "I can't bear to think I killed her—I can't bear it!"

Winton got up in the discomfort of these sudden confidences; a blackbird, startled by the movement, ceased his song. Gyp said in a hard voice:

"No; I don't want to have any children."

"Without that, I shouldn't have had you, Gyp."

"No; but I don't want to have them. And I don't —I don't want to love like that. I should be afraid."

Winton looked at her for a long time without speaking, his brows drawn down, frowning, puzzled, as though over his own past.

"Love," he said, "it catches you, and you're gone. When it comes, you welcome it, whether it's to kill you or not. Shall we start back, my child?"

When she got home, it was not quite noon. She hurried over her bath and dressing, and ran out to the music-room. Its walls had been hung with Willesden scrim gilded over; the curtains were silver-grey; there was a divan covered with silver-and-gold stuff, and a beaten brass fireplace. It was a study in silver, and gold, save for two touches of fantasy—a screen round the piano-head, covered with brilliantly painted peacocks' tails, and a blue Persian vase, in which were flowers of various hues of red.

Fiorsen was standing at the window in a fume of cigarette smoke. He did not turn round. Gyp put her hand within his arm, and said:

"So sorry, dear. But it's only just half-past twelve."

His face was as if the whole world had injured him.

"Pity you came back! Very nice, riding, I'm sure!"

Could she not go riding with her own father? What insensate jealousy and egomania! She turned away, without a word, and sat down at the piano. She was not good at standing injustice—not good at all! The scent of brandy, too, was mixed with the fumes of his cigarette. Drink in the morning was so ugly—really horrid! She sat at the piano, waiting. He would be like this till he had played away the fumes of his ill mood, and then he would come and paw her shoulders and put his lips to her neck. Yes; but it was not the way to behave, not the way to make her love him. And she said suddenly:

"Gustav; what exactly have I done that you dislike?"

"You have had a father."

Gyp sat quite still for a few seconds, and then began to laugh. He looked so like a sulky child, standing there. He turned swiftly on her and put his hand over her mouth. She looked up over that hand which smelled of tobacco. Her heart was doing the *grand écart* within her, this way in compunction, that way in resentment. His eyes fell before hers; he dropped his hand.

"Well, shall we begin?" she said.

He answered roughly: " No," and went out into the garden.

Gyp was left dismayed, disgusted. Was it possible that she could have taken part in such a horrid little scene? She remained sitting at the piano, playing over and over a single passage, without heeding what it was.

IV

So far, they had seen nothing of Rosek at the little house. She wondered if Fiorsen had passed on to him her remark, though if he had, he would surely say he hadn't; she had learned that her husband spoke the truth when convenient, not when it caused him pain. About music, or any art, however, he could be implicitly relied on; and his frankness was appalling when his nerves were ruffled.

But at the first concert she saw Rosek's unwelcome figure on the other side of the gangway, two rows back. He was talking to a young girl, whose face, short and beautifully formed, had the opaque transparency of alabaster. With her round blue eyes fixed on him, and her lips just parted, she had a slightly vacant look. Her laugh, too, was just a little vacant. And yet her features were so beautiful, her hair so smooth and fair, her colouring so pale and fine, her neck so white and round, the poise of her body so perfect that Gyp found it difficult to take her glance away. She had refused her aunt's companionship. It might irritate Fiorsen and affect his playing to see her with "that stiff English creature." She wanted, too, to feel again the sensations of Wiesbaden. There would be a kind of sacred pleasure in knowing that she had helped to perfect sounds which touched the hearts and senses of so many listeners. She had looked forward to this concert so long. And she sat scarcely breathing, abstracted from consciousness of those about her, soft and still, radiating warmth and eagerness.

Fiorsen looked his worst, as ever, when first coming before an audience—cold, furtive, defensive, defiant, half turned away, with those long fingers tightening the screws, touching the strings. It seemed queer to think that only six hours ago she had stolen out of bed from beside him. Wiesbaden! No; this was not like Wiesbaden! And when he played she had not the same emotions. She had heard him now too often, knew too exactly how he produced those sounds; knew that their fire and sweetness and nobility sprang from fingers, ear, brain—not from his soul. Nor was it possible any longer to drift off on those currents of sound into new worlds, to hear bells at dawn, and the dews of evening as they fell, to feel the divinity of wind and sunlight. The romance and ecstasy that at Wiesbaden had soaked her spirit came no more. She was watching for the weak spots, the passages with which he had struggled and she had struggled; she was distracted by memories of petulance, black moods, and sudden caresses. And then she caught his eye. The look was like, yet how unlike, those looks at Wiesbaden. It had the old love-hunger, but had lost the adoration, its spiritual essence. And she thought: ' Is it my fault, or is it only because he has me now to do what he likes with ?' It was all another disillusionment, perhaps the greatest yet. But she kindled and flushed at the applause, and lost herself in pleasure at his success. At the interval, she slipped out at once, for her first visit to the artist's room, the mysterious enchantment of a peep behind the scenes. He was coming down from his last recall; and at sight of her his look of bored contempt vanished;

lifting her hand, he kissed it. Gyp felt happier than
she had since her marriage. Her eyes shone, and she
whispered:

" Beautiful !"

He whispered back:

" So ! Do you love me, Gyp ?"

She nodded. And at that moment she did, or
thought so.

Then people began to come; amongst them her old
music-master, Monsieur Harmost, grey and mahogany
as ever, who, after a " *Merveilleux*," " *Très fort* " or
two to Fiorsen, turned his back on him to talk to his
old pupil.

So she had married Fiorsen—dear, dear ! That
was extraordinary, but extraordinary ! And what was
it like, to be always with him—a little funny—not so ?
And how was her music ? It would be spoiled now.
Ah, what a pity ! No ? She must come to him, then;
yes, come again. All the time he patted her arm, as
if playing the piano, and his fingers, that had the
touch of an angel, felt the firmness of her flesh, as
though debating whether she were letting it deteriorate.
He seemed really to have missed " his little friend,"
to be glad at seeing her again; and Gyp, who never
could withstand appreciation, smiled at him. More
people came. She saw Rosek talking to her husband,
and the young alabaster girl standing silent, her lips
still a little parted, gazing up at Fiorsen. A perfect
figure, though rather short; a dovelike face, whose
exquisitely shaped, just-opened lips seemed to be
demanding sugar-plums. She could not be more than
nineteen. Who was she ?

A voice said almost in her ear:

" How do you do, Mrs. Fiorsen ? I am fortunate
to see you again at last."

She was obliged to turn.   If Gustav had given her away, one would never know it from this velvet-masked creature, with his suave watchfulness and ready composure, who talked away so smoothly. What was it that she so disliked in him ? Gyp had acute instincts, the natural intelligence deep in certain natures, not over intellectual, but whose " feelers " are too delicate to be deceived.   And, for something to say, she asked:

" Who is the girl you were talking to, Count Rosek ? Her face is so lovely."

He smiled, exactly the smile she had so disliked at Wiesbaden; following his glance, she saw her husband talking to the girl, whose lips at that moment seemed more than ever to ask for sugar-plums.

" A young dancer, Daphne Wing—she will make a name.   A dove flying ! So you admire her, Madame Gyp ?"

Gyp said, smiling:

" She's very pretty—I can imagine her dancing beautifully."

" Will you come one day and see her ? She has still to make her début."

Gyp answered:

" Thank you.   I don't know.   I love dancing, of course."

" Good !   I will arrange it."

And Gyp thought: ' No, no ! I don't want to have anything to do with you !   Why do I speak the truth ? Why didn't I say I hate dancing ?'

Just then a bell sounded; people began hurrying away.   The girl came up to Rosek.

" Miss Daphne Wing—Mrs. Fiorsen."

Gyp put out her hand with a smile—this girl was

certainly a picture. Miss Daphne Wing smiled, too, and said, with the intonation of those who have been carefully corrected of an accent:

" Oh, Mrs. Fiorsen, how beautifully your husband plays—doesn't he ?"

It was not merely the careful speech but something lacking when the perfect mouth moved—spirit, sensibility, who could say ? And Gyp felt sorry, as at blight on a perfect flower. With a friendly nod, she turned away to Fiorsen, who was waiting to go up on to the platform. Was it at her or at the girl he had been looking ? She smiled at him and slid away. In the corridor, Rosek, in attendance, said:

" Why not this evening ? Come with Gustav to my rooms. She shall dance to us, and we will all have supper. She admires you, Madame Gyp. She will love to dance for you."

Gyp longed for the simple brutality to say: " I don't want to come. I don't like you !" But all she could manage was:

" Thank you. I—I will ask Gustav."

Once in her seat again, she rubbed the cheek that his breath had touched. A girl was singing now— one of those faces that Gyp always admired, reddish-gold hair, blue eyes—the very antithesis of herself— and the song was " The Bens of Jura," that strange outpouring from a heart broken by love:

" And my heart reft of its own sun "——

Tears rose in her eyes, and the shiver of some very deep response passed through her. What was it Dad had said: " Love catches you, and you're gone !"

She, who was the result of love like that, did not want to love !

The girl finished singing. There was little applause.
Yet she had sung beautifully; and what more wonderful song in the world? Was it too tragic, too painful,
too strange—not " pretty " enough? Gyp felt sorry
for her. Her head ached now. She would so have
liked to slip away when it was all over. But she had
not the needful rudeness. She would have to go
through with this evening at Rosek's and be gay.
And why not? Why this shadow over everything?
But it was no new sensation, that of having entered
by her own free will on a life which, for all effort,
would not give her a feeling of anchorage or home.
Of her own accord she had stepped into the cage !

On the way to Rosek's rooms, she disguised from
Fiorsen her headache and depression. He was in one
of his boy-out-of-school moods, elated by applause,
mimicking her old master, the idolatries of his wor-
shippers, Rosek, the girl dancer's upturned expectant
lips. And he slipped his arm round Gyp in the cab,
crushing her against him and sniffing at her cheek
as if she had been a flower.

Rosek had the first floor of an old-time mansion in
Russell Square. The smell of incense or some kindred
perfume was at once about one; and, on the walls of
the dark hall, electric light burned, in jars of alabaster
picked up in the East. The whole place was in fact
a sanctum of the collector's spirit. Its owner had a
passion for black—the walls, divans, picture-frames,
even some of the tilings were black, with glimmerings
of gold, ivory, and moonlight. On a round black
table there stood a golden bowl filled with moonlight-
coloured velvety " palm " and " honesty"; from a black
wall gleamed out the ivory mask of a faun's face;
from a dark niche the little silver figure of a dancing

girl. It was beautiful, but deathly. And Gyp,
though excited always by anything new, keenly alive
to every sort of beauty, felt a longing for air and sunlight. It was a relief to get close to one of the black-
curtained windows, and see the westering sun shower
warmth and light on the trees of the Square gardens.
She was introduced to a Mr. and Mrs. Gallant, a dark-
faced, cynical-looking man with clever, malicious eyes,
and one of those large cornucopias of women with avid
blue stares. The little dancer was not there. She
had " gone to put on nothing," Rosek informed them.

He took Gyp the round of his treasures, scarabs,
Rops drawings, death-masks, Chinese pictures, and
queer old flutes, with an air of displaying them for the
first time to one who could truly appreciate. And
she kept thinking of that saying, " *Une technique
merveilleuse.*" Her instinct apprehended the refined
bone-viciousness of this place, where nothing, save
perhaps taste, would be sacred. It was her first
glimpse into that gilt-edged bohemia, whence the
generosities, the *élans*, the struggles of the true bohemia
are as rigidly excluded as from the spheres where
bishops moved. But she talked and smiled; and no
one could have told that her nerves were crisping as
if at contact with a corpse. While showing her those
alabaster jars, her host had laid his hand softly on her
wrist, and in taking it away, he let his fingers, with
a touch softer than a kitten's paw, ripple over the
skin, then put them to his lips. Ah, there it was—
the—the *technique!* A desperate desire to laugh
seized her. And he saw it—oh, yes, he saw it! He
gave her one look, passed that same hand over his
smooth face, and—behold!—it showed as before, un-
mortified, unconscious. A deadly little man!

When they returned to the salon, as it was called, Miss Daphne Wing in a black kimono, whence her face and arms emerged more like alabaster than ever, was sitting on a divan beside Fiorsen. She rose at once and came across to Gyp.

"Oh, Mrs. Fiorsen"—why did everything she said begin with "Oh!"—"isn't this room lovely? It's perfect for dancing. I only brought cream, and flame-colour; they go so beautifully with black."

She threw back her kimono for Gyp to inspect her dress—a girdled cream-coloured shift, which made her ivory arms and neck seem more than ever dazzling; and her mouth opened, as if for a sugar-plum of praise. Then, lowering her voice, she murmured:

"Do you know, I'm rather afraid of Count Rosek."

"Why?"

"Oh, I don't know; he's so critical, and smooth, and he comes up so quietly. I do think your husband plays wonderfully. Oh, Mrs. Fiorsen, you are beautiful, aren't you?" Gyp laughed. "What would you like me to dance first. A waltz of Chopin's?"

"Yes; I love Chopin."

"Then I shall. I shall dance exactly what you like, because I do admire you, and I'm sure you're awfully sweet. Oh, yes; you are; I can see that! And I think your husband is awfully in love with you. I should be, if I were a man. You know, I've been studying five years, and I haven't come out yet. But now Count Rosek's going to back me, I expect it'll be very soon. Will you come to my first night? Mother says I've got to be awfully careful. She only let me come this evening because you were going to be here. Would you like me to begin?"

She slid across to Rosek, and Gyp heard her say:

" Oh, Mrs. Fiorsen wants me to begin; a Chopin waltz, please. The one that goes like this."

Rosek went to the piano, the little dancer to the centre of the room. Gyp sat down beside Fiorsen.

Rosek began playing, his eyes fixed on the girl, and his mouth loosened from compression in a sweetish smile. Miss Daphne Wing was standing with her finger-tips joined at her breast—a perfect statue of ebony and palest wax. Suddenly she flung away the black kimono. A thrill swept Gyp from head to foot. She *could* dance—that common little girl! Every movement of her round, sinuous body, of her bare limbs, had the ecstasy of natural genius, controlled by the quivering balance of a really fine training. " A dove flying!" So she was. Her face had lost its vacancy, or rather its vacancy had become divine, having that look—not lost but gone before—which dance demands. Yes, she was a gem, even if she had a common soul. Tears came up in Gyp's eyes. It was so lovely—like a dove, when it flings itself up in the wind, breasting on up, up—wings bent back, poised. Abandonment, freedom—chastened, shaped, controlled !

When, after the dance, the girl came and sat down beside her, she squeezed her hot little hand, but the caress was for her art, not for this moist little person with the lips avid of sugar-plums.

' Oh, did you like it ? I'm so glad. Shall I go and put on my flame-colour, now ?"

The moment she was gone, comment broke out freely. The dark and cynical Gallant thought the girl's dancing like a certain Napierkowska whom he had seen in Moscow, without her fire—the touch of passion would have to be supplied. She wanted love !

Love! And suddenly Gyp was back in the concert-
hall, listening to that other girl singing the song of a
broken heart.

> " Thy kiss, dear love——
> Like watercress gathered fresh from cool streams."

Love! in this abode—of fauns' heads, deep cushions,
silver dancing girls! Love! She had a sudden sense
of deep abasement. What was she, herself, but just
a feast for a man's senses? Her home, what but a
place like this? Miss Daphne Wing was back again.
Gyp looked at her husband's face while she was
dancing. His lips! How was it that she could see
that disturbance in him, and not care. If she had
really loved him, to see his lips like that would have
hurt her, but she might have understood perhaps, and
forgiven. Now she neither quite understood nor quite
forgave.

And that night, when he kissed her, she murmured:
" Would you rather it were that girl—not me?"
" That girl! I could swallow her at a draught.
But you, my Gyp—I want to drink for ever!"
Was that true? *If* she had loved him—how good
to hear!

V

AFTER this, Gyp was daily more and more in contact with high bohemia, that curious composite section of society which embraces the neck of music, poetry, and the drama. She was a success, but secretly she felt that she did not belong to it, nor, in truth, did Fiorsen, who was much too genuine a bohemian, and artist, and mocked at the Gallants and even the Roseks of this life, as he mocked at Winton, Aunt Rosamund, and their world. Life with him had certainly one effect on Gyp; it made her feel less and less a part of that old orthodox, well-bred world which she had known before she married him; but to which she had confessed to Winton she had never felt that she belonged, since she knew the secret of her birth. She was, in truth, much too impressionable, too avid of beauty, and perhaps too naturally critical to accept the dictates of their fact-and-form-governed routine; only, of her own accord, she would never have had initiative enough to step out of its circle. Loosened from those roots, unable to attach herself to this new soil, and not spiritually leagued with her husband, she was more and more lonely. Her only truly happy hours were those spent with Winton or at her piano or with her puppies. She was always wondering at what she had done, longing to find the deep, the sufficient reason for having done it. But the more she sought and longed, the deeper grew her bewilderment, her feeling of being in a cage. Of late, too,

another and more definite uneasiness had come
to her.

She spent much time in her garden, where the
blossoms had all dropped, lilac was over, acacias coming
into bloom, and blackbirds silent.

Winton, who, by careful experiment, had found that
from half-past three to six there was little or no chance
of stumbling across his son-in-law, came in nearly
every day for tea and a quiet cigar on the lawn. He
was sitting there with Gyp one afternoon, when Betty,
who usurped the functions of parlour-maid whenever
the whim moved her, brought out a card on which
were printed the words, " Miss Daphne Wing."

" Bring her out, please, Betty dear, and some fresh
tea, and buttered toast—plenty of buttered toast;
yes, and the chocolates, and any other sweets there are,
Betty darling."

Betty, with that expression which always came over
her when she was called " darling," withdrew across
the grass, and Gyp said to her father:

" It's the little dancer I told you of, Dad. Now
you'll see something perfect. Only, she'll be dressed.
It's a pity."

She was. The occasion had evidently exercised her
spirit. In warm ivory, shrouded by leaf-green chiffon,
with a girdle of tiny artificial leaves, and a lightly
covered head encircled by other green leaves, she was
somewhat like a nymph peering from a bower. If
rather too arresting, it was charming, and, after all,
no frock could quite disguise the beauty of her figure.
She was evidently nervous.

" Oh, Mrs. Fiorsen, I thought you wouldn't mind
my coming. I did so want to see you again. Count
Rosek said he thought I might. It's all fixed for my

coming out. Oh, how do you do?" And with lips
and eyes opening at Winton, she sat down in the chair
he placed for her. Gyp, watching his expression, felt
inclined to laugh. Dad, and Daphne Wing! And
the poor girl so evidently anxious to make a good
impression! Presently she asked:

"Have you been dancing at Count Rosek's again
lately?"

"Oh, yes, haven't you—didn't you—I——" And
she stopped.

The thought flashed through Gyp: 'So Gustav's
been seeing her, and hasn't told me!' But she said
at once:

"Ah, yes, of course; I forgot. When is the night of
your coming-out?"

"Next Friday week. Fancy! The Octagon. Isn't
it splendid? They've given me such a good engagement. I do so want you and Mr. Fiorsen to come,
though!"

Gyp, smiling, murmured:

"Of course we will. My father loves dancing, too;
don't you, Dad?"

Winton took his cigar from his mouth.

"When it's good," he said, urbanely.

"Oh, mine *is* good; isn't it, Mrs. Fiorsen? I mean,
I *have* worked—ever since I was thirteen, you know.
I simply love it. I think *you* would dance beautifully,
Mrs. Fiorsen. You've got such a perfect figure. I
simply love to see you walk."

Gyp flushed, and said:

"Do have one of these, Miss Wing—they've got
whole raspberries inside."

The little dancer put one in her mouth.

"Oh, but please don't call me Miss Wing! I

wish you'd call me Daphne. Mr. Fior—everybody
does."

Conscious of her father's face, Gyp murmured:

" It's a lovely name. Won't you have another ?
These are apricot."

" They're perfect. You know, my first dress is
going to be all orange-blossom; Mr. Fiorsen suggested
that. But I expect he told you. Perhaps you suggested it really; did you ?" Gyp shook her head.
" Count Rosek says the world is waiting for me——"
She paused with a sugar-plum half-way to her lips,
and added doubtfully: " Do you think that's
true ?"

Gyp answered with a soft: " I hope so."

" He says I'm something new. It would be nice to
think that. He has great taste; so has Mr. Fiorsen,
hasn't he ?"

Conscious of the compression in the lips behind the
smoke of her father's cigar, and with a sudden longing
to get up and walk away, Gyp nodded.

The little dancer placed the sweet in her mouth,
and said complacently:

" Of course he has; because he married you."

Then, seeming to grow conscious of Winton's eyes
fixed so intently on her, she became confused, swal-
lowed hastily, and said:

" Oh, isn't it lovely here—like the country ! I'm
afraid I must go; it's my practice-time. It's so important for me not to miss any now, isn't it ?" And
she rose.

Winton got up, too. Gyp saw the girl's eyes,
lighting on his rigid hand, grow round and rounder;
and from her, walking past the side of the house, the
careful voice floated back.

" Oh, I do hope——" But what, could not be heard.

Sinking back in her chair, Gyp sat motionless. Bees were murmurous among her flowers, pigeons murmurous among the trees; the sunlight warmed her knees, and her stretched-out feet through the open-work of her stockings. The maid's laughter, the delicious growling of the puppies at play in the kitchen came drifting down the garden, with the distant cry of a milkman up the road. All was very peaceful. But in her heart were such curious, baffled emotions, such strange, tangled feelings. This moment of en-lightenment regarding the measure of her husband's frankness came close on the heels of the moment fate had chosen for another revelation, for clinching within her a fear felt for weeks past. She had said to Winton that she did not want to have a child. In those conscious that their birth has caused death or even too great suffering, there is sometimes this hostile instinct. She had not even the consolation that Fiorsen wanted children; she knew that he did not. And now she was sure one was coming. But it was more than that. She had not reached, and knew she could not reach, that point of spirit-union which alone makes marriage sacred, and the sacrifices demanded by motherhood a joy. She was fairly caught in the web of her foolish and presumptuous mistake ! So few months of marriage—and so sure that it was a failure, so hopeless for the future ! In the light of this new certainty, it was terrifying. A hard, natural fact is needed to bring a yearning and bewildered spirit to knowledge of the truth. Disillusionment is not welcome to a woman's heart; the less welcome when it is disillusionment with self as much as with another. Her great dedication—her scheme of life! She had been going to—what?—save Fiorsen from himself! It was laughable. She had only lost herself. Already she felt in prison, and by a child would be all the more bound. To some women, the knowledge that a thing must be brings assuagement of the nerves. Gyp was the opposite of those. To force her was the way to stiver up every contrary emotion. She might will herself to acquiesce, but—one cannot change one's nature.

And so, while the pigeons cooed and the sunlight warmed her feet, she spent the bitterest moments of her life—so far. Pride came to her help. She had made a miserable mess of it, but no one must know— certainly not her father, who had warned her so desperately! She had made her bed, and she would have to lie on it.

When Winton came back, he found her smiling, and said:

" I don't see the fascination, Gyp."

" Don't you think her face really rather perfect ?"

" Common."

" Yes; but that drops off when she's dancing."

Winton looked at her from under half-closed eyelids.

" With her clothes ? What does Fiorsen think of her ?"

Gyp smiled.

" Does he think of her ? I don't know."

She could feel the watchful tightening of his face. And suddenly he said:

" Daphne Wing! By George !"

The words were a masterpiece of resentment and distrust. His daughter in peril from—such as that!

After he was gone Gyp sat on till the sun had quite

vanished and the dew was stealing through her thin frock. She would think of anything, anybody except herself! To make others happy was the way to be happy—or so they said. She would try—must try. Betty—so stout, and with that rheumatism in her leg —did she ever think of herself? Or Aunt Rosamund, with her perpetual rescuings of lost dogs, lame horses, and penniless musicians? And Dad, for all his man-of-the-world ways, was he not always doing little things for the men of his old regiment, always thinking of her, too, and what he could do to give her pleasure? To love everybody, and bring them happiness! Was it not possible? Only, people were hard to love, different from birds and beasts and flowers, to love which seemed natural and easy.

She went up to her room and began to dress for dinner. Which of her frocks did he like best? The pale, low-cut amber, or that white, soft one, with the coffee-dipped lace? She decided on the latter. Scrutinizing her supple, slender image in the glass, a shudder went through her. That would all go; she would be like those women taking careful exercise in the streets, who made her wonder at their hardihood in showing themselves. It wasn't fair that one must become unsightly, offensive to the eye, in order to bring life into the world. Some women seemed proud to be like that. How was that possible? She would never dare to show herself in the days coming.

She finished dressing and went downstairs. It was nearly eight, and Fiorsen had not come in. When the gong was struck, she turned from the window with a sigh, and went in to dinner. That sigh had been relief. She ate her dinner with the two pups beside her, sent them off, and sat down at her piano. She played Chopin—studies, waltzes, mazurkas, preludes, a polonaise or two. And Betty, who had a weakness for that composer, sat on a chair by the door which partitioned off the back premises, having opened it a little. She wished she could go and take a peep at her "pretty" in her white frock, with the candle-flames on each side, and those lovely lilies in the vase close by, smelling beautiful. And one of the maids coming too near, she shooed her angrily away.

It grew late. The tray had been brought up; the maids had gone to bed. Gyp had long stopped play-ing, had turned out, ready to go up, and, by the French window, stood gazing out into the dark. How warm it was—warm enough to draw forth the scent of the jessamine along the garden wall! Not a star. There always seemed so few stars in London. A sound made her swing round. Something tall was over there in the darkness, by the open door. She heard a sigh, and called out, frightened:

"Is that you, Gustav?"

He spoke some words that she could not understand. Shutting the window quickly, she went toward him. Light from the hall lit up one side of his face and figure. He was pale; his eyes shone strangely; his sleeve was all white. He said thickly:

"Little ghost!" and then some words that must be Swedish. It was the first time Gyp had ever come to close quarters with drunkenness. And her thought was simply: 'How awful if anybody were to see—how awful!' She made a rush to get into the hall and lock the door leading to the back regions, but he caught her frock, ripping the lace from her neck, and his entangled fingers clutched her shoulder. She stopped dead, fearing to make a noise or pull him over, and his other hand clutched her other shoulder, so that he stood steadying himself by her. Why was she not shocked, smitten to the ground with grief and shame and rage? She only felt: 'What am I to do? How get him upstairs without anyone knowing?' And she looked up into his face—it seemed to her so pathetic with its shining eyes and its staring whiteness that she could have burst into tears. She said gently:

"Gustav, it's all right. Lean on me; we'll go up."

His hands, that seemed to have no power or purpose, touched her cheeks, mechanically caressing. More than disgust, she felt that awful pity. Putting her arm round his waist, she moved with him toward the stairs. If only no one heard; if only she could get him quietly up! And she murmured:

"Don't talk; you're not well. Lean on me hard."

He seemed to make a big effort; his lips puffed out, and with an expression of pride that would have been comic if not so tragic, he muttered something.

Holding him close with all her strength, as she might have held one desperately loved, she began to mount. It was easier than she had thought. Only across the landing now, into the bedroom, and then the danger would be over. Done! He was lying across the bed, and the door shut. Then, for a moment, she gave way to a fit of shivering so violent that she could hear her teeth chattering yet could not stop them. She caught sight of herself in the big mirror. Her pretty lace was all torn; her shoulders were red where his hands had gripped her, holding himself up. She threw off her dress, put on a wrapper, and went up to him. He was lying in a sort of stupor, and with difficulty she got him to sit up and lean against the bed-rail. Taking off his tie and collar, she racked her brains for

what to give him. Sal volatile! Surely that must
be right. It brought him to himself, so that he even
tried to kiss her. At last he was in bed, and she stood
looking at him. His eyes were closed; he would not
see if she gave way now. But she would not cry—
she would not. One sob came—but that was all.
Well, there was nothing to be done now but get into
bed too. She undressed, and turned out the light.
He was in a stertorous sleep. And lying there, with
eyes wide open, staring into the dark, a smile came
on her lips—a very strange smile! She was thinking
of all those preposterous young wives she had read of,
who, blushing, trembling, murmur into the ears of their
young husbands that they "have something—something to tell them!"

VI

LOOKING at Fiorsen, next morning, still sunk in heavy sleep, her first thought was: "He looks exactly the same." And, suddenly, it seemed queer to her that she had not been, and still was not, disgusted. It was all too deep for disgust, and somehow, too natural. She took this new revelation of his unbridled ways without resentment. Besides, she had long known of this taste of his—one cannot drink brandy and not betray it.

She stole noiselessly from bed, noiselessly gathered up his boots and clothes all tumbled on to a chair, and took them forth to the dressing-room. There she held the garments up to the early light and brushed them, then, noiseless, stole back to bed, with needle and thread and her lace. No one must know; not even he must know. For the moment she had forgotten that other thing so terrifically important. It came back to her, very sudden, very sickening. So long as she could keep it secret, no one should know that either—he least of all.

The morning passed as usual; but when she came to the music-room at noon, she found that he had gone out. She was just sitting down to lunch when Betty, with the broad smile which prevailed on her moon-face when someone had tickled the right side of her, announced:

"Count Rosek."

Gyp got up, startled.

" Say that Mr. Fiorsen is not in, Betty. But—but ask if he will come and have some lunch, and get a bottle of hock up, please."

In the few seconds before her visitor appeared, Gyp experienced the sort of excitement one has entering a field where a bull is grazing.

But not even his severest critics could accuse Rosek of want of tact. He had hoped to see Gustav, but it was charming of her to give him lunch—a great delight !

He seemed to have put off, as if for her benefit, his corsets, and some, at all events, of his offending looks —seemed simpler, more genuine. His face was slightly browned, as if, for once, he had been taking his due of air and sun. He talked without cynical sub-meanings, was most appreciative of her " charming little house," and even showed some warmth in his sayings about art and music. Gyp had never disliked him less. But her instincts were on the watch. After lunch, they went out across the garden to see the music-room, and he sat down at the piano. He had the deep, caressing touch that lies in fingers of steel worked by a real passion for tone. Gyp sat on the divan and listened. She was out of his sight there; and she looked at him, wondering. He was playing Schumann's Child Music. How could one who produced such fresh idyllic sounds have sinister intentions ? And presently she said:

" Count Rosek !"

" Madame ?"

" Will you please tell me why you sent Daphne Wing here yesterday ?"

" *I* send her ?"

" Yes."

But instantly she regretted having asked that question. He had swung round on the music-stool and was looking full at her. His face had changed.

"Since you ask me, I thought you should know that Gustav is seeing a good deal of her."

He had given the exact answer she had divined.

"Do you think I mind that?"

A flicker passed over his face. He got up and said quietly:

"I am glad that you do not."

"Why glad?"

She, too, had risen. Though he was little taller than herself, she was conscious suddenly of how thick and steely he was beneath his dapper garments, and of a kind of snaky will-power in his face. Her heart beat faster.

He came toward her and said:

"I am glad you understand that it is over with Gustav—finished——" He stopped dead, seeing at once that he had gone wrong, and not knowing quite where. Gyp had simply smiled. A flush coloured his cheeks, and he said:

"He is a volcano soon extinguished. You see, I know him. Better you should know him, too. Why do you smile?"

"Why is it better I should know?"

He went very pale, and said between his teeth:

"That you may not waste your time; there is love waiting for you."

But Gyp still smiled.

"Was it from love of me that you made him drunk last night?"

His lips quivered.

"Gyp!" Gyp turned. But with the merest change

of front, he had put himself between her and the door.
" You never loved him. That is my excuse. You
have given him too much already—more than he is
worth. Ah ! God ! I am tortured by you; I am
possessed."

He had gone white through and through like a
flame, save for his smouldering eyes. She was afraid,
and because she was afraid, she stood her ground.
Should she make a dash for the door that opened into
the little lane and escape that way ? Then suddenly
he seemed to regain control; but she could feel that
he was trying to break through her defences by the
sheer intensity of his gaze—by a kind of mesmerism,
knowing that he had frightened her.

Under the strain of this duel of eyes, she felt herself
beginning to sway, to get dizzy. Whether or no he
really moved his feet, he seemed coming closer inch
by inch. She had a horrible feeling—as if his arms
were already round her.

With an effort, she wrenched her gaze from his, and
suddenly his crisp hair caught her eyes. Surely—
surely it was curled with tongs ! A kind of spasm of
amusement was set free in her heart, and, almost
inaudibly, the words escaped her lips : " *Une technique
merveilleuse !*" His eyes wavered; he uttered a little
gasp; his lips fell apart. Gyp walked across the room
and put her hand on the bell. She had lost her fear.
Without a word, he turned, and went out into the
garden. She watched him cross the lawn. Gone !
She had beaten him by the one thing not even violent
passions can withstand—ridicule, almost unconscious
ridicule. Then she gave way and pulled the bell with
nervous violence. The sight of the maid, in her trim
black dress and spotless white apron, coming from

the house completed her restoration. Was it possible that she had really been frightened, nearly failing in that encounter, nearly dominated by that man—in her own house, with her own maids down there at hand? And she said quietly:

" I want the puppies, please."

" Yes, ma'am."

Over the garden, the day brooded in the first-gathered warmth of summer. Mid-June of a fine year. The air was drowsy with hum and scent.

And Gyp, sitting in the shade, while the puppies rolled and snapped, searched her little world for comfort and some sense of safety, and could not find it; as if there were all round her a hot heavy fog in which things lurked, and where she kept erect only by pride and the will not to cry out that she was struggling and afraid.

Fiorsen, leaving his house that morning, had walked till he saw a taxi-cab. Leaning back therein, with hat thrown off, he caused himself to be driven rapidly, at random. This was one of his habits when his mind was not at ease—an expensive idiosyncracy, ill-afforded by a pocket that had holes. The swift motion and titillation by the perpetual close shaving of other vehicles were sedative to him. He needed sedatives this morning. To wake in his own bed without the least remembering how he had got there was no more new to him than to many another man of twenty-eight, but it was new since his marriage. If he had remembered even less he would have been more at ease. But he could just recollect standing in the dark drawing-room, seeing and touching a ghostly Gyp quite close to him. And, somehow, he was afraid.

8

And when he was afraid—like most people—he was at his worst.

If she had been like all the other women in whose company he had eaten passion-fruit, he would not have felt this carking humiliation. If she had been like them, at the pace he had been going since he obtained possession of her, he would already have "finished," as Rosek had said. And he knew well enough that he had not "finished." He might get drunk, might be loose-ended in every way, but Gyp was hooked into his senses, and, for all that he could not get near her, into his spirit. Her very passivity was her strength, the secret of her magnetism. In her, he felt some of that mysterious sentiency of nature, which, even in yielding to man's fevers, lies apart with a faint smile—the uncapturable smile of the woods and fields by day or night, that makes one ache with longing. He felt in her some of the unfathomable, soft, vibrating indifference of the flowers and trees and streams, of the rocks, of bird-songs, and the eternal hum, under sunshine or starshine. Her dark, half-smiling eyes enticed him, inspired an unquench-able thirst. And his was one of those natures which, encountering spiritual difficulty, at once jib off, seek anodynes, try to bandage wounded egoism with ex-cess—a spoiled child, with the desperations and the inherent pathos, the something repulsive and the something lovable that belong to all such. Having wished for this moon, and got her, he now did not know what to do with her, kept taking great bites at her, with a feeling all the time of getting further and further away. At moments, he desired revenge for his failure to get near her spiritually, and was ready to commit follies of all kinds. He was only kept in

control at all by his work. For he did work hard;
though, even there, something was lacking. He had
all the qualities of making good, except the moral back-
bone holding them together, which alone could give
him his rightful—as he thought—pre-eminence. It
often surprised and vexed him to find that some contemporary held higher rank than himself.

Threading the streets in his cab, he mused:

"Did I do anything that really shocked her last
night ? Why didn't I wait for her this morning and
find out the worst ?" And his lips twisted awry—for
to find out the worst was not his forte. Meditation,
seeking as usual a scapegoat, lighted on Rosek. Like
most egoists addicted to women, he had not many
friends. Rosek was the most constant. But even for
him, Fiorsen had at once the contempt and fear that
a man naturally uncontrolled and yet of greater scope
has for one of less talent but stronger will-power. He
had for him, too, the feeling of a wayward child for
its nurse, mixed with the need that an artist, especially
an executant artist, feels for a connoisseur and patron
with well-lined pockets.

'Curse Paul !' he thought. 'He must know—he
does know—that brandy of his goes down like water.
Trust him, he saw I was getting silly ! He had some
game on. Where did I go after ? How did I get
home ?' And again: 'Did I hurt Gyp ?' If the
servants had seen—that would be the worst; that
would upset her fearfully ! And he laughed. Then
he had a fresh access of fear. He didn't know her,
never knew what she was thinking or feeling, never
knew anything about her. And he thought angrily:
'That's not fair ! I don't hide myself from her. I
am as free as nature; I let her see everything. What

did I do? That maid looked very queerly at me this morning!' And suddenly he said to the driver: "Bury Street, St. James's." He could find out, at all events, whether Gyp had been to her father's. The thought of Winton ever afflicted him; and he changed his mind several times before the cab reached that little street, but so swiftly that he had not time to alter his instructions to the driver. A light sweat broke out on his forehead while he was waiting for the door to be opened.

"Mrs. Fiorsen here?"

"No, sir."

"Not been here this morning?"

"No, sir."

He shrugged away the thought that he ought to give some explanation of his question, and got into the cab again, telling the man to drive to Curzon Street. If she had not been to "that Aunt Rosamund" either it would be all right. She had not. There was no one else she would go to. And, with a sigh of relief, he began to feel hungry, having had no breakfast. He would go to Rosek's, borrow the money to pay his cab, and lunch there. But Rosek was not in. He would have to go home to get the cab paid. The driver seemed to eye him queerly now, as though conceiving doubts about the fare.

Going in under the trellis, Fiorsen passed a man coming out, who held in his hand a long envelope and eyed him askance.

Gyp, who was sitting at her bureau, seemed to be adding up the counterfoils in her cheque-book. She did not turn round, and Fiorsen paused. How was she going to receive him?

" Is there any lunch ?" he said.

She reached out and rang the bell. He felt sorry for himself. He had been quite ready to take her in his arms and say: " Forgive me, little Gyp; I'm sorry !"

Betty answered the bell.

" Please bring up some lunch for Mr. Fiorsen."

He heard the stout woman sniff as she went out. She was a part of his ostracism. And, with sudden rage, he said:

" What do you want for a husband—a bourgeois who would die if he missed his lunch ?"

Gyp turned round to him and held out her cheque-book.

" I don't in the least mind about meals; but I do about this." He read on the counterfoil:

" Messrs. Travers & Sanborn, Tailors, Account rendered: £54 3s. 7d." " Are there many of these, Gustav ?"

Fiorsen had turned the peculiar white that marked deep injury to his self-esteem. He said violently:

" Well, what of that ? A bill ! Did you pay it ? You have no business to pay my bills."

" The man said if it wasn't paid this time, he'd sue you." Her lips quivered. " I think owing money is horrible. It's undignified. Are there many others ? Please tell me !"

" I shall not tell you. What is it to you ?"

" It is a lot to me. I have to keep this house and pay the maids and everything, and I want to know how I stand. I am not going to make debts. That's hateful."

Her face had a hardness that he did not know. He perceived dimly that she was different from the Gyp of this hour yesterday—the last time when, in possession of his senses, he had seen or spoken to her. The novelty of her revolt stirred him in strange ways, wounded his self-conceit, inspired a curious fear, and yet excited his senses. He came up to her, said softly:

"Money! Curse money! Kiss me!" With a certain amazement at the sheer distaste in her face, he heard her say:

"It's childish to curse money. I will spend all the income I have; but I will not spend more, and I will not ask Dad."

He flung himself down in a chair.

"Ho! Ho! Virtue!"

"No—pride."

He said gloomily:

"So you don't believe in me. You don't believe I can earn as much as I want—more than you have—any time? You never have believed in me."

"I think you earn now as much as you are ever likely to earn."

"That is what you think! I don't want money—your money! I can live on nothing, any time. I have done it—often."

"Hssh!"

He looked round and saw the maid in the doorway.

"Please, sir, the driver says can he have his fare, or do you want him again? Twelve shillings."

Fiorsen stared at her a moment in the way that—as the maid often said—made you feel like a silly.

"No. Pay him."

The girl glanced at Gyp, answered: "Yes, sir," and went out.

Fiorsen laughed; he laughed, holding his sides. It

was droll coming on the top of his assertion, too droll !
And, looking up at her, he said:

" That was good, wasn't it, Gyp ?"

But her face had not abated its gravity; and, knowing that she was even more easily tickled by the incongruous than himself, he felt again that catch of
fear. Something was different. Yes; something was
really different.

" Did I hurt you last night ?"

She shrugged her shoulders and went to the window.
He looked at her darkly, jumped up, and swung out
past her into the garden. And, almost at once, the
sound of his violin, furiously played in the music-room,
came across the lawn.

Gyp listened with a bitter smile. Money, too !
But what did it matter ? She could not get out of
what she had done. She could never get out. To-night
he would kiss her; and she would pretend it was all
right. And so it would go on and on ! Well, it was
her own fault. Taking twelve shillings from her purse,
she put them aside on the bureau to give the maid.
And suddenly she thought: ' Perhaps he'll get tired
of me. If only he would get tired !' That was a
long way the furthest she had yet gone.

VII

THEY who have known the doldrums—how the sails of the listless ship droop, and the hope of escape dies day by day—may understand something of the life Gyp began living now. On a ship, even doldrums come to an end. But a young woman of twenty-three, who has made a mistake in her marriage, and has only herself to blame, looks forward to no end, unless she be the new woman, which Gyp was not. Having settled that she would not admit failure, and clenched her teeth on the knowledge that she was going to have a child, she went on keeping things sealed up even from Winton. To Fiorsen, she managed to behave as usual, making material life easy and pleasant for him —playing for him, feeding him well, indulging his amorousness. It did not matter; she loved no one else. To count herself a martyr would be silly! Her *malaise*, successfully concealed, was deeper—of the spirit; the subtle utter discouragement of one who has done for herself, clipped her own wings.

As for Rosek, she treated him as if that little scene had never taken place. The idea of appealing to her husband in a difficulty was gone for ever since the night he came home drunk. And she did not dare to tell her father. He would—what would he not do? But she was always on her guard, knowing that Rosek would not forgive her for that dart of ridicule. His insinuations about Daphne Wing she put out of mind, as she never could have if she had loved Fiorsen.

She set up for herself the idol of pride, and became its faithful worshipper. Only Winton, and perhaps Betty, could tell she was not happy. Fiorsen's debts and irresponsibility about money did not worry her much, for she paid everything in the house—rent, wages, food, and her own dress—and had so far made ends meet; and what he did outside the house she could not help.

So the summer wore on till concerts were over, and it was supposed to be impossible to stay in London. But she dreaded going away. She wanted to be left quiet in her little house. It was this which made her tell Fiorsen her secret one night, after the theatre. He had begun to talk of a holiday, sitting on the edge of the settee, with a glass in his hand and a cigarette between his lips. His cheeks, white and hollow from too much London, went a curious dull red; he got up and stared at her. Gyp made an involuntary movement with her hands.

" You needn't look at me. It's true."

He put down glass and cigarette and began to tramp the room. And Gyp stood with a little smile, not even watching him. Suddenly he clasped his forehead and broke out:

" But I don't want it; I won't have it—spoiling my Gyp." Then quickly going up to her with a scared face: " I don't want it; I'm afraid of it. Don't have it."

In Gyp's heart came the same feeling as when he had stood there drunk, against the wall—compassion, rather than contempt of his childishness. And taking his hand she said:

" All right, Gustav. It shan't bother you. When I begin to get ugly, I'll go away with Betty till it's over."

He went down on his knees.

"Oh, no! Oh, no! Oh, no! My beautiful Gyp!'

And Gyp sat like a sphinx, for fear that she too might let slip those words: "Oh, no!"

The windows were open, and moths had come in. One had settled on the hydrangea plant that filled the hearth. Gyp looked at the soft, white, downy thing, whose head was like a tiny owl's against the bluish petals; looked at the purple-grey tiles down there, and the stuff of her own frock, in the shaded gleam of the lamps. And all her love of beauty rebelled, called up by his: "Oh, no!" She would be unsightly soon, and suffer pain, and perhaps die of it, as her own mother had died. She set her teeth, listening to that grown-up child revolting against what he had brought on her, and touched his hand, protectingly.

It interested, even amused her this night and next day to watch his treatment of the disconcerting piece of knowledge. For when at last he realized that he had to acquiesce in nature, he began, as she had known he would, to jib away from all reminder of it. She was careful not to suggest that he should go away without her, knowing his perversity. But when he proposed that she should come to Ostend with him and Rosek, she answered, after seeming deliberation, that she thought she had better not—she would rather stay at home quite quietly; but he must certainly go and get a good holiday.

When he was really gone, peace fell on Gyp—peace such as one feels, having no longer the tight, banded sensations of a fever. To be without that strange, disorderly presence in the house! When she woke in the sultry silence of the next morning, she utterly failed to persuade herself that she was missing him, missing the sound of his breathing, the sight of his rumpled hair on the pillow, the outline of his long form under the sheet. Her heart was devoid of any emptiness or ache; she only felt how pleasant and cool and tranquil it was to lie there alone. She stayed quite late in bed. It was delicious, with window and door wide open and the puppies running in and out, to lie and doze off, or listen to the pigeons' cooing, and the distant sounds of traffic, and feel in command once more of herself, body and soul. Now that she had told Fiorsen, she had no longer any desire to keep her condition secret. Feeling that it would hurt her father to learn of it from anyone but herself, she telephoned to tell him she was alone, and asked if she might come to Bury Street and dine with him.

Winton had not gone away, because, between Goodwood and Doncaster there was no racing that he cared for; one could not ride at this time of year, so might just as well be in London. In fact, August was perhaps the pleasantest of all months in town; the club was empty, and he could sit there without some old bore buttonholing him. Little Boncarte, the fencing-master, was always free for a bout— Winton had long learned to make his left hand what his right hand used to be; the Turkish baths in Jermyn Street were nearly void of their fat clients; he could saunter over to Covent Garden, buy a melon, and carry it home without meeting any but the most inferior duchesses in Piccadilly; on warm nights he could stroll the streets or the parks, smoking his cigar, his hat pushed back to cool his forehead, thinking vague thoughts, recalling vague memories. He received the news that his daughter was alone and free from that fellow with something like delight. Where should he dine her? Mrs. Markey was on her holiday. Why not Blafard's? Quiet—small rooms—not too respectable—quite fairly cool—good things to eat. Yes; Blafard's!

When she drove up, he was ready in the doorway, his thin brown face with its keen, half-veiled eyes the picture of composure, but feeling at heart like a schoolboy off for an exeat. How pretty she was looking—though pale from London—her dark eyes, her smile! And stepping quickly to the cab, he said:

"No; I'm getting in—dining at Blafard's, Gyp—a night out!"

It gave him a thrill to walk into that little restaurant behind her; and passing through its low red rooms to mark the diners turn and stare with envy—taking him, perhaps, for a different sort of relation. He settled her into a far corner by a window, where she could see the people and be seen. He wanted her to be seen; while he himself turned to the world only the short back wings of his glossy greyish hair. He had no notion of being disturbed in his enjoyment by the sight of Hivites and Amorites, or whatever they might be, lapping champagne and shining in the heat. For, secretly, he was living not only in this evening but in a certain evening of the past, when, in this very corner, he had dined with her mother. *His* face then had borne the brunt; hers had been turned away from inquisition. But he did not speak of this to Gyp.

She drank two full glasses of wine before she told him her news. He took it with the expression she knew so well—tightening his lips and staring a little upward. Then he said quietly:

"When?"

" November, Dad."

A shudder, not to be repressed, went through Winton. The very month ! And stretching his hand across the table, he took hers and pressed it tightly.

" It'll be all right, child; I'm glad."

Clinging to his hand, Gyp murmured:

" I'm not; but I won't be frightened—I promise."

Each was trying to deceive the other; and neither was deceived. But both were good at putting a calm face on things. Besides, this was " a night out "— for her, the first since her marriage—of freedom, of feeling somewhat as she used to feel with all before her in a ballroom of a world; for him, the unfettered resumption of a dear companionship and a stealthy revel in the past. After his, " So he's gone to Ostend ?" and his thought: ' He would !' they never alluded to Fiorsen, but talked of horses, of Mildenham —it seemed to Gyp years since she had been there— of her childish escapades. And, looking at him quizzically, she asked:

" What were you like as a boy, Dad ? Aunt Rosamund says that you used to get into white rages when nobody could go near you. She says you were always climbing trees, or shooting with a catapult, or stalking things, and that you never told anybody what you didn't want to tell them. And weren't you desperately in love with your nursery-governess ?"

Winton smiled. How long since he had thought of that first affection. Miss Huntley ! Helena Huntley —with crinkly brown hair, and blue eyes, and fascinating frocks ! He remembered with what grief and sense of bitter injury he heard in his first schoolholidays that she was gone. And he said:

" Yes, yes. By Jove, what a time ago ! And my

father's going off to India. He never came back; killed in that first Afghan business. When I was fond, I *was* fond. But I didn't feel things like you— not half so sensitive. No; not a bit like you, Gyp."

And watching her unconscious eyes following the movements of the waiters, never staring, but taking in all that was going on, he thought: ' Prettiest creature in the world !'

" Well," he said: " What would you like to do now —drop into a theatre, or music-hall, or what ?"

Gyp shook her head. It was so hot. Could they just drive, and then perhaps sit in the park ? That would be lovely. It had gone dark, and the air was not quite so exhausted—a little freshness of scent from the trees in the squares and parks mingled with the fumes of dung and petrol. Winton gave the same order he had given that long past evening: " Knightsbridge Gate." It had been a hansom then, and the night air had blown in their faces, instead of as now in these infernal taxis, down the back of one's neck. They left the cab and crossed the Row; passed the end of the Long Water, up among the trees. There, on two chairs covered by Winton's coat, they sat side by side. No dew was falling yet; the heavy leaves hung unstirring; the air was warm, sweet-smelling. Blotted against trees or on the grass were other couples darker than the darkness, very silent. All was quiet save for the never-ceasing hum of traffic. From Winton's lips, the cigar smoke wreathed and curled. He was dreaming. The cigar between his teeth trembled; a long ash fell. Mechanically he raised his hand to brush it off—his right hand ! A voice said softly in his ear:

" Isn't it delicious, and warm, and gloomy black ?"

Winton shivered, as one shivers recalled from dreams; and, carefully brushing off the ash with his left hand, he answered:

"Yes; very jolly. My cigar's out, though, and I haven't a match."

Gyp's hand slipped through his arm.

"All these people in love, and so dark and whispery —it makes a sort of strangeness in the air. Don't you feel it ?"

Winton murmured:

"No moon to-night !"

Again they were silent. A puff of wind ruffled the leaves; the night, for a moment, seemed full of whispering; then the sound of a giggle jarred out and a girl's voice:

"Oh ! Chuck it, 'Arry."

Gyp rose.

"I feel the dew now, Dad. Can we walk on ?"

They went along paths, so as not to wet her feet in her thin shoes. And they talked. The spell was over; the night again but a common London night; the park a space of parching grass and gravel; the people just clerks and shop-girls walking out.

VIII

Fiorsen's letters were the source of one long smile to Gyp. He missed her horribly; if only she were there!—and so forth—blended in the queerest way with the impression that he was enjoying himself uncommonly. There were requests for money, and careful omission of any real account of what he was doing. Out of a balance running rather low, she sent him remittances; this was her holiday, too, and she could afford to pay for it. She even sought out a shop where she could sell jewelry, and, with a certain malicious joy, forwarded him the proceeds. It would give him and herself another week.

One night she went with Winton to the Octagon, where Daphne Wing was still performing. Remembering the girl's squeaks of rapture at her garden, she wrote next day, asking her to lunch and spend a lazy afternoon under the trees.

The little dancer came with avidity. She was pale, and droopy from the heat, but happily dressed in Liberty silk, with a plain turn-down straw hat. They lunched off sweetbreads, ices, and fruit, and then, with coffee, cigarettes, and plenty of sugar-plums, settled down in the deepest shade of the garden, Gyp in a low wicker chair, Daphne Wing on cushions and the grass. Once past the exclamatory stage, she seemed a great talker, laying bare her little soul with perfect liberality. And Gyp—excellent listener—enjoyed it, as one enjoys all confidential revelations of existences very different from one's own, especially when regarded as a superior being.

" Of course I don't mean to stay at home any longer than I can help; only it's no good going out into life " —this phrase she often used—" till you know where you are. In my profession, one has to be so careful. Of course, people think it's worse than it is; Father gets fits sometimes. But you know, Mrs. Fiorsen, home's awful. We have mutton—you know what mutton is—it's really awful in your bedroom in hot weather. And there's nowhere to practise. What I should like would be a studio. It would be lovely, somewhere down by the river, or up here near you. That *would* be lovely. You know, I'm putting by. As soon as ever I have two hundred pounds, I shall skip. What I think would be perfectly lovely would be to inspire painters and musicians. I don't want to be just a common ' turn '—ballet business year after year, and that; I want to be something rather special. But Mother's so silly about me; she thinks I oughtn't to take any risks at all. I shall never get on that way. It *is* so nice to talk to you, Mrs. Fiorsen, because you're young enough to know what I feel; and I'm sure you'd never be shocked at anything. You see, about men: Ought one to marry, or ought one to take a lover ? They say you can't be a perfect artist till you've felt passion. But, then, if you marry, that means mutton over again, and perhaps babies, and perhaps the wrong man after all. Ugh ! But then, on the other hand, I don't want to be raffish. I hate raffish people—I simply hate them. What do you think ? It's awfully difficult, isn't it ?"

Gyp, perfectly grave, answered:

9

"That sort of thing settles itself. I shouldn't bother beforehand."

Miss Daphne Wing buried her perfect chin deeper in her hands, and said meditatively:

"Yes; I rather thought that, too; of course I could do either now. But, you see, I really don't care for men who are not distinguished. I'm sure I shall only fall in love with a really distinguished man. That's what you did—isn't it?—so you *must* understand. I think Mr. Fiorsen is wonderfully distinguished."

Sunlight, piercing the shade, suddenly fell warm on Gyp's neck where her blouse ceased, and fortunately stilled the medley of emotion and laughter a little lower down. She continued to look gravely at Daphne Wing, who resumed:

"Of course, Mother would have fits if I asked her such a question, and I don't know what Father would do. Only it is important, isn't it? One may go all wrong from the start; and I do really want to get on. I simply adore my work. I don't mean to let love stand in its way; I want to make it help, you know. Count Rosek says my dancing lacks passion. I wish you'd tell me if you think it does. I should believe *ou*."

Gyp shook her head.

"I'm not a judge."

Daphne Wing looked up reproachfully.

"Oh, I'm sure you are! If I were a man, I should be passionately in love with you. I've got a new dance where I'm supposed to be a nymph pursued by a faun; it's so difficult to feel like a nymph when you know it's only the ballet-master. Do you think I ought to put passion into that? You see, I'm supposed to be flying all the time; but it would be much more subtle, wouldn't it, if I could give the impression that I wanted to be caught. Don't you think so?"

Gyp said suddenly:

"Yes, I think it *would* do you good to be in love."

Miss Daphne's mouth fell a little open; her eyes grew round. She said:

"You frightened me when you said that. You looked so different—so—intense."

A flame indeed had leaped up in Gyp. This fluffy, flabby talk of love set her instincts in revolt. She did not want to love; she had failed to fall in love. But, whatever love was like, it did not bear talking about. How was it that this little suburban girl, when she once got on her toes, could twirl one's emotions as she did?

"D'you know what I should simply revel in?" Daphne Wing went on: "To dance to you here in the garden some night. It must be wonderful to dance out of doors; and the grass is nice and hard now. Only, I suppose it would shock the servants. Do they look out this way?" Gyp skook her head. "I could dance over there in front of the drawing-room window. Only it would have to be moonlight. I could come any Sunday. I've got a dance where I'm supposed to be a lotus flower—that would do splendidly. And there's my real moonlight dance that goes to Chopin. I could bring my dresses, and change in the music-room, couldn't I?" She wriggled up, and sat cross-legged, gazing at Gyp, and clasping her hands. "Oh, may I?"

Her excitement infected Gyp. A desire to give pleasure, the queerness of the notion, and her real love of seeing this girl dance, made her say:

"Yes; next Sunday."

Daphne Wing got up, made a rush, and kissed her. Her mouth was soft, and she smelled of orange blossom; but Gyp recoiled a little—she hated promiscuous kisses. Somewhat abashed, Miss Daphne hung her head, and said:

"You did look so lovely; I couldn't help it, really."

And Gyp gave her hand the squeeze of compunction.

They went indoors, to try over the music of the two dances; and soon after Daphne Wing departed, full of sugar-plums and hope.

She arrived punctually at eight o'clock next Sunday, carrying an exiguous green linen bag, which contained her dresses. She was subdued, and, now that it had come to the point, evidently a little scared. Lobster salad, hock, and peaches restored her courage. She ate heartily. It did not apparently matter to her whether she danced full or empty; but she would not smoke.

"It's bad for the——" She checked herself.

When they had finished supper, Gyp shut the dogs into the back premises; she had visions of their rending Miss Wing's draperies, or calves. Then they went into the drawing-room, not lighting up, that they might tell when the moonlight was strong enough outside. Though it was the last night of August, the heat was as great as ever—a deep, unstirring warmth; the climbing moon shot as yet but a thin shaft here and there through the heavy foliage. They talked in low voices, unconsciously playing up to the nature of the escapade. As the moon drew up, they stole out across the garden to the music-room. Gyp lighted the candles.

"Can you manage?"

Miss Daphne had already shed half her garments.

"Oh, I'm so excited, Mrs. Fiorsen! I do hope I shall dance well."

Gyp stole back to the house; it being Sunday evening, the servants had been easily disposed of. She sat down at the piano, turning her eyes toward the garden. A blurred white shape flitted suddenly across the darkness at the far end and became motionless, as it might be a whiteflowering bush under the trees. Miss Daphne had come out, and was waiting for the moon. Gyp began to play. She pitched on a little Sicilian pastorale that the herdsmen play on their pipes coming down from the hills, softly, from very far, rising, rising, swelling to full cadence, and failing, failing away again to nothing. The moon rose over the trees; its light flooded the face of the house, down on to the grass, and spread slowly back toward where the girl stood waiting. It caught the border of sunflowers along the garden wall with a stroke of magical, unearthly colour—gold that was not gold.

Gyp began to play the dance. The pale blurr in the darkness stirred. The moonlight fell on the girl now, standing with arms spread, holding out her drapery—a white, winged statue. Then, like a gigantic moth she fluttered forth, blanched and noiseless flew over the grass, spun and hovered. The moonlight etched out the shape of her head, painted her hair with pallid gold. In the silence, with that unearthly gleam of colour along the sunflowers and on the girl's head, it was as if a spirit had dropped into the garden and was fluttering to and fro, unable to get out.

A voice behind Gyp said: "My God! What's this? An angel?"

Fiorsen was standing half-way in the darkened room staring out into the garden, where the girl had halted, transfixed before the window, her eyes as round as saucers, her mouth open, her limbs rigid with interest and affright. Suddenly she turned and, gathering her garment, fled, her limbs gleaming in the moonlight.

And Gyp sat looking up at the apparition of her husband. She could just see his eyes straining after that flying nymph. Miss Daphne's faun! Why, even his ears were pointed! Had she never noticed before how like a faun he was? Yes—on her wedding-night! And she said quietly:

"Daphne Wing was rehearsing her new dance. So you're back! Why didn't you let me know? Are you all right—you look splendid!"

Fiorsen bent down and clutched her by the shoulders. "My Gyp! Kiss me!"

But even while his lips were pressed on hers, she felt rather than saw his eyes straying to the garden, and thought, "He would like to be kissing that girl!"

The moment he had gone to get his things from the cab, she slipped out to the music-room.

Miss Daphne was dressed, and stuffing her garments into the green linen bag. She looked up, and said piteously:

"Oh! Does he mind? It's awful, isn't it?"

Gyp strangled her desire to laugh.

"It's for you to mind."

"Oh, *I* don't, if you don't! How did you like the dance?"

"Lovely! When you're ready—come along!"

"Oh, I think I'd rather go home, please! It must seem so funny!"

"Would you like to go by this back way into the lane? You turn to the right, into the road."

" Oh, yes; please. It would have been better if he could have seen the dance properly, wouldn't it? What will he think?"

Gyp smiled, and opened the door into the lane.

When she returned, Fiorsen was at the window, gazing out. Was it for her or for that flying nymph?

IX

September and October passed. There were more concerts, not very well attended. Fiorsen's novelty had worn off, nor had his playing sweetness and sentiment enough for the big Public. There was also a financial crisis. It did not seem to Gyp to matter. Everything seemed remote and unreal in the shadow of her coming time. Unlike most mothers to be, she made no garments, no preparations of any kind. Why make what might never be needed? She played for Fiorsen a great deal, for herself not at all, read many books—poetry, novels, biographies—taking them in at the moment, and forgetting them at once, as one does with books read just to distract the mind. Winton and Aunt Rosamund, by tacit agreement, came on alternate afternoons. And Winton, almost as much under that shadow as Gyp herself, would take the evening train after leaving her, and spend the next day racing or cub-hunting, returning the morning of the day after to pay his next visit. He had no dread just then like that of an unoccupied day face to face with anxiety.

Betty, who had been present at Gyp's birth, was in a queer state. The obvious desirability of such events to one of motherly type defrauded by fate of children was terribly impinged on by that old memory, and a solicitude for her " pretty " far exceeding what she would have had for a daughter of her own. What a peony regards as a natural happening to a peony, she watches with awe when it happens to the lily. That other single lady of a certain age, Aunt Rosamund, the very antithesis to Betty—a long, thin nose and a mere button, a sense of divine rights and no sense of rights at all, a drawl and a comforting wheeze, length and circumference, decision and the curtsey to providence, humour and none, dyspepsia, and the digestion of an ostrich, with other oppositions—Aunt Rosamund was also uneasy, as only one could be who disapproved heartily of uneasiness, and habitually joked and drawled it into retirement.

But of all those round Gyp, Fiorsen gave the most interesting display. He had not even an elementary notion of disguising his state of mind. And his state of mind was weirdly, wistfully primitive. He wanted Gyp as she had been. The thought that she might never become herself again terrified him so at times that he was forced to drink brandy, and come home only a little less far gone than that first time. Gyp had often to help him go to bed. On two or three occasions, he suffered so that he was out all night. To account for this, she devised the formula of a room at Count Rosek's, where he slept when music kept him late, so as not to disturb her. Whether the servants believed her or not, she never knew. Nor did she ever ask him where he went—too proud, and not feeling that she had the right.

Deeply conscious of the unæsthetic nature of her condition, she was convinced that she could no longer be attractive to one so easily upset in his nerves, so intolerant of ugliness. As to deeper feelings about her—had he any ? He certainly never gave anything up, or sacrificed himself in any way. If she had loved, she felt she would want to give up everything to the loved one; but then—she would never love ! And yet he seemed frightened about her. It was puzzling ! But perhaps she would not be puzzled much longer about that or anything; for she often had the feeling that she would die. How could she be going to live, grudging her fate ? What would give her strength to go through with it ? And, at times, she felt as if she would be glad to die. Life had defrauded her, or she had defrauded herself of life. Was it really only a year since that glorious day's hunting when Dad and she, and the young man with the clear eyes and the irrepressible smile, had slipped away with the hounds ahead of all the field—the fatal day Fiorsen descended from the clouds and asked for her ? An overwhelming longing for Mildenham came on her, to get away there with her father and Betty.

She went at the beginning of November.

Over her departure, Fiorsen behaved like a tired child that will not go to bed. He could not bear to be away from her, and so forth; but when she had gone, he spent a furious bohemian evening. At about five, he woke with " an awful cold feeling in my heart," as he wrote to Gyp next day—" an awful feeling, my Gyp; I walked up and down for hours " (in reality, half an hour at most). " How shall I bear to be away from you at this time ? I feel lost." Next day, he found himself in Paris with Rosek. " I could not stand," he wrote, " the sight of the streets, of the garden, of our room. When I come back I shall stay with Rosek. Nearer to the day I will come; I must come to you." But Gyp, when she read the letter, said to Winton: " Dad, when it comes, don't send for him. I don't want him here."

With those letters of his, she buried the last remnants

of her feeling that somewhere in him there must be something as fine and beautiful as the sounds he made with his violin. And yet she felt those letters genuine in a way, pathetic, and with real feeling of a sort.

From the moment she reached Mildenham, she began to lose that hopelessness about herself; and, for the first time, had the sensation of wanting to live in the new life within her. She first felt it, going into her old nursery, where everything was the same as it had been when she first saw it, a child of eight; there was her old red doll's house, the whole side of which opened to display the various floors ; the worn Venetian blinds, the rattle of whose fall had sounded in her ears so many hundred times; the high fender, near which she had lain so often on the floor, her chin on her hands, reading Grimm, or " Alice in Wonderland," or histories of England. Here, too, perhaps this new child would live amongst the old familiars. And the whim seized her to face her hour in her old nursery, not in the room where she had slept as a girl. She would not like the daintiness of that room deflowered. Let it stay the room of her girlhood. But in the nursery—there was safety, comfort ! And when she had been at Mildenham a week, she made Betty change her over.

No one in that house was half so calm to look at in those days as Gyp. Betty was not guiltless of sitting on the stairs and crying at odd moments. Mrs. Markey had never made such bad soups. Markey so far forgot himself as frequently to talk. Winton lamed a horse trying an impossible jump that he might get home the quicker, and, once back, was like an unquiet spirit. If Gyp were in the room, he would make the pretence of wanting to warm his feet or hand, just to stroke her shoulder as he went back to his chair. His voice, so measured and dry, had a ring in it, that too plainly disclosed the anxiety of his heart. Gyp, always sensitive to atmosphere, felt cradled in all the love about her. Wonderful that they should all care so much! What had she done for anyone, that people should be so sweet—he especially, whom she had so grievously distressed by her wretched marriage? She would sit staring into the fire with her wide, dark eyes, unblinking as an owl's at night— wondering what she could do to make up to her father, whom already once she had nearly killed by coming into life. And she began to practise the bearing of the coming pain, trying to project herself into this unknown suffering, so that it should not surprise from her cries and contortions.

She had one dream, over and over again, of sinking and sinking into a feather bed, growing hotter and more deeply walled in by that which had no stay in it, yet through which her body could not fall and reach anything more solid. Once, after this dream, she got up and spent the rest of the night wrapped in a blanket and the eider-down, on the old sofa, where, as a child, they had made her lie flat on her back from twelve to one every day. Betty was aghast at finding her there asleep in the morning. Gyp's face was so like the child-face she had seen lying there in the old days, that she bundled out of the room and cried bitterly into the cup of tea. It did her good. Going back with the tea, she scolded her " pretty " for sleeping out there, with the fire out, too !

But Gyp only said:

" Betty, darling, the tea's awfully cold ! Please get me some more !"

X

FROM the day of the nurse's arrival, Winton gave up hunting. He could not bring himself to be out of doors for more than half an hour at a time. Distrust of doctors did not prevent him having ten minutes every morning with the old practitioner who had treated Gyp for mumps, measles, and the other blessings of childhood. The old fellow—his name was Rivershaw—was a most peculiar survival. He smelled of mackintosh, had round purplish cheeks, a rim of hair which people said he dyed, and bulging grey eyes slightly bloodshot. He was short in body and wind, drank port wine, was suspected of taking snuff, read *The Times*, spoke always in a husky voice, and used a very small brougham with a very old black horse. But he had a certain low cunning, which had defeated many ailments, and his reputation for assisting people into the world stood extremely high. Every morning punctually at twelve, the crunch of his little brougham's wheels would be heard. Winton would get up, and, taking a deep breath, cross the hall to the dining-room, extract from a sideboard a decanter of port, a biscuit-canister, and one glass. He would then stand with his eyes fixed on the door, till, in due time, the doctor would appear, and he could say:

" Well, doctor ? How is she ?"

" Nicely; quite nicely."

" Nothing to make one anxious ?"

The doctor, puffing out his cheeks, with eyes straying to the decanter, would murmur:

"Cardiac condition, capital—a little—um—not to matter. Taking its course. These things!"

And Winton, with another deep breath, would say:

"Glass of port, doctor?"

An expression of surprise would pass over the doctor's face.

"Cold day—ah, perhaps——" And he would blow his nose on his purple-and-red bandanna.

Watching him drink his port, Winton would remark:

"We can get you at any time, can't we?"

And the doctor, sucking his lips, would answer:

"Never fear, my dear sir! Little Miss Gyp—old friend of mine. At her service day and night. Never fear!"

A sensation of comfort would pass through Winton, which would last quite twenty minutes after the crunching of the wheels and the mingled perfumes of him had died away.

In these days, his greatest friend was an old watch that had been his father's before him; a gold repeater from Switzerland, with a chipped dial-plate, and a case worn wondrous thin and smooth—a favourite of Gyp's childhood. He would take it out about every quarter of an hour, look at its face without discovering the time, finger it, all smooth and warm from contact with his body, and put it back. Then he would listen. There was nothing whatever to listen to, but he could not help it. Apart from this, his chief distraction was to take a foil and make passes at a leather cushion, set up on the top of a low bookshelf. In these occupations, varied by constant visits to the room next the nursery, where—to save her the stairs—Gyp was now

established, and by excursions to the conservatory to
see if he could not find some new flower to take her,
he passed all his time, save when he was eating, sleeping, or smoking cigars, which he had constantly to
be relighting.

By Gyp's request, they kept from him knowledge
of when her pains began. After that first bout was
over and she was lying half asleep in the old nursery,
he happened to go up. The nurse—a bonny creature
—one of those free, independent, economic agents
that now abound—met him in the sitting-room.
Accustomed to the " fuss and botheration of men "
at such times, she was prepared to deliver him a little
lecture. But, in approaching, she became affected
by the look on his face, and, realizing somehow that
she was in the presence of one whose self-control was
proof, she simply whispered:

" It's beginning; but don't be anxious—she's not
suffering just now. We shall send for the doctor
soon. She's very plucky;" and with an unaccustomed
sensation of respect and pity she repeated: " Don't
be anxious, sir."

" If she wants to see me at any time, I shall be in
my study. Save her all you can, nurse."

The nurse was left with a feeling of surprise at having
used the word " Sir "; she had not done such a thing
since—since—— ! And, pensive, she returned to the
nursery, where Gyp said at once:

" Was that my father ?   I didn't want him to know."

The nurse answered mechanically:

" That's all right, my dear."

" How long do you think before—before it'll begin
again, nurse ?   I'd like to see him."

The nurse stroked her hair.

"Soon enough when it's all over and comfy. Men are always fidgety."

Gyp looked at her, and said quietly:

"Yes. You see, my mother died when I was born."

The nurse, watching those lips, still pale with pain, felt a queer pang. She smoothed the bedclothes and said:

"That's nothing—it often happens—that is, I mean, —you know it has no connection whatever."

And seeing Gyp smile, she thought: 'Well, I am a fool.'

"If by any chance I don't get through, I want to be cremated; I want to go back as quick as I can. I can't bear the thought of the other thing. Will you remember, nurse? I can't tell my father that just now; it might upset him. But promise me."

And the nurse thought: 'That can't be done without a will or something, but I'd better promise. It's a morbid fancy, and yet she's not a morbid subject, either.' And she said:

"Very well, my dear; only, you're not going to do anything of the sort. That's flat."

Gyp smiled again, and there was silence, till she said:

"I'm awfully ashamed, wanting all this attention, and making people miserable. I've read that Japanese women quietly go out somewhere by themselves and sit on a gate."

The nurse, still busy with the bedclothes, murmured abstractedly:

"Yes, that's a very good way. But don't you fancy you're half the trouble most of them are. You're very good, and you're going to get on splendidly." And she thought: 'Odd! She's never once spoken of her husband. I don't like it for this sort—too perfect, too sensitive; her face touches you so !'

Gyp murmured again:

" I'd like to see my father, please; and rather quick."

The nurse, after one swift look, went out.

Gyp, who had clenched her hands under the bed-clothes, fixed her eyes on the window. November ! Acorns and the leaves—the nice, damp, earthy smell ! Acorns all over the grass. She used to drive the old retriever in harness on the lawn covered with acorns and the dead leaves, and the wind still blowing them off the trees—in her brown velvet—that was a ducky dress ! Who was it had called her once " a wise little owl," in that dress ? And, suddenly, her heart sank. The pain was coming again. Winton's voice from the door said:

" Well, my pet ?"

" It was only to see how you are. I'm all right. What sort of a day is it ? You'll go riding, won't you ? Give my love to the horses. Good-bye, Dad; just for now."

Her forehead was wet to his lips.

Outside, in the passage, her smile, like something actual on the air, preceded him—the smile that had just lasted out. But when he was back in the study, he suffered—suffered ! Why could he not have that pain to bear instead ?

The crunch of the brougham brought his ceaseless march over the carpet to an end. He went out into the hall and looked into the doctor's face—he had forgotten that this old fellow knew nothing of his special reason for deadly fear. Then he turned back into his study. The wild south wind brought wet drift-leaves whirling against the panes. It was here that he had stood looking out into the ark, when Fiorsen came down to ask for Gyp a year go. Why had he not bundled the fellow out neck and crop, and taken her away?—India, Japan—anywhere would have done! She had not loved that fiddler, never really loved him. Monstrous—monstrous! The full bitterness of having missed right action swept over Winton, and he positively groaned aloud. He moved from the window and went over to the bookcase; there in one row were the few books he ever read, and he took one out. " Life of General Lee." He put it back and took another, a novel of Whyte Melville's: "Good for Nothing." Sad book—sad ending! The book dropped from his hand and fell with a flump on the floor. In a sort of icy discovery, he had seen his life as it would be if for a second time he had to bear such loss. She must not—could not die! If she did—then, for him——! In old times they buried a man with his horse and his dog, as if at the end of a good run. There was always that! The extremity of this thought brought relief. He sat down, and, for a long time, stayed staring into the fire in a sort of coma. Then his feverish fears began again. Why the devil didn't they come and tell him something, anything—rather than this silence, this deadly solitude and waiting? What was that? The front door shutting. Wheels? Had that hell-hound of an old doctor sneaked off? He started up. There at the door was Markey, holding in his hand some cards. Winton scanned them.

" Lady Summerhay; Mr. Bryan Summerhay. I said, ' Not at home,' sir."

Winton nodded.

" Well ?"

" Nothing at present. You have had no lunch, sir."

" What time is it ?"

" Four o'clock."

" Bring in my fur coat and the port, and make the fire up. I want any news there is."

Markey nodded.

Odd to sit in a fur coat before a fire, and the day not cold ! They said you lived on after death. He had never been able to feel that *she* was living on. *She* lived in Gyp. And now if Gyp——— ! Death— your own—no great matter ! But—for her ! The wind was dropping with the darkness. He got up and drew the curtains.

It was seven o'clock when the doctor came down into the hall, and stood rubbing his freshly washed hands before opening the study door. Winton was still sitting before the fire, motionless, shrunk into his fur coat. He raised himself a little and looked round dully.

The doctor's face puckered, his eyelids drooped half-way across his bulging eyes; it was his way of smiling. " Nicely," he said; " nicely—a girl. No complications."

Winton's whole body seemed to swell, his lips opened, he raised his hand. Then, the habit of a lifetime catching him by the throat, he stayed motionless. At last he got up and said:

" Glass of port, doctor ?"

The doctor spying at him above the glass thought: ' This is " the fifty-two." Give me " the sixty-eight " —more body.'

After a time, Winton went upstairs. Waiting in the outer room he had a return of his cold dread.

" Perfectly successful—the patient died from exhaustion!" The tiny squawking noise that fell on his ears entirely failed to reassure him. He cared nothing for that new being. Suddenly he found Betty just behind him, her bosom heaving horribly.

" What is it, woman ? Don't !"

She had leaned against his shoulder, appearing to have lost all sense of right and wrong, and, out of her sobbing, gurgled:

" She looks so lovely—oh dear, she looks so lovely !"

Pushing her abruptly from him, Winton peered in through the just-opened door. Gyp was lying extremely still, and very white; her eyes, very large, very dark, were fastened on her baby. Her face wore a kind of wonder. She did not see Winton, who stood stone-quiet, watching, while the nurse moved about her business behind a screen. This was the first time in his life that he had seen a mother with her just-born baby. That look on her face—gone right away somewhere, right away—amazed him. She had never seemed to like children, had said she did not want a child. She turned her head and saw him. He went in. She made a faint motion toward the baby, and her eyes smiled. Winton looked at that swaddled speckled mite; then, bending down, he kissed her hand and tiptoed away.

At dinner he drank champagne, and benevolence towards all the world spread in his being. Watching the smoke of his cigar wreathe about him, he thought: ' Must send that chap a wire.' After all, he was a fellow being—might be suffering, as he himself had suffered only two hours ago. To keep him in ignorance —it wouldn't do ! And he wrote out the form—

"All well, a daughter.—WINTON,"

and sent it out with the order that a groom should take it in that night.

Gyp was sleeping when he stole up at ten o'clock. He, too, turned in, and slept like a child.

RETURNING the next afternoon from the first ride for several days, Winton passed the station fly rolling away from the drive-gate with the light-hearted disillusionment peculiar to quite empty vehicles.

The sight of a fur coat and broad-brimmed hat in the hall warned him of what had happened.

" Mr. Fiorsen, sir; gone up to Mrs. Fiorsen."

Natural, but a d——d bore ! And bad, perhaps, for Gyp. He asked:

" Did he bring things ?"

" A bag, sir."

" Get a room ready, then."

To dine *tête-à-tête* with that fellow !

Gyp had passed the strangest morning in her life, so far. Her baby fascinated her, also the tug of its lips, giving her the queerest sensation, almost sensual; a sort of meltedness, an infinite warmth, a desire to grip the little creature right into her—which, of course one must not do. And yet, neither her sense of humour nor her sense of beauty were deceived. It was a queer little affair with a tuft of black hair, in grace greatly inferior to a kitten. Its tiny, pink, crisped fingers with their infinitesimal nails, its microscopic curly toes, and solemn black eyes—when they showed, its inimitable stillness when it slept, its incredible vigour when it fed, were all, as it were, miraculous. Withal, she had a feeling of gratitude to one that had not killed nor even hurt her so very desperately—

gratitude because she had succeeded, performed her part of mother perfectly—the nurse had said so— she, so distrustful of herself! Instinctively she knew, too, that this was *her* baby, not his, going "to take after her," as they called it. How it succeeded in giving that impression she could not tell, unless it were the passivity, and dark eyes of the little creature. Then from one till three they had slept together with perfect soundness and unanimity. She awoke to find the nurse standing by the bed, looking as if she wanted to tell her something.

"Someone to see you, my dear."

And Gyp thought: 'He! I can't think quickly; I ought to think quickly—I want to, but I can't.' Her face expressed this, for the nurse said at once:

"I don't think you're quite up to it yet."

Gyp answered:

"Yes. Only, not for five minutes, please."

Her spirit had been very far away, she wanted time to get it back before she saw him—time to know in some sort what she felt now; what this mite lying beside her had done for her and him. The thought that it was his, too—this tiny, helpless being—seemed unreal. No, it was not his! He had not wanted it, and now that she had been through the torture it was hers, not his—never his. The memory of the night when she first yielded to the certainty that the child was coming, and he had come home drunk, swooped on her, and made her shrink and shudder and put her arm round her baby. It had not made any difference. Only—— Back came the old accusing thought, from which these last days she had been free: 'But I married him—I chose to marry him. I can't get out of that!' And she felt as if she must cry out to the nurse: " Keep him away; I don't want to see him. Oh, please, I'm tired." She bit the words back. And presently, with a very faint smile, said:

" Now, I'm ready."

She noticed first what clothes he had on—his newest suit, dark grey, with little lighter lines—she had chosen it herself; that his tie was in a bow, not a sailor's knot, and his hair brighter than usual—as always just after being cut; and surely the hair was growing down again in front of his ears. Then, gratefully, almost with emotion, she realized that his lips were quivering, his whole face quivering. He came in on tiptoe, stood looking at her a minute, then crossed very swiftly to the bed, very swiftly knelt down, and, taking her hand, turned it over and put his face to it. The bristles of his moustache tickled her palm; his nose flattened itself against her fingers, and his lips kept murmuring words into the hand, with the moist warm touch of his lips. Gyp knew he was burying there all his remorse, perhaps the excesses he had committed while she had been away from him, burying the fears he had felt, and the emotion at seeing her so white and still. She felt that in a minute he would raise a quite different face. And it flashed through her: ' If I loved him I wouldn't mind what he did—ever ! Why don't I love him ? There's something lovable. Why don't I ?'

He did raise his face; his eyes lighted on the baby, and he grinned.

" Look at this !" he said. " Is it possible ? Oh, my Gyp, what a funny one ! Oh, oh, oh !" He went off into an ecstasy of smothered laughter; then his face grew grave, and slowly puckered into a sort of comic disgust. Gyp too had seen the humours of her

baby, of its queer little reddish pudge of a face, of
its twenty-seven black hairs, and the dribble at its
almost invisible mouth; but she had also seen it as a
miracle; she had felt it, and there surged up from her
all the old revolt and more against his lack of consideration. It was not a funny one—her baby! It
was not ugly! Or, if it were, she was not fit to be
told of it. Her arm tightened round the warm bundled
thing against her. Fiorsen put his finger out and
touched its cheek.

"It *is* real—so it is. Mademoiselle Fiorsen. Tk,
tk!"

The baby stirred. And Gyp thought: 'If I loved
I wouldn't even mind his laughing at my baby. It
would be different.'

"Don't wake her!" she whispered. She felt his
eyes on her, knew that his interest in the baby had
ceased as suddenly as it came, that he was thinking,
'How long before I have you in my arms again?'
He touched her hair. And, suddenly, she had a
fainting, sinking sensation that she had never yet
known. When she opened her eyes again, the economic
agent was holding something beneath her nose and
making sounds that seemed to be the words: "Well,
I am a d——d fool!" repeatedly expressed. Fiorsen
was gone.

Seeing Gyp's eyes once more open, the nurse withdrew the ammonia, replaced the baby, and saying:
"Now go to sleep!" withdrew behind the screen.
Like all robust personalities, she visited on others her
vexations with herself. But Gyp did not go to sleep;
she gazed now at her sleeping baby, now at the pattern
of the wall-paper, trying mechanically to find the bird
caught at intervals amongst its brown-and-green

foliage—one bird in each alternate square of the pattern, so that there was always a bird in the centre of four other birds. And the bird was of green and yellow with a red beak.

On being turned out of the nursery with the assurance that it was " all right—only a little faint," Fiorsen went down-stairs disconsolate. The atmosphere of this dark house where he was a stranger, an unwelcome stranger, was insupportable. He wanted nothing in it but Gyp, and Gyp had fainted at his touch. No wonder he felt miserable. He opened a door. What room was this ? A piano ! The drawing-room. Ugh ! No fire—what misery ! He recoiled to the doorway and stood listening. Not a sound. Grey light in the cheerless room; almost dark already in the hall behind him. What a life these English lived—worse than the winter in his old country home in Sweden, where, at all events, they kept good fires. And, suddenly, all his being revolted. Stay here and face that father— and that image of a servant ! Stay here for a night of this ! Gyp was not his Gyp, lying there with that baby beside her, in this hostile house. Smothering his footsteps, he made for the outer hall. There were his coat and hat. He put them on. His bag ? He could not see it. No matter ! They could send it after him. He would write to her—say that her fainting had upset him—that he could not risk making her faint again—could not stay in the house so near her, yet so far. She would understand. And there came over him a sudden wave of longing. Gyp ! He wanted her. To be with her ! To look at her and kiss her, and feel her his own again ! And, opening the door, he passed out on to the drive and strode away, miserable and sick at heart. All the way to the station through the darkening lanes, and in the railway carriage going up, he felt that aching wretchedness. Only in the lighted street, driving back to Rosek's, did he shake it off a little. At dinner and after, drinking that special brandy he nearly lost it; but it came back when he went to bed, till sleep relieved him with its darkness and dreams.

XII

GYP'S recovery proceeded at first with a sure rapidity which delighted Winton. As the economic agent pointed out, she was beautifully made, and that had a lot to do with it !

Before Christmas Day, she was already out, and on Christmas morning the old doctor, by way of present, pronounced her fit and ready to go home when she liked. That afternoon, she was not so well, and next day back again upstairs. Nothing seemed definitely wrong, only a sort of desperate lassitude; as if the knowledge that to go back was within her power, only needing her decision, had been too much for her. And since no one knew her inward feelings, all were puzzled except Winton. The nursing of her child was promptly stopped.

It was not till the middle of January that she said to him :

" I must go home, Dad."

The word " home " hurt him, and he only answered: " Very well, Gyp; when ?"

" The house is quite ready. I think I had better go to-morrow. He's still at Rosek's. I won't let him know. Two or three days there by myself first would be better for settling baby in."

" Very well; I'll take you up."

He made no effort to ascertain her feelings toward Fiorsen. He knew too well.

They travelled next day, reaching London at half-

past two. Betty had gone up in the early morning
to prepare the way. The dogs had been with Aunt
Rosamund all this time. Gyp missed their greeting;
but the installation of Betty and the baby in the spare
room that was now to be the nursery, absorbed all
her first energies. Light was just beginning to fail
when, still in her fur, she took a key of the music-room
and crossed the garden, to see how all had fared
during her ten weeks' absence. What a wintry garden!
How different from that languorous, warm, moonlit
night when Daphne Wing had come dancing out of
the shadow of the dark trees. How bare and sharp
the boughs against the grey, darkening sky—and not
a song of any bird, not a flower! She glanced back
at the house. Cold and white it looked, but there
were lights in her room and in the nursery, and someone just drawing the curtains. Now that the leaves
were off, one could see the other houses of the road,
each different in shape and colour, as is the habit of
London houses. It was cold, frosty; Gyp hurried
down the path. Four little icicles had formed beneath
the window of the music-room. They caught her eye,
and, passing round to the side, she broke one off.
There must be a fire in there, for she could see the
flicker through the curtains not quite drawn. Thought-
ful Ellen had been airing it! But, suddenly, she
stood still. There was more than a fire in there!
Through the chink in the drawn curtains she had seen
two figures seated on the divan. Something seemed
to spin round in her head. She turned to rush away.
Then a kind of superhuman coolness came to her,
and she deliberately looked in. He and Daphne
Wing! His arm was round her neck. The girl's face
riveted her eyes. It was turned a little back and up,

gazing at him, the lips parted, the eyes hypnotized, adoring; and her arm round him seemed to shiver— with cold, with ecstasy?

Again that something went spinning through Gyp's head. She raised her hand. For a second it hovered close to the glass. Then, with a sick feeling, she dropped it and turned away.

Never! Never would she show him or that girl that they could hurt her! Never! They were safe from any scene she would make—safe in their nest! And blindly, across the frosty grass, through the un-lighted drawing-room, she went upstairs to her room, locked the door, and sat down before the fire. Pride raged within her. She stuffed her handkerchief between her teeth and lips; she did it unconsciously. Her eyes felt scorched from the fire-flames, but she did not trouble to hold her hand before them.

Suddenly she thought: ' Suppose I *had* loved him ?' and laughed. The handkerchief dropped to her lap, and she looked at it with wonder—it was blood-stained. She drew back in the chair, away from the scorching of the fire, and sat quite still, a smile on her lips. That girl's eyes, like a little adoring dog's— that girl, who had fawned on her so! She had got her " distinguished man " ! She sprang up and looked at herself in the glass; shuddered, turned her back on herself, and sat down again. In her own house ! Why not here—in this room ? Why not before her eyes ? Not yet a year married ! It was almost funny—almost funny ! And she had her first calm thought: ' I am free.'

But it did not seem to mean anything, had no value to a spirit so bitterly stricken in its pride. She moved her chair closer to the fire again. Why had she not

tapped on the window? To have seen that girl's
face ashy with fright! To have seen him—caught—
caught in the room she had made beautiful for him,
the room where she had played for him so many hours,
the room that was part of the house that she paid for!
How long had they used it for their meetings—sneak-
ing in by that door from the back lane? Perhaps
even before she went away—to bear his child! And
there began in her a struggle between mother instinct
and her sense of outrage—a spiritual tug-of-war so
deep that it was dumb, unconscious—to decide whether
her baby would be all hers, or would have slipped
away from her heart, and be a thing almost abhorrent.

She huddled nearer the fire, feeling cold and physically sick. And suddenly the thought came to her:
'If I don't let the servants know I'm here, they
might go out and see what I saw!' Had she shut the
drawing-room window when she returned so blindly?
Perhaps already——! In a fever, she rang the bell,
and unlocked the door. The maid came up.

"Please shut the drawing-room window, Ellen; and
tell Betty I'm afraid I got a little chill travelling.
I'm going to bed. Ask her if she can manage with
baby." And she looked straight into the girl's face.
It wore an expression of concern, even of commisera-
tion, but not that fluttered look which must have
been there if she had known.

"Yes, m'm; I'll get you a hot-water bottle, m'm.
Would you like a hot bath and a cup of hot tea at
once?"

Gyp nodded. Anything—anything! And when
the maid was gone, she thought mechanically: 'A
cup of hot tea! How quaint! What should it be
but hot?'

The maid came back with the tea; she was an affectionate girl, full of that admiring love servants and dogs always felt for Gyp, imbued, too, with the instinctive partisanship which stores itself one way or the other in the hearts of those who live in houses where the atmosphere lacks unity. To her mind, the mistress was much too good for him—a foreigner—and such 'abits! Manners—he hadn't any! And no good would come of it. Not if you took her opinion!

"And I've turned the water in, m'm. Will you have a little mustard in it?"

Again Gyp nodded. And the girl, going downstairs for the mustard, told cook there was "that about the mistress that makes you quite pathetic." The cook, who was fingering her concertina, for which she had a passion, answered:

"She 'ides up her feelin's, same as they all does. Thank 'eaven she haven't got that drawl, though, that 'er old aunt 'as—always makes me feel to want to say, 'Buck up, old dear, you ain't 'alf so precious as all that!'"

And when the maid Ellen had taken the mustard and gone, she drew out her concertina to its full length and, with cautionary softness, began to practise "Home, Sweet Home"!

To Gyp, lying in her hot bath, those muffled strains just mounted, not quite as a tune, rather as some far-away humming of large flies. The heat of the water, the pungent smell of the mustard, and that droning hum slowly soothed and drowsed away the vehemence of feeling. She looked at her body, silver-white in the yellowish water, with a dreamy sensation. Some day she, too, would love! Strange feeling she had never had before! Strange, indeed, that it should come at such a moment, breaking through the old instinctive shrinking. Yes; some day love would come to her. There floated before her brain the adoring look on Daphne Wing's face, the shiver that had passed along her arm, and pitifulness crept into her heart—a half-bitter, half-admiring pitifulness. Why should she grudge—she who did not love? The sounds, like the humming of large flies, grew deeper, more vibrating. It was the cook, in her passion swelling out her music on the phrase,

> " Be it ne-e-ver so humble,
> There's no-o place like home !"

XIII

THAT night, Gyp slept peacefully, as though nothing had happened, as though there were no future at all before her. She woke into misery. Her pride would never let her show the world what she had discovered, would force her to keep an unmoved face and live an unmoved life. But the struggle between mother-instinct and revolt was still going on within her. She was really afraid to see her baby, and she sent word to Betty that she thought it would be safer if she kept quite quiet till the afternoon.

She got up at noon and stole downstairs. She had not realized how violent was her struggle over *his* child till she was passing the door of the room where it was lying. If she had not been ordered to give up nursing, that struggle would never have come. Her heart ached, but a demon pressed her on and past the door. Downstairs she just pottered round, dusting her china, putting in order the books which, after house-cleaning, the maid had arranged almost too carefully, so that the first volumes of Dickens and Thackeray followed each other on the top shelf, and the second volumes followed each other on the bottom shelf. And all the time she thought dully : ' Why am I doing this ? What do I care how the place looks ? It is not my home. It can never be my home !'

For lunch she drank some beef tea, keeping up the fiction of her indisposition. After that, she sat down at her bureau to write. Something must be decided! There she sat, her forehead on her hand, and nothing came—not one word—not even the way to address him; just the date, and that was all. At a ring of the bell she started up. She could not see anybody! But the maid only brought a note from Aunt Rosamund, and the dogs, who fell frantically on their mistress and instantly began to fight for her possession. She went on her knees to separate them, and enjoin peace and good-will, and their little avid tongues furiously licked her cheeks. Under the eager touch of those wet tongues the band round her brain and heart gave way; she was overwhelmed with longing for her baby. Nearly a day since she had seen her— was it possible? Nearly a day without sight of those solemn eyes and crinkled toes and fingers! And, followed by the dogs, she went upstairs.

The house was invisible from the music-room; and, spurred on by thought that, until Fiorsen knew she was back, those two might be there in each other's arms any moment of the day or night, Gyp wrote that evening:

"DEAR GUSTAV,—We are back.—GYP."

What else in the world could she say? He would not get it till he woke about eleven. With the instinct to take all the respite she could, and knowing no more than before how she would receive his return, she went out in the forenoon and wandered about all day shopping and trying not to think. Returning at tea-time, she went straight up to her baby, and there heard from Betty that he had come, and gone out with his violin to the music-room.

Bent over the child, Gyp needed all her self-control

—but her self-control was becoming great. Soon, the girl would come fluttering down that dark, narrow lane; perhaps at this very minute her fingers were tapping at the door, and he was opening it to murmur: " No; she's back !" Ah, then the girl would shrink ! The rapid whispering—some other meeting-place ! Lips to lips, and that look on the girl's face; till she hurried away from the shut door, in the darkness, disappointed ! And he, on that silver-and-gold divan, gnawing his moustache, his eyes—catlike—staring at the fire ! And then, perhaps, from his violin would come one of those swaying bursts of sound, with tears in them, and the wind in them, that had of old bewitched her ! She said:

" Open the window just a little, Betty dear—it's hot."

There it was, rising, falling ! Music ! Why did it so move one even when, as now, it was the voice of insult ! And suddenly she thought: " He will expect me to go out there again and play for him. But I will not, never !"

She put her baby down, went into her bedroom, and changed hastily into a teagown for the evening, ready to go down-stairs. A little shepherdess in china on the mantel-shelf attracted her attention, and she took it in her hand. She had bought it three and more years ago, when she first came to London, at the beginning of that time of girl-gaiety when all life seemed a long cotillon, and she its leader. Its cool daintiness made it seem the symbol of another world, a world without depths or shadows, a world that did not feel—a happy world !

She had not long to wait before he tapped on the drawing-room window. She got up from the tea-table to let him in. Why do faces gazing in through glass from darkness always look hungry—searching, appealing for what you have and they have not? And while she was undoing the latch she thought: 'What am I going to say? I feel nothing!' The ardour of his gaze, voice, hands seemed to her so false as to be almost comic; even more comically false his look of disappointment when she said:

"Please take care; I'm still brittle!" Then she sat down again and asked:

"Will you have some tea?"

"Tea! I have you back, and you ask me if I will have tea! Gyp! Do you know what I have felt like all this time? No; you don't know. You know nothing of me—do you?"

A smile of sheer irony formed on her lips—without her knowing it was there. She said:

"Have you had a good time at Count Rosek's?" And, without her will, against her will, the words slipped out: "I'm afraid you've missed the music-room!"

His stare wavered; he began to walk up and down.

"Missed! Missed everything! I have been very miserable, Gyp. You've no idea how miserable. Yes, miserable, miserable, miserable!" With each repetition of that word, his voice grew gayer. And kneeling down in front of her, he stretched his long arms round her till they met behind her waist: "Ah, my Gyp! I shall be a different being, now."

And Gyp went on smiling. Between that, and stabbing these false raptures to the heart, there seemed to be nothing she could do. The moment his hands relaxed, she got up and said:

"You know there's a baby in the house?"

He laughed.

" Ah, the baby ! I'd forgotten. Let's go up and see it."

Gyp answered:

" You go."

She could feel him thinking: ' Perhaps it will make her nice to me !' He turned suddenly and went.

She stood with her eyes shut, seeing the divan in the music-room and the girl's arm shivering. Then, going to the piano, she began with all her might to play a Chopin polonaise.

That evening they dined out, and went to " The Tales of Hoffmann." By such devices it was possible to put off a little longer what she was going to do. During the drive home in the dark cab, she shrank away into her corner, pretending that his arm would hurt her dress; her exasperated nerves were already overstrung. Twice she was on the very point of crying out: " I am not Daphne Wing !" But each time pride strangled the words in her throat. And yet they would have to come. What other reason could she find to keep him from her room ?

But when in her mirror she saw him standing behind her—he had crept into the bedroom like a cat —fierceness came into her. She could see the blood rush up in her own white face, and, turning round she said:

" No, Gustav, go out to the music-room if you want a companion."

He recoiled against the foot of the bed and stared at her haggardly, and Gyp, turning back to her mirror, went on quietly taking the pins out of her hair. For fully a minute she could see him leaning there, moving his head and hands as though in pain. Then, to her surprise, he went. And a vague feeling of compunction mingled with her sense of deliverance. She lay awake a long time, watching the fire-glow brighten and darken on the ceiling, tunes from "The Tales of Hoffmann" running in her head; thoughts and fancies crisscrossing in her excited brain. Falling asleep at last, she dreamed she was feeding doves out of her hand, and one of them was Daphne Wing. She woke with a start. The fire still burned, and by its light she saw him crouching at the foot of the bed, just as he had on their wedding-night—the same hungry yearning in his face, and an arm outstretched. Before she could speak, he began:

"Oh, Gyp, you don't understand! All that is nothing—it is only you I want—always. I am a fool who cannot control himself. Think! It's a long time since you went away from me."

Gyp said, in a hard voice:

"I didn't want to have a child."

He said quickly:

"No; but now you have it you are glad. Don't be unmerciful, my Gyp! It is like you to be merciful. That girl—it is all over—I swear—I promise."

His hand touched her foot through the soft eiderdown. Gyp thought: 'Why does he come and whine to me like this? He has no dignity—none!' And she said:

"How can you promise? You have made the girl love you. I saw her face."

He drew his hand back.

"You saw her?"

"Yes."

He was silent, staring at her. Presently he began again:

" She is a little fool. I do not care for the whole of her as much as I care for your one finger. What does it matter what one does in that way if one does not care ? The soul, not the body, is faithful. A man satisfies appetite—it is nothing."

Gyp said:

" Perhaps not; but it is something when it makes others miserable."

" Has it made you miserable, my Gyp ?"

His voice had a ring of hope. She answered, startled:

" I ? No—her."

" Her ? Ho ! It is an experience for her—it is life. It will do her no harm."

" No; nothing will do anybody harm if it gives you pleasure."

At that bitter retort, he kept silence a long time, now and then heaving a long sigh. His words kept sounding in her heart: " The soul, not the body, is faithful." Was he, after all, more faithful to her than she had ever been, could ever be—who did not love, had never loved him ? What right had she to talk, who had married him out of vanity, out of—what ?

And suddenly he said:

" Gyp ! Forgive !"

She uttered a sigh, and turned away her face.

He bent down against the eider-down. She could hear him drawing long, sobbing breaths, and, in the midst of her lassitude and hopelessness, a sort of pity stirred her. What did it matter ? She said, in a choked voice:

" Very well, I forgive."

XIV

THE human creature has wonderful power of putting up with things. Gyp never really believed that Daphne Wing was of the past. Her sceptical instinct told her that what Fiorsen might honestly mean to do was very different from what he would do under stress of opportunity carefully put within his reach.

Since her return, Rosek had begun to come again, very careful not to repeat his mistake, but not deceiving her at all. Though his self-control was as great as Fiorsen's was small, she felt he had not given up his pursuit of her, and would take very good care that Daphne Wing was afforded every chance of being with her husband. But pride never let her allude to the girl. Besides, what good to speak of her? They would both lie—Rosek, because he obviously saw the mistaken line of his first attack; Fiorsen, because his temperament did not permit him to suffer by speaking the truth.

Having set herself to endure, she found she must live in the moment, never think of the future, never think much of anything. Fortunately, nothing so conduces to vacuity as a baby. She gave herself up to it with desperation. It was a good baby, silent, somewhat understanding. In watching its face, and feeling it warm against her, Gyp succeeded daily in getting away into the hypnotic state of mothers, and cows that chew the cud. But the baby slept a great deal, and much of its time was claimed by Betty.

Those hours, and they were many, Gyp found difficult. She had lost interest in dress and household elegance, keeping just enough to satisfy her fastidiousness; money, too, was scarce, under the drain of Fiorsen's irregular requirements. If she read, she began almost at once to brood. She was cut off from the music-room, had not crossed its threshold since her discovery. Aunt Rosamund's efforts to take her into society were fruitless—all the effervescence was out of that, and, though her father came, he never stayed long for fear of meeting Fiorsen. In this condition of affairs, she turned more and more to her own music, and one morning, after she had come across some compositions of her girlhood, she made a resolution. That afternoon she dressed herself with pleasure, for the first time for months, and sallied forth into the February frost.

Monsieur Edouard Harmost inhabited the ground floor of a house in the Marylebone Road. He received his pupils in a large back room overlooking a little sooty garden. A Walloon by extraction, and of great vitality, he grew old with difficulty, having a soft corner in his heart for women, and a passion for novelty, even for new music, that was unappeasable. Any fresh discovery would bring a tear rolling down his mahogany cheeks into his clipped grey beard, the while he played, singing wheezily to elucidate the wondrous novelty, or moved his head up and down, as if pumping.

When Gyp was shown into this well-remembered room he was seated, his yellow fingers buried in his stiff grey hair, grieving over a pupil who had just gone out. He did not immediately rise, but stared hard at Gyp.

" Ah," he said, at last, " my little old friend ! She has come back ! Now that is good !" And, patting her hand he looked into her face, which had a warmth and brilliance rare to her in these days. Then, making for the mantelpiece, he took therefrom a bunch of Parma violets, evidently brought by his last pupil, and thrust them under her nose. " Take them, take them—they were meant for me. Now—how much have you forgotten ? Come !" And, seizing her by the elbow, he almost forced her to the piano. " Take off your furs. Sit down !"

And while Gyp was taking off her coat, he fixed on her his prominent brown eyes that rolled easily in their slightly blood-shot whites, under squared eyelids and cliffs of brow. She had on what Fiorsen called her " humming-bird " blouse—dark blue, shot with pea-cock and old rose, and looked very warm and soft under her fur cap. Monsieur Harmost's stare seemed to drink her in; yet that stare was not unpleasant, having in it only the rather sad yearning of old men who love beauty and know that their time for seeing it is getting short.

" Play me the ' Carnival,' " he said. " We shall soon see !"

Gyp played. Twice he nodded; once he tapped his fingers on his teeth, and showed her the whites of his eyes—which meant: " That will have to be very different !" And once he grunted. When she had finished, he sat down beside her, took her hand in his, and, examining the fingers, began:

" Yes, yes, soon again ! Spoiling yourself, playing for that fiddler ! *Trop sympathique !* The back-bone, the back-bone—we shall improve that. Now, four hours a day for six weeks—and we shall have something again."

Gyp said softly:

"I have a baby, Monsieur Harmost."

Monsieur Harmost bounded.

"What! That is a tragedy!" Gyp shook her head. "You like it? A baby! Does it not squall?"

"Very little."

"*Mon Dieu!* Well, well, you are still as beautiful as ever. That is something. Now, what can you do with this baby? Could you get rid of it a little? This is serious. This is a talent in danger. A fiddler, and a baby! *C'est beaucoup! C'est trop!*"

Gyp smiled. And Monsieur Harmost, whose exterior covered much sensibility, stroked her hand.

"You have grown up, my little friend," he said gravely. "Never mind; nothing is wasted. But a baby!" And he chirruped his lips. "Well; courage! We shall do things yet!"

Gyp turned her head away to hide the quiver of her lips. The scent of latakia tobacco that had soaked into things, and of old books and music, a dark smell, like Monsieur Harmost's complexion; the old brown curtains, the sooty little back garden beyond, with its cat-runs, and its one stunted sumach tree; the dark-brown stare of Monsieur Harmost's rolling eyes brought back that time of happiness, when she used to come week after week, full of gaiety and importance, and chatter away, basking in his brusque admiration and in music, all with the glamourous feeling that she was making him happy, and herself happy, and going to play very finely some day.

The voice of Monsieur Harmost, softly gruff, as if he knew what she was feeling, increased her emotion; her breast heaved under the humming-bird blouse, water came into her eyes, and more than ever her lips quivered. He was saying:

" Come, come ! The only thing we cannot cure is age. You were right to come, my child. Music is your proper air. If things are not all what they ought to be, you shall soon forget. In music—in music, we can get away. After all, my little friend, they cannot take our dreams from us—not even a wife, not even a husband can do that. Come, we shall have good times yet !"

And Gyp, with a violent effort, threw off that sudden weakness. From those who serve art devotedly there radiates a kind of glamour. She left Monsieur Harmost that afternoon, infected by his passion for music. Poetic justice—on which all homeopathy is founded— was at work to try and cure her life by a dose of what had spoiled it. To music, she now gave all the hours she could spare. She went to him twice a week, determining to get on, but uneasy at the expense, for monetary conditions were ever more embarrassed. At home, she practised steadily and worked hard at composition. She finished several songs and studies during the spring and summer, and left still more unfinished. Monsieur Harmost was tolerant of these efforts, seeming to know that harsh criticism or dis- approval would cut her impulse down, as frost cuts the life of flowers. Besides, there was always some- thing fresh and individual in her things. He asked her one day:

" What does your husband think of these ?"

Gyp was silent a moment.

" I don't show them to him."

She never had; she instinctively kept back the knowledge that she composed, dreading his ruthless-

ness when anything grated on his nerves, and knowing
that a breath of mockery would wither her belief in
herself, frail enough plant already. The only person,
besides her master, to whom she confided her efforts
was—strangely enough—Rosek. But he had surprised
her one day copying out some music, and said at
once: " I knew. I was certain you composed. Ah,
do play it to me ! I am sure you have talent." The
warmth with which he praised that little " caprice "
was surely genuine; and she felt so grateful that she
even played him others, and then a song for him to
sing. From that day, he no longer seemed to her
odious; she even began to have for him a certain
friendliness, to be a little sorry, watching him, pale,
trim, and sphinxlike, in her drawing-room or garden,
getting no nearer to the fulfilment of his desire. He
had never again made love to her, but she knew that
at the least sign he would. His face and his invincible
patience made him pathetic to her. Women such as
Gyp cannot actively dislike those who admire them
greatly. She consulted him about Fiorsen's debts.
There were hundreds of pounds owing, it seemed, and,
in addition, much to Rosek himself. The thought of
these debts weighed unbearably on her. Why did
he, *how* did he get into debt like this ? What became
of the money he earned ? His fees, this summer,
were good enough. There was such a feeling of
degradation about debt. It was, somehow, so under-
bred to owe money to all sorts of people. Was it on
that girl, on other women, that he spent it all ? Or
was it simply that his nature had holes in every
pocket ?

Watching Fiorsen closely, that spring and early
summer, she was conscious of a change, a sort of

loosening, something in him had given way—as when, in winding a watch, the key turns on and on, the ratchet being broken. Yet he was certainly working hard—perhaps harder than ever. She would hear him, across the garden, going over and over a passage, as if he never would be satisfied. But his playing seemed to her to have lost its fire and sweep; to be stale, and as if disillusioned. It was all as though he had said to himself: " What's the use ?" In his face, too, there was a change. She knew—she was certain that he was drinking secretly. Was it his failure with her ? Was it the girl ? Was it simply heredity from a hard-drinking ancestry ?

Gyp never faced these questions. To face them would mean useless discussion, useless admission that she could not love him, useless asseveration from him about the girl, which she would not believe, useless denials of all sorts. Hopeless !

He was very irritable, and seemed especially to resent her music lessons, alluding to them with a sort of sneering impatience. She felt that he despised them as amateurish, and secretly resented it. He was often impatient, too, of the time she gave to the baby. His own conduct with the little creature was like all the rest of him. He would go to the nursery, much to Betty's alarm, and take up the baby; be charming with it for about ten minutes, then suddenly dump it back into its cradle, stare at it gloomily or utter a laugh, and go out. Sometimes, he would come up when Gyp was there, and after watching her a little in silence, almost drag her away.

Suffering always from the guilty consciousness of having no love for him, and ever more and more from her sense that, instead of saving him she was, as it were, pushing him down-hill—ironical nemesis for vanity!—Gyp was ever more and more compliant to his whims, trying to make up. But this compliance, when all the time she felt further and further away, was straining her to breaking-point. Hers was a nature that goes on passively enduring till something snaps; after that—no more.

Those months of spring and summer were like a long spell of drought, when moisture gathers far away, coming nearer, nearer, till, at last, the deluge bursts and sweeps the garden.

XV

THE tenth of July that year was as the first day of summer. There had been much fine weather, but always easterly or northerly; now, after a broken, rainy fortnight, the sun had come in full summer warmth with a gentle breeze, drifting here and there scent of the opening lime blossom. In the garden, under the trees at the far end, Betty sewed at a garment, and the baby in her perambulator had her seventh morning sleep. Gyp stood before a bed of pansies and sweet peas. How monkeyish the pansies' faces! The sweet peas, too, were like tiny bright birds fastened to green perches swaying with the wind. And their little green tridents, growing out from the queer, flat stems, resembled the antennæ of insects. Each of these bright frail, growing things had life and individuality like herself!

The sound of footsteps on the gravel made her turn. Rosek was coming from the drawing-room window. Rather startled, Gyp looked at him over her shoulder. What had brought him at eleven o'clock in the morning? He came up to her, bowed, and said:

" I came to see Gustav. He's not up yet, it seems. I thought I would speak to you first. Can we talk ?"

Hesitating just a second, Gyp drew off her gardening-gloves:

" Of course ! Here ? Or in the drawing-room ?"
Rosek answered:

" In the drawing-room, please."

A faint tremor passed through her, but she led the way, and seated herself where she could see Betty and the baby. Rosek stood looking down at her; his stillness, the sweetish gravity of his well-cut lips, his spotless dandyism stirred in Gyp a kind of unwilling admiration.

" What is it ?" she said.

" Bad business, I'm afraid. Something must be done at once. I have been trying to arrange things, but they will not wait. They are even threatening to sell up this house."

With a sense of outrage, Gyp cried:

" Nearly everything here is mine."

Rosek shook his head.

" The lease is in his name—you are his wife. They can do it, I assure you." A sort of shadow passed over his face, and he added: " I cannot help him any more—just now."

Gyp shook her head quickly.

" No—of course ! You ought not to have helped him at all. I can't bear——" He bowed, and she stopped, ashamed. " How much does he owe altogether ?"

" About thirteen hundred pounds. It isn't much, of course. But there is something else——"

" Worse ?"

Rosek nodded.

" I am afraid to tell you; you will think again perhaps that I am trying to make capital out of it. I can read your thoughts, you see. I cannot afford that you should think that, this time."

Gyp made a little movement as though putting away his words.

" No; tell me, please."

Rosek shrugged his shoulders.

"There is a man called Wagge, an undertaker—the father of someone you know——"

"Daphne Wing?"

"Yes. A child is coming. They have made her tell. It means the cancelling of her engagements, of course—and other things."

Gyp uttered a little laugh; then she said slowly:

"Can you tell me, please, what this Mr.—Wagge can do?"

Again Rosek shrugged his shoulders.

"He is rabid—a rabid man of his class is dangerous. A lot of money will be wanted, I should think—some blood, perhaps."

He moved swiftly to her, and said very low:

"Gyp, it is a year since I told you of this. You did not believe me then. I told you, too, that I loved you. I love you more, now, a hundred times! Don't move! I am going up to Gustav."

He turned, and Gyp thought he was really going; but he stopped and came back past the line of the window. The expression of his face was quite changed, so hungry that, for a moment, she felt sorry for him. And that must have shown in her face, for he suddenly caught at her, and tried to kiss her lips; she wrenched back, and he could only reach her throat, but that he kissed furiously. Letting her go as suddenly, he bent his head and went out without a look.

Gyp stood wiping his kisses off her throat with the back of her hand, dumbly, mechanically thinking: "What have I done to be treated like this? What *have* I done?" No answer came. And such rage against men flared up that she just stood there, twisting her garden-gloves in her hands, and biting the lips he would have kissed. Then, going to her bureau, she took up her address book and looked for the name; Wing, 88, Frankland Street, Fulham. Unhooking her little bag from off the back of the chair, she put her cheque-book into it. Then, taking care to make no sound, she passed into the hall, caught up her sun-shade, and went out, closing the door without noise.

She walked quickly toward Baker Street. Her gardening-hat was right enough, but she had come out without gloves, and must go into the first shop and buy a pair. In the choosing of them, she forgot her emotions for a minute. Out in the street again, they came back as bitterly as ever. And the day was so beautiful—the sun bright, the sky blue, the clouds dazzling white; from the top of her 'bus she could see all its brilliance. There rose up before her the memory of the man who had kissed her arm at the first ball. And now—this! But, mixed with her rage, a sort of unwilling compassion and fellow feeling kept rising for that girl, that silly, sugar-plum girl, brought to such a pass by—her husband. These feelings sustained her through that voyage to Fulham. She got down at the nearest corner, walked up a widish street of narrow grey houses till she came to number eighty-eight. On that newly scrubbed step, waiting for the door to open, she very nearly turned and fled. What exactly had she come to do?

The door was opened by a servant in an untidy frock. Mutton! The smell of mutton—there it was, just as the girl had said!

" Is Miss—Miss Daphne Wing at home?"

In that peculiar " I've given it up" voice of domestics in small households, the servant an-swered:

"Yes; Miss Disey's in. D'you want to see 'er? What nyme?"

Gyp produced her card. The maid looked at it, at Gyp, and at two brown-painted doors, as much as to say, "Where will you have it?" Then, opening the first of them, she said:

"Tyke a seat, please; I'll fetch her."

Gyp went in. In the middle of what was clearly the dining-room, she tried to subdue the tremor of her limbs and a sense of nausea. The table against which her hand rested was covered with red baize, no doubt to keep the stains of mutton from penetrating to the wood. On the mahogany sideboard reposed a cruet-stand and a green dish of very red apples. A bamboo-framed talc screen painted with white and yellow marguerites stood before a fireplace filled with pampas-grass dyed red. The chairs were of red morocco, the curtains a brownish-red, the walls green, and on them hung a set of Landseer prints. The peculiar sensation which red and green in juxtaposition produce on the sensitive was added to Gyp's distress. And, suddenly, her eyes lighted on a little deep-blue china bowl. It stood on a black stand on the mantel-piece, with nothing in it. To Gyp, in this room of red and green, with the smell of mutton creeping in, that bowl was like the crystallized whiff of another world. Daphne Wing—not Daisy Wagge—had surely put it there! And, somehow, it touched her—emblem of stifled beauty, emblem of all that the girl had tried to pour out to her that August afternoon in her garden nearly a year ago. Thin Eastern china, good and really beautiful! A wonder they allowed it to pollute this room!

A sigh made her turn round With her back against

the door and a white, scared face, the girl was standing. Gyp thought: 'She has suffered horribly.' And,
going impulsively up to her, she held out her hand.

Daphne Wing sighed out: "Oh, Mrs. Fiorsen!" and,
bending over that hand, kissed it. Gyp saw that her
new glove was wet. Then the girl relapsed, her feet
a little forward, her head a little forward, her back
against the door. Gyp, who knew why she stood thus,
was swept again by those two emotions—rage against
men, and fellow feeling for one about to go through
what she herself had just endured.

"It's all right," she said, gently; "only, what's to
be done?"

Daphne Wing put her hands up over her white face
and sobbed. She sobbed so quietly but so terribly
deeply that Gyp herself had the utmost difficulty not
to cry. It was the sobbing of real despair by a creature
bereft of hope and strength, above all, of love—the
sort of weeping which is drawn from desolate, suffering
souls only by the touch of fellow feeling. And,
instead of making Gyp glad or satisfying her sense of
justice, it filled her with more rage against her husband
—that he had taken this girl's infatuation for his
pleasure and then thrown her away. She seemed to
see him discarding that clinging, dove-fair girl, for
cloying his senses and getting on his nerves, discarding
her with caustic words, to abide alone the consequences
of her infatuation. She put her hand timidly on that
shaking shoulder, and stroked it. For a moment the
sobbing stopped, and the girl said brokenly:

"Oh, Mrs. Fiorsen, I do love him so!" At those
naïve words, a painful wish to laugh seized on
Gyp, making her shiver from head to foot. Daphne
Wing saw it, and went on: "I know—I know—it's

awful; but I do—and now he—he——" Her quiet but really dreadful sobbing broke out again. And again Gyp began stroking and stroking her shoulder. "And I have been so awful to you! Oh, Mrs. Fiorsen, do forgive me, please!"

All Gyp could find to answer, was:

"Yes, yes; that's nothing! Don't cry—don't cry!"

Very slowly the sobbing died away, till it was just a long shivering, but still the girl held her hands over her face and her face down. Gyp felt paralyzed. The unhappy girl, the red and green room, the smell of mutton—creeping!

At last, a little of that white face showed; the lips, no longer craving for sugar-plums, murmured:

"It's you he—he—really loves all the time. And you don't love him—that's what's so funny—and—and—I can't understand it. Oh, Mrs. Fiorsen, if I could see him—just see him! He told me never to come again; and I haven't dared. I haven't seen him for three weeks—not since I told him about *it*. What shall I do? What shall I do?"

His being her own husband seemed as nothing to Gyp at that moment. She felt such pity and yet such violent revolt that any girl should want to crawl back to a man who had spurned her. Unconsciously, she had drawn herself up and pressed her lips together. The girl, who followed every movement, said piteously:

"I don't seem to have any pride. I don't mind what he does to me, or what he says, if only I can see him."

Gyp's revolt yielded to her pity. She said:

"How long before?"

"Three months."

Three months—and in this state of misery!

"I think I shall do something desperate. Now that I can't dance, and *they* know, it's too awful! If I could see him, I wouldn't mind anything. But I know—I know he'll never want me again. Oh, Mrs. Fiorsen, I wish I was dead! I do!"

A heavy sigh escaped Gyp, and, bending suddenly, she kissed the girl's forehead. Still that scent of orange blossom about her skin or hair, as when she asked whether she ought to love or not; as when she came, moth-like, from the tree-shade into the moon-light, spun, and fluttered, with her shadow spinning and fluttering before her. Gyp turned away, feeling that she must relieve the strain, and pointing to the bowl, said:

"*You* put that there, I'm sure. It's beautiful."

The girl answered, with piteous eagerness:

"Oh, would you like it? Do take it. Count Rosek gave it me." She started away from the door. "Oh, that's papa. He'll be coming in!"

Gyp heard a man clear his throat, and the rattle of an umbrella falling into a stand; the sight of the girl wilting and shrinking against the sideboard steadied her. Then the door opened, and Mr. Wagge entered. Short and thick, in black frock coat and trousers, and a greyish beard, he stared from one to the other. He looked what he was, an Englishman and a chapelgoer, nourished on sherry and mutton, who could and did make his own way in the world. His features, coloured, as from a deep liverishness, were thick, like his body, and not ill-natured, except for a sort of anger in his small, rather piggy grey eyes. He said in a voice permanently gruff, but impregnated with a species of professional ingratiation:

"Ye-es? Whom 'ave I—— ?"

" Mrs. Fiorsen."

" Ow !" The sound of his breathing could be heard distinctly; he twisted a chair round and said:

" Take a seat, won't you ?"

Gyp shook her head.

In Mr. Wagge's face a kind of deference seemed to struggle with some more primitive emotion. Taking out a large, black-edged handkerchief, he blew his nose, passed it freely over his visage, and turning to his daughter, muttered:

" Go upstairs."

The girl turned quickly, and the last glimpse of her white face whipped up Gyp's rage against men.   When the door was shut, Mr. Wagge cleared his throat; the grating sound carried with it the suggestion of enormously thick linings.

He said more gruffly than ever:

" May I ask what 'as given us the honour ?"

" I came to see your daughter."

His little piggy eyes travelled from her face to her feet, to the walls of the room, to his own watch-chain to his hands that had begun to rub themselves together, back to her breast, higher than which they dared not mount.   Their infinite embarrassment struck Gyp. She could almost hear him thinking: ' Now, how can I discuss it with this attractive young female, wife of the scoundrel who's ruined my daughter ?   Delicate— that's what it is !'   Then the words burst hoarsely from him.

" This is an unpleasant business, ma'am.   I don't know what to say. Reelly I don't. It's awkward; it's very awkward."

Gyp said quietly:

" Your daughter is desperately unhappy; and that can't be good for her just now."

Mr. Wagge's thick figure seemed to writhe.

"Pardon me, ma'am," he spluttered, "but I must call your husband a scoundrel. I'm sorry to be impolite, but I must do it. If I had 'im 'ere, I don't know that I should be able to control myself—I don't indeed." Gyp made a movement of her gloved hands, which he seemed to interpret as sympathy, for he went on in a stream of husky utterance: "It's a delicate thing before a lady, and she the injured party; but one has feelings. From the first I said this dancin' was in the face of Providence; but women have no more sense than an egg. Her mother she would have it; and now she's got it! Career, indeed! Pretty career! Daughter of mine! I tell you, ma'am, I'm angry; there's no other word for it—I'm angry. If that scoundrel comes within reach of me, I shall mark 'im—I'm not a young man, but I shall mark 'im. An' what to say to you, I'm sure I don't know. That my daughter should be'ave like that! Well, it's made a difference to me. An' now I suppose her name'll be dragged in the mud. I tell you frankly I 'oped you wouldn't hear of it, because after all the girl's got her punishment. And this divorce-court—it's not nice—it's a horrible thing for respectable people. And, mind you, I won't see my girl married to that scoundrel, not if you do divorce 'im. No; she'll have her disgrace for nothing."

Gyp, who had listened with her head a little bent, raised it suddenly, and said:

"There'll be no public disgrace, Mr. Wagge, unless you make it yourself. If you send Daphne—Daisy—quietly away somewhere till her trouble's over, no one need know anything."

Mr. Wagge, whose mouth had opened slightly, and

whose breathing could certainly have been heard in the street, took a step forward and said:

"Do I understand you to say that you're not goin' to take proceedings, ma'am?"

Gyp shuddered, and shook her head.

Mr. Wagge stood silent, slightly moving his face up and down.

"Well," he said, at length, "it's more than she deserves; but I don't disguise it's a relief to me. And I must say, in a young lady like you, and—and handsome, it shows a Christian spirit." Again Gyp shivered, and shook her head. "It does. You'll allow me to say so, as a man old enough to be your father—and a regular attendant."

He held out his hand. Gyp put her gloved hand into it.

"I'm very, very sorry. Please be nice to her."

Mr. Wagge recoiled a little, and for some seconds stood ruefully rubbing his hands together and looking from side to side.

"I'm a domestic man," he said suddenly. "A domestic man in a serious line of life; and I never thought to have anything like this in my family— never! It's been—well, I can't tell you what it's been!"

Gyp took up her sunshade. She felt that she must get away; at any moment he might say something she could not bear—and the smell of mutton rising fast!

"I am sorry," she said again; "good-bye;" and moved past him to the door. She heard him breathing hard as he followed her to open it, and thought: ' If only—oh! please let him be silent till I get outside!' Mr. Wagge passed her and put his hand on the latch of the front door. His little piggy eyes scanned her almost timidly.

" Well," he said, " I'm very glad to have the privilege of your acquaintance; and, if I may say so, you 'ave —you 'ave my 'earty sympathy. Good-day."

The door once shut behind her, Gyp took a long breath and walked swiftly away. Her cheeks were burning; and, with a craving for protection, she put up her sunshade. But the girl's white face came up again before her, and the sound of her words:

" Oh, Mrs. Fiorsen, I wish I was dead ! I *do* !"

XVI

GYP walked on beneath her sunshade, making unconsciously for the peace of trees. Her mind was a whirl of impressions—Daphne Wing's figure against the door, Mr. Wagge's puggy grey-bearded countenance, the red pampas-grass, the blue bowl, Rosek's face swooping at her, her last glimpse of her baby asleep under the trees !

She reached Kensington Gardens, turned into that walk renowned for the beauty of its flowers and the plainness of the people who frequent it, and sat down on a bench. It was near the luncheon-hour; nursemaids, dogs, perambulators, old gentlemen—all were hurrying a little toward their food. They glanced with critical surprise at this pretty young woman, leisured and lonely at such an hour, trying to find out what was wrong with her, as one naturally does with beauty—bow legs or something, for sure, to balance a face like that ! But Gyp noticed none of them, except now and again a dog which sniffed her knees in passing. For months she had resolutely cultivated insensibility, resolutely refused to face reality; the barrier was forced now, and the flood had swept her away. " Proceedings !" Mr. Wagge had said. To those who shrink from letting their secret affairs be known even by their nearest friends, the notion of a public exhibition of troubles simply never comes, and it had certainly never come to Gyp. With a bitter smile she thought: ' I'm better off than she is, after all! Suppose I loved him, too? No, I never—never—want to love. Women who love suffer too much.'

She sat on that bench a long time before it came into her mind that she was due at Monsieur Harmost's for a music lesson at three o'clock. It was well past two already; and she set out across the grass. The summer day was full of murmurings of bees and flies, cooings of blissful pigeons, the soft swish and stir of leaves, and the scent of lime blossom under a sky so blue, with few white clouds, slow, and calm, and full. Why be unhappy? And one of those spotty spaniel dogs, that have broad heads, with frizzy topknots, and are always rascals, smelt at her frock and moved round and round her, hoping that she would throw her sunshade on the water for him to fetch, this being in his view the only reason why anything was carried in the hand.

She found Monsieur Harmost fidgeting up and down the room, whose opened windows could not rid it of the smell of latakia.

"Ah," he said, "I thought you were not coming! You look pale; are you not well? Is it the heat? Or"—he looked hard into her face—"has someone hurt you, my little friend?" Gyp shook her head. "Ah, yes," he went on irritably; "you tell me nothing; you tell nobody nothing! You close up your pretty face like a flower at night. At your age, my child, one should make confidences; a secret grief is to music as the east wind to the stomach. Put off your mask for once." He came close to her. "Tell me your troubles. It is a long time since I have been meaning to ask. Come! We are only once young; I want to see you happy."

But Gyp stood looking down. Would it be relief

to pour her soul out ? Would it ? His brown eyes questioned her like an old dog's. She did not want to hurt one so kind. And yet—impossible !

Monsieur Harmost suddenly sat down at the piano. Resting his hands on the keys, he looked round at her, and said:

" I am in love with you, you know. Old men can be very much in love, but they know it is no good— that makes them endurable. Still, we like to feel of use to youth and beauty; it gives us a little warmth. Come; tell me your grief !" He waited a moment, then said irritably: " Well, well, we go to music then !"

It was his habit to sit by her at the piano corner, but to-day he stood as if prepared to be exceptionally severe. And Gyp played, whether from over-excited nerves or from not having had any lunch, better than she had ever played. The Chopin polonaise in A flat, that song of revolution, which had always seemed so unattainable, went as if her fingers were being worked for her. When she had finished, Monsieur Harmost, bending forward, lifted one of her hands and put his lips to it. She felt the scrub of his little bristly beard, and raised her face with a deep sigh of satisfaction. A voice behind them said mockingly:

" Bravo !"

There, by the door, stood Fiorsen.

" Congratulations, *madame !* I have long wanted to see you under the inspiration of your—master !"

Gyp's heart began to beat desperately. Monsieur Harmost had not moved. A faint grin slowly settled in his beard, but his eyes were startled.

Fiorsen kissed the back of his own hand.

" To this old Pantaloon you come to give your heart. Ho—what a lover !"

Gyp saw the old man quiver; she sprang up and cried:

"You brute!"

Fiorsen ran forward, stretching out his arms toward Monsieur Harmost, as if to take him by the throat.

The old man drew himself up. "*Monsieur*," he said, "you are certainly drunk."

Gyp slipped between, right up to those outstretched hands till she could feel their knuckles against her. Had he gone mad? Would he strangle her? But her eyes never moved from his, and his began to waver; his hands dropped, and, with a kind of moan, he made for the door.

Monsieur Harmost's voice behind her said:

"Before you go, *monsieur*, give me some explanation of this imbecility!"

Fiorsen spun round, shook his fist, and went out muttering. They heard the front door slam. Gyp turned abruptly to the window, and there, in her agitation, she noticed little outside things as one does in moments of bewildered anger. Even into that back yard, summer had crept. The leaves of the sumach-tree were glistening; in a three-cornered little patch of sunlight, a black cat with a blue ribbon round its neck was basking. The voice of one hawking strawberries drifted melancholy from a side street. She was conscious that Monsieur Harmost was standing very still, with a hand pressed to his mouth, and she felt a perfect passion of compunction and anger. That kind and harmless old man—to be so insulted! This was indeed the culmination of all Gustav's outrages! She would never forgive him this! For he had insulted her as well, beyond what pride or meekness could put up with. She turned, and, running up to the old man, put both her hands into his.

"I'm so awfully sorry. Good-bye, dear, dear Monsieur Harmost; I shall come on Friday!" And, before he could stop her, she was gone.

She dived into the traffic; but, just as she reached the pavement on the other side, felt her dress plucked and saw Fiorsen just behind her. She shook herself free and walked swiftly on. Was he going to make a scene in the street? Again he caught her arm. She stopped dead, faced round on him, and said, in an icy voice:

"Please don't make scenes in the street, and don't follow me like this. If you want to talk to me, you can—at home."

Then, very calmly, she turned and walked on. But he was still following her, some paces off. She did not quicken her steps, and to the first taxi-cab driver that passed she made a sign, and saying:

"Bury Street—quick!" got in. She saw Fiorsen rush forward, too late to stop her. He threw up his hand and stood still, his face deadly white under his broad-brimmed hat. She was far too angry and upset to care.

From the moment she turned to the window at Monsieur Harmost's, she had determined to go to her father's. She would not go back to Fiorsen; and the one thought that filled her mind was how to get Betty and her baby. Nearly four! Dad was almost sure to be at his club. And leaning out, she said: "No; Hyde Park Corner, please."

The hall porter, who knew her, after calling to a page-boy: "Major Winton—sharp, now!" came specially out of his box to offer her a seat and *The Times*.

13

Gyp sat with it on her knee, vaguely taking in her surroundings—a thin old gentleman anxiously weighing himself in a corner, a white-calved footman crossing with a tea-tray; a number of hats on pegs; the green baize board with its white rows of tapelike paper, and three members standing before it. One of them, a tall, stout, good-humoured-looking man in *pince-nez* and a white waistcoat, becoming conscious, removed his straw hat and took up a position whence, without staring, he could gaze at her; and Gyp knew, without ever seeming to glance at him, that he found her to his liking. She saw her father's unhurried figure passing that little group, all of whom were conscious now, and, eager to get away out of this sanctum of masculinity, she met him at the top of the low steps, and said:

" I want to talk to you, Dad."

He gave her a quick look, selected his hat, and followed to the door. In the cab, he put his hand on hers and said:

" Now, my dear ? "

But all she could get out was:

" I want to come back to you. I can't go on there. It's—it's—I've come to an end."

His hand pressed hers tightly, as if he were trying to save her the need for saying more. Gyp went on:

" I must get baby; I'm terrified that he'll try to keep her, to get me back."

" Is he at home ? "

" I don't know. I haven't told him that I'm going to leave him."

Winton looked at his watch and asked:

" Does the baby ever go out as late as this ? "

" Yes; after tea. It's cooler."

"I'll take this cab on, then. You stay and get the room ready for her. Don't worry, and don't go out till I return."

And Gyp thought: 'How wonderful of him not to have asked a single question.'

The cab stopped at the Bury Street door. She took his hand, put it to her cheek, and got out. He said quietly:

"Do you want the dogs?"

"Yes—oh, yes! He doesn't care for them."

"All right. There'll be time to get you in some things for the night after I come back. I shan't run any risks to-day. Make Mrs. Markey give you tea."

Gyp watched the cab gather way again, saw him wave his hand; then, with a deep sigh, half anxiety, half relief, she rang the bell.

XVII

WHEN the cab debouched again into St. James' Street, Winton gave the order: " Quick as you can !" One could think better going fast ! A little red had come into his brown cheeks; his eyes under their half-drawn lids had a keener light; his lips were tightly closed; he looked as he did when a fox was breaking cover. Gyp could do no wrong, or, if she could, he would stand by her in it as a matter of course. But he was going to take no risks—make no frontal attack. Time for that later, if necessary. He had better nerves than most people, and that kind of steely determination and resource which makes many Englishmen of his class formidable in small operations. He kept his cab at the door, rang, and asked for Gyp, with a kind of pleasure in his ruse.

" She's not in yet, sir. Mr. Fiorsen's in."

" Ah ! And baby ?"

" Yes, sir."

" I'll come in and see her. In the garden ?"

" Yes, sir."

" Dogs there, too ?"

" Yes, sir. And will you have tea, please, sir ?"

" No, thanks." How to effect this withdrawal without causing gossip, and yet avoid suspicion of collusion with Gyp ? And he added: " Unless Mrs. Fiorsen comes in."

Passing out into the garden, he became aware that Fiorsen was at the dining-room window watching him, and decided to make no sign that he knew this. The baby was under the trees at the far end, and the dogs came rushing thence with a fury which lasted till they came within scent of him. Winton went leisurely up to the perambulator, and, saluting Betty, looked down at his grandchild. She lay under an awning of muslin, for fear of flies, and was awake. Her solemn, large brown eyes, already like Gyp's, regarded him with gravity. Clucking to her once or twice, as is the custom, he moved so as to face the house. In this position, he had Betty with her back to it. And he said quietly:

"I'm here with a message from your mistress, Betty. Keep your head; don't look round, but listen to me. She's at Bury Street and going to stay there; she wants you and baby and the dogs." The stout woman's eyes grew round and her mouth opened. Winton put his hand on the perambulator. "Steady, now! Go out as usual with this thing. It's about your time; and wait for me at the turning to Regent's Park. I'll come on in my cab and pick you all up. Don't get flurried; don't take anything; do exactly as you usually would. Understand?"

It is not in the nature of stout women with babies in their charge to receive such an order without question. Her colour, and the heaving of that billowy bosom made Winton add quickly:

"Now, Betty, pull yourself together; Gyp wants you. I'll tell you all about it in the cab."

The poor woman, still heaving vaguely, could only stammer:

"Yes, sir. Poor little thing! What about its night-things? And Miss Gyp's?"

Conscious of that figure still at the window, Winton

made some passes with his fingers at the baby, and said:

"Never mind them. As soon as you see me at the drawing-room window, get ready and go. Eyes front, Betty; don't look round; I'll cover your retreat! Don't fail Gyp now. Pull yourself together."

With a sigh that could have been heard in Kensington, Betty murmured: "Very well, sir; oh dear!" and began to adjust the strings of her bonnet. With nods, as if he had been the recipient of some sage remarks about the baby, Winton saluted, and began his march again towards the house. He carefully kept his eyes to this side and to that, as if examining the flowers, but noted all the same that Fiorsen had receded from the window. Rapid thought told him that the fellow would come back there to see if he were gone, and he placed himself before a rose-bush, where, at that reappearance, he could make a sign of recognition. Sure enough, he came; and Winton quietly raising his hand to the salute passed on through the drawing-room window. He went quickly into the hall, listened a second, and opened the dining-room door. Fiorsen was pacing up and down, pale and restless. He came to a standstill and stared haggardly at Winton, who said:

"How are you? Gyp not in?"

"No."

Something in the sound of that "No" touched Winton with a vague—a very vague—compunction. To be left by Gyp! Then his heart hardened again. The fellow was a rotter—he was sure of it, had always been sure.

"Baby looks well," he said.

Fiorsen turned and began to pace up and down again.

" Where is Gyp ?   I want her to come in.   I want
her."

Winton took out his watch.

" It's not late."   And suddenly he felt a great aversion from the part he was playing.   To get the baby;
to make Gyp safe—yes !   But, somehow, not this
pretence that he knew nothing about it.   He turned
on his heel and walked out.   It imperilled everything;
but he couldn't help it.   He could not stay and go on
prevaricating like this.   Had that woman got clear ?
He went back into the drawing-room.   There they were
—just passing the side of the house.   Five minutes,
and they would be down at the turning.   He stood at
the window, waiting.   If only that fellow did not come
in !   Through the partition wall he could hear him
still tramping up and down the dining-room.   What
a long time a minute was !   Three had gone when he
heard the dining-room door opened, and Fiorsen
crossing the hall to the front door.   What was he after,
standing there as if listening ?   And suddenly he heard
him sigh.   It was just such a sound as many times,
in the long-past days, had escaped himself, waiting,
listening for footsteps, in parched and sickening
anxiety.   Did this fellow then really love—almost as
he had loved ?   And in revolt at spying on him like
this, he advanced and said:

" Well, I won't wait any longer."

Fiorsen started; he had evidently supposed himself
alone.   And Winton thought: ' By Jove ! he does
look bad !'

" Good-bye !" he said; but the words: " Give my
love to Gyp," perished on their way up to his lips.

" Good-bye !" Fiorsen echoed.   And Winton went
out under the trellis, conscious of that forlorn figure

still standing at the half-opened door. Betty was nowhere in sight; she must have reached the turning. His mission had succeeded, but he felt no elation. Round the corner, he picked up his convoy, and, with the perambulator hoisted on to the taxi, journeyed on at speed. He had said he would explain in the cab, but the only remark he made was:

" You'll all go down to Mildenham to-morrow."

And Betty, who had feared him ever since their encounter so many years ago, eyed his profile, without daring to ask questions. Before he reached home, Winton stopped at a post-office, and sent this telegram:

" Gyp and the baby are with me letter follows.— WINTON."

It salved a conscience on which that fellow's figure in the doorway weighed; besides, it was necessary, lest Fiorsen should go to the police. The rest must wait till he had talked with Gyp.

There was much to do, and it was late before they dined, and not till Markey had withdrawn could they begin their talk.

Close to the open windows where Markey had placed two hydrangea plants—just bought on his own responsibility, in token of silent satisfaction—Gyp began. She kept nothing back, recounting the whole miserable fiasco of her marriage. When she came to Daphne Wing and her discovery in the music-room, she could see the glowing end of her father's cigar move convulsively. That insult to his adored one seemed to Winton so inconceivable that, for a moment, he stopped her recital by getting up to pace the room. In her own house—her own house ! And—after that, she had gone on with him! He came back to his chair and did not interrupt again, but his stillness almost frightened her.

Coming to the incidents of the day itself, she hesitated. Must she tell him, too, of Rosek—was it wise, or necessary? The all-or-nothing candour that was part of her nature prevailed, and she went straight on, and, save for the feverish jerking of his evening shoe, Winton made no sign. When she had finished, he got up and slowly extinguished the end of his cigar against the window-sill; then looking at her lying back in her chair as if exhausted, he said: "By God!" and turned his face away to the window.

At that hour before the theatres rose, a lull brooded in the London streets; in this quiet narrow one, the town's hum was only broken by the clack of a half-drunken woman bickering at her man as they lurched along for home, and the strains of a street musician's fiddle, trying to make up for a blank day. The sound vaguely irritated Winton, reminding him of those two damnable foreigners by whom she had been so treated. To have them at the point of a sword or pistol—to teach them a lesson! He heard her say:

"Dad, I should like to pay his debts. Then things would be as they were when I married him."

He emitted an exasperated sound. He did not believe in heaping coals of fire.

"I want to make sure, too, that the girl is all right till she's over her trouble. Perhaps I could use some of that—that other money, if mine is all tied up?"

It was sheer anger, not disapproval of her impulse, that made him hesitate; money and revenge would never be associated in his mind. Gyp went on:

"I want to feel as if I'd never let him marry me.

Perhaps his debts are all part of that—who knows?
Please!"

Winton looked at her. How like—when she said
that "Please!" How like—her figure sunk back
in the old chair, and the face lifted in shadow! A sort
of exultation came to him. He had got her back—
had got her back!

XVIII

FIORSEN's bedroom was—as the maid would remark—
" a proper pigsty "—until he was out of it and it could
be renovated each day. He had a talent for disorder, so
that the room looked as if three instead of one man had
gone to bed in it. Clothes and shoes, brushes, water,
tumblers, breakfast-tray, newspapers, French novels,
and cigarette-ends—none were ever where they should
have been; and the stale fumes from the many cigarettes
he smoked before getting up incommoded anyone
whose duty it was to take him tea and shaving-water.
When, on that first real summer day, the maid had
brought Rosek up to him, he had been lying a long
time on his back, dreamily watching the smoke from
his cigarette, and four flies waltzing in the sunlight that
filtered through the green sun-blinds. This hour,
before he rose, was his creative moment, when he could
best see the form of music and feel inspiration for its
rendering. Of late, he had been stale and wretched,
all that side of him dull; but this morning he felt again
the delicious stir of fancy, that vibrating, half-dreamy
state when emotion seems so easily to find shape and
the mind pierces through to new expression. Hearing
the maid's knock, and her murmured: " Count Rosek
to see you, sir," he thought: ' What the devil does he
want ?' A larger nature, drifting without control,
in contact with a smaller one, who knows his own mind
exactly, will instinctively be irritable, though he may
fail to grasp what his friend is after.

And pushing the cigarette-box toward Rosek, he turned away his head. It would be money he had come about, or—that girl! That girl—he wished she was dead! Soft, clinging creature! A baby! God! What a fool he had been—ah, what a fool! Such absurdity! Unheard of! First Gyp—then her! He had tried to shake the girl off. As well try to shake off a burr! How she clung! He had been patient—oh, yes—patient and kind, but how go on when one was tired—tired of her—and wanting only Gyp, only his own wife? That was a funny thing! And now, when, for an hour or two, he had shaken free of worry, had been feeling happy—yes, happy—this fellow must come, and stand there with his face of a sphinx! And he said pettishly:

"Well, Paul! sit down. What troubles have you brought?"

Rosek lit a cigarette but did not sit down. He struck even Fiorsen by his unsmiling pallor.

"You had better look out for Mr. Wagge, Gustav; he came to me yesterday. He has no music in his soul."

Fiorsen sat up.

"Satan take Mr. Wagge! What can he do?"

"I am not a lawyer, but I imagine he can be unpleasant—the girl is young."

Fiorsen glared at him, and said:

"Why did you throw me that cursed girl?"

Rosek answered, a little too steadily:

"I did not, my friend."

"What! You did. What was your game? You never do anything without a game. You know you did. Come; what was your game?"

"You like pleasure, I believe."

Fiorsen said violently:

"Look here: I have done with your friendship—you are no friend to me. I have never really known you, and I should not wish to. It is finished. Leave me in peace."

Rosek smiled.

"My dear, that is all very well, but friendships are not finished like that. Moreover, you owe me a thousand pounds."

"Well, I will pay it." Rosek's eyebrows mounted. "I will. Gyp will lend it to me."

"Oh! Is Gyp so fond of you as that? I thought she only loved her music-lessons."

Crouching forward with his knees drawn up, Fiorsen hissed out:

"Don't talk of Gyp! Get out of this! I will pay you your thousand pounds."

Rosek, still smiling, answered:

"Gustav, don't be a fool! With a violin to your shoulder, you are a man. Without—you are a child. Lie quiet, my friend, and think of Mr. Wagge. But you had better come and talk it over with me. Goodbye for the moment. Calm yourself." And, flipping the ash off his cigarette on to the tray by Fiorsen's elbow, he nodded and went.

Fiorsen, who had leaped out of bed, put his hand to his head. The cursed fellow! Cursed be every one of them—the father and the girl, Rosek and all the other sharks! He went out on to the landing. The house was quite still below. Rosek had gone—good riddance! He called, "Gyp!" No answer. He went into her room. Its superlative daintiness struck his fancy. A scent of cyclamen! He looked out into the garden. There was the baby at the end, and that fat woman. No Gyp! Never in when she was wanted. Wagge! He shivered; and, going back into his bedroom, took a brandy-bottle from a locked cupboard and drank some. It steadied him; he locked up the cupboard again, and dressed.

Going out to the music-room, he stopped under the trees to make passes with his fingers at the baby. Sometimes he felt that it was an adorable little creature, with its big, dark eyes so like Gyp's. Sometimes it excited his disgust—a discoloured brat. This morning, while looking at it, he thought suddenly of the other that was coming—and grimaced. Catching Betty's stare of horrified amazement at the face he was making at her darling, he burst into a laugh and turned away into the music-room.

While he was keying up his violin, Gyp's conduct in never having come there for so long struck him as bitterly unjust. The girl—who cared about the wretched girl? As if she made any real difference! It was all so much deeper than that. Gyp had never loved him, never given him what he wanted, never quenched his thirst of her! That was the heart of it. No other woman he had ever had to do with had been like that—kept his thirst unquenched. No; he had always tired of them before they tired of him. She gave him nothing really—nothing! Had she no heart or did she give it elsewhere? What was it Paul had said about her music-lessons? And suddenly it struck him that he knew nothing, absolutely nothing, of where she went or what she did. She never told him anything. Music-lessons? Every day, nearly, she went out, was away for hours. The thought that she might go to the arms of another man made him put down his violin with a feeling of actual sickness.

Why not? That deep and fearful whipping of the sexual instinct which makes the ache of jealousy so truly terrible was at its full in such a nature as Fiorsen's He drew a long breath and shuddered. The remembrance of her fastidious pride, her candour, above all her passivity cut in across his fear. No, not Gyp!

He went to a little table whereon stood a tantalus, tumblers, and a syphon, and pouring out some brandy, drank. It steadied him. And he began to practise. He took a passage from Brahms' violin concerto and began to play it over and over. Suddenly, he found he was repeating the same flaws each time; he was not attending. The fingering of that thing was ghastly! Music-lessons! Why did she take them? Waste of time and money—she would never be anything but an amateur! Ugh! Unconsciously, he had stopped playing. Had she gone there to-day? It was past lunch-time. Perhaps she had come in.

He put down his violin and went back to the house. No sign of her! The maid came to ask if he would lunch. No! Was the mistress to be in? She had not said. He went into the dining-room, ate a biscuit, and drank a brandy and soda. It steadied him. Lighting a cigarette, he came back to the drawing-room and sat down at Gyp's bureau. How tidy! On the little calendar, a pencil-cross was set against to-day— Wednesday, another against Friday. What for? Music-lessons! He reached to a pigeon-hole, and took out her address-book. "H—Harmost, 305A, Marylebone Road," and against it the words in pencil, "3 P.M."

Three o'clock. So that was her hour! His eyes rested idly on a little old coloured print of a Bacchante, with flowing green scarf, shaking a tambourine at

a naked Cupid, who with a baby bow and arrow in
his hands, was gazing up at her. He turned it over;
on the back was written in a pointed, scriggly hand,
"To my little friend.—E. H." Fiorsen drew smoke
deep down into his lungs, expelled it slowly, and went
to the piano. He opened it and began to play, staring
vacantly before him, the cigarette burned nearly to
his lips. He went on, scarcely knowing what he
played. At last he stopped, and sat dejected. A
great artist? Often, nowadays, he did not care if
he never touched a violin again. Tired of standing
up before a sea of dull faces, seeing the blockheads
knock their silly hands one against the other! Sick
of the sameness of it all! Besides—besides, were his
powers beginning to fail? What was happening to
him of late?

He got up, went into the dining-room, and drank
some brandy. Gyp could not bear his drinking.
Well, she shouldn't be out so much—taking music-
lessons. Music-lessons! Nearly three o'clock. If he
went for once and saw what she really did—— Went,
and offered her his escort home! An attention. It
might please her. Better, anyway, than waiting here
until she chose to come in with her face all closed up.
He drank a little more brandy—ever so little—took
his hat and went. Not far to walk, but the sun was
hot, and he reached the house feeling rather dizzy.
A maid-servant opened the door to him.

"I am Mr. Fiorsen. Mrs. Fiorsen here?"

"Yes, sir; will you wait?"

Why did she look at him like that? Ugly girl!
How hateful ugly people were! When she was gone,
he reopened the door of the waiting-room, and listened.

Chopin! The polonaise in A flat. Good! Could

that be Gyp? Very good! He moved out, down the passage, drawn on by her playing, and softly turned the handle. The music stopped. He went in.

When Winton had left him, an hour and a half later that afternoon, Fiorsen continued to stand at the front door, swaying his body to and fro. The brandy-nurtured burst of jealousy which had made him insult his wife and old Monsieur Harmost had died suddenly when Gyp turned on him in the street and spoke in that icy voice; since then he had felt fear, increasing every minute. Would she forgive? To one who always acted on the impulse of the moment, so that he rarely knew afterward exactly what he had done, or whom hurt, Gyp's self-control had ever been mysterious and a little frightening. Where had she gone? Why did she not come in? Anxiety is like a ball that rolls down-hill, gathering momentum. Suppose she did not come back! But she must—there was the baby —their baby!

For the first time, the thought of it gave him un-alloyed satisfaction. He left the door, and, after drinking a glass to steady him, flung himself down on the sofa in the drawing-room. And while he lay there, the brandy warm within him, he thought: ' I will turn over a new leaf; give up drink, give up every-thing, send the baby into the country, take Gyp to Paris, Berlin, Vienna, Rome—anywhere out of this England, anywhere, away from that father of hers and all these stiff, dull folk! She will like that—she loves travelling!' Yes, they would be happy! Delicious nights—delicious days—air that did not weigh you down and make you feel that you must drink—real inspiration—real music! The acrid wood-

14

smoke scent of Paris streets, the glistening cleanness of the Thiergarten, a serenading song in a Florence back street, fireflies in the summer dusk at Sorrento— he had intoxicating memories of them all! Slowly the warmth of the brandy died away, and, despite the heat, he felt chill and shuddery. He shut his eyes, thinking to sleep till she came in. But very soon he opened them, because—a thing usual with him of late—he saw such ugly things—faces, vivid, changing as he looked, growing ugly, uglier, becoming all holes—holes— horrible holes—— Corruption—matted, twisted, dark human-tree-roots of faces! Horrible! He opened his eyes, for when he did that, they always went. It was very silent. No sound from above. No sound of the dogs. He would go up and see the baby.

While he was crossing the hall, there came a ring. He opened the door himself. A telegram! He tore the envelope.

" Gyp and the baby are with me letter follows.— WINTON."

He gave a short laugh, shut the door in the boy's face, and ran up-stairs; why—heaven knew! There was nobody there now! Nobody! Did it mean that she had really left him—was not coming back? He stopped by the side of Gyp's bed, and flinging himself forward, lay across it, burying his face. And he sobbed, as men will, unmanned by drink. Had he lost her? Never to see her eyes closing and press his lips against them! Never to soak his senses in her loveliness! He leaped up, with the tears still wet on his face. Lost her? Absurd! That calm, prim, devilish Englishman, her father—he was to blame— he had worked it all—stealing the baby!

He went down-stairs and drank some brandy. It steadied him a little. What should he do? "Letter follows." Drink, and wait? Go to Bury Street? No. Drink! Enjoy himself!

He laughed, and, catching up his hat, went out, walking furiously at first, then slower and slower, for his head began to whirl, and, taking a cab, was driven to a restaurant in Soho. He had eaten nothing but a biscuit since his breakfast, always a small matter, and ordered soup and a flask of their best Chianti— solids he could not face. More than two hours he sat, white and silent, perspiration on his forehead, now and then grinning and flourishing his fingers, to the amusement and sometimes the alarm of those sitting near. But for being known there, he would have been regarded with suspicion. About half-past nine, there being no more wine, he got up, put a piece of gold on the table, and went out without waiting for his change.

In the streets, the lamps were lighted, but daylight was not quite gone. He walked unsteadily, toward Piccadilly. A girl of the town passed and looked up at him. Staring hard, he hooked his arm in hers without a word; it steadied him, and they walked on thus together. Suddenly he said:

" Well, girl, are you happy?" The girl stopped and tried to disengage her arm; a rather frightened look had come into her dark-eyed powdered face. Fiorsen laughed, and held it firm. " When the unhappy meet, they walk together. Come on! You are just a little like my wife. Will you have a drink?"

The girl shook her head, and, with a sudden movement, slipped her arm out of this madman's and dived away like a swallow through the pavement traffic. Fiorsen stood still and laughed with his head thrown back. The second time to-day *She* had slipped from his grasp. Passers looked at him, amazed. The ugly devils! And with a grimace, he turned out of Piccadilly, past St. James's Church, making for Bury Street. They wouldn't let him in, of course—not they! But he would look at the windows; they had flower-boxes—flower-boxes! And, suddenly, he groaned aloud—he had thought of Gyp's figure busy among the flowers at home. Missing the right turning, he came in at the bottom of the street. A fiddler in the gutter was scraping away on an old violin. Fiorsen stopped to listen. Poor devil! "Pagliacci!" Going up to the man—dark, lame, very shabby, he took out some silver, and put his other hand on the man's shoulder.

"Brother," he said, "lend me your fiddle. Here's money for you. Come; lend it to me. I am a great violinist."

"*Vraiment, monsieur!*"

"*Ah! Vraiment! Voyons! Donnez—un instant —vous verrez.*"

The fiddler, doubting but hypnotized, handed him the fiddle; his dark face changed when he saw this stranger fling it up to his shoulder and the ways of his fingers with bow and strings. Fiorsen had begun to walk up the street, his eyes searching for the flower-boxes. He saw them, stopped, and began playing "*Che faro?*" He played it wonderfully on that poor fiddle; and the fiddler, who had followed at his elbow, stood watching him, uneasy, envious, but a little entranced. *Sapristi!* This tall, pale *monsieur* with the strange face and the eyes that looked drunk and the hollow chest, played like an angel! Ah, but it was not so easy as all that to make money in the streets of this sacred town! You might play like forty angels

and not a copper ! He had begun another tune—like
little pluckings at your heart—*très joli*—*tout à fait
écœurant !* Ah, there it was—a *monsieur* as usual
closing the window, drawing the curtains ! Always
same thing ! The violin and the bow were thrust
back into his hands; and the tall strange *monsieur*
was off as if devils were after him—not badly drunk,
that one ! And not a *sou* thrown down ! With an
uneasy feeling that he had been involved in something
that he did not understand, the lame, dark fiddler
limped his way round the nearest corner, and for two
streets at least did not stop. Then, counting the
silver Fiorsen had put into his hand and carefully
examining his fiddle, he used the word, " *Bigre !*"
and started for home.

XIX

G<small>YP</small> hardly slept at all. Three times she got up, and, stealing to the door, looked in at her sleeping baby, whose face in its new bed she could just see by the night-light's glow. The afternoon had shaken her nerves. Nor was Betty's method of breathing while asleep conducive to the slumber of anything but babies. It was so hot, too, and the sound of the violin still in her ears. By that little air of Poise, she had known for certain it was Fiorsen; and her father's abrupt drawing of the curtains had clinched that certainty. If she had gone to the window and seen him, she would not have been half so deeply disturbed as she was by that echo of an old emotion. The link which yesterday she thought broken for good was reforged in some mysterious way. The sobbing of that old fiddle had been his way of saying, " Forgive me; forgive !" To leave him would have been so much easier if she had really hated him; but she did not. However difficult it may be to live with an artist, to hate him is quite as difficult. An artist is so flexible—only the rigid can be hated. She hated the things he did, and him when he was doing them; but afterward again could hate him no more than she could love him, and that was—not at all. Resolution and a sense of the practical began to come back with daylight. When things were hopeless, it was far better to recognize it and harden one's heart.

Winton, whose night had been almost as sleepless—

to play like a beggar in the street, under his windows, had seemed to him the limit !—announced at breakfast that he must see his lawyer, make arrangements for the payment of Fiorsen's debts, and find out what could be done to secure Gyp against persecution. Some deed was probably necessary; he was vague on all such matters. In the meantime, neither Gyp nor the baby must go out. Gyp spent the morning writing and rewriting to Monsieur Harmost, trying to express her chagrin, but not saying that she had left Fiorsen.

Her father came back from Westminster quiet and angry. He had with difficulty been made to understand that the baby was Fiorsen's property, so that, if the fellow claimed it, legally they would be unable to resist. The point opened the old wound, forced him to remember that his own daughter had once belonged to another—father. He had told the lawyer in a measured voice that he would see the fellow damned first, and had directed a deed of separation to be prepared, which should provide for the complete payment of Fiorsen's existing debts on condition that he left Gyp and the baby in peace. After telling Gyp this, he took an opportunity of going to the extempore nursery and standing by the baby's cradle. Until then, the little creature had only been of interest as part of Gyp; now it had for him an existence of its own—this tiny, dark-eyed creature, lying there, watching him so gravely, clutching his finger. Suddenly the baby smiled—not a beautiful smile, but it made on Winton an indelible impression.

Wishing first to settle this matter of the deed, he put off going down to Mildenham; but " not trusting those two scoundrels a yard "—for he never failed to bracket Rosek and Fiorsen—he insisted that the baby should not go out without two attendants, and that Gyp should not go out alone. He carried precaution to the point of accompanying her to Monsieur Harmost's on the Friday afternoon, and expressed a wish to go in and shake hands with the old fellow. It was a queer meeting. Those two had as great difficulty in finding anything to say as though they were denizens of different planets. And indeed, there *are* two planets on this earth! When, after a minute or so of the friendliest embarrassment, he had retired to wait for her, Gyp sat down to her lesson.

Monsieur Harmost said quietly:

" Your letter was very kind, my little friend—and your father is very kind. But, after all, it was a compliment your husband paid me." His smile smote Gyp; it seemed to sum up so many resignations. " So you stay again with your father!" And, looking at her very hard with his melancholy brown eyes: " When will you find your fate, I wonder ?"

" Never !"

Monsieur Harmost's eyebrows rose.

" Ah," he said, " you think ! No, that is impossible !" He walked twice very quickly up and down the room; then spinning round on his heel, said sharply: " Well, we must not waste your father's time. To work."

Winton's simple comment in the cab on the way home was:

" Nice old chap !"

At Bury Street, they found Gyp's agitated parlourmaid. Going to do the music-room that morning, she had " found the master sitting on the sofa, holding his head, and groaning awful. He's not been at home, ma'am, since you—you went on your visit, so I didn't know what to do. I ran for cook and we got him up to bed, and not knowing where you'd be, ma'am, I telephoned to Count Rosek, and he came—I hope I didn't do wrong—and he sent me down to see you. The doctor says his brain's on the touch and go, and he keeps askin' for you, ma'am. So I didn't know what to do."

Gyp, pale to the lips, said:

"Wait here a minute, Ellen," and went into the dining-room. Winton followed. She turned to him at once, and said:

"Oh, Dad, what am I to do? His brain! It would be too awful to feel I'd brought that about."

Winton grunted. Gyp went on:

"I must go and see. If it's really that, I couldn't bear it. I'm afraid I must go, Dad."

Winton nodded.

"Well, I'll come too," he said. "The girl can go back in the cab and say we're on the way."

Taking a parting look at her baby, Gyp thought bitterly: 'My fate? *This* is my fate, and no getting out of it!' On the journey, she and Winton were quite silent—but she held his hand tight. While the cook was taking up to Rosek the news of their arrival, Gyp stood looking out at her garden. Two days and six hours only since she had stood there above her pansies; since, at this very spot, Rosek had kissed her throat! Slipping her hand through Winton's arm, she said:

"Dad, please don't make anything of that kiss. He couldn't help himself, I suppose. What does it matter, too?"

A moment later Rosek entered. Before she could speak, Winton was saying:

" Thank you for letting us know, sir. But now that my daughter is here, there will be no further need for your kind services. Good-day !"

At the cruel curtness of those words, Gyp gave the tiniest start forward. She had seen them go through Rosek's armour as a sword through brown paper. He recovered himself with a sickly smile, bowed, and went out. Winton followed—precisely as if he did not trust him with the hats in the hall. When the outer door was shut, he said :

" I don't think he'll trouble you again."

Gyp's gratitude was qualified by a queer compassion. After all, his offence had only been that of loving her.

Fiorsen had been taken to her room, which was larger and cooler than his own; and the maid was standing by the side of the bed with a scared face. Gyp signed to her to go. He opened his eyes presently :

" Gyp ! Oh ! Gyp ! Is it you ? The devilish, awful things I see—don't go away again ! Oh, Gyp !" With a sob he raised himself and rested his forehead against her. And Gyp felt—as on the first night he came home drunk—a merging of all other emotions in the desire to protect and heal.

" It's all right, all right," she murmured. " I'm going to stay. Don't worry about anything. Keep quite quiet, and you'll soon be well."

In a quarter of an hour, he was asleep. His wasted look went to her heart, and that expression of terror which had been coming and going until he fell asleep ! Anything to do with the brain was so horrible ! Only too clear that she must stay—that his recovery depended on her. She was still sitting there, motionless, when the doctor came, and, seeing him asleep, beckoned her out. He looked a kindly man, with two waist-

coats, the top one unbuttoned; and while he talked, he
winked at Gyp involuntarily, and, with each wink,
Gyp felt that he ripped the veil off one more domestic
secret. Sleep was the ticket—the very ticket for him!
Had something on his mind—yes! And—er—a little
given to—brandy? Ah! all that must stop! Stomach
as well as nerves affected. Seeing things—nasty
things—sure sign. Perhaps not a very careful life
before marriage. And married—how long? His
kindly appreciative eyes swept Gyp from top to toe.
Year and a half! Quite so! Hard worker at his
violin, too? No doubt! Musicians always a little
inclined to be immoderate—too much sense of beauty
—burn the candle at both ends! She must see to
that. She had been away, had she not—staying with
her father? Yes. But—no one like a wife for nursing.
As to treatment? Well! One would shove in a dash
of what he would prescribe, night and morning. Perfect
quiet. No stimulant. A little cup of strong coffee
without milk, if he seemed low. Keep him in bed at
present. No worry; no excitement. Young man still.
Plenty of vitality. As to herself, no undue anxiety.
To-morrow they would see whether a night nurse
would be necessary. Above all, no violin for a month,
no alcohol—in every way the strictest moderation!
And with a last and friendliest wink, leaning heavily
on that word " moderation," he took out a stylographic
pen, scratched on a leaf of his note-book, shook Gyp's
hand, smiled whimsically, buttoned his upper waistcoat, and departed.

Gyp went back to her seat by the bed. Irony!
She whose only desire was to be let go free, was mainly
responsible for his breakdown! But for her, there
would be nothing on his mind, for he would not be

married! Brooding morbidly, she asked herself—his drinking, debts, even the girl—had she caused them, too? And when she tried to free him and herself— this was the result! Was there something fatal about her that must destroy the men she had to do with? She had made her father unhappy, Monsieur Harmost —Rosek, and her husband! Even before she married, how many had tried for her love, and gone away unhappy! And, getting up, she went to a mirror and looked at herself long and sadly.

XX

THREE days after her abortive attempt to break away, Gyp, with much heart-searching, wrote to Daphne Wing, telling her of Fiorsen's illness, and mentioning a cottage near Mildenham, where—if she liked to go— she would be quite comfortable and safe from all curiosity, and finally begging to be allowed to make good the losses from any broken dance-contracts.

Next morning, she found Mr. Wagge with a tall, crape-banded hat in his black-gloved hands, standing in the very centre of her drawing-room. He was staring into the garden, as if he had been vouchsafed a vision of that warm night when the moonlight shed its ghostly glamour on the sunflowers, and his daughter had danced out there. She had a perfect view of his thick red neck in its turn-down collar, crossed by a black bow over a shiny white shirt. And, holding out her hand, she said:

" How do you do, Mr. Wagge ? It was kind of you to come."

Mr. Wagge turned. His pug face wore a downcast expression.

" I hope I see you well, ma'am. Pretty place you 'ave 'ere. I'm fond of flowers myself. They've always been my 'obby."

" They're a great comfort in London, aren't they ?"

" Ye-es; I should think you might grow the dahlia here." And having thus obeyed the obscure instincts of *savoir faire*, satisfied some obscurer desire to flatter, he went on: " My girl showed me your letter. I didn't like to write; in such a delicate matter I'd rather be vivey vocey. Very kind, in your position; I'm sure I appreciate it. I always try to do the Christian thing myself. Flesh passes; you never know when you may have to take your turn. I said to my girl I'd come and see you."

" I'm very glad. I hoped perhaps you would."

Mr. Wagge cleared his throat, and went on, in a hoarser voice:

" I don't want to say anything harsh about a certain party in your presence, especially as I read he's indisposed, but really I hardly know how to bear the situation. I can't bring myself to think of money in relation to that matter; all the same, it's a serious loss to my daughter, very serious loss. I've got my family pride to think of. My daughter's name, well—it's my own; and, though I say it, I'm respected—a regular attendant—I think I told you. Sometimes, I assure you, I feel I can't control myself, and it's only that—and you, if I may say so, that keeps me in check."

During this speech, his black-gloved hands were clenching and unclenching, and he shifted his broad, shining boots. Gyp gazed at them, not daring to look up at his eyes thus turning and turning from Christianity to shekels, from his honour to the world, from his anger to herself. And she said:

" Please let me do what I ask, Mr. Wagge. I should be so unhappy if I mightn't do that little something."

Mr. Wagge blew his nose.

" It's a delicate matter," he said. " I don't know where my duty lays. I don't, reelly."

Gyp looked up then.

" The great thing is to save Daisy suffering, isn't it ?"

Mr. Wagge's face wore for a moment an expression of affront, as if from the thought: ' Sufferin' ! You must leave that to her father !' Then it wavered; the curious, furtive warmth of the attracted male came for a moment into his little eyes; he averted them, and coughed. Gyp said softly:

" To please me."

Mr. Wagge's readjusted glance stopped in confusion at her waist. He answered, in a voice that he strove to make bland:

" If you put it in that way, I don't reelly know 'ow to refuse; but it must be quite between you and me—I can't withdraw my attitude."

Gyp murmured:

" No, of course. Thank you so much; and you'll let me know about everything later. I mustn't take up your time now." And she held out her hand.

Mr. Wagge took it in a lingering manner.

" Well, I *have* an appointment," he said; " a gentleman at Campden Hill. He starts at twelve. I'm never late. *Good*-morning."

When she had watched his square, black figure pass through the outer gate, busily rebuttoning those shining black gloves, she went upstairs and washed her face and hands.

For several days, Fiorsen wavered; but his collapse had come just in time, and with every hour the danger lessened. At the end of a fortnight of a perfectly white life, there remained nothing to do in the words of the doctor but " to avoid all recurrence of the predisposing causes, and shove in sea air !" Gyp had locked up all brandy—and violins; she could control him so long as he was tamed by his own weakness. But she passed some very bitter hours before she sent for her baby, Betty, and the dogs, and definitely took up life in her little house again. His debts had been paid, including the thousand pounds to Rosek, and the losses of Daphne Wing. The girl had gone down to that cottage where no one had ever heard of her, to pass her time in lonely grief and terror, with the aid of a black dress and a gold band on her third finger.

August and the first half of September were spent near Bude. Fiorsen's passion for the sea, a passion Gyp could share, kept him singularly moderate and free from restiveness. He had been thoroughly frightened, and such terror is not easily forgotten. They stayed in a farmhouse, where he was at his best with the simple folk, and his best could be charming. He was always trying to get his " mermaid," as he took to calling Gyp, away from the baby, getting her away to himself, along the grassy cliffs and among the rocks and yellow sands of that free coast. His delight was to find every day some new nook where they could bathe, and dry themselves by sitting in the sun. And very like a mermaid she was, on a seaweedy rock, with her feet close together in a little pool, her fingers combing her drowned hair, and the sun silvering her wet body. If she had loved him, it would have been perfect. But though, close to nature like this—there are men to whom towns are poison—he was so much more easy to bear, even to like, her heart never opened to him, never fluttered at his voice, or beat more quickly under his kisses. One cannot regulate these things. The warmth in her eyes when they looked at her baby, and the coolness when they looked at him, were such that not even a man, and he an egoist, could help seeing; and secretly he began to hate that tiny rival, and she began to notice that he did.

As soon as the weather broke, he grew restless, craving his violin, and they went back to town, in robust health—all three. During those weeks, Gyp had never been free of the feeling that it was just a lull, of forces held up in suspense, and the moment they were back in their house, this feeling gathered density and darkness, as rain gathers in the sky after a fine spell. She had often thought of Daphne Wing, and had written twice, getting in return one naïve and pathetic answer:

" DEAR MRS. FIORSEN,

" Oh, it is kind of you to write, because I know what you must be feeling about me; and it was so kind of you to let me come here. I try not to think about things, but of course I can't help it; and I don't seem to care what happens now. Mother is coming down here later on. Sometimes I lie awake all night, listening to the wind. Don't you think the wind is the most melancholy thing in the world? I wonder if I shall die? I hope I shall. Oh, I do, really! Good-bye, dear Mrs. Fiorsen. I shall never forgive myself about you.

" Your grateful,
" DAPHNE WING."

The girl had never once been mentioned between her and Fiorsen since the night when he sat by her bed, begging forgiveness; she did not know whether he ever gave the little dancer and her trouble a thought, or even knew what had become of her. But now that

15

the time was getting near, Gyp felt more and more every day as if she must go down and see her. She wrote to her father, who, after a dose of Harrogate with Aunt Rosamund, was back at Mildenham. Winton answered that the nurse was there, and that there seemed to be a woman, presumably the mother, staying with her, but that he had not of course made direct inquiry. Could not Gyp come down? He was alone, and cubbing had begun. It was like him to veil his longings under such dry statements. But the thought of giving him pleasure, and of a gallop with hounds fortified intensely her feeling that she ought to go. Now that baby was so well, and Fiorsen still not drinking, she might surely snatch this little holiday and satisfy her conscience about the girl. Since the return from Cornwall, she had played for him in the music-room just as of old, and she chose the finish of a morning practice to say:

"Gustav, I want to go to Mildenham this afternoon for a week. Father's lonely."

He was putting away his violin, but she saw his neck grow red.

"To him? No. He will steal you as he stole the baby. Let him have the baby if he likes. Not you. No."

Gyp, who was standing by the piano, kept silence at this unexpected outburst, but revolt blazed up in her. She never asked him anything; he should not refuse this. He came up behind and put his arms round her.

"My Gyp, I want you here—I am lonely, too. Don't go away."

She tried to force his arms apart, but could not, and her anger grew. She said coldly :

" There's another reason why I must go."

" No, no ! No good reason—to take you from me."

" There is ! The girl who is just going to have your child is staying near Mildenham, and I want to see how she is."

He let go of her then, and recoiling against the divan, sat down. And Gyp thought: ' I'm sorry. I didn't mean to—but it serves him right.'

He muttered, in a dull voice:

" Oh, I hoped she was dead."

" Yes ! For all you care, she might be. I'm going, but you needn't be afraid that I shan't come back. I shall be back to-day week; I promise."

He looked at her fixedly.

" Yes. You don't break your promises; you will not break it." But, suddenly, he said again: " Gyp, don't go !"

" I must."

He got up and caught her in his arms.

" Say you love me, then !"

But she could not. It was one thing to put up with embraces, quite another to pretend that. When at last he was gone, she sat smoothing her hair, staring before her with hard eyes, thinking: " Here—where I saw him with that girl ! What animals men are !"

Late that afternoon, she reached Mildenham. Winton met her at the station. And on the drive up, they passed the cottage where Daphne Wing was staying. It stood in front of a small coppice, a creepered, plain-fronted, little brick house, with a garden still full of sunflowers, tenanted by the old jockey, Pettance, his widowed daughter, and her three small children. " That talkative old scoundrel," as Winton always called him, was still employed in the Mildenham stables, and his daughter was laundress to the establishment. Gyp had secured for Daphne Wing the same free, independent, economic agent who had watched over her own event; the same old doctor, too, was to be the presiding deity. There were no signs of life about the cottage, and she would not stop, too eager to be at home again, to see the old rooms, and smell the old savour of the house, to get to her old mare, and feel its nose nuzzling her for sugar. It was so good to be back once more, feeling strong and well and able to ride. The smile of the inscrutable Markey at the front door was a joy to her, even the darkness of the hall, where a gleam of last sunlight fell across the skin of Winton's first tiger, on which she had so often sunk down dead tired after hunting. Ah, it was nice to be at home !

In her mare's box, old Pettance was putting a last touch to cleanliness. His shaven, skin-tight, wicked old face, smiled deeply. He said in honeyed tones:

" Good-evenin', miss; beautiful evenin', ma'am !" And his little burning brown eyes, just touched by age, regarded her lovingly.

" Well, Pettance, how are you ? And how's Annie, and how are the children ? And how's this old darling ?"

" Wonderful, miss; artful as a kitten. Carry you like a bird to-morrow, if you're goin' out."

" How are her legs ?"

And while Gyp passed her hand down those iron legs, the old mare examined her down the back of her neck.

" They 'aven't filled not once since she come in—

she was out all July and August; but I've kept 'er well at it since, in 'opes you might be comin'."

"They feel splendid." And, still bending down, Gyp asked: "And how is your lodger—the young lady I sent you?"

"Well, ma'am, she's very young, and these very young ladies they get a bit excited, you know, at such times; I should say she've never been——" with obvious difficulty he checked the words, "to an 'orse before!" "Well, you must expect it. And her mother, she's a dreadful funny one, miss. She do needle me! Oh, she puts my back up properly! No class, of course—that's where it is. But this 'ere nurse—well, you know, miss, she won't 'ave no nonsense; so there we are. And, of course, you're bound to 'ave 'ighsteria, a bit—losin' her 'usband as young as that."

Gyp could feel his wicked old smile even before she raised herself. But what did it matter if he did guess? She knew he would keep a stable secret.

"Oh, we've 'ad some pretty flirts-up and cryin', dear me! I sleeps in the next room—oh, yes, at night-time—when you're a widder at that age, you can't expect nothin' else. I remember when I was ridin' in Ireland for Captain O'Neill, there was a young woman——"

Gyp thought: 'I mustn't let him get off—or I shall be late for dinner,' and she said:

"Oh, Pettance, who bought the young brown horse?"

"Mr. Bryn Summer'ay, ma'am, over at Widrington, for an 'unter, and 'ack in town, miss."

"Summerhay? Ah!" With a touch of the whip to her memory, Gyp recalled the young man with the

clear eyes and teasing smile, on the chestnut mare,
the bold young man who reminded her of somebody,
and she added:

"That'll be a good home for him, I should think."

"Oh, yes, miss; good 'ome—nice gentleman, too.
He come over here to see it, and asked after you. I
told 'im you was a married lady now, miss. 'Ah,' he
said; 'she rode beautiful!' And he remembered the
'orse well. The major, he wasn't 'ere just then, so I
let him try the young un; he popped 'im over a fence
or two, and when he come back he says, 'Well, I'm
goin' to have 'im.' Speaks very pleasant, an' don't
waste no time—'orse was away before the end of the
week. Carry 'im well; 'e's a strong rider, too, and a
good plucked one but bad 'ands, I should say."

"Yes, Pettance; I must go in now. Will you tell
Annie I shall be round to-morrow, to see her?"

"Very good, miss. 'Ounds meets at Filly Cross,
seven-thirty. You'll be goin' out?"

"Rather. Good-night."

Flying back across the yard, Gyp thought: "'She
rode beautiful!' How jolly! I'm glad he's got my
horse."

XXI

STILL glowing from her morning in the saddle, Gyp
started out next day at noon on her visit to the " old
scoundrel's " cottage. It was one of those lingering
mellow mornings of late September, when the air, just
warmed through, lifts off the stubbles, and the hedgerows are not yet dried of dew. The short cut led across
two fields, a narrow strip of village common, where
linen was drying on gorse bushes coming into bloom,
and one field beyond; she met no one. Crossing the
road, she passed into the cottage-garden, where sunflowers and Michaelmas daisies in great profusion
were tangled along the low red-brick garden-walls,
under some poplar trees yellow-flecked already. A
single empty chair, with a book turned face downward,
stood outside an open window. Smoke wreathing
from one chimney was the only sign of life. But,
standing undecided before the half-open door, Gyp
was conscious, as it were, of too much stillness, of
something unnatural about the silence. She was
raising her hand to knock when she heard the sound
of smothered sobbing. Peeping through the window,
she could just see a woman dressed in green, evidently
Mrs. Wagge, seated at a table, crying into her handkerchief. At that very moment, too, a low moaning
came from the room above. Gyp recoiled; then,
making up her mind, she went in and knocked at the
room where the woman in green was sitting. After
fully half a minute, it was opened, and Mrs. Wagge

stood there. The nose and eyes and cheeks of that thinnish, acid face were red, and in her green dress, and with her greenish hair (for it was going grey and she put on it a yellow lotion smelling of cantharides), she seemed to Gyp just like one of those green apples that turn reddish so unnaturally in the sun. She had rubbed over her face, which shone in streaks, and her handkerchief was still crumpled in her hand. It was horrible to come, so fresh and glowing, into the presence of this poor woman, evidently in bitter sorrow. And a desperate desire came over Gyp to fly. It seemed dreadful for anyone connected with him who had caused this trouble to be coming here at all. But she said as softly as she could:

" Mrs. Wagge ? Please forgive me—but is there any news ? I am—— It was I who got Daphne down here."

The woman before her was evidently being torn this way and that, but at last she answered, with a sniff:

" It—it—was born this morning—dead."

Gyp gasped. To have gone through it all for that ! Every bit of mother-feeling in her rebelled and sorrowed; but her reason said: Better so ! Much better ! And she murmured:

" How is she ?"

Mrs. Wagge answered, with profound dejection:

" Bad—very bad. I don't know I'm sure what to say—my feelings are all anyhow, and that's the truth. It's so dreadfully upsetting altogether."

" Is my nurse with her ?"

" Yes; she's there. She's a very headstrong woman, but capable, I don't deny. Daisy's very weak. Oh, it *is* upsetting ! And now I suppose there'll have to be a burial. There really seems no end to it. And all because of—of that man." And Mrs. Wagge turned away again to cry into her handkerchief.

Feeling she could never say or do the right thing to the poor lady, Gyp stole out. At the bottom of the stairs, she hesitated whether to go up or no. At last, she mounted softly. It must be in the front room that the bereaved girl was lying—the girl who, but a year ago, had debated with such naïve self-importance whether or not it was her duty to take a lover. Gyp summoned courage to tap gently. The economic agent opened the door an inch, but, seeing who it was, slipped her robust and handsome person through into the corridor.

" You, my dear ! " she said in a whisper. " That's nice ! "

" How is she ? "

" Fairly well—considering. You know about it."

" Yes; can I see her ? "

" I hardly think so. I can't make her out. She's got no spirit, not an ounce. She doesn't want to get well, I believe. It's the man, I expect." And, looking at Gyp with her fine blue eyes, she asked: " Is that it ? Is he tired of her ? "

Gyp met her gaze better than she had believed possible.

" Yes, nurse."

The economic agent swept her up and down.

" It's a pleasure to look at you. You've got quite a colour, for you. After all, I believe it *might* do her good to see you. Come in ! "

Gyp passed in behind her, and stood gazing, not daring to step forward. What a white face, with eyes closed, with fair hair still damp on the forehead, with one white hand lying on the sheet above her heart !

What a frail madonna of the sugar-plums! On the whole of that bed the only colour seemed the gold hoop round the wedding-finger.

The economic agent said very quietly:

"Look, my dear; I've brought you a nice visitor."

Daphne Wing's eyes and lips opened and closed again. And the awful thought went through Gyp: 'Poor thing! She thought it was going to be him, and it's only me!' Then the white lips said:

"Oh, Mrs. Fiorsen, it's you—it is kind of you!" And the eyes opened again, but very little, and differently.

The economic agent slipped away. Gyp sat down by the bed and timidly touched the hand.

Daphne Wing looked at her, and two tears slowly ran down her cheeks.

"It's over," she said just audibly, "and there's nothing now—it was dead, you know. I don't want to live. Oh, Mrs. Fiorsen, why can't they let me die, too?"

Gyp bent over and kissed the hand, unable to bear the sight of those two slowly rolling tears. Daphne Wing went on:

"You *are* good to me. I wish my poor little baby hadn't——"

Gyp, knowing her own tears were wetting that hand, raised herself and managed to get out the words:

"Bear up! Think of your work!"

"Dancing! Ho!" She gave the least laugh ever heard. "It seems so long ago."

"Yes; but now it'll all come back to you again, better than ever."

Daphne Wing answered by a feeble sigh.

There was silence. Gyp thought: 'She's falling asleep.'

With eyes and mouth closed like that, and all
alabaster white, the face was perfect, purged of its
little commonnesses. Strange freak that this white
flower of a face could ever have been produced by Mr.
and Mrs. Wagge!

Daphne Wing opened her eyes and said:

"Oh! Mrs. Fiorsen, I feel so weak. And I feel
much more lonely now. There's nothing anywhere."

Gyp got up; she felt herself being carried into the
mood of the girl's heart, and was afraid it would be
seen. Daphne Wing went on:

"Do you know, when nurse said she'd brought a
visitor, I thought it was him; but I'm glad now. If
he had looked at me like he used—I couldn't have
borne it."

Gyp bent down and put her lips to the damp forehead. Faint, very faint, there was still the scent of
orange-blossom.

When she was once more in the garden, she hurried
away; but instead of crossing the fields again, turned
past the side of the cottage into the coppice behind.
And, sitting down on a log, her hands pressed to her
cheeks and her elbows to her breast, she stared at the
sunlit bracken and the flies chasing each other over it.
Love! Was it always something hateful and tragic
that spoiled lives? Criss-cross! One darting on
another, taking her almost before she knew she was
seized, then darting away and leaving her wanting to
be seized again. Or darting on her, who, when seized,
was fatal to the darter, yet had never wanted to be
seized. Or darting one on the other for a moment,
then both breaking away too soon. Did never two
dart at each other, seize, and cling, and ever after
be one? Love! It had spoiled her father's life, and

Daphne Wing's; never came when it was wanted; always came when it was not. Malevolent wanderer, alighting here, there; tiring of the spirit before it tired of the body; or of the body before it tired of the spirit. Better to have nothing to do with it—far better! If one never loved, one would never feel lonely—like that poor girl. And yet! No—there was no "and yet." Who that was free would wish to become a slave? A slave—like Daphne Wing! A slave—like her own husband to his want of a wife who did not love him. A slave like her father had been—still was, to a memory. And watching the sunlight on the bracken, Gyp thought: 'Love! Keep far from me. I don't want you. I shall never want you!'

Every morning that week she made her way to the cottage, and every morning had to pass through the hands of Mrs. Wagge. The good lady had got over the upsetting fact that Gyp was the wife of that villain, and had taken a fancy to her, confiding to the economic agent, who confided it to Gyp, that she was "very distangey—and such pretty eyes, quite Italian." She was one of those numberless persons whose passion for distinction was just a little too much for their passionate propriety. It was that worship of distinction which had caused her to have her young daughter's talent for dancing fostered. Who knew to what it might lead in these days? At great length she explained to Gyp the infinite care with which she had always "brought Daisy up like a lady—and now this is the result." And she would look piercingly at Gyp's hair or ears, at her hands or her instep, to see how it was done. The burial worried her dreadfully. " I'm using the name of Daisy Wing; she was christened

' Daisy,' and the Wing's professional, so that takes them both in, and it's quite the truth. But I don't think anyone would connect it, would they ? About the father's name, do you think I might say the late Mr. Joseph Wing, this once ? You see, it never was alive, and I must put something if they're not to guess the truth, and that I couldn't bear; Mr. Wagge would be so distressed. It's in his own line, you see. Oh, it is upsetting !"

Gyp murmured desperately:

" Oh ! yes, anything."

Though the girl was so deathly white and spiritless, it soon became clear that she was going to pull through. With each day, a little more colour and a little more commonness came back to her. And Gyp felt instinctively that she would, in the end, return to Fulham purged of her infatuation, rather harder, perhaps rather deeper.

Late one afternoon toward the end of her week at Mildenham, Gyp wandered again into the coppice, and sat down on that same log. An hour before sunset, the light shone level on the yellowing leaves all round her; a startled rabbit pelted out of the bracken and pelted back again, and, from the far edge of the little wood, a jay cackled harshly, shifting its perch from tree to tree. Gyp thought of her baby, and of that which would have been its half-brother; and now that she was so near having to go back to Fiorsen, she knew that she had not been wise to come here. To have been in contact with the girl, to have touched, as it were, that trouble, had made the thought of life with him less tolerable even than it was before. Only the longing to see her baby made return seem possible. Ah, well—she would get used to it all again ! But the anticipation of his eyes fixed on her, then sliding away from the meeting with her eyes, of all—of all that would begin again, suddenly made her shiver. She was very near to loathing at that moment. He, the father of her baby! The thought was ridiculous and strange. That little creature seemed to bind him to her no more than if it were the offspring of some chance encounter, some pursuit of nymph by faun. No! It was hers alone. And a sudden feverish longing to get back to it overpowered all other thought. This longing grew in her so all night that at breakfast she told her father. Swallowing down whatever his feeling may have been, he said:

"Very well, my child; I'll come up with you."

Putting her into the cab in London, he asked:

"Have you still got your key of Bury Street? Good! Remember, Gyp—any time day or night— there it is for you."

She had wired to Fiorsen from Mildenham that she was coming, and she reached home soon after three. He was not in, and what was evidently her telegram lay unopened in the hall. Tremulous with expectation, she ran up to the nursery. The pathetic sound of some small creature that cannot tell what is hurting it, or why, met her ears. She went in, disturbed, yet with the half-triumphant thought: 'Perhaps that's for me!'

Betty, very flushed, was rocking the cradle, and examining the baby's face with a perplexed frown. Seeing Gyp, she put her hand to her side, and gasped:

"Oh, be joyful! Oh, my dear! I *am* glad. I can't do anything with baby since the morning. Whenever she wakes up, she cries like that. And till to-day she's been a little model. Hasn't she! There, there!"

Gyp took up the baby, whose black eyes fixed themselves on her mother in a momentary contentment; but, at the first movement, she began again her fretful plaint. Betty went on:

"She's been like that ever since this morning. Mr. Fiorsen's been in more than once, ma'am, and the fact is, baby don't like it. He stares at her so. But this morning I thought—well—I thought: ' You're her father. It's time she was getting used to you.' So I let them be a minute; and when I came back—I was only just across to the bathroom—he was comin' out lookin' quite fierce and white, and baby—oh, screamin' ! And except for sleepin', she's hardly stopped cryin' since."

Pressing the baby to her breast, Gyp sat very still, and queer thoughts went through her mind.

" How has he been, Betty ?" she said.

Betty plaited her apron; her moon-face was troubled.

" Well," she said, " I think he's been drinkin'. Oh, I'm sure he has—I've smelt it about him. The third day it began. And night before last he came in dreadfully late—I could hear him staggerin' about, abusing the stairs as he was comin' up. Oh dear—it *is* a pity !"

The baby, who had been still enough since she lay in her mother's lap, suddenly raised her little voice again. Gyp said:

" Betty, I believe something hurts her arm. She cries the moment she's touched there. Is there a pin or anything ? Just see. Take her things off. Oh— look !"

Both the tiny arms above the elbow were circled with dark marks, as if they had been squeezed by ruthless fingers. The two women looked at each other in horror; and under her breath Gyp said: " He !"

She had flushed crimson; her eyes filled but dried again almost at once. And, looking at her face, now gone very pale, and those lips tightened to a line, Betty stopped in her outburst of ejaculation. When they had wrapped the baby's arms in remedies and cotton-wool, Gyp went into her bedroom, and, throwing herself down on her bed, burst into a passion of weeping, smothering it deep in her pillow.

It was the crying of sheer rage. The brute ! Not to have control enough to stop short of digging his claws into that precious mite ! Just because the poor little thing cried at that cat's stare of his ! The brute ! The devil ! And he would come to her and whine about it, and say: " My Gyp, I never meant—how should I know I was hurting ? Her crying was so—— Why should she cry at me ? I was upset ! I wasn't thinking !" She could hear him pleading and sighing to her to forgive him. But she would not—not this time ! He had hurt a helpless thing once too often. Her fit of crying ceased, and she lay listening to the tick of the clock, and marshalling in her mind a hundred little evidences of his malevolence toward her baby— his own baby. How was it possible ? Was he really going mad ? And a fit of such chilly shuddering seized her that she crept under the eiderdown to regain warmth. In her rage, she retained enough sense of proportion to understand that he had done this, just as he had insulted Monsieur Harmost and her father— and others—in an ungovernable access of nerve-irritation; just as, perhaps, one day he would kill someone. But to understand this did not lessen her feeling. Her baby ! Such a tiny thing ! She hated him at last; and she lay thinking out the coldest, the cruellest, the most cutting things to say. She had been too long-suffering.

But he did not come in that evening; and, too upset to eat or do anything, she went up to bed at ten o'clock. When she had undressed, she stole across to the nursery; she had a longing to have the baby with her— a feeling that to leave her was not safe. She carried her off, still sleeping, and, locking her doors, got into bed. Having warmed a nest with her body for the little creature, she laid it there; and then for a long time lay awake, expecting every minute to hear him return. She fell asleep at last, and woke with a start. There were vague noises down below or on the stairs. It must be he ! She had left the light on in her room, and she leaned over to look at the baby's face. It was still sleeping, drawing its tiny breaths peacefully, little dog-shivers passing every now and then over its face. Gyp, shaking back her dark plaits of hair, sat up by its side, straining her ears.

Yes; he *was* coming up, and, by the sounds, he was not sober. She heard a loud creak, and then a thud, as if he had clutched at the banisters and fallen; she heard muttering, too, and the noise of boots dropped. Swiftly the thought went through her: ' If he were quite drunk, he would not have taken them off at all; —nor if he were quite sober. Does he know I'm back ?' Then came another creak, as if he were raising himself by support of the banisters, and then—or was it fancy ? —she could hear him creeping and breathing behind the door. Then—no fancy this time—he fumbled at the door and turned the handle. In spite of his state, he must know that she was back, had noticed her travelling-coat or seen the telegram. The handle was

tried again, then, after a pause, the handle of the door
between his room and hers was fiercely shaken. She
could hear his voice, too, as she knew it when he was
flown with drink, thick, a little drawling.

" Gyp—let me in—Gyp !"

The blood burned up in her cheeks, and she thought:
' No, my friend; you're not coming in !'

After that, sounds were more confused, as if he were
now at one door, now at the other; then creakings,
as if on the stairs again, and after that, no sound
at all.

For fully half an hour, Gyp continued to sit up,
straining her ears. Where was he ? What doing ?
On her over-excited nerves, all sorts of possibilities
came crowding. He must have gone downstairs
again. In that half-drunken state, where would his
baffled frenzies lead him ? And, suddenly, she thought
that she smelled burning. It went, and came again;
she got up, crept to the door, noiselessly turned the
key, and pulling it open a few inches, sniffed.

All was dark on the landing. There was no smell of
burning out there. Suddenly, a hand clutched her
ankle. All the blood rushed from her heart; she stifled
a scream, and tried to pull the door to. But his arm
and her leg were caught between, and she saw the
black mass of his figure lying full-length on its face.
Like a vice, his hand held her; he drew himself up on
to his knees, on to his feet, and forced his way through.
Panting, but in utter silence, Gyp struggled to drive
him out. His drunken strength seemed to come and
go in gusts, but hers was continuous, greater than she
had ever thought she had, and she panted:

" Go ! go out of my room—you—you—wretch !"

Then her heart stood still with horror, for he had

slued round to the bed and was stretching his hands
out above the baby. She heard him mutter:

" Ah-h-h !—*you*—in my place—*you* !"

Gyp flung herself on him from behind, dragging his
arms down, and, clasping her hands together, held
him fast. He twisted round in her arms and sat down
on the bed. In that moment of his collapse, Gyp
snatched up her baby and fled out, down the dark
stairs, hearing him stumbling, groping in pursuit. She
fled into the dining-room and locked the door. She
heard him run against it and fall down. Snuggling
her baby, who was crying now, inside her nightgown,
next to her skin for warmth, she stood rocking and
hushing it, trying to listen. There was no more
sound. By the hearth, whence a little heat still came
forth from the ashes, she cowered down. With
cushions and the thick white felt from the dining-table,
she made the baby snug, and wrapping her shivering
self in the table-cloth, sat staring wide-eyed before her
—and always listening. There were sounds at first,
then none. A long, long time she stayed like that,
before she stole to the door. She did not mean to
make a second mistake. She could hear the sound
of heavy breathing. And she listened to it, till she
was quite certain that it was really the breathing of
sleep. Then stealthily she opened, and looked. He
was over there, lying against the bottom stair, in a
heavy, drunken slumber. She knew that sleep so well;
he would not wake from it.

It gave her a sort of evil pleasure that they would
find him like that in the morning when she was gone.
She went back to her baby and, with infinite precaution,
lifted it, still sleeping, cushion and all, and stole past
him up the stairs that, under her bare feet, made no

sound. Once more in her locked room, she went to the window and looked out. It was just before dawn; her garden was grey and ghostly, and she thought: ' The last time I shall see you. Good-bye !'

Then, with the utmost speed, she did her hair and dressed. She was very cold and shivery, and put on her fur coat and cap. She hunted out two jerseys for the baby, and a certain old camel's-hair shawl. She took a few little things she was fondest of and slipped them into her wrist-bag with her purse, put on her hat and a pair of gloves. She did everything very swiftly, wondering, all the time, at her own power of knowing what to take. When she was quite ready, she scribbled a note to Betty to follow with the dogs to Bury Street, and pushed it under the nursery door. Then, wrapping the baby in the jerseys and shawl, she went downstairs. The dawn had broken, and, from the long narrow window above the door with spikes of iron across it, grey light was striking into the hall. Gyp passed Fiorsen's sleeping figure safely, and, for one moment, stopped for breath. He was lying with his back against the wall, his head in the hollow of an arm raised against a stair, and his face turned a little upward. That face which, hundreds of times, had been so close to her own, and something about this crumpled body, about his tumbled hair, those cheekbones, and the hollows beneath the pale lips just parted under the dirt-gold of his moustache—something of lost divinity in all that inert figure—clutched for a second at Gyp's heart. Only for a second. It was over, this time ! No more—never again ! And, turning very stealthily, she slipped her shoes on, undid the chain, opened the front door, took up her burden, closed the door softly behind her, and walked away.

PART III

I

GYP was going up to town. She sat in the corner of a first-class carriage, alone. Her father had gone up by an earlier train, for the annual June dinner of his old regiment, and she had stayed to consult the doctor concerning "little Gyp," aged nearly nineteen months, to whom teeth were making life a burden.

Her eyes wandered from window to window, obeying the faint excitement within her. All the winter and spring, she had been at Mildenham, very quiet, riding much, and pursuing her music as best she could, seeing hardly anyone except her father; and this departure for a spell of London brought her the feeling that comes on an April day, when the sky is blue, with snow-white clouds, when in the fields the lambs are leaping, and the grass is warm for the first time, so that one would like to roll in it. At Widrington, a porter entered, carrying a kit-bag, an overcoat, and some golf-clubs; and round the door a little group, such as may be seen at any English wayside station, clustered, filling the air with their clean, slightly drawling voices. Gyp noted a tall woman whose blonde hair was going grey, a young girl with a fox-terrier on a lead, a young man with a Scotch terrier under his arm and his back to the carriage. The girl was kissing the Scotch terrier's head.

"Good-bye, old Ossy! Was he nice! Tumbo, keep *down!* *You're* not going!"

"Good-bye, dear boy! Don't work too hard!"

The young man's answer was not audible, but it was followed by irrepressible gurgles and a smothered:

"Oh, Bryan, you *are*—— Good-bye, dear Ossy!"

"Good-bye!" "Good-bye!" The young man who had got in, made another unintelligible joke in a rather high-pitched voice, which was somehow familiar, and again the gurgles broke forth. Then the train moved. Gyp caught a side view of him, waving his hat from the carriage window. It was her acquaintance of the hunting-field—the "Mr. Bryn Summer'ay," as old Pettance called him, who had bought her horse last year. Seeing him pull down his overcoat, to bank up the old Scotch terrier against the jolting of the journey, she thought: 'I like men who think first of their dogs.' His round head, with curly hair, broad brow, and those clean-cut lips, gave her again the wonder: 'Where *have* I seen someone like him?' He raised the window, and turned round.

"How would you like—— Oh, how d'you do! We met out hunting. You don't remember me, I expect."

"Yes; perfectly. And you bought my horse last summer. How is he?"

"In great form. I forgot to ask what you called him; I've named him Hotspur—he'll never be steady at his fences. I remember how he pulled with you that day."

They were silent, smiling, as people will in remembrance of a good run.

Then, looking at the dog, Gyp said softly:

"*He* looks rather a darling. How old?"

" Twelve. Beastly when dogs get old ! "

There was another little silence while he contemplated her steadily with his clear eyes.

" I came over to call once—with my mother; November the year before last. Somebody was ill."

" Yes—I."

" Badly ? "

Gyp shook her head.

" I heard you were married——" The little drawl in his voice had increased, as though covering the abruptness of that remark. Gyp looked up.

" Yes; but my little daughter and I live with my father again." What " came over " her—as they say —to be so frank, she could not have told.

He said simply:

" Ah ! I've often thought it queer I've never seen you since. What a run that was ! "

" Perfect ! Was that your mother on the platform ? "

" Yes—and my sister Edith. Extraordinary deadalive place, Widrington; I expect Mildenham isn't much better ? "

" It's very quiet, but I like it."

" By the way, I don't know your name now ? "

" Fiorsen."

" Oh, yes ! The violinist. Life's a bit of a gamble, isn't it ? "

Gyp did not answer that odd remark, did not quite know what to make of this audacious young man, whose hazel eyes and lazy smile were queerly lovable, but whose face in repose had such a broad gravity. He took from his pocket a little red book.

" Do you know these ? I always take them travelling. Finest things ever written, aren't they ? "

The book—Shakespeare's Sonnets—was open at that which begins:

> " Let me not to the marriage of true minds
> Admit impediments.   Love is not love
> Which alters when it alteration finds,
> Or bends with the remover to remove——"

Gyp read on as far as the lines:

> " Love's not Time's fool, though rosy lips and cheeks
> Within his bending sickle's compass come.
> Love alters not with his brief hours and weeks
> But bears it out even to the edge of doom——"

and looked out of the window.   The train was passing through a country of fields and dykes, where the sun, far down in the west, shone almost level over wide, whitish-green space, and the spotted cattle browsed or stood by the ditches, lazily flicking their tufted tails. A shaft of sunlight flowed into the carriage, filled with dust motes; and, handing the little book back through that streak of radiance, she said softly:

" Yes; that's wonderful. Do you read much poetry ?"

" More law, I'm afraid.   But it is about the finest thing in the world, isn't it ?"

" No; I think music."

" Are you a musician ?"

" Only a little."

" You look as if you might be."

" What ?   A little ?"

" No; I should think you had it badly."

" Thank you.   And you haven't it at all ?"

" I like opera."

" The hybrid form—and the lowest !"

" That's why it suits me.   Don't you like it, though ?"

" Yes; that's why I'm going up to London."

" Really ?   Are you a subscriber ?"

" This season."

" So am I.   Jolly—I shall see you."

Gyp smiled.   It was so long since she had talked
to a man of her own age, so long since she had seen
a face that roused her curiosity and admiration, so
long since she had been admired.   The sun-shaft,
shifted by a westward trend of the train, bathed her
from the knees up; and its warmth increased her light-
hearted sense of being in luck—above her fate, instead
of under it.

Astounding how much can be talked of in two or
three hours of a railway journey !   And what a friendly
after-warmth clings round those hours !   Does the
difficulty of making oneself heard provoke confidential
utterance ?   Or is it the isolation or the continual
vibration that carries friendship faster and further
than will a spasmodic acquaintanceship of weeks ?
But in that long talk he was far the more voluble.
There was, too, much of which she could not speak.
Besides, she liked to listen.   His slightly drawling
voice fascinated her—his audacious, often witty way
of putting things, and the irrepressible bubble of
laughter that would keep breaking from him.   He
disclosed his past, such as it was, freely—public-school
and college life, efforts at the bar, ambitions, tastes,
even his scrapes.   And in this spontaneous unfolding
there was perpetual flattery; Gyp felt through it all,
as pretty women will, a sort of subtle admiration.
Presently he asked her if she played piquet.

" Yes; I play with my father nearly every evening."

" Shall we have a game, then ?"

She knew he only wanted to play because he could

sit nearer, joined by the evening paper over their knees, hand her the cards after dealing, touch her hand by accident, look in her face. And this was not unpleasant; for she, in turn, liked looking at his face, which had what is called " charm "—that something light and unepiscopal, entirely lacking to so many solid, handsome, admirable faces.

But even railway journeys come to an end; and when he gripped her hand to say good-bye, she gave his an involuntary little squeeze. Standing at her cab window, with his hat raised, the old dog under his arm, and a look of frank, rather wistful, admiration on his face, he said:

" I shall see you at the opera, then, and in the Row perhaps; and I may come along to Bury Street, sometime, mayn't I ?"

Nodding to those friendly words, Gyp drove off through the sultry London evening. Her father was not back from the dinner, and she went straight to her room. After so long in the country, it seemed very close in Bury Street; she put on a wrapper and sat down to brush the train-smoke out of her hair.

For months after leaving Fiorsen, she had felt nothing but relief. Only of late had she begun to see her new position, as it was—that of a woman married yet not married, whose awakened senses have never been gratified, whose spirit is still waiting for unfoldment in love, who, however disillusioned, is—even if in secret from herself—more and more surely seeking a real mate, with every hour that ripens her heart and beauty. To-night—gazing at her face, reflected, intent and mournful, in the mirror—she saw that position more clearly, in all its aridity, than she had ever seen it. What was the use of being pretty ? No longer

use to anyone ! Not yet twenty-six, and in a nunnery !
With a shiver, but not of cold, she drew her wrapper
close. This time last year she had at least been in
the main current of life, not a mere derelict. And yet
—better far be like this than go back to him whom
memory painted always standing over her sleeping
baby, with his arms stretched out and his fingers
crooked like claws.

After that early-morning escape, Fiorsen had lurked
after her for weeks, in town, at Mildenham, followed
them even to Scotland, where Winton had carried her
off. But she had not weakened in her resolution a
second time, and suddenly he had given up pursuit,
and gone abroad. Since then—nothing had come
from him, save a few wild or maudlin letters, written
evidently during drinking-bouts. Even they had
ceased, and for four months she had heard no word.
He had " got over " her, it seemed, wherever he was—
Russia, Sweden—who knew—who cared ?

She let the brush rest on her knee, thinking again
of that walk with her baby through empty, silent
streets, in the early misty morning last October, of
waiting dead-tired outside here, on the pavement,
ringing till they let her in. Often, since, she had
wondered how fear could have worked her up to that
weird departure. She only knew that it had not been
unnatural at the time. Her father and Aunt Rosamund had wanted her to try for a divorce, and no
doubt they had been right. But her instincts had
refused, still refused to let everyone know her secrets
and sufferings—still refused the hollow pretence
involved, that she had loved him when she never had.
No, it had been her fault for marrying him without
love—

> " Love is not love
> Which alters when it alteration finds ! "

What irony—giving her that to read—if her fellow traveller had only known !

She got up from before the mirror, and stood looking round her room, the room she had always slept in as a girl. So he had remembered her all this time ! It had not seemed like meeting a stranger. They were not strangers now, anyway. And, suddenly, on the wall before her, she saw his face; or, if not, what was so like that she gave a little gasp. Of course ! How stupid of her not to have known at once ! There, in a brown frame, hung a photograph of the celebrated Botticelli or Masaccio " Head of a Young Man " in the National Gallery. She had fallen in love with it years ago, and on the wall of her room it had been ever since. That broad face, the clear eyes, the bold, clean-cut mouth, the audacity—only, the live face was English, not Italian, had more humour, more " breeding," less poetry—something " old Georgian " about it. How he would laugh if she told him he was like that peasant acolyte with fluffed-out hair, and a little ruching round his neck ! And, smiling, Gyp plaited her own hair and got into bed.

But she could not sleep; she heard her father come in and go up to his room, heard the clocks strike midnight, and one, and two, and always the dull roar of Piccadilly. She had nothing over her but a sheet, and still it was too hot. There was a scent in the room, as of honeysuckle. Where could it come from ? She got up at last, and went to the window. There, on the window-sill, behind the curtains, was a bowl of jessamine. Her father must have brought it up for her—just like him to think of that !

And, burying her nose in those white blossoms, she was visited by a memory of her first ball—that evening of such delight and disillusionment. Perhaps Bryan Summerhay had been there—all that time ago! If he had been introduced to her then, if she had happened to dance with him instead of with that man who had kissed her arm, might she not have felt different toward all men? And if he had admired her —and had not everyone, that night—might she not have liked, perhaps more than liked, him in return? Or would she have looked on him as on all her swains before she met Fiorsen, so many moths fluttering round a candle, foolish to singe themselves, not to be taken seriously? Perhaps she had been bound to have her lesson, to be humbled and brought low!

Taking a sprig of jessamine and holding it to her nose, she went up to that picture. In the dim light, she could just see the outline of the face and the eyes gazing at her. The scent of the blossom penetrated her nerves; in her heart, something faintly stirred, as a leaf turns over, as a wing flutters. And, blossom and all, she clasped her hands over her breast, where again her heart quivered with that faint, shy tremor.

It was late, no—early, when she fell asleep and had a strange dream. She was riding her old mare through a field of flowers. She had on a black dress, and round her head a crown of bright, pointed crystals; she sat without saddle, her knee curled up, perched so lightly that she hardly felt the mare's back, and the reins she held were long twisted stems of honeysuckle. Singing as she rode, her eyes flying here and there, over the field, up to the sky, she felt happier, lighter than thistledown. While they raced along, the old mare kept turning her head and biting at the

honeysuckle flowers; and suddenly that chestnut face
became the face of Summerhay, looking back at her
with his smile. She awoke. Sunlight, through the
curtains where she had opened them to find the flowers,
was shining on her.

II

VERY late that same night, Summerhay came out of the little Chelsea house, which he inhabited, and walked toward the river. In certain moods men turn insensibly toward any space where nature rules a little —downs, woods, waters—where the sky is free to the eye and one feels the broad comradeship of primitive forces. A man is alone when he loves, alone when he dies; nobody cares for one so absorbed, and he cares for nobody, no—not he! Summerhay stood by the river-wall and looked up at the stars through the plane-tree branches. Every now and then he drew a long breath of the warm, unstirring air, and smiled, without knowing that he smiled. And he thought of little, of nothing; but a sweetish sensation beset his heart, a kind of quivering lightness his limbs. He sat down on a bench and shut his eyes. He saw a face —only a face. The lights went out one by one in the houses opposite; no cabs passed now, and scarce a passenger was afoot, but Summerhay sat like a man in a trance, the smile coming and going on his lips; and behind him the air that ever stirs above the river faintly moved with the tide flowing up.

It was nearly three, just coming dawn, when he went in, and, instead of going to bed, sat down to a case in which he was junior on the morrow, and worked right on till it was time to ride before his bath and breakfast. He had one of those constitutions, not uncommon among barristers—fostered perhaps by ozone in the Courts of Law—that can do this sort of thing and take no harm. Indeed, he worked best in such long spurts of vigorous concentration. With real capacity and a liking for his work, this young man was certainly on his way to make a name; though, in the intervals of energy, no one gave a more complete impression of imperturbable drifting on the tides of the moment. Altogether, he was rather a paradox. He chose to live in that little Chelsea house which had a scrap of garden rather than in the Temple or St. James's, because he often preferred solitude; and yet he was an excellent companion, with many friends, who felt for him the affectionate distrust inspired by those who are prone to fits and starts of work and play, conviviality and loneliness. To women, he was almost universally attractive. But if he had scorched his wings a little once or twice, he had kept heart-free on the whole. He was, it must be confessed, a bit of a gambler, the sort of gambler who gets in deep, and then, by a plucky, lucky plunge, gets out again, until some day perhaps—he stays there. His father, a diplomatist, had been dead fifteen years; his mother was well known in the semi-intellectual circles of society. He had no brothers, two sisters, and an income of his own. Such was Bryan Summerhay at the age of twenty-six, his wisdom-teeth to cut, his depths unplumbed.

When he started that morning for the Temple, he had still a feeling of extraordinary lightness in his limbs, and he still saw that face—its perfect regularity, its warm pallor, and dark smiling eyes rather wide apart, its fine, small, close-set ears, and the sweep of the black-brown hair across the low brow. Or was it something much less definite he saw—an emanation

or expression, a trick, a turn, an indwelling grace, a
something that appealed, that turned, and touched
him ? Whatever it was, it would not let him be, and
he did not desire that it should. For this was in his
character; if he saw a horse that he liked, he put his
money on it whenever it ran; if charmed by an opera,
he went over and over again; if by a poem, he almost
learned it by heart. And while he walked along the
river—his usual route—he had queer and unaccustomed
sensations, now melting, now pugnacious. And he felt
happy.

He was rather late, and went at once into court.
In wig and gown, that something "old Georgian"
about him was very visible. A beauty-spot or two,
a full-skirted velvet coat, a sword and snuff-box, with
that grey wig or its equivalent, and there would have
been a perfect eighteenth-century specimen of the less
bucolic stamp—the same strong, light build, breadth
of face, brown pallor, clean and unpinched cut of lips,
the same slight insolence and devil-may-caredom, the
same clear glance, and bubble of vitality. It was
almost a pity to have been born so late.

Except that once or twice he drew a face on blotting-
paper and smeared it over, he remained normally
attentive to his "lud" and the matters in hand all
day, conducted without error the examination of two
witnesses and with terror the cross-examination of
one; lunched at the Courts in perfect amity with the
sucking barrister on the other side of the case, for they
had neither, as yet, reached that maturity which
enables an advocate to call his enemy his "friend,"
and treat him with considerable asperity. Though
among his acquaintances Summerhay always provoked
badinage, in which he was scarcely ever defeated, yet

in chambers and court, on circuit, at his club, in society
or the hunting-field, he had an unfavourable effect on
the grosser sort of stories. There are men—by no
means strikingly moral—who exercise this blighting
influence. They are generally what the French call
" *spirituel*," and often have rather desperate love-
affairs which they keep very closely to themselves.

When at last in chambers, he had washed off that
special reek of clothes, and parchment, far-away
herrings, and distemper, which clings about the law,
dipping his whole curly head in water, and towelling
vigorously, he set forth alone along the Embankment,
his hat tilted up, smoking a cigar. It was nearly seven.
Just this time yesterday he had got into the train,
just this time yesterday turned and seen the face
which had refused to leave him since. Fever recurs
at certain hours, just so did the desire to see her
mount within him, becoming an obsession, because it
was impossible to gratify it. One could not call at
seven o'clock ! The idea of his club, where at this
time of day he usually went, seemed flat and stale,
until he remembered that he might pass up Bury
Street to get to it. But, near Charing Cross, a hand
smote him on the shoulder, and the voice of one of his
intimates said:

" Hallo, Bryan !"

Odd, that he had never noticed before how vacuous
this fellow was—with his talk of politics, and racing,
of this ass and that ass—subjects hitherto of primary
importance ! And, stopping suddenly, he drawled out:

" Look here, old chap, you go on; see you at the
club—presently."

" Why ? What's up ?"

With his lazy smile, Summerhay answered:

" ' There are more things in heaven and earth, Horatio,' " and turned on his heel.

When his friend had disappeared, he resumed his journey toward Bury Street. He passed his boot shop, where, for some time, he had been meaning to order two pairs, and went by thinking: ' I wonder where *she* goes for things.' Her figure came to him so vividly— sitting back in that corner, or standing by the cab, her hand in his. The blood rushed up in his cheeks. She had been scented like flowers, and—and a rainy wind ! He stood still before a plate-glass window, in confusion, and suddenly muttered aloud: " Damn it ! I believe I am !" An old gentleman, passing, turned so suddenly, to see what he was, that he ricked his neck.

But Summerhay still stood, not taking in at all the reflected image of his frowning, rueful face, and of the cigar extinct between his lips. Then he shook his head vigorously and walked on. He walked faster, his mind blank, as it is sometimes for a short space after a piece of self-revelation that has come too soon for adjustment or even quite for understanding. And when he began to think, it was irritably and at random. He had come to Bury Street, and, while he passed up it, felt a queer, weak sensation down the back of his legs. No flower-boxes this year broke the plain front of Winton's house, and nothing whatever but its number and the quickened beating of his heart marked it out for Summerhay from any other dwelling. The moment he turned into Jermyn Street, that beating of the heart subsided, and he felt suddenly morose. He entered his club at the top of St. James' Street and passed at once into the least used room. This was the library; and going to the French section, he took down " The Three Musketeers " and seated himself in a window, with his back to anyone who might come in. He had taken this—his favourite romance, feeling in want of warmth and companionship; but he did not read. From where he sat he could throw a stone to where she was sitting perhaps; except for walls he could almost reach her with his voice, could certainly see her. This was imbecile! A woman he had only met twice. Imbecile! He opened the book. . . .

> " Oh, no; it is an ever-fixed mark
>   That looks on tempests and is never shaken.
> It is the star to every wandering bark,
>   Whose worth's unknown altho' its height be taken."

" Point of five! Three queens—three knaves! Do you know that thing of Dowson's: ' I have been faithful to thee, Cynara, in my fashion '? Better than any Verlaine, except ' *Les sanglots longs.*' What have you got?"

" Only quart to the queen. Do you like the name ' Cynara '?"

" Yes; don't you?"

" Cynara! Cynara! Ye-es—an autumn, rose-petal, whirling, dead-leaf sound."

" Good! Pipped. Shut up, Ossy—don't snore!"

" Ah, poor old dog! Let him. Shuffle for me, please. Oh! there goes another card!" Her knee was touching his—— ! . . .

The book had dropped—Summerhay started.

Dash it! Hopeless! And, turning round in that huge armchair, he snoozed down into its depths. In a few minutes, he was asleep. He slept without a dream.

It was two hours later when the same friend, seeking distraction, came on him, and stood grinning down at that curly head and face which just then had the sleepy abandonment of a small boy's. Maliciously he gave the chair a little kick.

Summerhay stirred, and thought: ' What ! Where am I ?'

In front of the grinning face, above him, floated another, filmy, charming. He shook himself, and sat up. " Oh, damn you !"

" Sorry, old chap !"

" What time is it ?"

" Ten o'clock."

Summerhay uttered an unintelligible sound, and, turning over on the other arm, pretended to snooze down again. But he slept no more. Instead, he saw her face, heard her voice, and felt again the touch of her warm, gloved hand.

III

At the opera, that Friday evening, they were playing
" Cavalleria " and " Pagliacci "—works of which Gyp
tolerated the first and loved the second, while Winton
found them, with " Faust " and " Carmen," about
the only operas he could not sleep through.

Women's eyes, which must not stare, cover more
space than the eyes of men, which must not stare, but
do; women's eyes have less method, too, seeing all
things at once, instead of one thing at a time. Gyp
had seen Summerhay long before he saw her; seen him
come in and fold his opera hat against his white waistcoat, looking round, as if for—someone. Her eyes
criticized him in this new garb—his broad head, and
its crisp, dark, shining hair, his air of sturdy, lazy,
lovable audacity. He looked well in evening clothes.
When he sat down, she could still see just a little of
his profile; and, vaguely watching the stout Santuzza
and the stouter Turiddu, she wondered whether, by
fixing her eyes on him, she could make him turn and
see her. Just then he did see her, and his face lighted
up. She smiled back. Why not? She had not so
many friends nowadays. But it was rather startling
to find, after that exchange of looks, that she at once
began to want another. Would he like her dress?
Was her hair nice? She wished she had not had it
washed that morning. But when the interval came,
she did not look round, until his voice said:

" How d'you do, Major Winton ? Oh, how d'you do ?"

Winton had been told of the meeting in the train. He was pining for a cigarette, but had not liked to desert his daughter. After a few remarks, he got up and said:

" Take my pew a minute, Summerhay, I'm going to have a smoke."

He went out, thinking, not for the first time by a thousand: ' Poor child, she never sees a soul ! Twenty-five, pretty as paint, and clean out of the running. What the devil am I to do about her ?'

Summerhay sat down. Gyp had a queer feeling, then, as if the house and people vanished, and they two were back again in the railway-carriage—alone together. Ten minutes to make the most of ! To smile and talk, and enjoy the look in his eyes, the sound of his voice and laugh. To laugh, too, and be warm and nice to him. Why not ? They were friends. And, presently, she said, smiling:

" Oh, by the way, there's a picture in the National Gallery, I want you to look at."

" Yes ? Which ? Will you take me ?"

" If you like."

" To-morrow's Saturday; may I meet you there ? What time ? Three ?"

Gyp nodded. She knew she was flushing, and, at that moment, with the warmth in her cheeks and the smile in her eyes, she had the sensation, so rare and pleasant, of feeling beautiful. Then he was gone ! Her father was slipping back into his stall; and, afraid of her own face, she touched his arm, and murmured:

" Dad, do look at that head-dress in the next row but one; did you ever see anything so delicious !"

And while Winton was star-gazing, the orchestra struck up the overture to " Pagliacci." Watching that heart-breaking little plot unfold, Gyp had something more than the old thrill, as if for the first time she understood it with other than her æsthetic sense. Poor Nedda ! and poor Canio ! Poor Silvio ! Her breast heaved, and her eyes filled with tears. Within those doubled figures of the tragi-comedy she seemed to see, to feel that passionate love—too swift, too strong, too violent, sweet and fearful within them.

" Thou hast my heart, and I am thine for ever—
   To-night and for ever I am thine !
   What is there left to me ? What have I but a heart that
      is broken ?"

And the clear, heart-aching music mocking it all, down to those last words:

La commedia e finita !

While she was putting on her cloak, her eyes caught Summerhay's. She tried to smile—could not, gave a shake of her head, slowly forced her gaze away from his, and turned to follow Winton.

At the National Gallery, next day, she was not late by coquetry, but because she had changed her dress at the last minute, and because she was afraid of letting him think her eager. She saw him at once standing under the colonnade, looking by no means imperturbable, and marked the change in his face when he caught sight of her, with a little thrill. She led him straight up into the first Italian room to contemplate his counterfeit. A top hat and modern collar did not improve the likeness, but it was there still.

" Well ! Do you like it ?"

" Yes. What are you smiling at ?"

" I've had a photograph of that, ever since I was fifteen; so you see I've known you a long time."

He stared.

" Great Scott ! Am I like that ? All right; I shall try and find *you* now."

But Gyp shook her head.

" No. Come and look at my very favourite picture ' The Death of Procris.' What is it makes one love it so ? Procris is out of drawing, and not beautiful; the faun's queer and ugly. What is it—can you tell ?"

Summerhay looked not at the picture, but at her. In æsthetic sense, he was not her equal. She said softly:

" The wonder in the faun's face, Procris's closed eyes; the dog, and the swans, and the pity for what might have been !"

Summerhay repeated:

" Ah, for what might have been ! Did you enjoy ' Pagliacci ' ?"

Gyp shivered.

" I think I felt it too much."

" I thought you did. I watched you."

" Destruction by—love—seems such a terrible thing ! Now show me your favourites. I believe I can tell you what they are, though."

" Well ?"

" The ' Admiral,' for one."

" Yes. What others ?"

" The two Bellini's."

" By Jove, you *are* uncanny !"

Gyp laughed.

" You want decision, clarity, colour, and fine

texture. Is that right? Here's another of *my* favourites."

On a screen was a tiny "Crucifixion" by da Messina —the thinnest of high crosses, the thinnest of simple, humble, suffering Christs, lonely, and actual in the clear, darkened landscape.

"I think that touches one more than the big, idealized sort. One feels it *was* like that. Oh! And look—the Francesca's! Aren't they lovely?"

He repeated:

"Yes; lovely!" But his eyes said: "And so are you."

They spent two hours among those endless pictures, talking a little of art and of much besides, almost as alone as in the railway carriage. But, when she had refused to let him walk back with her, Summerhay stood stock-still beneath the colonnade. The sun streamed in under; the pigeons preened their feathers; people passed behind him and down there in the square, black and tiny against the lions and the great column. He took in nothing of all that. What was it in her? She was like no one he had ever known— not one! Different from girls and women in society as—— Simile failed. Still more different from anything in the half-world he had met! Not the new sort—college, suffrage! Like no one! And he knew so little of her! Not even whether she had ever really been in love. Her husband—where was he; what was he to her? "The rare, the mute, the inexpressive She!" When she smiled; when her eyes—but her eyes were so quick, would drop before he could see right into them! How beautiful she had looked, gazing at that picture—her favourite, so softly, her lips just smiling! If he could kiss them, would he not go nearly mad? With a deep sigh, he moved down the wide, grey steps into the sunlight. And London, throbbing, overflowing with the season's life, seemed to him empty. To-morrow—yes, to-morrow he could call!

IV

AFTER that Sunday call, Gyp sat in the window at
Bury Street close to a bowl of heliotrope on the window-
sill. She was thinking over a passage of their conversation.

"Mrs. Fiorsen, tell me about yourself."

"Why? What do you want to know?"

"Your marriage?"

"I made a fearful mistake—against my father's
wish. I haven't seen my husband for months; I shall
never see him again if I can help it. Is that
enough?"

"And you love him?"

"No."

"It must be like having your head in chancery.
Can't you get it out?"

"No."

"Why?"

"Divorce-court! Ugh! I couldn't!"

"Yes, I know—it's hellish!"

Was he, who gripped her hand so hard and said
that, really the same nonchalant young man who had
leaned out of the carriage window, gurgling with
laughter? And what had made the difference? She
buried her face in the heliotrope, whose perfume
seemed the memory of his visit; then, going to the
piano, began to play. She played Debussy, McDowell,
Ravel; the chords of modern music suited her
feelings just then. And she was still playing,

when her father came in. During these last nine
months of his daughter's society, he had regained a
distinct measure of youthfulness, an extra twist in his
little moustache, an extra touch of dandyism in his
clothes, and the gloss of his short hair. Gyp stopped
playing at once, and shut the piano.

"Mr. Summerhay's been here, Dad. He was sorry
to miss you."

There was an appreciable pause before Winton
answered:

"My dear, I doubt it."

And there passed through Gyp the thought that
she could never again be friends with a man without
giving that pause. Then, conscious that her father
was gazing at her, she turned and said:

"Well, was it nice in the Park?"

"Thirty years ago they were all nobs and snobs;
now God himself doesn't know what they are!"

"But weren't the flowers nice?"

"Ah—and the trees, and the birds—but, by Jove,
the humans do their best to dress the balance!"

"What a misanthrope you're getting!"

"I'd like to run a stud for two-leggers; they want
proper breeding. What sort of a fellow is young
Summerhay? Not a bad face."

She answered impassively:

"Yes; it's so alive."

In spite of his self-control, she could always read
her father's thoughts quicker than he could read hers,
and knew that he was struggling between the wish
that she should have a good time and the desire to
convey some kind of warning. He said, with a sigh:

"What does a young man's fancy turn to in summer,
Gyp?" But Gyp did not answer.

Women who have subtle instincts and some experience are able to impose their own restraint on those
who, at the lifting of a hand, would become their
lovers. From that afternoon on, Gyp knew that a
word from her would change everything; but she was
far from speaking it. And yet, except at week-ends,
when she went back to her baby at Mildenham, she
saw Summerhay most days—in the Row, at the opera,
or at Bury Street. She had a habit of going to St.
James's Park in the late afternoon and sitting there
by the water. Was it by chance that he passed one
day on his way home from chambers, and that, after
this, they sat there together constantly? Why make
her father uneasy—when there was nothing to be
uneasy about—by letting him come too often to Bury
Street? It was so pleasant, too, out there, talking
calmly of many things, while in front of them the
small ragged children fished and put the fishes into
clear glass bottles, to eat, or watch on rainy days, as
is the custom of man with the minor works of God.

So, in nature, when the seasons are about to change,
the days pass, tranquil, waiting for the wind that brings
in the new. And was it not natural to sit under the
trees, by the flowers and the water, the pigeons and
the ducks, that wonderful July? For all was peaceful
in Gyp's mind, except, now and then, when a sort of
remorse possessed her, a sort of terror, and a sort of
troubling sweetness.

V

SUMMERHAY did not wear his heart on his sleeve, and when, on the closing-day of term, he left his chambers to walk to that last meeting, his face was much as usual under his grey top hat. But, in truth, he had come to a pretty pass. He had his own code of what was befitting to a gentleman. It was perhaps a trifle "old Georgian," but it included doing nothing to distress a woman. All these weeks he had kept himself in hand; but to do so had cost him more than he liked to reflect on. The only witness of his struggles was his old Scotch terrier, whose dreams he had disturbed night after night, tramping up and down the long back-to-front sitting-room of his little house. She knew—must know—what he was feeling. If she wanted his love, she had but to raise her finger; and she had not raised it. When he touched her, when her dress disengaged its perfume or his eyes traced the slow, soft movement of her breathing, his head would go round, and to keep calm and friendly had been torture.

While he could see her almost every day, this control had been just possible; but now that he was about to lose her—for weeks—his heart felt sick within him. He had been hard put to it before the world. A man passionately in love craves solitude, in which to alternate between fierce exercise and that trance-like stillness when a lover simply aches or is busy conjuring her face up out of darkness or the sunlight.

He had managed to do his work, had been grateful
for having it to do; but to his friends he had not given
attention enough to prevent them saying: "What's
up with old Bryan?" Always rather elusive in his
movements, he was now too elusive altogether for
those who had been accustomed to lunch, dine, dance,
and sport with him. And yet he shunned his own
company—going wherever strange faces, life, anything
distracted him a little, without demanding real attention. It must be confessed that he had come un-
willingly to discovery of the depth of his passion,
aware that it meant giving up too much. But there
are women who inspire feeling so direct and simple
that reason does not come into play; and he had never
asked himself whether Gyp was worth loving, whether
she had this or that quality, such or such virtue. He
wanted her exactly as she was; and did not weigh her
in any sort of balance. It is possible for men to love
passionately, yet know that their passion is but desire,
possible for men to love for sheer spiritual worth,
feeling that the loved one lacks this or that charm.

Summerhay's love had no such divided consciousness. About her past, too, he dismissed speculation.
He remembered having heard in the hunting-field that
she was Winton's natural daughter; even then it had
made him long to punch the head of that covertside
scandal-monger. The more there might be against
the desirability of loving her, the more he would love
her; even her wretched marriage only affected him in
so far as it affected her happiness. It did not matter
—nothing mattered except to see her and be with her
as much as she would let him. And now she was
going to the sea for a month, and he himself—curse it !
—was due in Perthshire to shoot grouse. A month !

He walked slowly along the river. Dared he speak? At times, her face was like a child's when it expects some harsh or frightening word. One could not hurt her—impossible! But, at times, he had almost thought she would like him to speak. Once or twice he had caught a slow soft glance—gone the moment he had sight of it.

He was before his time, and, leaning on the river parapet, watched the tide run down. The sun shone on the water, brightening its yellowish swirl, and little black eddies—the same water that had flowed along under the willows past Eynsham, past Oxford, under the church at Clifton, past Moulsford, past Sonning. And he thought: 'My God! To have her to myself one day on the river—one whole long day!' Why had he been so pusillanimous all this time? He passed his hand over his face. Broad faces do not easily grow thin, but his felt thin to him, and this gave him a kind of morbid satisfaction. If she knew how he was longing, how he suffered! He turned away, toward Whitehall. Two men he knew stopped to bandy a jest. One of them was just married. They, too, were off to Scotland for the twelfth. Pah! How stale and flat seemed that which till then had been the acme of the whole year to him! Ah, but if he had been going to Scotland *with her!* He drew his breath in with a sigh, and walked on rapidly.

Oblivious of the gorgeous sentries at the Horse Guards, oblivious of all beauty, he passed irresolute along the water, making for their usual seat; already, in fancy, he was sitting there, prodding at the gravel, a nervous twittering in his heart, and that eternal question: Dare I speak? asking itself within him. And suddenly he saw that she was before him, sitting there already. His heart gave a jump. No more craning—he *would* speak!

She was wearing a maize-coloured muslin to which the sunlight gave a sort of transparency, and sat, leaning back, her knees crossed, one hand resting on the knob of her furled sunshade, her face half hidden by her shady hat. Summerhay clenched his teeth, and went straight up to her.

"Gyp! No, I won't call you anything else. This can't go on! You know it can't. You know I worship you! If you can't love me, I've got to break away. All day, all night, I think and dream of nothing but you. Do you want me to go, Gyp?"

Suppose she said: "Yes, go!" She made a little movement, as if in protest, and without looking at him, answered very low:

"Of course I don't want you to go. How could I?" Summerhay gasped.

"Then you *do* love me?"

She turned her face away.

"Wait, please. Wait a little longer. When we come back I'll tell you: I promise!"

"So long?"

"A month. Is that long? Please! It's not easy for me." She smiled faintly, lifted her eyes to him just for a second. "Please not any more now."

That evening at his club, through the bluish smoke of cigarette after cigarette, he saw her face as she had lifted it for that one second; and now he was in heaven, now in hell.

VI

THE verandahed bungalow on the South Coast, built
and inhabited by an artist friend of Aunt Rosamund's,
had a garden of which the chief feature was one pine-
tree which had strayed in advance of the wood behind.
The little house stood in solitude, just above a low
bank of cliff whence the beach sank in sandy ridges.
The verandah and thick pine wood gave ample
shade, and the beach all the sun and sea air needful
to tan little Gyp, a fat, tumbling soul, as her mother
had been at the same age, incurably fond and fearless
of dogs or any kind of beast, and speaking words already
that required a glossary.

At night, Gyp, looking from her bedroom through
the flat branches of the pine, would get a feeling of
being the only creature in the world. The crinkled,
silvery sea, that lonely pine-tree, the cold moon, the
sky dark corn-flower blue, the hiss and sucking rustle
of the surf over the beach pebbles, even the salt, chill
air, seemed lonely. By day, too—in the hazy heat
when the clouds merged, scarce drifting, into the blue,
and the coarse sea-grass tufts hardly quivered, and
sea-birds passed close above the water with chuckle
and cry—it all often seemed part of a dream. She
bathed, and grew as tanned as her little daughter, a
regular Gypsy, in her broad hat and linen frocks;
and yet she hardly seemed to be living down here at
all, for she was never free of the memory of that last
meeting with Summerhay. Why had he spoken and

put an end to their quiet friendship, and left her to such heart-searchings all by herself? But she did not want his words unsaid. Only, how to know whether to recoil and fly, or to pass beyond the dread of letting herself go, of plunging deep into the unknown depths of love—of that passion, whose nature for the first time she had tremulously felt, watching "Pagliacci"—and had ever since been feeling and trembling at! Must it really be neck or nothing? Did she care enough to break through all barriers, fling herself into midstream? When they could see each other every day, it was so easy to live for the next meeting—not think of what was coming after. But now, with all else cut away, there was only the future to think about—hers and his. But need she trouble about his? Would he not just love her as long as he liked?

Then she thought of her father—still faithful to a memory—and felt ashamed. Some men loved on—yes—even beyond death! But, sometimes, she would think: 'Am I a candle-flame again? Is he just going to burn himself? What real good can I be to him—I, without freedom, and with my baby, who will grow up?' Yet all these thoughts were, in a way, unreal. The struggle was in herself, so deep that she could hardly understand it; as might be an effort to subdue the instinctive dread of a precipice. And she would feel a kind of resentment against all the happy life around her these summer days—the sea-birds, the sunlight, and the waves; the white sails far out; the calm sun-steeped pine-trees; her baby, tumbling and smiling and softly twittering; and Betty and the other servants—all this life that seemed so simple and untortured.

To the one post each day she looked forward terribly. And yet his letters, which began like hers: " My dear friend," might have been read by anyone—almost. She spent a long time over her answers. She was not sleeping well; and, lying awake, she could see his face very distinct before her closed eyes—its teasing, lazy smile, its sudden intent gravity. Once she had a dream of him, rushing past her down into the sea. She called, but, without turning his head, he swam out further, further, till she lost sight of him, and woke up suddenly with a pain in her heart. " If you can't love me, I've got to break away !" His face, his flung-back head reminded her too sharply of those words. Now that he was away from her, would he not feel that it was best to break, and forget her ? Up there, he would meet girls untouched by life—not like herself. He had everything before him; could he possibly go on wanting one who had nothing before her ? Some blue-eyed girl with auburn hair—that type so superior to her own—would sweep, perhaps had already swept him, away from her ! What then ? No worse than it used to be ? Ah, so much worse that she dared not think of it !

Then, for five days, no letter came. And, with each blank morning, the ache in her grew—a sharp, definite ache of longing and jealousy, utterly unlike the mere feeling of outraged pride when she had surprised Fiorsen and Daphne Wing in the music-room—a hundred years ago, it seemed. When on the fifth day the postman left nothing but a bill for little Gyp's shoes, and a note from Aunt Rosamund at Harrogate, where she had gone with Winton for the annual cure, Gyp's heart sank to the depths. Was this the end ? And, with a blind, numb feeling, she wandered out into the wood, where the fall of the pine-needles, season after season, had made of the ground one soft, dark, dust-coloured bed, on which the sunlight traced the pattern of the pine boughs, and ants rummaged about their great heaped dwellings.

Gyp went along till she could see no outer world for the grey-brown tree-stems streaked with gum-resin; and, throwing herself down on her face, dug her elbows deep into the pine dust. Tears, so rare with her, forced their way up, and trickled slowly to the hands whereon her chin rested. No good—crying! Crying only made her ill; crying was no relief. She turned over on her back and lay motionless, the sunbeams warm on her cheeks. Silent here, even at noon! The sough of the calm sea could not reach so far; the flies were few; no bird sang. The tall bare pine stems rose up all round like columns in a temple roofed with the dark boughs and sky. Cloud-fleeces drifted slowly over the blue. There should be peace—but in her heart there was none!

A dusky shape came padding through the trees a little way off, another—two donkeys loose from somewhere, who stood licking each other's necks and noses. Those two humble beasts, so friendly, made her feel ashamed. Why should she be sorry for herself, she who had everything in life she wanted—except love— the love she had thought she would never want? Ah, but she wanted it now, wanted it at last with all her being!

With a shudder, she sprang up; the ants had got to her, and she had to pick them off her neck and dress. She wandered back towards the beach. If he had truly found someone to fill his thoughts, and drive her out, all the better for him; she would never, by word

or sign, show him that she missed, and wanted him—
never! She would sooner die!

She came out into the sunshine. The tide was low;
and the wet foreshore gleamed with opal tints; there
were wandering tracks on the sea, as of great serpents
winding their way beneath the surface; and away to
the west the archwayed, tawny rock that cut off the
line of coast was like a dream-shape. All was dreamy.
And, suddenly her heart began beating to suffocation
and the colour flooded up in her cheeks. On the edge
of the low cliff bank, by the side of the path, Summerhay was sitting!

He got up and came toward her. Putting her hands
up to her glowing face, she said:

"Yes; it's me. Did you ever see such a gipsified
object? I thought you were still in Scotland. How's
dear Ossy?" Then her self-possession failed, and she
looked down.

"It's no good, Gyp. I must know."

It seemed to Gyp that her heart had given up
beating; she said quietly: "Let's sit down a minute";
and moved under the cliff bank where they could not
be seen from the house. There, drawing the coarse
grass blades through her fingers, she said, with a
shiver:

"I didn't try to make you, did I? I never tried."

"No; never."

"It's wrong."

"Who cares? No one could care who loves as I
do. Oh, Gyp, can't you love me? I know I'm
nothing much." How quaint and boyish! "But it's
eleven weeks to-day since we met in the train. I
don't think I've had one minute's let-up since."

"Have you tried?"

" Why should I, when I love you ? "

Gyp sighed; relief, delight, pain—she did not know.

" Then what is to be done ? Look over there—that bit of blue in the grass is my baby daughter. There's her—and my father—and——"

" And what ? "

" I'm afraid—afraid of love, Bryan ! "

At that first use of his name, Summerhay turned pale and seized her hand.

" Afraid—how—afraid ? "

Gyp said very low:

" I might love too much. Don't say any more now. No; don't ! Let's go in and have lunch." And she got up.

He stayed till tea-time, and not a word more of love did he speak. But when he was gone, she sat under the pine-tree with little Gyp on her lap. Love ! If her mother had checked love, she herself would never have been born. The midges were biting before she went in. After watching Betty give little Gyp her bath, she crossed the passage to her bedroom and leaned out of the window. Could it have been to-day she had lain on the ground with tears of despair running down on to her hands ? Away to the left of the pine-tree, the moon had floated up, soft, barely visible in the paling sky. A new world, an enchanted garden ! And between her and it—what was there ?

That evening she sat with a book on her lap, not reading; and in her went on the strange revolution which comes in the souls of all women who are not half-men when first they love—the sinking of ' I ' into ' Thou,' the passionate, spiritual subjection, the intense, unconscious giving-up of will, in preparation for completer union.

She slept without dreaming, awoke heavy and oppressed. Too languid to bathe, she sat listless on the beach with little Gyp all the morning. Had she energy or spirit to meet him in the afternoon by the rock archway, as she had promised? For the first time since she was a small and naughty child, she avoided the eyes of Betty. One could not be afraid of that stout, devoted soul, but one could feel that she knew too much. When the time came, after early tea, she started out; for if she did not go, he would come, and she did not want the servants to see him two days running.

This last day of August was warm and still, and had a kind of beneficence—the corn all gathered in, the apples mellowing, robins singing already, a few slumberous, soft clouds, a pale blue sky, a smiling sea. She went inland, across the stream, and took a foot-path back to the shore. No pines grew on that side, where the soil was richer—of a ruddy brown. The second crops of clover were already high; in them humblebees were hard at work; and, above, the white-throated swallows dipped and soared. Gyp gathered a bunch of chicory flowers. She was close above the shore before she saw him standing in the rock arch-way, looking for her across the beach. After the hum of the bees and flies, it was very quiet here—only the faintest hiss of tiny waves. He had not yet heard her coming, and the thought flashed through her: 'If I take another step, it is for ever!' She stood there scarcely breathing, the chicory flowers held before her lips. Then she heard him sigh, and, moving quickly forward, said:

" Here I am."

He turned round, seized her hand, and, without a

word, they passed through the archway. They walked
on the hard sand, side by side, till he said:

"Let's go up into the fields."

They scrambled up the low cliff and went along the
grassy top to a gate into a stubble field. He held it
open for her, but, as she passed, caught her in his
arms and kissed her lips as if he would never stop.
To her, who had been kissed a thousand times, it was
the first kiss. Deadly pale, she fell back from him
against the gate; then, her lips still quivering, her eyes
very dark, she looked at him distraught with passion,
drunk on that kiss. And, suddenly turning round to
the gate, she laid her arms on the top bar and buried
her face on them. A sob came up in her throat that
seemed to tear her to bits, and she cried as if her heart
would break. His timid despairing touches, his voice
close to her ear:

"Gyp, Gyp! My darling! My love! Oh, don't,
Gyp!" were not of the least avail; she could not stop.
That kiss had broken down something in her soul,
swept away her life up to that moment, done something terrible and wonderful. At last, she struggled
out:

"I'm sorry—so sorry! Don't—don't look at me!
Go away a little, and I'll—I'll be all right."

He obeyed without a word, and, passing through
the gate, sat down on the edge of the cliff with his
back to her, looking out over the sea.

Gripping the wood of the old grey gate till it hurt
her hands, Gyp gazed at the chicory flowers and
poppies that had grown up again in the stubble field,
at the butterflies chasing in the sunlight over the hedge
toward the crinkly foam edging the quiet sea till they
were but fluttering white specks in the blue.

But when she had rubbed her cheeks and smoothed her face, she was no nearer to feeling that she could trust herself. What had happened in her was too violent, too sweet, too terrifying. And going up to him she said:

"Let me go home now by myself. Please, let me go, dear. To-morrow!"

Summerhay looked up.

"Whatever you wish, Gyp—always!"

He pressed her hand against his cheek, then let it go, and, folding his arms tight, resumed his meaningless stare at the sea. Gyp turned away. She crossed back to the other side of the stream, but did not go in for a long time, sitting in the pine wood till the evening gathered and the stars crept out in a sky of that mauve-blue which the psychic say is the soul-garment colour of the good.

Late that night, when she had finished brushing her hair, she opened her window and stepped out on to the verandah. How warm! How still! Not a sound from the sleeping house—not a breath of wind! Her face, framed in her hair, her hands, and all her body, felt as if on fire. The moon behind the pine-tree branches was filling every cranny of her brain with wakefulness. The soft shiver of the wellnigh surfless sea on a rising tide, rose, fell, rose, fell. The sand cliff shone like a bank of snow. And all was inhabited, as a moonlit night is wont to be, by a magical Presence. A big moth went past her face, so close that she felt the flutter of its wings. A little night beast somewhere was scruttling in bushes or the sand. Suddenly, across the wan grass the shadow of the pine-trunk moved. It moved—ever so little—moved! And, petrified—Gyp stared. There, joined to the trunk, Summerhay was standing, his face just visible against the stem, the moonlight on one cheek, a hand shading his eyes. He moved that hand, held it out in supplication. For long—how long—Gyp did not stir, looking straight at that beseeching figure. Then, with a feeling she had never known, she saw him coming. He came up to the verandah and stood looking up at her. She could see all the workings of his face—passion, reverence, above all amazement; and she heard his awed whisper:

"Is it you, Gyp? Really you? You look so young—so young!"

VII

FROM the moment of surrender, Gyp passed straight into a state the more enchanted because she had never believed in it, had never thought that she could love as she now loved. Days and nights went by in a sort of dream, and when Summerhay was not with her, she was simply waiting with a smile on her lips for the next hour of meeting. Just as she had never felt it possible to admit the world into the secrets of her married life, so, now she did not consider the world at all. Only the thought of her father weighed on her conscience. He was back in town. And she felt that she must tell him. When Summerhay heard this he only said: " All right, Gyp, whatever you think best."

And two days before her month at the bungalow was up, she went, leaving Betty and little Gyp to follow on the last day. Winton, pale and somewhat languid, as men are when they have been cured, found her when he came in from the club. She had put on evening dress, and above the pallor of her shoulders, her sunwarmed face and throat had almost the colour of a nectarine. He had never seen her look like that, never seen her eyes so full of light. And he uttered a quiet grunt of satisfaction. It was as if a flower, which he had last seen in close and elegant shape, had bloomed in full perfection. She did not meet his gaze quite steadily and all that evening kept putting

her confession off and off. It was not easy—far from
easy. At last, when he was smoking his " go-to-bed "
cigarette, she took a cushion and sank down on it
beside his chair, leaning against his knee, where her
face was hidden from him, as on that day after her
first ball, when she had listened to *his* confession.
And she began:

" Dad, do you remember my saying once that I
didn't understand what you and my mother felt for
each other ?" Winton did not speak; misgiving had
taken possession of him. Gyp went on: " I know
now how one would rather die than give someone up."

Winton drew his breath in sharply:

" Who ? Summerhay ?"

" Yes; I used to think I should never be in love, but
you knew better."

Better !

In disconsolate silence, he thought rapidly:
' What's to be done ? What can I do ? Get her a
divorce ?'

Perhaps because of the ring in her voice, or the
sheer seriousness of the position, he did not feel resentment as when he lost her to Fiorsen. Love ! A
passion such as had overtaken her mother and himself !
And this young man ? A decent fellow, a good
rider—comprehensible ! Ah, if the course had only
been clear ! He put his hand on her shoulder and
said:

" Well, Gyp, we must go for the divorce, then,
after all."

She shook her head.

" It's too late. Let *him* divorce me, if he only
will !"

Winton needed all his self-control at that moment. Too late? Already! Sudden recollection that he had not the right to say a word alone kept him silent. Gyp went on:

"I love him, with every bit of me. I don't care what comes—whether it's open or secret. I don't care what anybody thinks."

She had turned round now, and if Winton had doubt of her feeling, he lost it. This was a Gyp he had never seen! A glowing, soft, quick-breathing creature, with just that lithe watchful look of the mother cat or lioness whose whelps are threatened. There flashed through him a recollection of how, as a child, with face very tense, she would ride at fences that were too big. At last he said:

"I'm sorry you didn't tell me sooner."

"I couldn't. I didn't know. Oh, Dad, I'm always hurting you! Forgive me!"

She was pressing his hand to her cheek that felt burning hot. And he thought: 'Forgive! Of course I forgive. That's not the point; the point is——'

And a vision of his loved one talked about, besmirched, bandied from mouth to mouth, or else—for her what there had been for him, a hole-and-corner life, an underground existence of stealthy meetings kept dark, above all from her own little daughter. Ah, not that! And yet—was not even that better than the other, which revolted to the soul his fastidious pride in her, roused in advance his fury against tongues that would wag, and eyes that would wink or be uplifted in righteousness? Summerhay's world was more or less his world; scandal, which—like all parasitic growths—flourishes in enclosed spaces, would have every chance. And, at once, his brain began to search steely and quick, for some way out; and the expression as when a fox broke covert, came on his face.

" Nobody knows, Gyp ?"

" No; nobody."

That was something ! With an irritation that rose from his very soul, he muttered:

" I can't stand it that you should suffer, and that fellow Fiorsen go scot-free. Can you give up seeing Summerhay while we get you a divorce ? We might do it, if no one knows. I think you owe it to me, Gyp."

Gyp got up and stood by the window a long time without answering. Winton watched her face. At last she said:

" I couldn't. We might stop seeing each other; it isn't that. It's what I should feel. I shouldn't respect myself after; I should feel so mean. Oh, Dad, don't you see ? He really loved me in his way. And to pretend ! To make out a case for myself, tell about Daphne Wing, about his drinking, and baby; pretend that I wanted him to love me, when I got to hate it and didn't care really whether he was faithful or not—and knowing all the while that I've been everything to someone else ! I couldn't. I'd much rather let him know, and ask him to divorce me."

Winton replied:

" And suppose he won't ?"

" Then my mind would be clear, anyway; and we would take what we could.

" And little Gyp ?"

Staring before her as if trying to see into the future, she said slowly:

" Some day, she'll understand, as I do. Or perhaps it will be all over before she knows. Does happiness ever last ?"

And, going up to him, she bent over, kissed his forehead, and went out. The warmth from her lips, and the scent of her remained with Winton like a sensation wafted from the past.

Was there then nothing to be done—nothing? Men of his stamp do not, as a general thing, see very deep even into those who are nearest to them; but to-night he saw his daughter's nature more fully perhaps than ever before. No use to importune her to act against her instincts—not a bit of use! And yet—how to sit and watch it all—watch his own passion with its ecstasy and its heart-burnings re-enacted with her—perhaps for many years? And the old vulgar saying passed through his mind: " What's bred in the bone will come out in the meat." Now she had given, she would give with both hands—beyond measure—beyond!—as he himself, as her mother had given! Ah, well, she was better off than his own loved one had been. One must not go ahead of trouble, or cry over spilled milk!

VIII

Gyp had a wakeful night. The question she herself
had raised, of telling Fiorsen, kept her thoughts in
turmoil. Was he likely to divorce her if she did ?
His contempt for what he called " these *bourgeois*
morals," his instability, the very unpleasantness, and
offence to his vanity—all this would prevent him.
No; he would not divorce her, she was sure, unless by
any chance he wanted legal freedom, and that was
quite unlikely. What then would be gained ? Ease
for her conscience ? But had she any right to
ease her conscience if it brought harm to her lover ?
And was it not ridiculous to think of conscience in
regard to one who, within a year of marriage, had
taken to himself a mistress, and not even spared the
home paid for and supported by his wife ? No; if
she told Fiorsen, it would only be to salve her pride,
wounded by doing what she did not avow. Besides,
where was he ? At the other end of the world for all
she knew.

She came down to breakfast, dark under the eyes
and no whit advanced toward decision. Neither of
them mentioned their last night's talk, and Gyp went
back to her room to busy herself with dress, after
those weeks away. It was past noon when, at a
muffled knock, she found Markey outside her door.

" Mr. Fiorsen, m'm."

Gyp beckoned him in, and closed the door.

"In the hall, m'm—slipped in when I answered the bell; short of shoving, I couldn't keep him out."

Gyp stood full half a minute before she said:

"Is my father in?"

"No, m'm; the major's gone to the fencin'-club."

"What did you say?"

"Said I would see. So far as I was aware, nobody was in. Shall I have a try to shift him, m'm?"

With a faint smile Gyp shook her head.

"Say no one can see him."

Markey's woodcock eyes, under their thin, dark, twisting brows, fastened on her dolefully; he opened the door to go. Fiorsen was standing there, and, with a quick movement, came in. She saw Markey raise his arms as if to catch him round the waist, and said quietly:

"Markey—wait outside, please."

When the door was shut, she retreated against her dressing-table and stood gazing at her husband, while her heart throbbed as if it would leap through its coverings.

He had grown a short beard, his cheeks seemed a little fatter, and his eyes surely more green; otherwise, he looked much as she remembered him. And the first thought that passed through her was: 'Why did I ever pity him? He'll never fret or drink himself to death—he's got enough vitality for twenty men.'

His face, which had worn a fixed, nervous smile, grew suddenly grave as her own, and his eyes roved round the room in the old half-fierce, half-furtive way.

"Well, Gyp," he said, and his voice shook a little: "At last! Won't you kiss me?"

The question seemed to Gyp idiotic; and suddenly she felt quite cool.

"If you want to speak to my father, you must come later; he's out."

Fiorsen gave one of his fierce shrugs.

"Is it likely? Look, Gyp! I returned from Russia yesterday. I was a great success, made a lot of money out there. Come back to me! I will be good—I swear it! Now I have seen you again, I can't be without you. Ah, Gyp, come back to me! And see how good I will be. I will take you abroad, you and the *bambina*. We will go to Rome—anywhere you like—live how you like. Only come back to me!"

Gyp answered stonily:

"You are talking nonsense."

"Gyp, I swear to you I have not seen a woman— not one fit to put beside you. Oh, Gyp, be good to me once more. This time I will not fail. Try me! Try me, my Gyp!"

Only at this moment of his pleading, whose tragic tones seemed to her both false and childish, did Gyp realize the strength of the new feeling in her heart. And the more that feeling throbbed within her, the harder her face and her voice grew. She said:

"If that is all you came to say—please go. I will never come back to you. Once for all, understand, *please*."

The silence in which he received her words, and his expression, impressed her far more than his appeal; with one of his stealthy movements he came quite close, and, putting his face forward till it almost touched her, said:

"You are my wife. I want you back. I must have

you back. If you do not come, I will kill either you
or myself."

And suddenly she felt his arms knotted behind her
back, crushing her to him. She stifled a scream; then,
very swiftly, took a resolve, and, rigid in his arms, said:

"Let go; you hurt me. Sit down quietly. I will
tell you something."

The tone of her voice made him loosen his grasp and
crane back to see her face. Gyp detached his arms
from her completely, sat down on an old oak chest,
and motioned him to the window-seat. Her heart
thumped pitifully; cold waves of almost physical
sickness passed through and through her. She had
smelt brandy in his breath when he was close to her.
It was like being in the cage of a wild beast; it was
like being with a madman! The remembrance of
him with his fingers stretched out like claws above her
baby was so vivid at that moment that she could
scarcely see him as he was, sitting there quietly, waiting
for what she was going to say. And fixing her eyes
on him, she said softly:

"You say you love me, Gustav. I tried to love you,
too, but I never could—never from the first. I tried
very hard. Surely you care what a woman feels, even
if she happens to be your wife."

She could see his face quiver; and she went on:

"When I found I couldn't love you, I felt I had no
right over you. I didn't stand on my rights. Did I ?"

Again his face quivered, and again she hurried on:

"But you wouldn't expect me to go all through my
life without ever feeling love—you who've felt it so
many times?" Then, clasping her hands tight, with
a sort of wonder at herself, she murmured: "I *am* in
love. I've given myself."

He made a queer, whining sound, covering his face. And the beggar's tag: "''Ave a feelin' 'eart, gentleman—'ave a feelin' 'eart!'' passed idiotically through Gyp's mind. Would he get up and strangle her? Should she dash to the door—escape? For a long, miserable moment, she watched him swaying on the window-seat, with his face covered. Then, without looking at her, he crammed a clenched hand up against his mouth, and rushed out.

Through the open door, Gyp had a glimpse of Markey's motionless figure, coming to life as Fiorsen passed. She drew a long breath, locked the door, and lay down on her bed. Her heart beat dreadfully. For a moment, something had checked his jealous rage. But if on this shock he began to drink, what might not happen? He had said something wild. And she shuddered. But what right had he to feel jealousy and rage against her? What right? She got up and went to the glass, trembling, mechanically tidying her hair. Miraculous that she had come through unscathed!

Her thoughts flew to Summerhay. They were to meet at three o'clock by the seat in St. James's Park. But all was different, now; difficult and dangerous! She must wait, take counsel with her father. And yet if she did not keep that tryst, how anxious he would be—thinking that all sorts of things had happened to her; thinking perhaps—oh, foolish!—that she had forgotten, or even repented of her love. What would she herself think, if he were to fail her at their first tryst after those days of bliss? Certainly that he had changed his mind, seen she was not worth it, seen that a woman who could give herself so soon, so easily, was one to whom he could not sacrifice his life.

In this cruel uncertainty, she spent the next two hours, till it was nearly three. If she did not go out, he would come on to Bury Street, and that would be still more dangerous. She put on her hat and walked swiftly towards St. James's Palace. Once sure that she was not being followed, her courage rose, and she passed rapidly down toward the water. She was ten minutes late, and seeing him there, walking up and down, turning his head every few seconds so as not to lose sight of the bench, she felt almost lightheaded from joy. When they had greeted with that pathetic casualness of lovers which deceives so few, they walked on together past Buckingham Palace, up into the Green Park, beneath the trees. During this progress, she told him about her father; but only when they were seated in that comparative refuge, and his hand was holding hers under cover of the sunshade that lay across her knee, did she speak of Fiorsen.

He tightened his grasp of her hand; then, suddenly dropping it, said:

" Did he touch you, Gyp ?"

Gyp heard that question with a shock. Touch her ! Yes ! But what did it matter ?

He made a little shuddering sound; and, wondering, mournful, she looked at him. His hands and teeth were clenched. She said softly :

" Bryan ! Don't ! I wouldn't let him kiss me."

He seemed to have to force his eyes to look at her.

" It's all right," he said, and, staring before him, bit his nails.

Gyp sat motionless, cut to the heart. She was soiled, and spoiled for him ! Of course ! And yet a sense of injustice burned in her. Her heart had never been touched; it was his utterly. But that was not enough for a man—he wanted an untouched body, too. That she could not give; he should have thought of that sooner, instead of only now. And, miserably, she, too, stared before her, and her face hardened.

A little boy came and stood still in front of them, regarding her with round, unmoving eyes. She was conscious of a slice of bread and jam in his hand, and that his mouth and cheeks were smeared with red. A woman called out: " Jacky! Come on, now!" and he was hauled away, still looking back, and holding out his bread and jam as though offering her a bite. She felt Summerhay's arm slipping round her.

" It's over, darling. Never again—I promise you!"

Ah, he might promise—might even keep that promise. But he would suffer, always suffer, thinking of that other. And she said:

" You can only have me as I am, Bryan. I can't make myself new for you; I wish I could—oh, I wish I could!"

" I ought to have cut my tongue out first! Don't think of it! Come home to me and have tea—there's no one there. Ah, do, Gyp—come!"

He took her hands and pulled her up. And all else left Gyp but the joy of being close to him, going to happiness.

IX

FIORSEN, passing Markey like a blind man, made his way out into the street, but had not gone a hundred yards before he was hurrying back. He had left his hat. The servant, still standing there, handed him that wide-brimmed object and closed the door in his face. Once more he moved away, going towards Piccadilly. If it had not been for the expression on Gyp's face, what might he not have done? And, mixed with sickening jealousy, he felt a sort of relief, as if he had been saved from something horrible. So she had never loved him! Never at all? Impossible! Impossible that a woman on whom he had lavished such passion should never have felt passion for him— never any! Innumerable images of her passed before him—surrendering, always surrendering. It could not all have been pretence! He was not a common man —she herself had said so; he had charm—or, other women thought so! She had lied; she must have lied, to excuse herself!

He went into a café and asked for a *fine champagne*. They brought him a carafe, with the measures marked. He sat there a long time. When he rose, he had drunk nine, and he felt better, with a kind of ferocity that was pleasant in his veins and a kind of nobility that was pleasant in his soul. Let her love, and be happy with her lover! But let him get his fingers on that fellow's throat! Let her be happy, if she could keep her lover from him! And suddenly, he stopped in his tracks, for there on a sandwich-board just in front of him were the words: "Daphne Wing. Pantheon. Daphne Wing. Plastic Danseuse. Poetry of Motion. To-day at three o'clock. Pantheon. Daphne Wing."

Ah, *she* had loved him—little Daphne! It was past three. Going in, he took his place in the stalls, close to the stage, and stared before him, with a sort of bitter amusement. This was irony indeed! Ah—and here she came! A Pierrette—in short, diaphanous muslin, her face whitened to match it; a Pierrette who stood slowly spinning on her toes, with arms raised and hands joined in an arch above her glistening hair.

Idiotic pose! Idiotic! But there was the old expression on her face, limpid, dovelike. And that something of the divine about her dancing smote Fiorsen through all the sheer imbecility of her posturings. Across and across she flitted, pirouetting, caught up at intervals by a Pierrot in black tights with a face as whitened as her own, held upside down, or right end up with one knee bent sideways, and the toe of a foot pressed against the ankle of the other, and arms arched above her. Then, with Pierrot's hands grasping her waist, she would stand upon one toe and slowly twiddle, lifting her other leg toward the roof, while the trembling of her form manifested cunningly to all how hard it was; then, off the toe, she capered out to the wings, and capered back, wearing on her face that divine, lost, dovelike look, while her perfect legs gleamed white up to the very thigh-joint. Yes; on the stage she was adorable! And raising his hands high, Fiorsen clapped and called out: "*Brava!*" He marked the sudden roundness of

her eyes, a tiny start—no more. She had seen him.
' Ah ! Some don't forget me !' he thought.

And now she came on for her second dance, assisted
this time only by her own image reflected in a little
weedy pool about the middle of the stage. From the
programme Fiorsen read, " Ophelia's last dance," and
again he grinned. In a clinging sea-green gown, cut
here and there to show her inevitable legs, with marguerites and corn-flowers in her unbound hair, she
circled her own reflection, languid, pale, desolate; then
slowly gaining the abandon needful to a full display,
danced with frenzy till, in a gleam of limelight, she
sank into the apparent water and floated among paper
water-lilies on her back. Lovely she looked there,
with her eyes still open, her lips parted, her hair trailing
behind. And again Fiorsen raised his hands high to
clap, and again called out: ' Brava !' But the curtain
fell, and Ophelia did not reappear. Was it the sight
of him, or was she preserving the illusion that she
was drowned ? That " arty " touch would be just
like her.

Averting his eyes from two comedians in calico,
beating each other about the body, he rose with an
audible " Pish !" and made his way out. He stopped
in the street to scribble on his card, " Will you see
me ?—G. F." and took it round to the stage-door.
The answer came back:

" Miss Wing will see you in a minute, sir."

And leaning against the distempered wall of the
draughty corridor, a queer smile on his face, Fiorsen
wondered why the devil he was there, and what the
devil she would say.

When he was admitted, she was standing with her
hat on, while her " dresser " buttoned her patent-

leather shoes. Holding out her hand above the woman's back, she said:

"Oh, Mr. Fiorsen, how do you do?"

Fiorsen took the little moist hand; and his eyes passed over her, avoiding a direct meeting with her eyes. He received an impression of something harder, more self-possessed, than he remembered. Her face was the same, yet not the same; only her perfect, supple little body was as it had been. The dresser rose, murmured: "Good-afternoon, miss," and went.

Daphne Wing smiled faintly.

"I haven't seen you for a long time, have I?"

"No; I've been abroad. You dance as beautifully as ever."

"Oh, yes; it hasn't hurt my dancing."

With an effort, he looked her in the face. Was this really the same girl who had clung to him, cloyed him with her kisses, her tears, her appeals for love—just a little love? Ah, but she was more desirable, much more desirable than he had remembered! And he said:

"Give me a kiss, little Daphne!"

Daphne Wing did not stir; her white teeth rested on her lower lip; she said:

"Oh, no, thank you! How is Mrs. Fiorsen?"

Fiorsen turned abruptly.

"There is none."

"Oh, has she divorced you?"

"No. Stop talking of her; stop talking, I say!"

Daphne Wing, still motionless in the centre of her little crowded dressing-room, said, in a matter-of-fact voice:

"You are polite, aren't you? It's funny; I can't tell whether I'm glad to see you. I had a bad time, you know; and Mrs. Fiorsen was an angel. Why do you come to see me now?"

Exactly! Why had he come? The thought flashed through him: 'She'll help me to forget.' And he said:

"I was a great brute to you, Daphne. I came to make up, if I can."

"Oh, no; you can't make up—thank you!" A shudder ran through her, and she began drawing on her gloves. "You taught me a lot, you know. I ought to be quite grateful. Oh, you've grown a little beard! D'you think that improves you? It makes you look rather like Mephistopheles, I think."

Fiorsen stared fixedly at that perfectly shaped face, where a faint, underdone pink mingled with the fairness of the skin. Was she mocking him? Impossible! She looked too matter of fact.

"Where do you live now?" he said.

"I'm on my own, in a studio. You can come and see it, if you like."

"With pleasure."

"Only, you'd better understand. I've had enough of love."

Fiorsen grinned.

"Even for another?" he said.

Daphne Wing answered calmly:

"I wish you would treat me like a lady."

Fiorsen bit his lip, and bowed.

"May I have the pleasure of giving you some tea?"

"Yes, thank you; I'm very hungry. I don't eat lunch on matinée-days; I find it better not. Do you like my Ophelia dance?"

"It's artificial."

"Yes, it *is* artificial—it's done with mirrors and

wire netting, you know. But do I give you the illusion of being mad?" Fiorsen nodded. "I'm so glad. Shall we go? I do want my tea."

She turned round, scrutinized herself in the glass, touched her hat with both hands, revealing, for a second, all the poised beauty of her figure, took a little bag from the back of a chair, and said:

" I think, if you don't mind going on, it's less conspicuous. I'll meet you at Ruffel's—they have lovely things there. *Au revoir.*"

In a state of bewilderment, irritation, and queer meekness, Fiorsen passed down Coventry Street, and entering the empty Ruffel's, took a table near the window. There he sat staring before him, for the sudden vision of Gyp sitting on that oaken chest, at the foot of her bed, had blotted the girl clean out. The attendant coming to take his order, gazed at his pale, furious face, and said mechanically:

" What can I get you, please?"

Looking up, Fiorsen saw Daphne Wing outside, gazing at the cakes in the window. She came in.

" Oh, here you are! I should like iced coffee and walnut cake, and some of those marzipan sweets—oh, and some whipped cream with my cake. Do you mind?" And, sitting down, she fixed her eyes on his face and asked:

" Where have you been abroad?"

" Stockholm, Budapest, Moscow, other places."

" How perfect! Do you think I should make a success in Budapest or Moscow?"

" You might; you are English enough."

" Oh! Do you think I'm very English?"

" Utterly. Your kind of——" But even he was not quite capable of finishing that sentence—" your kind of vulgarity could not be produced anywhere else." Daphne Wing finished it for him:

" My kind of beauty ?"

Fiorsen grinned and nodded.

" Oh, I think that's the nicest thing you ever said to me ! Only, of course, I should like to think I'm more of the Greek type—pagan, you know."

She fell silent, casting her eyes down. Her profile at that moment, against the light, was very pure and soft in line. And he said:

" I suppose you hate me, little Daphne ? You ought to hate me."

Daphne Wing looked up; her round, blue-grey eyes passed over him much as they had been passing over the marzipan.

" No; I don't hate you—now. Of course, if I had any love left for you, I should. Oh, isn't that Irish ? But one can think anybody a rotter without hating them, can't one ?"

Fiorsen bit his lips.

" So you think me a ' rotter ' ? "

Daphne Wing's eyes grew rounder.

" But aren't you ? You couldn't be anything else —could you ?—with the sort of things you did."

" And yet you don't mind having tea with me ?"

Daphne Wing, who had begun to eat and drink, said with her mouth full:

" You see, I'm independent now, and I know life. That makes you harmless."

Fiorsen stretched out his hand and seized hers just where her little warm pulse was beating very steadily. She looked at it, changed her fork over, and went on eating with the other hand. Fiorsen drew his hand away as if he had been stung.

"Ah, you *have* changed—that is certain!"

"Yes; you wouldn't expect anything else, would you? You see, one doesn't go through that for nothing. I think I was a dreadful little fool——" She stopped, with her spoon on its way to her mouth—"and yet——"

"I love you still, little Daphne."

She slowly turned her head toward him, and a faint sigh escaped her.

"Once I would have given a lot to hear that."

And turning her head away again, she picked a large walnut out of her cake and put it in her mouth.

"Are you coming to see my studio? I've got it rather nice and new. I'm making twenty-five a week; my next engagement, I'm going to get thirty. I should like Mrs. Fiorsen to know—— Oh, I forgot; you don't like me to speak of her! Why not? I wish you'd tell me!" Gazing, as the attendant had, at his furious face, she went on: "I don't know how it is, but I'm not a bit afraid of you now. I used to be. Oh, how is Count Rosek? Is he as pale as ever? Aren't you going to have anything more? You've had hardly anything. D'you know what I should like —a chocolate éclair and a raspberry ice-cream soda with a slice of tangerine in it."

When she had slowly sucked up that beverage, prodding the slice of tangerine with her straws, they went out and took a cab. On that journey to her studio, Fiorsen tried to possess himself of her hand, but, folding her arms across her chest, she said quietly:

"It's very bad manners to take advantage of cabs." And, withdrawing sullenly into his corner, he watched her askance. Was she playing with him? Or had she really ceased to care the snap of a finger? It seemed incredible. The cab, which had been threading the maze of the Soho streets, stopped. Daphne Wing alighted, proceeded down a narrow passage to a green door on the right, and, opening it with a latch-key, paused to say:

"I like it's being in a little sordid street—it takes away all amateurishness. It wasn't a studio, of course; it was the back part of a paper-maker's. Any space conquered for art is something, isn't it?" She led the way up a few green-carpeted stairs, into a large room with a skylight, whose walls were covered in Japanese silk the colour of yellow azaleas. Here she stood for a minute without speaking, as though lost in the beauty of her home: then, pointing to the walls, she said:

"It took me ages, I did it all myself. And look at my little Japanese trees; aren't they dickies?" Six little dark abortions of trees were arranged scrupulously on a lofty window-sill, whence the skylight sloped. She added suddenly: "I think Count Rosek would like this room. There's something bizarre about it, isn't there? I wanted to surround myself with that, you know—to get the bizarre note into my work. It's so important nowadays. But through there I've got a bedroom and a bathroom and a little kitchen with everything to hand, all quite domestic; and hot water always on. My people are *so* funny about this room. They come sometimes, and stand about. But they can't get used to the neighbourhood; of course it *is* sordid, but I think an artist ought to be superior to that."

Suddenly touched, Fiorsen answered gently:

"Yes, little Daphne."

She looked at him, and another tiny sigh escaped her.

20

" Why did you treat me like you did ?" she said.
" It's such a pity, because now I can't feel anything
at all." And turning, she suddenly passed the back
of her hand across her eyes. Really moved by that,
Fiorsen went towards her, but she had turned round
again, and putting out her hand to keep him off,
stood shaking her head, with half a tear glistening on
her eyelashes.

" Please sit down on the divan," she said. " Will
you smoke ? These are Russians." And she took a
white box of pink-coloured cigarettes from a little
golden birchwood table. " I have everything Russian
and Japanese so far as I can; I think they help more
than anything with atmosphere. I've got a balalaika;
you can't play on it, can you ? What a pity ! If
only I had a violin ! I *should* have liked to hear you
play again." She clasped her hands: " Do you remember when I danced to you before the fire ?"

Fiorsen remembered only too well. The pink
cigarette trembled in his fingers, and he said rather
hoarsely:

" Dance to me now, Daphne !"

She shook her head.

" I don't trust you a yard. Nobody would—would
they ?"

Fiorsen started up.

" Then why did you ask me here ? What are you
playing at, you little——" At sight of her round,
unmoving eyes, he stopped. She said calmly:

" I thought you'd like to see that I'd mastered my
fate—that's all. But, of course, if you don't, you
needn't stop."

Fiorsen sank back on the divan. A conviction that
everything she said was literal had begun slowly to

sink into him. And taking a long pull at that pink cigarette he puffed the smoke out with a laugh.

" What are you laughing at ?"

" I was thinking, little Daphne, that you are as great an egoist as I."

" I want to be. It's the only thing, isn't it ?"

Fiorsen laughed again.

" You needn't worry. You always were."

She had seated herself on an Indian stool covered with a bit of Turkish embroidery, and, joining her hands on her lap, answered gravely:

" No; I think I wasn't, while I loved you. But it didn't pay, did it ?"

Fiorsen stared at her.

" It has made a woman of you, Daphne. Your face is different. Your mouth is prettier for my kisses —or the want of them. All over, you are prettier."

Pink came up in Daphne Wing's cheeks. And, encouraged by that flush, he went on warmly: " If you loved me now, I should not tire of you. Oh, you can believe me ! I——"

She shook her head.

" We won't talk about love, will we ? Did you have a big triumph in Moscow and St. Petersburg ? It must be wonderful to have really great triumphs !"

Fiorsen answered gloomily:

" Triumphs ? I made a lot of money."

Daphne Wing purred:

" Oh, I expect you're very happy."

Did she mean to be ironic ?

" I'm miserable."

He got up and went towards her. She looked up in his face.

" I'm sorry if you're miserable. I know what it feels like."

" You can help me not to be. Little Daphne, you can help me to forget." He had stopped, and put his hands on her shoulders. Without moving Daphne Wing answered:

" I suppose it's Mrs. Fiorsen you want to forget, isn't it ?"

" As if she were dead. Ah, let it all be as it was, Daphne ! You have grown up; you are a woman, an artist, and you——"

Daphne Wing had turned her head toward the stairs.

" That was the bell," she said. " Suppose it's my people ? It's just their time ! Oh, isn't that awkward ?"

Fiorsen dropped his grasp of her and recoiled against the wall. There with his head touching one of the little Japanese trees, he stood biting his fingers. She was already moving toward the door.

" My mother's got a key, and it's no good putting you anywhere, because she always has a good look round. But perhaps it isn't them. Besides, I'm not afraid now; it makes a wonderful difference being on one's own."

She disappeared. Fiorsen could hear a woman's acid voice, a man's, rather hoarse and greasy, the sound of a smacking kiss. And, with a vicious shrug, he stood at bay. Trapped ! The little devil ! The little dovelike devil ! He saw a lady in a silk dress, green shot with beetroot colour, a short, thick gentleman with a round, greyish beard, in a grey suit, having a small dahlia in his buttonhole, and, behind them, Daphne Wing, flushed, and very round-eyed. He took a step, intending to escape without more ado. The gentleman said:

"Introduce us, Daisy. I didn't quite catch—Mr. Dawson? How do you do, sir? One of my daughter's impresarios, I think. 'Appy to meet you, I'm sure."

Fiorsen took a long breath, and bowed. Mr. Wagge's small piggy eyes had fixed themselves on the little trees.

"She's got a nice little place here for her work—quiet and unconventional. I hope you think well of her talent, sir? You might go further and fare worse, I believe."

Again Fiorsen bowed.

"You may be proud of her," he said; "she is the rising star."

Mr. Wagge cleared his throat.

"Ow," he said; "ye'es! From a little thing, we thought she had stuff in her. I've come to take a great interest in her work. It's not in my line, but I think she's a sticker; I like to see perseverance. Where you've got that, you've got half the battle of success. So many of these young people seem to think life's all play. You must see a lot of that in your profession, sir."

"Robert!"

A shiver ran down Fiorsen's spine.

"Ye-es?"

"The name was not *Daw*son!"

There followed a long moment. On the one side was that vinegary woman poking her head forward like an angry hen, on the other, Daphne Wing, her eyes rounder and rounder, her cheeks redder and redder, her lips opening, her hands clasped to her perfect breast, and, in the centre, that broad, grey-bearded figure, with reddening face and angry eyes and hoarsening voice:

"You scoundrel! You infernal scoundrel!" It lurched forward, raising a pudgy fist. Fiorsen sprang down the stairs and wrenched open the door. He walked away in a whirl of mortification. Should he go back and take that pug-faced vulgarian by the throat? As for that minx! But his feelings about *her* were too complicated for expression. And then— so dark and random are the ways of the mind—his thoughts darted back to Gyp, sitting on the oaken chest, making her confession; and the whips and stings of it scored him worse than ever.

X

THAT same evening, standing at the corner of Bury Street, Summerhay watched Gyp going swiftly to her father's house. He could not bring himself to move while there was still a chance to catch a glimpse of her face, a sign from her hand. Gone! He walked away with his head down. The more blissful the hours just spent, the greater the desolation when they are over. Of such is the nature of love, as he was now discerning. The longing to have her always with him was growing fast. Since her husband knew— why wait? There would be no rest for either of them in an existence of meetings and partings like this, with the menace of that fellow. She must come away with him at once—abroad—until things had declared themselves; and then he must find a place where they could live and she feel safe and happy. He must show he was in dead earnest, set his affairs in order. And he thought: 'No good doing things by halves. Mother must know. The sooner the better. Get it over—at once!' And, with a grimace of discomfort, he set out for his aunt's house in Cadogan Gardens, where his mother always stayed when she was in town.

Lady Summerhay was in the boudoir, waiting for dinner and reading a book on dreams. A red-shaded lamp cast a mellow tinge over the grey frock, over one reddish cheek and one white shoulder. She was a striking person, tall and well built, her very blonde

hair only just turning grey, for she had married young
and been a widow fifteen years—one of those women
whose naturally free spirits have been netted by
association with people of public position. Bubbles
were still rising from her submerged soul, but it was
obvious that it would not again set eyes on the horizon.
With views neither narrow nor illiberal, as views in
society go, she judged everything now as people of
public position must—discussion, of course, but no
alteration in one's way of living. Speculation and
ideas did not affect social usage. The countless movements in which she and her friends were interested for
the emancipation and benefit of others were, in fact,
only channels for letting off her superfluous good-will,
conduit-pipes, for the directing spirit bred in her. She
thought and acted in terms of the public good, regu-
lated by what people of position said at luncheon and
dinner. And it was surely not her fault that such
people must lunch and dine. When her son had bent
and kissed her, she held up the book to him and said:

" Well, Bryan, I think this man's book disgraceful;
he simply runs his sex-idea to death. Really, we aren't
all quite so obsessed as that. I do think he ought to
be put in his own lunatic asylum."

Summerhay, looking down at her gloomily, ans-
swered:

" I've got bad news for you, Mother."

Lady Summerhay closed the book and searched his
face with apprehension. She knew that expression.
She knew that poise of his head, as if butting at something. He looked like that when he came to her in
gambling scrapes. Was this another? Bryan had
always been a pickle. His next words took her breath
away.

" The people at Mildenham, Major Winton and his daughter—you know. Well, I'm in love with her—I'm—I'm her lover."

Lady Summerhay uttered a gasp.

" But—but—Bryan——"

" That fellow she married drinks. He's impossible. She had to leave him a year ago, with her baby—other reasons, too. Look here, Mother: This is hateful, but you'd got to know. I can't talk of her. There's no chance of a divorce." His voice grew higher. " Don't try to persuade me out of it. It's no good."

Lady Summerhay, from whose comely face a frock, as it were, had slipped, clasped her hands together on the book.

Such a swift descent of " life " on one for whom it had for so long been a series of " cases " was cruel, and her son felt this without quite realizing why. In the grip of his new emotions, he still retained enough balance to appreciate what an abominably desolate piece of news this must be to her, what a disturbance and disappointment. And, taking her hand, he put it to his lips.

" Cheer up, Mother ! It's all right. She's happy, and so am I."

Lady Summerhay could only press her hand against his kiss, and murmur:

" Yes; that's not everything, Bryan. Is there—is there going to be a scandal ?"

" I don't know. I hope not; but, anyway, *he* knows about it."

" Society doesn't forgive."

Summerhay shrugged his shoulders.

" Awfully sorry for *you*, Mother."

" Oh, Bryan !"

This repetition of her plaint jarred his nerves.

"Don't run ahead of things. You needn't tell Edith or Flo. You needn't tell anybody. We don't know what'll happen yet."

But in Lady Summerhay all was too sore and blank. This woman she had never seen, whose origin was doubtful, whose marriage must have soiled her, who was some kind of a siren, no doubt. It really was too hard! She believed in her son, had dreamed of public position for him, or, rather, felt he would attain it as a matter of course. And she said feebly:

"This Major Winton is a man of breeding, isn't he?"

"Rather!" And, stopping before her, as if he read her thoughts, he added: "You think she's not good enough for me? She's good enough for anyone on earth. And she's the proudest woman I've ever met. If you're bothering as to what to do about her—don't! She won't want anything of anybody—I can tell you that. She won't accept any crumbs."

"That's lucky!" hovered on Lady Summerhay's lips; but, gazing at her son, she became aware that she stood on the brink of a downfall in his heart. Then the bitterness of her disappointment rising up again, she said coldly:

"Are you going to live together openly?"

"Yes; if she will."

"You don't know yet?"

"I shall—soon."

Lady Summerhay got up, and the book on dreams slipped off her lap with a thump. She went to the fireplace, and stood there looking at her son. He had altered. His merry look was gone; his face was strange to her. She remembered it like that, once in the park at Widrington, when he lost his temper with a pony and came galloping past her, sitting back, his curly hair stivered up like a little demon's. And she said sadly:

" You can hardly expect me to like it for you, Bryan, even if she is what you say. And isn't there some story about——"

" My dear mother, the more there is against her, the more I shall love her—that's obvious."

Lady Summerhay sighed again.

" What is this man going to do ? I heard him play once."

" I don't know. Nothing, I dare say. Morally and legally, he's out of court. I only wish to God he *would* bring a case, and I could marry her; but Gyp says he won't."

Lady Summerhay murmured:

" Gyp ? Is that her name ?" And a sudden wish, almost a longing, not a friendly one, to see this woman seized her. " Will you bring her to see me ? I'm alone here till Wednesday."

" I'll ask her, but I don't think she'll come." He turned his head away. " Mother, she's wonderful !"

An unhappy smile twisted Lady Summerhay's lips. No doubt ! Aphrodite herself had visited her boy. Aphrodite ! And—afterward ? She asked desolately:

" Does Major Winton know ?"

" Yes."

" What does he say to it ?"

" Say ? What can anyone say ? From your point of view, or his, it's rotten, of course. But in her position, anything's rotten."

At that encouraging word, the flood-gates gave way in Lady Summerhay, and she poured forth a stream of words.

" Oh, my dear, can't you pull up ? I've seen so many of these affairs go wrong. It really is not for nothing that law and conventions are what they are— believe me ! Really, Bryan, experience does show that the pressure's too great. It's only once in a way —very exceptional people, very exceptional circumstances. You mayn't think now it'll hamper you, but you'll find it will—most fearfully. It's not as if you were a writer or an artist, who can take his work where he likes and live in a desert if he wants. You've got to do yours in London, your whole career is bound up with society. Do think, before you go butting up against it ! It's all very well to say it's no affair of anyone's, but you'll find it is, Bryan. And then, can you—can you possibly make her happy in the long-run ?"

She stopped at the expression on his face. It was as if he were saying: " I have left your world. Talk to your fellows; all this is nothing to me."

" Look here, Mother: you don't seem to understand. I'm devoted—devoted so that there's nothing else for me."

" How long will that last, Bryan ? You mean bewitched."

Summerhay said, with passion:

" I don't. I mean what I said. Good-night !" And he went to the door.

" Won't you stay to dinner, dear ?"

But he was gone, and the full of vexation, anxiety, and wretchedness came on Lady Summerhay. It was too hard ! She went down to her lonely dinner, desolate and sore. And to the book on dreams, opened beside her plate, she turned eyes that took in nothing.

Summerhay went straight home. The lamps were brightening in the early-autumn dusk, and a draughty, ruffling wind flicked a yellow leaf here and there from off the plane trees. It was just the moment when evening blue comes into the colouring of the town— that hour of fusion when day's hard and staring shapes are softening, growing dark, mysterious, and all that broods behind the lives of men and trees and houses comes down on the wings of illusion to repossess the world—the hour when any poetry in a man wells up. But Summerhay still heard his mother's : " Oh, Bryan !" and, for the first time, knew the feeling that his hand was against everyone's. There was a difference already, or so it seemed to him, in the expression of each passer-by. Nothing any more would be a matter of course; and he was of a class to whom everything has always been a matter of course. Perhaps he did not realize this clearly yet; but he had begun to take what the nurses call " notice," as do those only who are forced on to the defensive against society.

Putting his latch-key into the lock, he recalled the sensation with which, that afternoon, he had opened to Gyp for the first time—half furtive, half defiant. It would be all defiance now. This was the end of the old order ! And, lighting a fire in his sitting-room, he began pulling out drawers, sorting and destroying. He worked for hours, burning, making lists, packing papers and photographs. Finishing at last, he drank a stiff whisky and soda, and sat down to smoke. Now that the room was quiet, Gyp seemed to fill it again with her presence. Closing his eyes, he could see her there by the hearth, just as she stood before they left, turning her face up to him, murmuring: " You won't stop loving me, now you're so sure I love you ?"

Stop loving her! The more she loved him, the more he would love her. And he said aloud: "By God! I won't!" At that remark, so vehement for the time of night, the old Scotch terrier, Ossian, came from his corner and shoved his long black nose into his master's hand.

"Come along up, Ossy! Good dog, Oss!" And, comforted by the warmth of that black body beside him in the chair, Summerhay fell asleep in front of the fire smouldering with blackened fragments of his past.

XI

THOUGH Gyp had never seemed to look round, she had been quite conscious of Summerhay still standing where they had parted, watching her into the house in Bury Street. The strength of her own feeling surprised her, as a bather in the sea is surprised, finding her feet will not touch bottom, that she is carried away helpless—only, these were the waters of ecstasy.

For the second night running, she hardly slept, hearing the clocks of St. James's strike, and Big Ben boom, hour after hour. At breakfast, she told her father of Fiorsen's reappearance. He received the news with a frown and a shrewd glance.

" Well, Gyp ?"

" I told him."

His feelings, at that moment, were perhaps as mixed as they had ever been—curiosity, parental disapproval, to which he knew he was not entitled, admiration of her pluck in letting that fellow know, fears for the consequences of this confession, and, more than all, his profound disturbance at knowing her at last launched into the deep waters of love. It was the least of these feelings that found expression.

" How did he take it ?"

" Rushed away. The only thing I feel sure of is that he won't divorce me."

" No, by George; I don't suppose even he would have that impudence !" And Winton was silent, trying to penetrate the future. "Well," he said suddenly, "it's on the knees of the gods then. But be careful, Gyp."

About noon, Betty returned from the sea, with a solemn, dark-eyed, cooing little Gyp, brown as a roasted coffee-berry. When she had been given all that she could wisely eat after the journey, Gyp carried her off to her own room, undressed her for sheer delight of kissing her from head to foot, and admiring her plump brown legs, then cuddled her up in a shawl and lay down with her on the bed. A few sleepy cooes and strokings, and little Gyp had left for the land of Nod, while her mother lay gazing at her black lashes with a kind of passion. She was not a child-lover by nature; but this child of her own, with her dark softness, plump delicacy, giving disposition, her cooing voice, and constant adjurations to "dear mum," was adorable. There was something about her insidiously seductive. She had developed so quickly, with the graceful roundness of a little animal, the perfection of a flower. The Italian blood of her great great-grandmother was evidently prepotent in her as yet; and, though she was not yet two years old, her hair, which had lost its baby darkness, was already curving round her neck and waving on her forehead. One of her tiny brown hands had escaped the shawl and grasped its edge with determined softness. And while Gyp gazed at the pinkish nails and their absurdly wee half-moons, at the sleeping tranquillity stirred by breathing no more than a rose-leaf on a windless day, her lips grew fuller, trembled, reached toward the dark lashes, till she had to rein her neck back with a jerk to stop such self-indulgence. Soothed, hypnotized, almost in a dream, she lay there beside her baby.

That evening, at dinner, Winton said calmly:

"Well, I've been to see Fiorsen, and warned him off. Found him at that fellow Rosek's." Gyp received the news with a vague sensation of alarm. "And I met that girl, the dancer, coming out of the house as I was going in—made it plain I'd seen her, so I don't think he'll trouble you."

An irresistible impulse made her ask:

"How was she looking, Dad?"

Winton smiled grimly. How to convey his impression of the figure he had seen coming down the steps—of those eyes growing rounder and rounder at sight of him, of that mouth opening in an: "Oh!"

"Much the same. Rather flabbergasted at seeing me, I think. A white hat—very smart. Attractive in her way, but common, of course. Those two were playing the piano and fiddle when I went up. They tried not to let me in, but I wasn't to be put off. Queer place, that!"

Gyp smiled. She could see it all so well. The black walls, the silver statuettes, Rops drawings, scent of dead rose-leaves and pastilles and cigarettes—and those two by the piano—and her father so cool and dry!

"One can't stand on ceremony with fellows like that. I hadn't forgotten that Polish chap's behaviour to you, my dear."

Through Gyp passed a quiver of dread, a vague return of the feelings once inspired by Rosek.

"I'm almost sorry you went, Dad. Did you say anything very——"

"Did I? Let's see! No; I think I was quite polite." He added, with a grim, little smile: "I won't swear I didn't call one of them a ruffian. I know

21

they said something about my presuming on being a cripple."

" Oh, darling !"

" Yes; it was that Polish chap—and so he is !"

Gyp murmured:

" I'd almost rather it had been—the other." Rosek's pale, suave face, with the eyes behind which there were such hidden things, and the lips sweetish and restrained and sensual—he would never forgive ! But Winton only smiled again, patting her arm. He was pleased with an encounter which had relieved his feelings.

Gyp spent all that evening writing her first real love-letter. But when, next afternoon at six, in fulfilment of its wording, she came to Summerhay's little house, her heart sank; for the blinds were down and it had a deserted look. If he had been there, he would have been at the window, waiting. Had he, then, not got her letter, not been home since yesterday ? And that chill fear which besets lovers' hearts at failure of a tryst smote her for the first time. In the three-cornered garden stood a decayed statue of a naked boy with a broken bow—a sparrow was perching on his greenish shoulder; sooty, heart-shaped lilac leaves hung round his head, and at his legs the old Scotch terrier was sniffing. Gyp called: " Ossian ! Ossy !" and the old dog came, wagging his tail feebly.

" Master ! Where is your master, dear ?"

Ossian poked his long nose into her calf, and that gave her a little comfort. She passed, perforce, away from the deserted house and returned home; but all manner of frightened thoughts beset her. Where had he gone ? Why had he gone ? Why had he not let her know ? Doubts—those hasty attendants on passion—came thronging, and scepticism ran riot. What did she know of his life, of his interests, of him, except that he said he loved her? Where had he gone? To Widrington, to some smart house-party, or even back to Scotland? The jealous feelings that had so besieged her at the bungalow when his letters ceased came again now with redoubled force. There must be some woman who, before their love began, had claim on him, or some girl that he admired. He never told her of any such—of course, he would not! She was amazed and hurt by her capacity for jealousy. She had always thought she would be too proud to feel jealousy—a sensation so dark and wretched and undignified, but—alas!—so horribly real and clinging.

She had said she was not dining at home; so Winton had gone to his club, and she was obliged to partake of a little trumped-up lonely meal. She went up to her room after it, but there came on her such restlessness that presently she put on her things and slipped out. She went past St. James's Church into Piccadilly, to the further, crowded side, and began to walk toward the park. This was foolish; but to do a foolish thing was some relief, and she went along with a faint smile, mocking her own recklessness. Several women of the town—ships of night with sails set—came rounding out of side streets or down the main stream, with their skilled, rapid-seeming slowness. And at the discomfited, half-hostile stares on their rouged and powdered faces, Gyp felt a wicked glee. She was disturbing, hurting them—and she wanted to hurt.

Presently, a man, in evening dress, with overcoat thrown open, gazed pointblank into her face, and, raising his hat, ranged up beside her. She walked straight on, still with that half-smile, knowing him puzzled and fearfully attracted. Then an insensate wish to stab him to the heart made her turn her head and look at him. At the expression on her face, he wilted away from her, and again she felt that wicked glee at having hurt him.

She crossed out into the traffic, to the park side, and turned back toward St. James's; and now she was possessed by profound, black sadness. If only her lover were beside her that beautiful evening, among the lights and shadows of the trees, in the warm air ! Why was he not among these passers-by ? She who could bring any casual man to her side by a smile could not conjure up the only one she wanted from this great desert of a town ! She hurried along, to get in and hide her longing. But at the corner of St. James's Street, she stopped. That was his club, nearly opposite. Perhaps he was there, playing cards or billiards, a few yards away, and yet as in another world. Presently he would come out, go to some music-hall, or stroll home thinking of her—perhaps not even thinking of her ! Another woman passed, giving her a furtive glance. But Gyp felt no glee now. And, crossing over, close under the windows of the club, she hurried home. When she reached her room, she broke into a storm of tears. How could she have liked hurting those poor women, hurting that man—who was only paying her a man's compliment, after all ? And with these tears, her jealous, wild feelings passed, leaving only her longing.

Next morning brought a letter. Summerhay wrote from an inn on the river, asking her to come down by the eleven o'clock train, and he would meet her at the station. He wanted to show her a house that he

had seen; and they could have the afternoon on the
river ! Gyp received this letter, which began: " My
darling !" with an ecstasy that she could not quite
conceal. And Winton, who had watched her face, said
presently:

" I think I shall go to Newmarket, Gyp. Home
to-morrow evening."

In the train on the way down, she sat with closed
eyes, in a sort of trance. If her lover had been there
holding her in his arms, he could not have seemed
nearer.

She saw him as the train ran in; but they met
without a hand-clasp, without a word, simply looking
at each other and breaking into smiles.

A little victoria " dug up "—as Summerhay said—
" horse, driver and all," carried them slowly upward.
Under cover of the light rugs their hands were clasped,
and they never ceased to look into each other's faces,
except for those formal glances of propriety which
deceive no one.

The day was beautiful, as only early September days
can be—when the sun is hot, yet not too hot, and its
light falls in a silken radiance on trees just losing the
opulent monotony of summer, on silvery-gold reaped
fields, silvery-green uplands, golden mustard; when
shots ring out in the distance, and, as one gazes, a
leaf falls, without reason, as it would seem. Presently
they branched off the main road by a lane past a clump
of beeches and drew up at the gate of a lonely house,
built of very old red brick, and covered by Virginia
creeper just turning—a house with an ingle-nook and
low, broad chimneys. Before it was a walled, neglected
lawn, with poplars and one large walnut-tree. The
sunlight seemed to have collected in that garden, and

there was a tremendous hum of bees. Above the
trees, the downs could be seen where racehorses, they
said, were trained. Summerhay had the keys of the
house, and they went in. To Gyp, it was like a child's
" pretending "—to imagine they were going to live
there together, to sort out the rooms and consecrate
each. She would not spoil this perfect day by argu-
ment or admission of the need for a decision. And
when he asked:

" Well, darling, what do you think of it ?" she only
answered:

" Oh, lovely, in a way; but let's go back to the river
and make the most of it."

They took boat at " The Bowl of Cream," the river
inn where Summerhay was staying. To him, who had
been a rowing man at Oxford, the river was known
from Lechlade to Richmond; but Gyp had never in
her life been on it, and its placid magic, unlike that
of any other river in the world, almost overwhelmed
her. On this glistening, windless day, to drift along
past the bright, flat water-lily leaves over the greenish
depths, to listen to the pigeons, watch the dragon-
flies flitting past, and the fish leaping lazily, not even
steering, letting her hand dabble in the water, then
cooling her sun-warmed cheek with it, and all the time
gazing at Summerhay, who, dipping his sculls gently,
gazed at her—all this was like a voyage down some
river of dreams, the very fulfilment of felicity. There
is a degree of happiness known to the human heart
which seems to belong to some enchanted world—a
bright maze into which, for a moment now and then,
we escape and wander. To-day, he was more than ever
like her Botticelli " Young Man," with his neck bare,
and his face so clear-eyed and broad and brown.

Had she really had a life with another man ? And only a year ago ? It seemed inconceivable !

But when, in the last backwater, he tied the boat up and came to sit with her once more, it was already getting late, and the vague melancholy of the now shadowy river was stealing into her. And, with a sort of sinking in her heart, she heard him begin:

" Gyp, we *must* go away together. We can never stand it, going on apart, snatching hours here and there."

Pressing his hand to her cheeks, she murmured:

" Why not, darling ? Hasn't this been perfect ? What could we ever have more perfect ? It's been paradise itself !"

" Yes; but to be thrown out every day ! To be whole days and nights without you ! Gyp, you must —you must ! What is there against it ? Don't you love me enough ?"

She looked at him, and then away into the shadows.

" Too much, I think. It's tempting Providence to change. Let's go on as we are, Bryan. No; don't look like that—don't be angry !"

" Why are you afraid ? Are you sorry for our love ?"

" No; but let it be like this. Don't let's risk anything."

" Risk ? Is it people—society—you're afraid of ? I thought *you* wouldn't care."

Gyp smiled.

" Society ? No; I'm not afraid of that."

" What, then ? Of me ?"

" I don't know. Men soon get tired. I'm a doubter, Bryan; I can't help it."

"As if anyone could get tired of you! Are you afraid of yourself?"

Again Gyp smiled.

"Not of loving too little, I told you."

"How can one love too much?"

She drew his head down to her. But when that kiss was over, she only said again:

"No, Bryan; let's go on as we are. I'll make up to you when I'm with you. If you were to tire of me, I couldn't bear it."

For a long time more he pleaded—now with anger, now with kisses, now with reasonings; but, to all, she opposed that same tender, half-mournful "No," and, at last, he gave it up, and, in dogged silence, rowed her to the village, whence she was to take train back. It was dusk when they left the boat, and dew was falling. Just before they reached the station, she caught his hand and pressed it to her breast.

"Darling, don't be angry with me! Perhaps I will —some day."

And, in the train, she tried to think herself once more in the boat, among the shadows and the whispering reeds and all the quiet wonder of the river.

XII

On reaching home she let herself in stealthily, and, though she had not had dinner, went up at once to her room. She was just taking off her blouse when Betty entered, her round face splotched with red, and tears rolling down her cheeks.

" Betty ! What is it ? "

" Oh, my dear, where *have* you been ? Such a dreadful piece of news ! They've stolen her ! That wicked man—your husband—he took her right out of her pram—and went off with her in a great car—he and that other one ! I've been half out of my mind ! " Gyp stared aghast. " I hollered to a policeman. ' He's stolen her—her father ! Catch them ! ' I said. ' However shall I face my mistress ? ' " She stopped for breath, then burst out again. " ' He's a bad one,' I said. ' A foreigner ! They're both foreigners ! ' ' Her father ? ' he said. ' Well, why shouldn't he ? He's only givin' her a joy ride. He'll bring her back, never you fear.' And I ran home—I didn't know where you were. Oh dear ! The major away and all —what was I to do ? I'd just turned round to shut the gate of the square gardens, and I never saw him till he'd put his great long arm over the pram and snatched her out." And, sitting on the bed, she gave way utterly.

Gyp stood still. Nemesis for her happiness ? That vengeful wretch, Rosek ! This was his doing. And she said :

" Oh, Betty, she must be crying !"

A fresh outburst of moans was the only answer. Gyp remembered suddenly what the lawyer had said over a year ago—it had struck her with terror at the time. In law, Fiorsen owned and could claim her child. She could have got her back, then, by bringing a horrible case against him, but now, perhaps, she had no chance. Was it her return to Fiorsen that they aimed at—or the giving up of her lover ? She went over to her mirror, saying:

" We'll go at once, Betty, and get her back somehow. Wash your face."

While she made ready, she fought down those two horrible fears—of losing her child, of losing her lover; the less she feared, the better she could act, the more subtly, the swifter. She remembered that she had somewhere a little stiletto, given her a long time ago. She hunted it out, took off its red leather sheath, and, stabbing the point into a tiny cork, slipped it beneath her blouse. If they could steal her baby, they were capable of anything. She wrote a note to her father, telling him what had happened, and saying where she had gone. Then, in a taxi, they set forth. Cold water and the calmness of her mistress had removed from Betty the main traces of emotion; but she clasped Gyp's hand hard and gave vent to heavy sighs.

Gyp would not think. If she thought of her little one crying, she knew she would cry, too. But her hatred for those who had dealt this cowardly blow grew within her. She took a resolution and said quietly:

" Mr. Summerhay, Betty — that's why they've stolen our darling. I suppose you know he and I care for each other. They've stolen her so as to make me do anything they like."

A profound sigh answered her.

Behind that moon-face with the troubled eyes, what conflict was in progress—between unquestioning morality and unquestioning belief in Gyp, between fears for her and wishes for her happiness, between the loyal retainer's habit of accepting and the old nurse's feeling of being in charge? She said faintly:

"Oh dear! He's a nice gentleman, too!" And suddenly, wheezing it out with unexpected force: "To say truth, I never did hold you was rightly married to that foreigner in that horrible registry place—no music, no flowers, no blessin' asked, nor nothing. I cried me eyes out at the time."

Gyp said quietly:

"No; Betty, I never was. I only thought I was in love." A convulsive squeeze and creaking, whiffling sounds heralded a fresh outburst. "Don't cry; we're just there. Think of our darling!"

The cab stopped. Feeling for her little weapon, she got out, and with her hand slipped firmly under Betty's arm, led the way upstairs. Chilly shudders ran down her spine—memories of Daphne Wing and Rosek, of that large woman—what was her name?— of many other faces, of unholy hours spent up there, in a queer state, never quite present, never comfortable in soul; memories of late returnings down these wide stairs out to their cab, of Fiorsen beside her in the darkness, his dim, broad-cheekboned face moody in the corner or pressed close to hers. Once they had walked a long way homeward in the dawn, Rosek with them, Fiorsen playing on his muted violin, to

the scandal of the policemen and the cats. Dim,
unreal memories! Grasping Betty's arm more firmly,
she rang the bell. When the man servant, whom she
remembered well, opened the door, her lips were so
dry that they could hardly form the words:

" Is Mr. Fiorsen in, Ford ?"

" No, ma'am; Mr. Fiorsen and Count Rosek went
into the country this afternoon. I haven't their
address at present." She must have turned white,
for she could hear the man saying: " Anything I can
get you, ma'am ?"

" When did they start, please ?"

" One o'clock, ma'am—by car. Count Rosek was
driving himself. I should say they won't be away
long—they just had their bags with them." Gyp put
out her hand helplessly; she heard the servant say in
a concerned voice: " I could let you know the moment
they return, ma'am, if you'd kindly leave me your
address."

Giving her card, and murmuring:

" Thank you, Ford; thank you very much," she
grasped Betty's arm again and leaned heavily on her
going down the stairs.

It was real, black fear now. To lose helpless things
—children—dogs—and know for certain that one
cannot get to them, no matter what they may be
suffering! To be pinned down to ignorance and have
in her ears the crying of her child—this horror, Gyp
suffered now. And nothing to be done! Nothing but
to go to bed and wait—hardest of all tasks! Mercifully
—thanks to her long day in the open—she fell at last
into a dreamless sleep, and when she was called,
there was a letter from Fiorsen on the tray with
her tea.

" GYP,

" I am not a baby-stealer like your father.
The law gives me the right to my own child. But
swear to give up your lover, and the baby shall come
back to you at once. If you do not give him up, I
will take her away out of England. Send me an answer
to this post-office, and do not let your father try any
tricks upon me.

" GUSTAV FIORSEN."

Beneath was written the address of a West End
post-office.

When Gyp had finished reading, she went through
some moments of such mental anguish as she had
never known, but—just as when Betty first told her
of the stealing—her wits and wariness came quickly
back. Had he been drinking when he wrote that
letter ? She could almost fancy that she smelled
brandy, but it was so easy to fancy what one wanted
to. She read it through again—this time, she felt
almost sure that it had been dictated to him. If he
had composed the wording himself, he would never
have resisted a gibe at the law, or a gibe at himself
for thus safeguarding her virtue. It was Rosek's
doing. Her anger flamed up anew. Since they used
such mean, cruel ways, why need she herself be scrupu-
lous ? She sprang out of bed and wrote:

" How *could* you do such a brutal thing ? At all
events, let the darling have her nurse. It's not like
you to let a little child suffer. Betty will be ready to
come the minute you send for her. As for myself,
you must give me time to decide. I will let you know
within two days.

" GYP."

When she had sent this off, and a telegram to her
father at Newmarket, she read Fiorsen's letter once
more, and was more than ever certain that it was
Rosek's wording. And, suddenly, she thought of
Daphne Wing, whom her father had seen coming out
of Rosek's house. Through her there might be a
way of getting news. She seemed to see again the
girl lying so white and void of hope when robbed by
death of her own just-born babe. Yes; surely it was
worth trying.

An hour later, her cab stopped before the Wagges'
door in Frankland Street. But just as she was about
to ring the bell, a voice from behind her said:—

"Allow me; I have a key. What may I—— Oh,
it's you!" She turned. Mr. Wagge, in professional
habiliments, was standing there. "Come in; come
in," he said. "I was wondering whether perhaps we
shouldn't be seeing you after what's transpired."

Hanging his tall black hat, craped nearly to the
crown, on a knob of the mahogany stand, he said
huskily:

"I *did* think we'd seen the last of that," and opened
the dining-room door. "Come in, ma'am. We can
put our heads together better in here."

In that too well remembered room, the table was
laid with a stained white cloth, a cruet-stand, and
bottle of Worcestershire sauce. The little blue bowl
was gone, so that nothing now marred the harmony of
red and green. Gyp said quickly:

"Doesn't Daph—Daisy live at home, then, now?"

The expression on Mr. Wagge's face was singular;
suspicion, relief, and a sort of craftiness were blended
with that furtive admiration which Gyp seemed always
to excite in him.

" Do I understand that you—er——"

" I came to ask if Daisy would do something for me."

Mr. Wagge blew his nose.

" You didn't know—— ." he began again.

" Yes; I dare say she sees my husband, if that's what you mean; and I don't mind—he's nothing to me now."

Mr. Wagge's face became further complicated by the sensations of a husband.

" Well," he said, " it's not to be wondered at, perhaps, in the circumstances. I'm sure I always thought——"

Gyp interrupted swiftly.

" Please, Mr. Wagge—please ! Will you give me Daisy's address ?"

Mr. Wagge remained a moment in deep thought; then he said, in a gruff, jerky voice:

" Seventy-three Comrade Street, So'o.   Up to seeing him there on Tuesday, I must say I cherished every hope.   Now I'm sorry I didn't strike him—he was too quick for me——"   He had raised one of his gloved hands and was sawing it up and down.   The sight of that black object cleaving the air nearly made Gyp scream, her nerves were so on edge.   " It's her blasted independence—I beg pardon—but who wouldn't ?" he ended suddenly.

Gyp passed him.

" Who wouldn't ?" she heard his voice behind her " I did think she'd have run straight this time——". And while she was fumbling at the outer door, his red, pudgy face, with its round grey beard, protruded almost over her shoulder.   " If you're going to see her, I hope you'll——"

Gyp was gone. In her cab she shivered. Once she had lunched with her father at a restaurant in the Strand. It had been full of Mr. Wagges. But, suddenly, she thought: 'It's hard on him, poor man!'

XIII

SEVENTY-THREE Comrade Street, Soho, was difficult to find; but, with the aid of a milk-boy, Gyp discovered the alley at last, and the right door. There her pride took sudden alarm, and, but for the milk-boy's eyes fixed on her while he let out his professional howl, she might have fled. A plump white hand and wrist emerging took the can, and Daphne Wing's voice said:

" Oh, where's the cream ?"

" Ain't got none."

" Oh ! I told you always—two pennyworth at twelve o'clock."

" Two penn'orth." The boy's eyes goggled.

" Didn't you want to speak to her, miss ?" He beat the closing door. " Lidy wants to speak to you ! Good-mornin', miss."

The figure of Daphne Wing in a blue kimono was revealed. Her eyes peered round at Gyp.

" Oh !" she said.

" May I come in ?"

" Oh, yes ! Oh, do ! I've been practising. Oh, I am glad to see you !"

In the middle of the studio, a little table was laid for two. Daphne Wing went up to it, holding in one hand the milk-can and in the other a short knife, with which she had evidently been opening oysters. Placing the knife on the table, she turned round to Gyp. Her face was deep pink, and so was her neck, which ran

22

V-shaped down into the folds of her kimono. Her eyes, round as saucers, met Gyp's, fell, met them again. She said:

"Oh, Mrs. Fiorsen, I am glad! I really am. I wanted you so much to see my room—do you like it? How *did* you know where I was?" She looked down and added: "I think I'd better tell you. Mr. Fiorsen came here, and, since then, I've seen him at Count Rosek's—and—and——"

"Yes; but don't trouble to tell me, please."

Daphne Wing hurried on.

"Of course, I'm quite mistress of myself now." Then, all at once, the uneasy woman-of-the-world mask dropped from her face and she seized Gyp's hand. "Oh, Mrs. Fiorsen, I shall never be like you!"

With a little shiver, Gyp said:

"I hope not." Her pride rushed up in her. How could she ask this girl anything? She choked back that feeling, and said stonily: "Do you remember my baby? No, of course; you never saw her. *He* and Count Rosek have just taken her away from me."

Daphne Wing convulsively squeezed the hand of which she had possessed herself.

"Oh, what a wicked thing! When?"

"Yesterday afternoon."

"Oh, I *am* glad I haven't seen him since! Oh, I *do* think that was wicked! Aren't you dreadfully distressed?" The least of smiles played on Gyp's mouth. Daphne Wing burst forth: "D'you know—— I think—I think your self-control is something awful. It frightens me. If my baby had lived and been stolen like that, I should have been half dead by now."

Gyp answered stonily as ever:

"Yes; I want her back, and I wondered——"

Daphne Wing clasped her hands.

"Oh, I expect I can make him——" She stopped, confused, then added hastily: "Are you sure you don't mind?"

"I shouldn't mind if he had fifty loves. Perhaps he has."

Daphne Wing uttered a little gasp; then her teeth came down rather viciously on her lower lip.

"I mean him to do what *I* want now, not what he wants me. That's the only way when you love. Oh, don't smile like that, please; you do make me feel so —uncertain."

"When are you going to see him next?"

Daphne Wing grew very pink.

"I don't know. He might be coming in to lunch. You see, it's not as if he were a stranger, is it?" Casting up her eyes a little, she added: "He won't even let me speak your name; it makes him mad. That's why I'm sure he still loves you; only, his love is so funny." And, seizing Gyp's hand: "I shall never forget how good you were to me. I do hope you— you love somebody else." Gyp pressed those damp, clinging fingers, and Daphne Wing hurried on: "I'm sure your baby's a darling. How you must be suffering! You look quite pale. But it isn't any good suffering. I learned that."

Her eyes lighted on the table, and a faint ruefulness came into them, as if she were going to ask Gyp to eat the oysters.

Gyp bent forward and put her lips to the girl's forehead.

"Good-bye. My baby would thank you if she knew."

And she turned to go. She heard a sob. Daphne

Wing was crying; then, before Gyp could speak, she struck herself on the throat, and said, in a strangled voice:

" Tha—that's idiotic! I—I haven't cried since— since, you know. I—I'm perfect mistress of myself; only, I—only—I suppose you reminded me—— I *never* cry!"

Those words and the sound of a hiccough accompanied Gyp down the alley to her cab.

When she got back to Bury Street, she found Betty sitting in the hall with her bonnet on. She had not been sent for, nor had any reply come from New-market. Gyp could not eat, could settle to nothing. She went up to her bedroom to get away from the servants' eyes, and wen ont mechanically with a frock of little Gyp's she had begun on the fatal morning Fiorsen had come back. Every other minute she stopped to listen to sounds that never meant anything, went a hundred times to the window to look at nothing. Betty, too, had come upstairs, and was in the nursery opposite; Gyp could hear her moving about restlessly among her household gods. Presently, those sounds ceased, and, peering into the room, she saw the stout woman still in her bonnet, sitting on a trunk, with her back turned, uttering heavy sighs. Gyp stole back into her own room with a sick, trembling sensation. If—if her baby really could not be recovered except by that sacrifice! If that cruel letter were the last word, and she forced to decide between them! Which would she give up? Which follow—her lover or her child?

She went to the window for air—the pain about her heart was dreadful. And, leaning there against the shutter, she felt quite dizzy from the violence of a

struggle that refused coherent thought or feeling, and
was just a dumb pull of instincts, both so terribly
strong—how terribly strong she had not till then
perceived.

Her eyes fell on the picture that reminded her of
Bryan; it seemed now to have no resemblance—none.
He was much too real, and loved, and wanted. Less
than twenty-four hours ago, she had turned a deaf ear
to his pleading that she should go to him for ever.
How funny! Would she not rush to him now—go
when and where he liked? Ah, if only she were back
in his arms! Never could she give him up—never!
But then in her ears sounded the cooing words: " Dear
Mum!" Her baby—that tiny thing—how could she
give her up, and never again hold close and kiss that
round, perfect little body, that grave little dark-eyed
face?

The roar of London came in through the open window. So much life, so many people—and not a soul
could help! She left the window and went to the
cottage-piano she had there, out of Winton's way.
But she only sat with arms folded, looking at the
keys. The song that girl had sung at Fiorsen's concert
—song of the broken heart—came back to her.

No, no; she couldn't—couldn't! It was to her
lover she would cling. And tears ran down her
cheeks.

A cab had stopped below, but not till Betty came
rushing in did she look up.

XIV

WHEN, trembling all over, she entered the dining-room, Fiorsen was standing by the sideboard, holding the child.

He came straight up and put her into Gyp's arms.

"Take her," he said, "and do what you will. Be happy."

Hugging her baby, close to the door as she could get, Gyp answered nothing. Her heart was in such a tumult that she could not have spoken a word to save her life; relieved, as one dying of thirst by unexpected water; grateful, bewildered, abashed, yet instinctively aware of something evanescent and unreal in his altruism. Daphne Wing! What bargain did this represent?

Fiorsen must have felt the chill of this instinctive vision, for he cried out:

"Yes! You never believed in me; you never thought me capable of good! Why didn't you?"

Gyp bent her face over her baby to hide the quivering of her lips.

"I am sorry—very, very sorry."

Fiorsen came closer and looked into her face.

"By God, I am afraid I shall never forget you—never!"

Tears had come into his eyes, and Gyp watched them, moved, troubled, but still deeply mistrusting.

He brushed his hand across his face; and the thought flashed through her: ' He means me to see them! Ah, what a cynical wretch I am !'

Fiorsen saw that thought pass, and muttering suddenly:

" Good-bye, Gyp ! I am not all bad. *I am not !*" he tore the door open and was gone.

That passionate " I am not !" saved Gyp from a breakdown. No; even at his highest pitch of abnegation, he could not forget himself.

Relief, if overwhelming, is slowly realized; but when, at last, what she had escaped and what lay before her were staring full in each other's face, it seemed to her that she must cry out, and tell the whole world of her intoxicating happiness. And the moment little Gyp was in Betty's arms, she sat down and wrote to Summerhay:

" DARLING,

" I've had a fearful time. My baby was stolen by him while I was with you. He wrote me a letter saying that he would give her back to me if I gave you up. But I found I couldn't give you up, not even for my baby. And then, a few minutes ago, he brought her—none the worse. To-morrow we shall all go down to Mildenham; but very soon, if you still want me, I'll come with you wherever you like. My father and Betty will take care of my treasure till we come back; and then, perhaps, the old red house we saw—after all. Only—now is the time for you to draw back. Look into the future—look far ! Don't let any foolish pity—or honour—weigh with you; be utterly sure, I do beseech you. I can just bear it now if I know it's for your good. But afterward it'll be too late. It would be the worst misery of all if I made you unhappy. Oh, make sure—make sure! I shall understand. I mean this with every bit of me. And now, good-night, and perhaps—good-bye.

"Your

"GYP."

She read it over and shivered. Did she really mean that she could bear it if he drew back—if he did look far, far into the future, and decided that she was not worth the candle? Ah, but better now—than later.

She closed and sealed the letter, and sat down to wait for her father. And she thought: 'Why does one have a heart? Why is there in one something so much too soft?'

Ten days later, at Mildenham station, holding her father's hand, Gyp could scarcely see him for the mist before her eyes. How good he had been to her all those last days, since she told him that she was going to take the plunge! Not a word of remonstrance or complaint.

"Good-bye, my love! Take care of yourself; wire from London, and again from Paris." And, smiling up at her, he added: "He has luck; I had none."

The mist became tears, rolled down, fell on his glove.

"Not too long out there, Gyp!"

She pressed her wet cheek passionately to his. The train moved, but, so long as she could see, she watched him standing on the platform, waving his grey hat, then, in her corner, sat down, blinded with tears behind her veil. She had not cried when she left him the day of her fatal marriage; she cried now that she was leaving him to go to her incredible happiness.

Strange ! But her heart had grown since then.

tears behind her veil. She had not cried when she
left him the day of her fatal marriage; she cried now
that she was leaving him to go to her incredible
happiness.

Strange! But her heart had grown since then.

PART IV

I

LITTLE Gyp, aged nearly four and a half that first of May, stood at the edge of the tulip border, bowing to two hen turkeys who were poking their heads elegantly here and there among the flowers. She was absurdly like her mother, the same oval-shaped face, dark arched brows, large and clear brown eyes; but she had the modern child's open-air look; her hair, that curled over at the ends, was not allowed to be long, and her polished brown legs were bare to the knees.

"Turkeys! You aren't good, are you? Come *on!*" And, stretching out her hands with the palms held up, she backed away from the tulip-bed. The turkeys, trailing delicately their long-toed feet and uttering soft, liquid interrogations moved after her in hopes of what she was not holding in her little brown hands. The sun, down in the west, for it was past tea-time, slanted from over the roof of the red house, and painted up that small procession—the deep blue frock of little Gyp, the glint of gold in the chestnut of her hair; the daisy-starred grass; the dark birds with translucent red dewlaps, and checkered tails and the tulip background, puce and red and yellow. When she had lured them to the open gate, little Gyp raised herself, and said:

"Aren't you duffies, dears? Shoo!" And on the tails of the turkeys she shut the gate. Then she went to where, under the walnut-tree—the one large tree of that walled garden—a very old Scotch terrier was lying, and sitting down beside him, began stroking his white muzzle, saying:

"Ossy, Ossy, do you love me?"

Presently, seeing her mother in the porch, she jumped up, and crying out: "Ossy—Ossy! Walk!" rushed to Gyp and embraced her legs, while the old Scotch terrier slowly followed.

Thus held prisoner, Gyp watched the dog's approach. Nearly three years had changed her a little. Her face was softer, and rather more grave, her form a little fuller, her hair, if anything, darker, and done differently—instead of waving in wings and being coiled up behind, it was smoothly gathered round in a soft and lustrous helmet, by which fashion the shape of her head was better revealed.

"Darling, go and ask Pettance to put a fresh piece of sulphur in Ossy's water-bowl, and to cut up his meat finer. You can give Hotspur and Brownie two lumps of sugar each; and then we'll go out." Going down on her knees in the porch, she parted the old dog's hair, and examined his eczema, thinking: "I must rub some more of that stuff in to-night. Oh, ducky, you're not smelling your best! Yes; only—not my face!"

A telegraph-boy was coming from the gate. Gyp opened the missive with the faint tremor she always felt when Summerhay was not with her.

"Detained; shall be down by last train; need not come up to-morrow.—BRYAN."

When the boy was gone, she stooped down and stroked the old dog's head.

"Master home all day to-morrow, Ossy—master home!"

A voice from the path said: "Beautiful evenin', ma'am."

The "old scoundrel," Pettance, stiffer in the ankle-joints, with more lines in his gargoyle's face, fewer stumps in his gargoyle's mouth, more film over his dark, burning little eyes, was standing before her, and, behind him, little Gyp, one foot rather before the other, as Gyp had been wont to stand, waited gravely.

"Oh, Pettance, Mr. Summerhay will be at home all to-morrow, and we'll go a long ride: and when you exercise, will you call at the inn, in case I don't go that way, and tell Major Winton I expect him to dinner to-night?"

"Yes, ma'am; and I've seen the pony for little Miss Gyp this morning, ma'am. It's a mouse pony, five year old, sound, good temper, pretty little paces. I says to the man: ' Don't you come it over me,' I says; ' I was born on an 'orse. Talk of twenty pounds for that pony! Ten, and lucky to get it!' ' Well,' he says, ' Pettance, it's no good to talk round an' round with you. Fifteen!' he says. ' I'll throw you one in,' I says, ' Eleven! Take it or leave it.' ' Ah!' he says, ' Pettance, *you* know 'ow to buy an 'orse. All right,' he says; ' twelve!' She's worth all of fifteen, ma'am, and the major's passed her. So if you likes to have 'er, there she is!"

Gyp looked at her little daughter, who had given one excited hop, but now stood still, her eyes flying up at her mother and her lips parted; and she thought: "The darling! She never begs for anything!"

" Very well, Pettance; buy her."

The " old scoundrel " touched his forelock:

" Yes, ma'am—very good, ma'am. Beautiful
evenin', ma'am." And, withdrawing at his gait of
one whose feet are at permanent right angles to the
legs, he mused: ' And that'll be two in my pocket.'

Ten minutes later Gyp, little Gyp, and Ossian
emerged from the garden gate for their evening walk.
They went, not as usual, up to the downs, but toward
the river, making for what they called " the wild."
This was an outlying plot of neglected ground belonging to their farm, two sedgy meadows, hedged by
banks on which grew oaks and ashes. An old stone
linhay, covered to its broken thatch by a huge ivy
bush, stood at the angle where the meadows met.
The spot had a strange life to itself in that smooth,
kempt, countryside of cornfields, grass, and beech-
clumps; it was favoured by beasts and birds, and
little Gyp had recently seen two baby hares there.
From an oak-tree, where the crinkled leaves were not
yet large enough to hide him, a cuckoo was calling
and they stopped to look at the grey bird till he flew
off. The singing and serenity, the green and golden
oaks and ashes, the flowers—marsh-orchis, ladies'
smocks, and cuckoo-buds, starring the rushy grass—
all brought to Gyp that feeling of the uncapturable
spirit which lies behind the forms of nature, the
shadowy, hovering smile of life that is ever vanishing
and ever springing again out of death. While they
stood there close to the old linhay a bird came flying
round them in wide circles, uttering shrill cries. It
had a long beak and long, pointed wings, and seemed
distressed by their presence. Little Gyp squeezed her
mother's hand.

"Poor bird! Isn't it a poor bird, mum?"

"Yes, dear, it's a curlew—I wonder what's the matter with it. Perhaps its mate is hurt."

"What is its mate?"

"The bird it lives with."

"It's afraid of us. It's not like other birds. Is it a real bird, Mum? Or one out of the sky?"

"I think it's real. Shall we go on and see if we can find out what's the matter?"

"Yes."

They went on into the sedgy grass and the curlew continued to circle, vanishing and reappearing from behind the trees, always uttering those shrill cries. Little Gyp said:

"Mum, could we speak to it? Because we're not going to hurt nothing, are we?"

"Of course not, darling! But I'm afraid the poor bird's too wild. Try, if you like. Call to it: ' Courlie! Courlie!' "

Little Gyp's piping joined the curlew's cries and other bird-songs in the bright shadowy quiet of the evening till Gyp said:

"Oh, look; it's dipping close to the ground, over there in that corner—it's got a nest! We won't go near, will we?"

Little Gyp echoed in a hushed voice:

"It's got a nest."

They stole back out of the gate close to the linhay, the curlew still flighting and crying behind them.

"Aren't we glad the mate isn't hurt, Mum?"

Gyp answered with a shiver:

"Yes, darling, fearfully glad. Now then, shall we go down and ask Grandy to come up to dinner?"

Little Gyp hopped. And they went toward the river.

At " The Bowl of Cream," Winton had for two years had rooms, which he occupied as often as his pursuits permitted. He had refused to make his home with Gyp, desiring to be on hand only when she wanted him; and a simple life of it he led in those simple quarters, riding with her when Summerhay was in town, visiting the cottagers, smoking cigars, laying plans for the defence of his daughter's position, and devoting himself to the whims of little Gyp. This moment, when his grandchild was to begin to ride, was in a manner sacred to one for whom life had scant meaning apart from horses. Looking at them, hand in hand, Gyp thought: ' Dad loves her as much as he loves me now—more, I think.'

Lonely dinner at the inn was an affliction which he studiously concealed from Gyp, so he accepted their invitation without alacrity, and they walked on up the hill, with little Gyp in the middle, supported by a hand on each side.

The Red House contained nothing that had been in Gyp's married home except the piano. It had white walls, furniture of old oak, and for pictures reproductions of her favourites. " The Death of Procris " hung in the dining-room. Winton never failed to scrutinize it when he came in to a meal—that " deuced rum affair " appeared to have a fascination for him. He approved of the dining-room altogether; its narrow oak " last supper " table made gay by a strip of blue linen, its old brick hearth, casement windows hung with flowered curtains—all had a pleasing austerity, uncannily redeemed to softness. He got on well enough with Summerhay, but he enjoyed himself much more when he was there alone with his daughter. And this evening he was especially glad to have her to himself, for she had seemed of late rather grave and absent-minded. When dinner was over and they were undisturbed, he said:

"It must be pretty dull for you, my dear, sometimes. I wish you saw more people."

"Oh no, Dad."

Watching her smile, he thought: 'That's not "sour grapes"—What is the trouble, then?'

"I suppose you've not heard anything of that fellow Fiorsen lately?"

"Not a word. But he's playing again in London this season, I see."

"Is he? Ah, that'll cheer them." And he thought: 'It's not that, then. But there's something—I'll swear!'

"I hear that Bryan's going ahead. I met a man in town last week who spoke of him as about the most promising junior at the bar."

"Yes; he's doing awfully well." And a sound like a faint sigh caught his ears. "Would you say he's changed much since you knew him, Dad?"

"I don't know—perhaps a little less jokey."

"Yes; he's lost his laugh."

It was very evenly and softly said, yet it affected Winton.

"Can't expect him to keep that," he answered, "turning people inside out, day after day—and most of them rotten. By George, what a life!"

But when he had left her, strolling back in the bright moonlight, he reverted to his suspicions and wished he had said more directly: "Look here, Gyp, are you worrying about Bryan—or have people been making themselves unpleasant?"

He had, in these last three years, become uncon-

sciously inimical to his own class and their imitators,
and more than ever friendly to the poor—visiting the
labourers, small farmers, and small tradesmen, doing
them little turns when he could, giving their children
sixpences, and so forth. The fact that they could
not afford to put on airs of virtue escaped him; he
perceived only that they were respectful and friendly
to Gyp and this warmed his heart toward them in
proportion as he grew exasperated with the two or
three landed families, and that *parvenu* lot in the
riverside villas.

When he first came down, the chief landowner—a
man he had known for years—had invited him to
lunch. He had accepted with the deliberate intention
of finding out where he was, and had taken the first
natural opportunity of mentioning his daughter. She
was, he said, devoted to her flowers; the Red House
had quite a good garden. His friend's wife, slightly
lifting her brows, had answered with a nervous smile:
" Oh ! yes; of course—yes." A silence had, not unnaturally, fallen. Since then, Winton had saluted his
friend and his friend's wife with such frigid politeness
as froze the very marrow in their bones. He had not
gone there fishing for Gyp to be called on, but to
show these people that his daughter could not be
slighted with impunity. Foolish of him, for, man of
the world to his finger-tips, he knew perfectly well that
a woman living with a man to whom she was not
married could not be recognized by people with any
pretensions to orthodoxy; Gyp was beyond even the
debatable ground on which stood those who have
been divorced and are married again. But even a
man of the world is not proof against the warping of

devotion, and Winton was ready to charge any wind-mill at any moment on her behalf.

Outside the inn door, exhaling the last puffs of his good-night cigarette, he thought: ' What wouldn't I give for the old days, and a chance to wing some of these moral upstarts !'

II

THE last train was not due till eleven-thirty, and
having seen that the evening tray had sandwiches,
Gyp went to Summerhay's study, the room at right
angles to the body of the house, over which was their
bedroom. Here, if she had nothing to do, she always
came when he was away, feeling nearer to him. She
would have been horrified if she had known of her
father's sentiments on her behalf. Her instant denial
of the wish to see more people had been quite genuine.
The conditions of her life, in that respect, often seemed
to her ideal. It was such a joy to be free of people
one did not care two straws about, and of all empty
social functions. Everything she had now was real—
love, and nature, riding, music, animals, and poor
people. What else was worth having? She would
not have changed for anything. It often seemed to
her that books and plays about the unhappiness of
women in her position were all false. If one loved,
what could one want better? Such women, if unhappy, could have no pride; or else could not really
love! She had recently been reading " Anna Kare-
nina," and had often said to herself: " There's something not true about it—as if Tolstoy wanted to make
us believe that Anna was secretly feeling remorse.
If one loves, one doesn't feel remorse. Even if my
baby had been taken away, I shouldn't have felt
remorse. One gives oneself to love—or one does not."

She even derived a positive joy from the feeling that

her love imposed a sort of isolation; she liked to be
apart—for him. Besides, by her very birth she was
outside the fold of society, her love beyond the love
of those within it—just as her father's love had been.
And her pride was greater than theirs, too. How
could women mope and moan because they were cast
out, and try to scratch their way back where they
were not welcome? How could any woman do that?
Sometimes, she wondered whether, if Fiorsen died, she
would marry her lover. What difference would it
make? She could not love him more. It would only
make him feel, perhaps, too sure of her, make it all
a matter of course. For herself, she would rather go
on as she was. But for him, she was not certain, of
late had been less and less certain. He was not bound
now, could leave her when he tired! And yet—did
he perhaps feel himself more bound than if they were
married—unfairly bound? It was this thought—
barely more than the shadow of a thought—which had
given her, of late, the extra gravity noticed by her
father.

In that unlighted room with the moonbeams drifting
in, she sat down at Summerhay's bureau, where he
often worked too late at his cases, depriving her of
himself. She sat there resting her elbows on the bare
wood, crossing her finger-tips, gazing out into the
moonlight, her mind drifting on a stream of memories
that seemed to have beginning only from the year
when he came into her life. A smile crept out on her
face, and now and then she uttered a little sigh of
contentment.

So many memories, nearly all happy! Surely, the
most adroit work of the jeweller who put the human
soul together was his provision of its power to forget

the dark and remember sunshine. The year and a
half of her life with Fiorsen, the empty months that
followed it were gone, dispersed like mist by the
radiance of the last three years in whose sky had hung
just one cloud, no bigger than a hand, of doubt whether
Summerhay really loved her as much as she loved
him, whether from her company he got as much as
the all she got from his. She would not have been
her distrustful self if she could have settled down in
complacent security; and her mind was ever at stretch
on that point, comparing past days and nights with
the days and nights of the present. Her prevision
that, when she loved, it would be desperately, had
been fulfilled. He had become her life. When this
befalls one whose besetting strength and weakness
alike is pride—no wonder that she doubts.

For their Odyssey they had gone to Spain—that
brown un-European land of, "lyrio" flowers, and
cries of "Agua!" in the streets, where the men seem
cleft to the waist when they are astride of horses,
under their wide black hats, and the black-clothed
women with wonderful eyes still look as if they missed
their Eastern veils. It had been a month of gaiety
and glamour, last days of September and early days
of October, a revel of enchanted wanderings in the
streets of Seville, of embraces and laughter, of strange
scents and stranger sounds, of orange light and velvety
shadows, and all the warmth and deep gravity of
Spain. The Alcazar, the cigarette-girls, the Gipsy
dancers of Triana, the old brown ruins to which they
rode, the streets, and the square with its grave talkers
sitting on benches in the sun, the water-sellers and
the melons; the mules, and the dark ragged man out
of a dream, picking up the ends of cigarettes, the wine

of Malaga, burnt fire and honey! Seville had bewitched them—they got no further. They had come
back across the brown uplands of Castile to Madrid
and Goya and Velasquez, till it was time for Paris,
before the law-term began. There, in a queer little
French hotel—all bedrooms, and a lift, coffee and
carved beds, wood fires, and a chambermaid who
seemed all France, and down below a restaurant, to
which such as knew about eating came, with waiters
who looked like monks, both fat and lean—they had
spent a week. Three special memories of that week
started up in the moonlight before Gyp's eyes: The
long drive in the Bois among the falling leaves of trees
flashing with colour in the crisp air under a brilliant
sky. A moment in the Louvre before the Leonardo
"Bacchus," when—his "restored" pink skin forgotten—all the world seemed to drop away while she
listened, with the listening figure before her, to some
mysterious music of growing flowers, and secret life.
And that last most disconcerting memory, of the
night before they returned. They were having supper
after the theatre in their restaurant, when, in a mirror
she saw three people come in and take seats at a table
a little way behind—Fiorsen, Rosek, and Daphne
Wing! How she managed to show no sign she never
knew! While they were ordering, she was safe, for
Rosek was a *gourmet*, and the girl would certainly
be hungry; but after that, she knew that nothing
could save her being seen—Rosek would mark down
every woman in the room! Should she pretend to
feel faint and slip out into the hotel? Or let Bryan
know? Or sit there laughing and talking, eating and
drinking, as if nothing were behind her?

Her own face in the mirror had a flush, and her

eyes were bright. When they saw her, they would see that she was happy, safe in her love. Her foot sought Summerhay's beneath the table. How splendid and brown and fit he looked, compared with those two pale, towny creatures! And he was gazing at her as though just discovering her beauty. How could she ever—that man with his little beard and his white face and those eyes—how could she ever! Ugh! And then, in the mirror, she saw Rosek's dark-circled eyes fasten on her and betray their recognition by a sudden gleam, saw his lips compressed, and a faint red come up in his cheeks. What would he do? The girl's back was turned—her perfect back—and she was eating. And Fiorsen was staring straight before him in that moody way she knew so well. All depended on that deadly little man, who had once kissed her throat. A sick feeling seized on Gyp. If her lover knew that within five yards of him were those two men! But she still smiled and talked, and touched his foot. Rosek had seen that she was conscious—was getting from it a kind of satisfaction. She saw him lean over and whisper to the girl, and Daphne Wing turning to look, and her mouth opening for a smothered "Oh!" Gyp saw her give an uneasy glance at Fiorsen, and then begin again to eat. Surely she would want to get away before he saw. Yes; very soon she rose. What little airs of the world she had now—quite mistress of the situation! The wrap must be placed exactly on her shoulders; and how she walked, giving just one startled look back from the door. Gone! The ordeal over! And Gyp said: "Let's go up, darling."

She felt as if they had both escaped a deadly peril —not from anything those two could do to him or her, but from the cruel ache and jealousy of the past, which the sight of that man would have brought him.

Women, for their age, are surely older than men— married women, at all events, than men who have not had that experience. And all through those first weeks of their life together, there was a kind of wise watchfulness in Gyp. He was only a boy in know- ledge of life as she saw it, and though his character was so much more decided, active, and insistent than her own, she felt it lay with her to shape the course and avoid the shallows and sunken rocks. The house they had seen together near the river, under the Berkshire downs, was still empty; and while it was being got ready, they lived at a London hotel. She had insisted that he should tell no one of their life together. If that must come, she wanted to be firmly settled in, with little Gyp and Betty and the horses, so that it should all be for him as much like respectable married life as possible. But, one day, in the first week after their return, while in her room, just back from a long day's shopping, a card was brought up to her: " Lady Summerhay." Her first impulse was to be " not at home;" her second, " I'd better face it. Bryan would wish me to see her!" When the page- boy was gone, she turned to the mirror and looked at herself doubtfully. She seemed to know exactly what that tall woman whom she had seen on the platform would think of her—too soft, not capable, not right for him!—not even if she were legally his wife. And touching her hair, laying a dab of scent on her eyebrows, she turned and went downstairs fluttering, but outwardly calm enough.

In the little low-roofed inner lounge of that old hotel, whose rooms were all " entirely renovated,"

Gyp saw her visitor standing at a table, rapidly turning the pages of an illustrated magazine, as people will when their minds are set upon a coming operation. And she thought: ' I believe she's more frightened than I am!'

Lady Summerhay held out a gloved hand.

"How do you do?" she said. "I hope you'll forgive my coming."

Gyp took the hand.

"Thank you. It was very good of you. I'm sorry Bryan isn't in yet. Will you have some tea?"

"I've had tea; but do let's sit down. How do you find the hotel?"

"Very nice."

On a velvet lounge that had survived the renovation, they sat side by side, screwed round toward each other.

"Bryan's told me what a pleasant time you had abroad. He's looking very well, I think. I'm devoted to him, you know."

Gyp answered softly:

"Yes, you must be." And her heart felt suddenly as hard as flint.

Lady Summerhay gave her a quick look.

"I—I hope you won't mind my being frank—I've been so worried. It's an unhappy position, isn't it?" Gyp did not answer, and she hurried on. "If there's anything I can do to help, I should be so glad—it must be horrid for you."

Gyp said very quietly:

"Oh! no. I'm perfectly happy—couldn't be happier." And she thought: ' I suppose she doesn't believe that.'

Lady Summerhay was looking at her fixedly.

" One doesn't realize these things at first—neither of you will, till you see how dreadfully Society can cold-shoulder."

Gyp made an effort to control a smile.

" One can only be cold-shouldered if one puts oneself in the way of it. I should never wish to see or speak to anyone who couldn't take me just for what I am. And I don't really see what difference it will make to Bryan; most men of his age have someone, somewhere." She felt malicious pleasure watching her visitor jib and frown at the cynicism of that soft speech; a kind of hatred had come on her of this society woman, who—disguise it as she would— was at heart her enemy, who regarded her, must regard her, as an enslaver, as a despoiler of her son's worldly chances, a Dalilah dragging him down. She said still more quietly: " He need tell no one of my existence; and you can be quite sure that if ever he feels he's had enough of me, he'll never be troubled by the sight of me again."

And she got up. Lady Summerhay also rose.

" I hope you don't think—I really am only too anxious to——"

" I think it's better to be quite frank. You will never like me, or forgive me for ensnaring Bryan. And so it had better be, please, as it would be if I were just his common mistress. That will be per- fectly all right for both of us. It was very good of you to come, though. Thank you—and good-bye."

Lady Summerhay literally faltered with speech and hand.

With a malicious smile, Gyp watched her retirement among the little tables and elaborately modern chairs till her tall figure had disappeared behind a column.

Then she sat down again on the lounge, pressing her hands to her burning ears. She had never till then known the strength of the pride-demon within her; at the moment, it was almost stronger than her love. She was still sitting there, when the page-boy brought her another card—her father's. She sprang up saying:

"Yes, here, please."

Winton came in all brisk and elated at sight of her after this long absence; and, throwing her arms round his neck, she hugged him tight. He was doubly precious to her after the encounter she had just gone through. When he had given her news of Mildenham and little Gyp, he looked at her steadily, and said:

"The coast'll be clear for you both down there, and at Bury Street, whenever you like to come, Gyp. I shall regard this as your real marriage. I shall have the servants in and make that plain."

A row like family prayers—and Dad standing up very straight, saying in his dry way: "You will be so good in future as to remember——" "I shall be obliged if you will," and so on; Betty's round face pouting at being brought in with all the others; Markey's soft, inscrutable; Mrs. Markey's demure and goggling; the maids' rabbit-faces; old Pettance's carved grin, the film lifting from his little burning eyes: "Ha! Mr. Bryn Summer'ay; he bought her 'orse, and so she's gone to 'im!" And she said:

"Darling, I don't know! It's awfully sweet of you. We'll see later."

Winton patted her hand. "We must stand up to 'em, you know, Gyp. You mustn't get your tail down."

Gyp laughed.

" No, Dad; never ! . . ."

That same night, across the strip of blackness between their beds, she said:

" Bryan, promise me something !"

" It depends. I know you too well."

" No; it's quite reasonable, and possible. Promise !"

" All right; if it is."

" I want you to let me take the lease of the Red House—let it be mine, the whole thing—let me pay for everything there."

" Reasonable ! What's the point ?"

" Only that I shall have a proper home of my own. I can't explain, but your mother's coming to-day made me feel I must."

" My child, how could I possibly live on *you* there ? It's absurd !"

" You can pay for everything else; London— travelling—clothes, if you like. We can make it square up. It's not a question of money, of course. I only want to feel that if, at any moment, you don't need me any more, you can simply stop coming."

" I think that's brutal, Gyp."

" No, no; so many women lose men's love because they seem to claim things of them. I don't want to lose yours that way—that's all."

" That's silly, darling !"

" It's not. Men—and women, too—always tug at chains. And when there is no chain——"

" Well then; let me take the house, and you can go away when you're tired of me." His voice sounded smothered, resentful; she could hear him turning and turning, as if angry with his pillows. And she murmured:

" No; I can't explain. But I really mean it."

" We're just beginning life together, and you talk as if you want to split it up. It hurts, Gyp, and that's all about it."

She said gently:

" Don't be angry, dear."

" Well! Why don't you trust me more?"

" I do. Only I must make as sure as I can."

The sound came again of his turning and turning.

" I can't!"

Gyp said slowly:

" Oh! Very well!"

A dead silence followed, both lying quiet in the darkness, trying to get the better of each other by sheer listening. An hour perhaps passed before he sighed, and, feeling his lips on hers, she knew that she had won. . . .

III

THERE, in the study, the moonlight had reached her face; an owl was hooting not far away, and still more memories came—the happiest of all, perhaps—of first days in this old house together.

Summerhay damaged himself out hunting that first winter. The memory of nursing him was strangely pleasant, now that it was two years old. For convalescence they had gone to the Pyrenees—Argelès in March, all almond-blossom and snows against the blue —a wonderful fortnight. In London on the way back they had their first awkward encounter. Coming out of a theatre one evening, Gyp heard a woman's voice, close behind, say: "Why, it's Bryan! What ages!" And his answer defensively drawled out:

"Hallo! How are you, Diana?"

"Oh, awfully fit. Where are you, nowadays? Why don't you come and see us?"

Again the drawl:

"Down in the country. I will, some time. Good-bye."

A tall woman or girl—red-haired, with one of those wonderful white skins that go therewith; and brown —yes, brown eyes; Gyp could see those eyes sweeping her up and down with a sort of burning-live curiosity. Bryan's hand was thrust under her arm at once.

"Come on, let's walk and get a cab."

As soon as they were clear of the crowd, she pressed his hand to her breast, and said:

" Did you mind ?"

" Mind ? Of course not. It's for you to mind."

" Who was it ?"

" A second cousin. Diana Leyton."

" Do you know her very well ?"

" Oh yes—used to."

" And do you like her very much ?"

" Rather !"

He looked round into her face, with laughter bubbling up behind his gravity. Ah, but could one tease on such a subject as their love ? And to this day the figure of that tall girl with the burning-white skin, the burning-brown eyes, the burning-red hair was not quite a pleasant memory to Gyp. After that night, they gave up all attempt to hide their union, going to whatever they wished, whether they were likely to meet people or not. Gyp found that nothing was so easily ignored as Society when the heart was set on other things. Besides, they were seldom in London, and in the country did not wish to know anyone, in any case. But she never lost the feeling that what was ideal for her might not be ideal for him. He ought to go into the world, ought to meet people. It would not do for him to be cut off from social pleasures and duties, and then some day feel that he owed his starvation to her. To go up to London, too, every day was tiring, and she persuaded him to take a set of residential chambers in the Temple, and sleep there three nights a week. In spite of all his entreaties, she herself never went to those chambers, staying always at Bury Street when she came up. A kind of superstition prevented her; she would not risk making him feel that she was hanging round his neck. Besides, she wanted to keep herself desirable—

so little a matter of course that he would hanker after
her when he was away. And she never asked him
where he went or whom he saw. But, sometimes, she
wondered whether he could still be quite faithful to
her in thought, love her as he used to; and joy would
go down behind a heavy bank of clouds, till, at his
return, the sun came out again. Love such as hers—
passionate, adoring, protective, longing to sacrifice
itself, to give all that it had to him, yet secretly demanding all his love in return—for how could a proud
woman love one who did not love her?—such love
as this is always longing for a union more complete
than it is likely to get in a world where all things
move and change. But against the grip of this love
she never dreamed of fighting now. From the moment
when she knew she must cling to him rather than to
her baby, she had made no reservations; all her eggs
were in one basket, as her father's had been before her
—all! . . .

The moonlight was shining full on the old bureau
and a vase of tulips standing there, giving those
flowers colour that was not colour, and an unnamed
look, as if they came from a world which no human
enters. It glinted on a bronze bust of old Voltaire,
which she had bought him for a Christmas present, so
that the great writer seemed to be smiling from the
hollows of his eyes. Gyp turned the bust a little, to
catch the light on its far cheek; a letter was disclosed
between it and the oak. She drew it out thinking:
'Bless him! He uses everything for paper-weights;'
and, in the strange light, its first words caught her eyes:

"DEAR BRYAN,
        "But *I* say—you *are* wasting yourself——"

24

She laid it down, methodically pushing it back under the bust. Perhaps he had put it there on purpose! She got up and went to the window, to check the temptation to read the rest of that letter and see from whom it was. No! She did not admit that she was tempted. One did not read letters. Then the full import of those few words struck into her: " Dear Bryan. But *I* say—you *are* wasting yourself." A letter in a chain of correspondence, then! A woman's hand; but not his mother's, nor his sisters'—she knew their writings. Who had dared to say he was wasting himself? A letter in a chain of letters! An intimate correspondent, whose name she did not know, because —he had not told her! Wasting himself—on what? —on his life with her down here? And was he? Had she herself not said that very night that he had lost his laugh? She began searching her memory. Yes, last Christmas vacation—that clear, cold, wonderful fortnight in Florence, he had been full of fun. It was May now. Was there no memory since—of his old infectious gaiety? She could not think of any. " But *I* say—you *are* wasting yourself." A sudden hatred flared up in her against the unknown woman who had said that thing—and fever, running through her veins, made her ears burn. She longed to snatch forth and tear to pieces the letter, with its guardian-ship of which that bust seemed mocking her; and she turned away with the thought: ' I'll go and meet him; I can't wait here.'

Throwing on a cloak she walked out into the moonlit garden, and went slowly down the whitened road toward the station. A magical, dewless night! The moonbeams had stolen in to the beech clump, frosting the boles and boughs, casting a fine ghostly grey over the shadow-patterned beech-mast. Gyp took the short cut through it. Not a leaf moved in there, no living thing stirred; so might an earth be where only trees inhabited! She thought: 'I'll bring him back through here.' And she waited at the far corner of the clump, where he must pass, some little distance from the station. She never gave people unnecessary food for gossip—any slighting of her irritated him, she was careful to spare him that. The train came in; a car went whizzing by, a cyclist, then the first foot-passenger, at a great pace, breaking into a run. She saw that it was he, and, calling out his name, ran back into the shadow of the trees. He stopped dead in his tracks, then came rushing after her. That pursuit did not last long, and, in his arms, Gyp said:

" If you aren't too hungry, darling, let's stay here a little—it's so wonderful!"

They sat down on a great root, and leaning against him, looking up at the dark branches, she said:

" Have you had a hard day?"

" Yes; got hung up by a late consultation; and old Leyton asked me to come and dine."

Gyp felt a sensation as when feet happen on ground that gives a little.

" The Leytons—that's Eaton Square, isn't it? A big dinner?"

" No. Only the old people, and Bertie and Diana."

" Diana? That's the girl we met coming out of the theatre, isn't it?"

" When? Oh—ah—what a memory, Gyp!"

" Yes; it's good for things that interest me."

" Why? Did she interest you?"

Gyp turned and looked into his face.

" Yes. Is she clever?"

" H'm ! I suppose you might call her so."

" And in love with you ?"

" Great Scott ! Why ?"

" Is it very unlikely ? I am."

He began kissing her lips and hair. And, closing her eyes, Gyp thought: ' If only that's not because he doesn't want to answer !' Then, for some minutes, they were silent as the moonlit beech clump.

" Answer me truly, Bryan. Do you never—never —feel as if you were wasting yourself on me ?"

She was certain of a quiver in his grasp; but his face was open and serene, his voice as usual when he was teasing.

" Well, hardly ever ! Aren't you funny, dear ?"

" Promise me faithfully to let me know when you've had enough of me. Promise !"

" All right ! But don't look for fulfilment in this life."

" I'm not so sure."

" I am."

Gyp put up her lips, and tried to drown for ever in a kiss the memory of those words: " But *I* say—you *are* wasting yourself."

IV

SUMMERHAY, coming down next morning, went straight to his bureau; his mind was not at ease. "Wasting yourself!" What had he done with that letter of Diana's? He remembered Gyp's coming in just as he finished reading it. Searching the pigeon-holes and drawers, moving everything that lay about, he twitched the bust—and the letter lay disclosed. He took it up with a sigh of relief:

"DEAR BRYAN,

"But *I* say—you *are* wasting yourself. Why, my dear, of course! '*Il faut se faire valoir !*' You have only one foot to put forward; the other is planted in I don't know what mysterious hole. One foot in the grave—at thirty! Really, Bryan! Pull it out. There's such a lot waiting for you. It's no good your being hoity-toity, and telling me to mind my business. I'm speaking for everyone who knows you. We all feel the blight on the rose. Besides, you always were my favourite cousin, ever since I was five and you a horrid little bully of ten; and I simply hate to think of you going slowly down instead of quickly up. Oh! I know 'D——n the world!' But—are you? I should have thought it was 'd——ning' you! Enough! When are you coming to see us? I've read that book. The man seems to think love is nothing but passion, and passion always fatal. I wonder! Perhaps you know.

"Don't be angry with me for being such a grand-mother.

"*Au revoir*.

"Your very good cousin,

"DIANA LEYTON."

He crammed the letter into his pocket, and sat there, appalled. It must have lain two days under that bust! Had Gyp seen it? He looked at the bronze face; and the philosopher looked back from the hollows of his eyes, as if to say: "What do you know of the human heart, my boy—your own, your mistress's, that girl's, or anyone's? A pretty dance the heart will lead you yet! Put it in a packet, tie it round with string, seal it up, drop it in a drawer, lock the drawer! And to-morrow it will be out and skipping on its wrappings. Ho! Ho!" And Summerhay thought: 'You old goat. You never had one!' In the room above, Gyp would still be standing as he had left her, putting the last touch to her hair—a man would be a scoundrel who, even in thought, could—— "Hallo!" the eyes of the bust seemed to say. "Pity! That's queer, isn't it? Why not pity that red-haired girl, with the skin so white that it burns you, and the eyes so brown that they burn you—don't they?" Old Satan! Gyp had his heart; no one in the world would ever take it from her!

And in the chair where she had sat last night conjuring up memories, he too now conjured. How he had loved her, did love her! She would always be what she was and had been to him. And the sage's mouth seemed to twist before him with the words: "Quite so, my dear! But the heart's very funny— very—capacious!" A tiny sound made him turn.

Little Gyp was standing in the doorway.

"Hallo!" he said.

"Hallo, Baryn!" She came flying to him, and he caught her up so that she stood on his knees with the sunlight shining on her fluffed out hair.

"Well, Gipsy! Who's getting a tall girl?"

"I'm goin' to ride."

"Ho, ho!"

"Baryn, let's do Humpty-Dumpty!"

"All right; come on!" He rose and carried her upstairs.

Gyp was still doing one of those hundred things which occupy women for a quarter of an hour after they are "quite ready," and at little Gyp's shout of, "Humpty!" she suspended her needle to watch the sacred rite.

Summerhay had seated himself on the foot-rail of the bed, rounding his arms, sinking his neck, blowing out his cheeks to simulate an egg; then, with an unexpectedness that even little Gyp could always see through, he rolled backward on to the bed.

And she, simulating "all the king's horses," tried in vain to put him up again. This immemorial game, watched by Gyp a hundred times, had to-day a special preciousness. If he could be so ridiculously young, what became of her doubts? Looking at his face pulled this way and that, lazily imperturbable under the pommelings of those small fingers, she thought: 'And that girl dared to say he was *wasting himself!*' For in the night conviction had come to her that those words were written by the tall girl with the white skin, the girl of the theatre—the Diana of his last night's dinner. Humpty-Dumpty was up on the bed-rail again for the finale; all the king's horses were clasped to him, making the egg more round, and over they both went with shrieks and gurgles. What a boy he was! She would not—no, she would not brood and spoil her day with him.

But that afternoon, at the end of a long gallop on the downs, she turned her head away and said suddenly:

"Is she a huntress?"

"Who?"

"Your cousin—Diana."

In his laziest voice, he answered:

"I suppose you mean—does she hunt me?"

She knew that tone, that expression on his face, knew he was angry; but could not stop herself.

"I did."

"So you're going to become jealous, Gyp?"

It was one of those cold, naked sayings that should never be spoken between lovers—one of those sayings at which the heart of the one who speaks sinks with a kind of dismay, and the heart of the one who hears quivers. She cantered on. And he, perforce, after her. When she reined in again, he glanced into her face and was afraid. It was all closed up against him. And he said softly:

"I didn't mean that, Gyp."

But she only shook her head. He *had* meant it—had wanted to hurt her! It didn't matter—she wouldn't give him the chance again. And she said:

"Look at that long white cloud, and the apple-green in the sky—rain to-morrow. One ought to enjoy any fine day as if it were the last."

Uneasy, ashamed, yet still a little angry, Summerhay rode on beside her.

That night, she cried in her sleep; and, when he awakened her, clung to him and sobbed out:

"Oh! such a dreadful dream! I thought you'd left off loving me!"

For a long time he held and soothed her. Never, never! He would never leave off loving her!

But a cloud no broader than your hand can spread and cover the whole day.

V

The summer passed, and always there was that little
patch of silence in her heart, and in his. The tall,
bright days grew taller, slowly passed their zenith,
slowly shortened. On Saturdays and Sundays, sometimes with Winton and little Gyp, but more often
alone, they went on the river. For Gyp, it had never
lost the magic of their first afternoon upon it—never
lost its glamour as of an enchanted world. All the
week she looked forward to these hours of isolation
with him, as if the surrounding water secured her not
only against a world that would take him from her,
if it could, but against that side of his nature, which,
so long ago she had named "old Georgian." She had
once adventured to the law courts by herself, to see
him in his wig and gown. Under that stiff grey
crescent on his broad forehead, he seemed so hard and
clever—so of a world to which she never could belong,
so of a piece with the brilliant bullying of the whole
proceeding. She had come away feeling that she only
possessed and knew one side of him. On the river,
she had that side utterly—her lovable, lazy, im-
pudently loving boy, lying with his head in her lap,
plunging in for a swim, splashing round her; or with
his sleeves rolled up, his neck bare, and a smile on his
face, plying his slow sculls down-stream, singing,
"Away, my rolling river," or pulling home like a
demon in want of his dinner. It was such a blessing
to lose for a few hours each week this growing con-

sciousness that she could never have the whole of him. But all the time the patch of silence grew, for doubt in the heart of one lover reacts on the heart of the other.

When the long vacation came, she made an heroic resolve. He must go to Scotland, must have a month away from her, a good long rest. And while Betty was at the sea with little Gyp, she would take her father for his cure. She held so inflexibly to this resolve, that, after many protests, he said with a shrug:

" Very well, I will then—if you're so keen to get rid of me."

" Keen to get rid !" When she could not bear to be away from him ! But she forced her feeling back, and said, smiling:

" At last ! There's a good boy !" Anything ! If only it would bring him back to her exactly as he had been. She asked no questions as to where, or to whom, he would go.

Tunbridge Wells, that charming purgatory where the retired prepare their souls for a more permanent retirement, was dreaming on its hills in long rows of adequate villas. Its commons and woods had remained unscorched, so that the retired had not to any extent deserted it, that August, for the sea. They still shopped in the Pantiles, strolled the uplands, or flourished their golf-clubs in the grassy parks; they still drank tea in each other's houses and frequented the many churches. One could see their faces, as it were, goldened by their coming glory, like the chins of children by reflection from buttercups. From every kind of life they had retired, and, waiting now for a

more perfect day, were doing their utmost to postpone
it. They lived very long.

Gyp and her father had rooms in a hotel where he
could bathe and drink the waters without having to
climb three hills. This was the first cure she had
attended since the long-past time at Wiesbaden.
Was it possible that was only six years ago? She
felt so utterly, so strangely different! Then life had
been sparkling sips of every drink, and of none too
much; now it was one long still draft, to quench a
thirst that would not be quenched.

During these weeks she held herself absolutely at
her father's disposal, but she lived for the post, and
if, by any chance, she did not get her daily letter, her
heart sank to the depths. She wrote every day,
sometimes twice, then tore up that second letter,
remembering for what reason she had set herself to
undergo this separation. During the first week, his
letters had a certain equanimity; in the second week
they became ardent; in the third, they were fitful—
now beginning to look forward, now moody and
dejected; and they were shorter. During this third
week Aunt Rosamund joined them. The good lady
had become a staunch supporter of Gyp's new existence, which, in her view, served Fiorsen right. Why
should the poor child's life be loveless? She had a
definitely low opinion of men, and a lower of the state
of the marriage-laws; in her view, any woman who
struck a blow in that direction was something of a
heroine. And she was oblivious of the fact that Gyp
was quite guiltless of the desire to strike a blow against
the marriage-laws, or anything else. Aunt Rosamund's aristocratic and rebellious blood boiled with
hatred of what she called the "stuffy people" who

still held that women were men's property. It had made her specially careful never to put herself in that position.

She had brought Gyp a piece of news.

" I was walking down Bond Street past that tea-and-tart shop, my dear—you know, where they have those special coffee-creams, and who should come out of it but Miss Daphne Wing and our friend Fiorsen; and pretty hangdog he looked. He came up to me, with his little lady watching him like a lynx. Really, my dear, I was rather sorry for him; he'd got that hungry look of his; she'd been doing all the eating, I'm sure. He asked me how you were. I told him, ' Very well.'

" ' When you see her,' he said, ' tell her I haven't forgotten her, and never shall. But she was quite right; this is the sort of lady that I'm fit for.' And the way he looked at that girl made me feel quite uncomfortable. Then he gave me one of his little bows; and off they went, she as pleased as Punch. I really was sorry for him."

Gyp said quietly:

" Ah! you needn't have been, Auntie; he'll always be able to be sorry for himself."

A little shocked at her niece's cynicism, Aunt Rosamund was silent. The poor lady had not lived with Fiorsen!

That same afternoon, Gyp was sitting in a shelter on the common, a book on her knee—thinking her one long thought: ' To-day is Thursday—Monday week! Eleven days—still!'—when three figures came slowly toward her, a man, a woman, and what should have been a dog. English love of beauty and the rights of man had forced its nose back, deprived it of half its ears, and all but three inches or so of tail. It had asthma—and waddled in disillusionment. A voice said:

"This'll do, Maria. We can take the sun 'ere."

But for that voice, with the permanent cold hoarseness caught beside innumerable graves, Gyp might not have recognized Mr. Wagge, for he had taken off his beard, leaving nothing but side-whiskers, and Mrs. Wagge had filled out wonderfully. They were some time settling down beside her.

"You sit here, Maria; you won't get the sun in your eyes."

"No, Robert; I'll sit here. You sit there."

"No, *you* sit there."

"No, *I* will. Come, Duckie!"

But the dog, standing stockily on the pathway was gazing at Gyp, while what was left of its broad nose moved from side to side. Mr. Wagge followed the direction of its glance.

"Oh!" he said, "oh, this is a surprise!" And fumbling at his straw hat, he passed his other hand over his sleeve and held it out to Gyp. It felt almost dry, and fatter than it had been. While she was shaking it, the dog moved forward and sat down on her feet. Mrs. Wagge also extended her hand, clad in a shiny glove.

"This is a—a—pleasure," she murmured. "Who *would* have thought of meeting you! Oh, don't let Duckie sit against your pretty frock! Come, Duckie!"

But Duckie did not move, resting his back against Gyp's shin-bones. Mr. Wagge, whose tongue had been passing over a mouth which she saw to its full advantage for the first time, said abruptly:

"You 'aven't come to live here, 'ave you?"

" Oh no ! I'm only with my father for the baths."

" Ah, I thought not, never havin' seen you. We've been retired here ourselves a matter of twelve months. A pretty spot."

" Yes; lovely, isn't it ?"

" We wanted nature. The air suits us, though a bit—er—too irony, as you might say. But it's a long-lived place. We were quite a time lookin' round."

Mrs. Wagge added in her thin voice:

" Yes—we'd thought of Wimbledon, you see, but Mr. Wagge liked this better; he can get his walk, here; and it's more—select, perhaps. We have several friends. The church is very nice."

Mr. Wagge's face assumed an uncertain expression. He said bluffly:

" I was always a chapel man; but—I don't know how it is—there's something in a place like this that makes church seem more—more suitable; my wife always had a leaning that way. I never conceal my actions."

Gyp murmured:

" It's a question of atmosphere, isn't it ?"

Mr. Wagge shook his head.

" No; I don't hold with incense—we're not 'Igh Church. But how are *you*, ma'am ? We often speak of you. You're looking well."

His face had become a dusky orange, and Mrs. Wagge's the colour of a doubtful beetroot. The dog on Gyp's feet stirred, snuffled, turned round, and fell heavily against her legs again. She said quietly:

" I was hearing of Daisy only to-day. She's quite a star now, isn't she ?"

Mrs. Wagge sighed. Mr. Wagge looked away and answered:

" It's a sore subject. There she is, making her forty and fifty pound a week, and run after in all the papers. She's a success—no doubt about it. And she works. Saving a matter of fifteen 'undred a year, I shouldn't be surprised. Why, at my best, the years the influenza was so bad, I never cleared a thousand nett. No, she's a success."

Mrs. Wagge added:

" Have you seen her last photograph—the one where she's standing between two hydrangea-tubs. It was her own idea."

Mr. Wagge mumbled suddenly:

" I'm always glad to see her when she takes a run down in a car. But I've come here for quiet after the life I've led, and I don't want to think about it, especially before you, ma'am. I don't—that's a fact."

A silence followed, during which Mr. and Mrs. Wagge looked at their feet, and Gyp looked at the dog.

" Ah !—here you are !" It was Winton, who had come up from behind the shelter, and stood, with eyebrows slightly raised. Gyp could not help a smile. Her father's weathered, narrow face, half-veiled eyes, thin nose, little crisp, grey moustache that did not hide his firm lips, his lean, erect figure, the very way he stood, his thin, dry, clipped voice were the absolute antithesis of Mr. Wagge's thick-set, stoutly planted form, thick-skinned, thick-featured face, thick, rather hoarse yet oily voice. It was as if Providence had arranged a demonstration of the extremes of social type. And she said:

" Mr. and Mrs. Wagge—my father."

Winton raised his hat. Gyp remained seated, the dog Duckie being still on her feet.

" 'Appy to meet you, sir. I hope you have benefit

from the waters. They're supposed to be most power-ful, I believe."

" Thank you—not more deadly than most. Are you drinking them ?"

Mr. Wagge smiled.

" Nao !" he said, " we live here."

" Indeed ! Do you find anything to do ?"

" Well, as a fact, I've come here for rest. But I take a Turkish bath once a fortnight—find it refresh-ing; keeps the pores of the skin acting."

Mrs. Wagge added gently:

" It seems to suit my husband wonderfully."

Winton murmured:

" Yes ! Is this your dog ? Bit of a philosopher, isn't he ?"

Mrs. Wagge answered:

" Oh, he's a naughty dog, aren't you, Duckie ?"

The dog Duckie, feeling himself the cynosure of every eye, rose and stood panting into Gyp's face. She took the occasion to get up.

" We must go, I'm afraid. Good-bye. It's been very nice to meet you again. When you see Daisy, will you please give her my love ?"

Mrs. Wagge unexpectedly took a handkerchief from her reticule. Mr. Wagge cleared his throat heavily. Gyp was conscious of the dog Duckie waddling after them, and of Mrs. Wagge calling, " Duckie, Duckie !" from behind her handkerchief.

Winton said softly:

" So those two got that pretty filly ! Well, she didn't show much quality, when you come to think of it. She's still with our friend, according to your aunt."

Gyp nodded.

" Yes; and I do hope she's happy."

" *He* isn't, apparently.   Serves him right."

Gyp shook her head.

" Oh no, Dad !"

" Well, one oughtn't to wish any man worse than he's likely to get.   But when I see people daring to look down their noses at you—by Jove !"

" Darling, what does that matter ?"

Winton answered testily:

" It matters very much to me—the impudence of it !"   His mouth relaxed in a grim little smile: " Ah, well—there's not much to choose between us so far as condemning our neighbours goes.   ' Charity Stakes— also ran, Charles Clare Winton, the Church, and Mrs. Grundy.' "

They opened out to each other more in those few days at Tunbridge Wells than they had for years. Whether the process of bathing softened his crust, or the air that Mr. Wagge found " a bit—er—too irony, as you might say," had upon Winton the opposite effect, he certainly relaxed that first duty of man, the concealment of his spirit, and disclosed his activities as he never had before—how such and such a person had been set on his feet, so and so sent out to Canada, this man's wife helped over her confinement, that man's daughter started again after a slip.   And Gyp's child-worship of him bloomed anew.

On the last afternoon of their stay, she strolled out with him through one of the long woods that stretched away behind their hotel.   Excited by the coming end of her self-inflicted penance, moved by the beauty among those sunlit trees, she found it difficult to talk. But Winton, about to lose her, was quite loquacious. Starting from the sinister change in the racing-world

—so plutocratic now, with the American seat, the increase of book-making owners, and other tragic occurrences—he launched forth into a jeremiad on the condition of things in general. Parliament, he thought, especially now that members were paid, had lost its self-respect; the towns had eaten up the country; hunting was threatened; the power and vulgarity of the press were appalling; women had lost their heads; and everybody seemed afraid of having any " breeding." By the time little Gyp was Gyp's age, they would all be under the thumb of Watch Committees, live in Garden Cities, and have to account for every half-crown they spent, and every half-hour of their time; the horse, too, would be an extinct animal, brought out once a year at the lord-mayor's show. He hoped—the deuce—he might not be alive to see it. And suddenly he added: " What do you think happens after death, Gyp ?"

They were sitting on one of those benches that crop up suddenly in the heart of nature. All around them briars and bracken were just on the turn; and the hum of flies, the vague stir of leaves and life formed but a single sound. Gyp, gazing into the wood, answered:

" Nothing, Dad. I think we just go back."

" Ah—— My idea, too !"

Neither of them had ever known what the other thought about it before !

Gyp murmured:

> " La vie est vaine—
> Un peu d'amour,
> Un peu de haine,
> Et puis bonjour !"

Not quite a grunt nor quite a laugh emerged from the depths of Winton, and, looking up at the sky, he said:

"And what they call 'God,' after all, what is it?
Just the very best you can get out of yourself—
nothing more, so far as I can see. Dash it, you can't
imagine anything more than you can imagine. One
would like to die in the open, though, like Whyte-
Melville. But there's one thing that's always puzzled
me, Gyp. All one's life one's tried to have a
single heart. Death comes, and out you go! Then
why did one love, if there's to be no meeting
after?"

"Yes; except for that, who would care? But does
the wanting to meet make it any more likely, Dad?
The world couldn't go on without love; perhaps loving
somebody or something with all your heart is all in
itself."

Winton stared; the remark was a little deep.

"Ye-es," he said at last. "I often think the
religious johnnies are saving their money to put on a
horse that'll never run after all. I remember those
Yogi chaps in India. There they sat, and this jolly
world might rot round them for all they cared—they
thought they were going to be all right themselves, in
Kingdom Come. But suppose it doesn't come?"

Gyp murmured with a little smile:

"Perhaps they were trying to love everything at
once."

"Rum way of showing it. And, hang it, there are
such a lot of things one can't love! Look at that!"
He pointed upwards. Against the grey bole of a
beech-tree hung a board, on which were the freshly
painted words:

PRIVATE.

TRESPASSERS WILL BE PROSECUTED.

" That board is stuck up all over this life and the next. Well, *we* won't give them the chance to **warn** us off, Gyp."

Slipping her hand through his arm, she pressed close up to him.

" No, Dad; you and I will go off with the wind and the sun, and the trees and the waters, like Procris in my picture."

VI

THE curious and complicated nature of man in matters of the heart is not sufficiently conceded by women, professors, clergymen, judges, and other critics of his conduct. And, naturally so, since they all have vested interests in his simplicity. Even journalists are in the conspiracy to make him out less wayward than he is, and dip their pens in epithets, if his heart diverges inch or ell.

Bryan Summerhay was neither more curious nor more complicated than those of his own sex who would condemn him for getting into the midnight express from Edinburgh with two distinct emotions in his heart—a regretful aching for the girl, his cousin, whom he was leaving behind, and a rapturous anticipation of the woman whom he was going to rejoin. How was it possible that he could feel both at once? "Against all the rules," women and other moralists would say. Well, the fact is, a man's heart knows no rules. And he found it perfectly easy, lying in his bunk, to dwell on memories of Diana handing him tea, or glancing up at him, while he turned the leaves of her songs, with that enticing mockery in her eyes and about her lips; and yet the next moment to be swept from head to heel by the longing to feel Gyp's arms around him, to hear her voice, look in her eyes, and press his lips on hers. If, instead of being on his way to rejoin a mistress, he had been going home to a wife, he would not have felt a particle more of

spiritual satisfaction, perhaps not so much. He was
returning to the feelings and companionship that he
knew were the most deeply satisfying spiritually and
bodily he would ever have. And yet he could ache
a little for that red-haired girl, and this without any
difficulty. How disconcerting! But, then, truth is.

From that queer seesawing of his feelings, he fell
asleep, dreamed of all things under the sun as men
only can in a train, was awakened by the hollow silence
in some station, slept again for hours, it seemed, and
woke still at the same station, fell into a sound sleep
at last that ended at Willesden in broad daylight.
Dressing hurriedly, he found he had but one emotion
now, one longing—to get to Gyp. Sitting back in his
cab, hands deep-thrust into the pockets of his ulster,
he smiled, enjoying even the smell of the misty London
morning. Where would she be—in the hall of the
hotel waiting, or upstairs still?

Not in the hall! And asking for her room, he made
his way to its door.

She was standing in the far corner motionless, deadly
pale, quivering from head to foot; and when he flung
his arms round her, she gave a long sigh, closing her
eyes. With his lips on hers, he could feel her almost
fainting; and he too had no consciousness of anything
but that long kiss.

Next day, they went abroad to a little place not
far from Fécamp, in that Normandy countryside
where all things are large—the people, the beasts, the
unhedged fields, the courtyards of the farms guarded
so squarely by tall trees, the skies, the sea, even the
blackberries large. And Gyp was happy. But twice
there came letters, in that too-well-remembered hand-
writing, which bore a Scottish postmark. A phantom

increases in darkness, solidifies when seen in mist. Jealousy is rooted not in reason, but in the nature that feels it—in her nature that loved desperately, felt proudly. And jealousy flourishes on scepticism. Even if pride would have let her ask—what good? She would not have believed the answers. Of course he would say—if only out of pity—that he never let his thoughts rest on another woman. But, after all, it was only a phantom. There were many hours in those three weeks when she felt he really loved her, and so—was happy.

They went back to the Red House at the end of the first week in October. Little Gyp, home from the sea, was now an almost accomplished horsewoman. Under the tutelage of old Pettance, she had been riding steadily round and round those rough fields by the linhay which they called "the wild," her firm brown legs astride of the mouse-coloured pony, her little brown face, with excited, dark eyes, very erect, her auburn crop of short curls flopping up and down on her little straight back. She wanted to be able to "go out riding" with Grandy and Mum and Baryn. And the first days were spent by them all more or less in fulfilling her new desires. Then term began, and Gyp sat down again to the long sharing of Summerhay with his other life.

VII

ONE afternoon at the beginning of November, the old
Scotch terrier, Ossian, lay on the path in the pale sunshine. He had lain there all the morning since his
master went up by the early train. Nearly sixteen
years old, he was deaf now and disillusioned, and
every time that Summerhay left him, his eyes seemed
to say: " You will leave me once too often !" The
blandishments of the other nice people about the
house were becoming to him daily less and less a
substitute for that which he felt he had not much
time left to enjoy; nor could he any longer bear a
stranger within the gate. From her window, Gyp
saw him get up and stand with his back ridged, growling at the postman, and, fearing for the man's calves,
she hastened out.

Among the letters was one in that dreaded hand-
writing marked " Immediate," and forwarded from
his chambers. She took it up, and put it to her nose.
A scent—of what ? Too faint to say. Her thumb
nails sought the edge of the flap on either side. She
laid the letter down. Any other letter, but not that
—she wanted to open it too much. Readdressing it,
she took it out to put with the other letters. And
instantly the thought went through her: ' What a
pity ! If I read it, and there was nothing !' All her
restless, jealous misgivings of months past would then
be set at rest ! She stood, uncertain, with the letter
in her hand. Ah—but if there *were* something ! She

would lose at one stroke her faith in him, and her
faith in herself—not only his love but her own self-
respect. She dropped the letter on the table. Could
she not take it up to him herself? By the three
o'clock slow train, she could get to him soon after five.
She looked at her watch. She would just have time
to walk down. And she ran upstairs. Little Gyp
was sitting on the top stair—her favourite seat—
looking at a picture-book.

"I'm going up to London, darling. Tell Betty I
may be back to-night, or perhaps I may not. Give
me a good kiss."

Little Gyp gave the good kiss, and said:

"Let me see you put your hat on, Mum."

While Gyp was putting on hat and furs, she thought:
'I shan't take a bag; I can always make shift at
Bury Street if——" She did not finish the thought,
but the blood came up in her cheeks. "Take care of
Ossy, darling!" She ran down, caught up the letter,
and hastened away to the station. In the train, her
cheeks still burned. Might not this first visit to his
chambers be like her old first visit to the little house
in Chelsea? She took the letter out. How she hated
that large, scrawly writing for all the thoughts and
fears it had given her these past months! If that girl
knew how much anxiety and suffering she had caused,
would she stop writing, stop seeing him? And Gyp
tried to conjure up her face, that face seen only for
a minute, and the sound of that clipped, clear voice
but once heard—the face and voice of one accustomed
to have her own way. No! It would only make her
go on all the more. Fair game, against a woman with
no claim—but that of love. Thank heaven she had
not taken him away from any woman—unless—that

girl perhaps thought she had! Ah! Why, in all
these years, had she never got to know his secrets, so
that she might fight against what threatened her?
But would she have fought? To fight for love was
degrading, horrible! And yet—if one did not? She
got up and stood at the window of her empty carriage.
There was the river—and there—yes, the very backwater where he had begged her to come to him for
good. It looked so different, bare and shorn, under
the light grey sky; the willows were all polled, the
reeds cut down. And a line from one of his favourite
sonnets came into her mind:

> "Bare ruined choirs where late the sweet birds sang."

Ah, well! Time enough to face things when they
came. She would only think of seeing him! And
she put the letter back to burn what hole it liked in
the pocket of her fur coat.

The train was late; it was past five, already growing
dark, when she reached Paddington and took a cab
to the Temple. Strange to be going there for the first
time—not even to know exactly where Harcourt
Buildings were. At Temple Lane, she stopped the
cab and walked down that narrow, ill-lighted, busy
channel into the heart of the Great Law.

"Up those stone steps, miss; along the railin',
second doorway." Gyp came to the second doorway
and in the doubtful light scrutinized the names.
"Summerhay—second floor." She began to climb
the stairs. Her heart beat fast. What would he say?
How greet her? Was it not absurd, dangerous, to
have come? He would be having a consultation
perhaps. There would be a clerk or someone to
beard, and what name could she give? On the first

floor she paused, took out a blank card, and pencilled
on it:

"Can I see you a minute ?—G."

Then, taking a long breath to quiet her heart, she
went on up. There was the name, and there the
door. She rang—no one came; listened—could hear
no sound. All looked so massive and bleak and dim
—the iron railings, stone stairs, bare walls, oak door.
She rang again. What should she do? Leave the
letter? Not see him after all—her little romance all
come to naught—just a chilly visit to Bury Street,
where perhaps there would be no one but Mrs. Markey,
for her father, she knew, was at Mildenham, hunting,
and would not be up till Sunday! And she thought:
'I'll leave the letter, go back to the Strand, have some
tea, and try again.'

She took out the letter, with a sort of prayer pushed
it through the slit of the door, heard it fall into its
wire cage; then slowly descended the stairs to the
outer passage into Temple Lane. It was thronged
with men and boys, at the end of the day's work.
But when she had nearly reached the Strand, a woman's
figure caught her eye. She was walking with a man
on the far side; their faces were turned toward each
other. Gyp heard their voices, and, faint, dizzy, stood
looking back after them. They passed under a lamp;
the light glinted on the woman's hair, on a trick of
Summerhay's, the lift of one shoulder, when he was
denying something; she heard his voice, high-pitched.
She watched them cross, mount the stone steps she
had just come down, pass along the railed stone passage,
enter the doorway, disappear. And such horror
seized on her that she could hardly walk away.

"Oh no! Oh no! Oh no!" So it went in her mind—a kind of moaning, like that of a cold, rainy wind through dripping trees. What did it mean? Oh, what did it mean? In this miserable tumult, the only thought that did not come to her was that of going back to his chambers. She hurried away. It was a wonder she was not run over, for she had no notion what she was doing, where going, and crossed the streets without the least attention to traffic. She came to Trafalgar Square, and stood leaning against its parapet in front of the National Gallery. Here she had her first coherent thought: So that was why his chambers had been empty! No clerk—no one! That they might be alone. Alone, where she had dreamed of being alone with him! And only that morning he had kissed her and said, "Good-bye, treasure!" A dreadful little laugh got caught in her throat, confused with a sob. Why—why had she a heart? Down there, against the plinth of one of the lions, a young man leaned, with his arms round a girl, pressing her to him. Gyp turned away from the sight and resumed her miserable wandering. She went up Bury Street. No light; not any sign of life! It did not matter; she could not have gone in, could not stay still, must walk! She put up her veil to get more air, feeling choked.

The trees of the Green Park, under which she was passing now, had still a few leaves, and they gleamed in the lamplight copper-coloured as that girl's hair. All sorts of torturing visions came to her. Those empty chambers! She had seen one little minute of their intimacy. A hundred kisses might have passed between them—a thousand words of love! And he would lie to her. Already he had acted a lie! She

had not deserved that. And this sense of the injustice done her was the first relief she felt—this
definite emotion of a mind clouded by sheer misery.
She had not deserved that he should conceal things
from her. She had not had one thought or look for
any man but him since that night down by the sea,
when he came to her across the garden in the moonlight—not one thought—and never would! Poor
relief enough! She was in Hyde Park now, wandering
along a pathway which cut diagonally across the grass.
And with more resolution, more purpose, she began
searching her memory for signs, proofs of *when* he had
changed to her. She could not find them. He had
not changed in his ways to her; not at all. Could one
act love, then? Act passion, or—horrible thought!—
when he kissed her nowadays, was he thinking of that
girl?

She heard the rustling of leaves behind. A youth
was following her along the path, some ravening
youth, whose ungoverned breathing had a kind of
pathos in it. Heaven! What irony! She was too
miserable to care, hardly even knew when, in the
main path again, she was free from his pursuit. Love!
Why had it such possession of her, that a little thing
—yes, a little thing—only the sight of him with
another, should make her suffer so? She came out
on the other side of the park. What should she do?
Crawl home, creep into her hole, and lie there stricken!
At Paddington she found a train just starting and got
in. There were other people in the carriage, business
men from the city, lawyers, from that—place where
she had been. And she was glad of their company,
glad of the crackle of evening papers and stolid faces
giving her looks of stolid interest from behind them,

glad to have to keep her mask on, afraid of the violence of her emotion. But one by one they got out, to their cars or their constitutionals, and she was left alone to gaze at darkness and the deserted river just visible in the light of a moon smothered behind the sou'-westerly sky. And for one wild moment she thought: 'Shall I open the door and step out—one step—peace !'

She hurried away from the station. It was raining, and she drew up her veil to feel its freshness on her hot face. There was just light enough for her to see the pathway through the beech clump. The wind in there was sighing, soughing, driving the dark boughs, tearing off the leaves, little black wet shapes that came whirling at her face. The wild melancholy in that swaying wood was too much for Gyp; she ran thrusting her feet through the deep rustling drifts of leaves not yet quite drenched. They clung all wet round her thin stockings, and the rainy wind beat her forehead. At the edge, she paused for breath, leaning against the bole of a beech, peering back, where the wild whirling wind was moaning and tearing off the leaves. Then, bending her head to the rain, she went on in the open, trying to prepare herself to show nothing when she reached home.

She got in and upstairs to her room, without being seen. If she had possessed any sedative drug she would have taken it. Anything to secure oblivion from this aching misery ! Huddling before the freshly lighted fire, she listened to the wind driving through the poplars; and once more there came back to her the words of that song sung by the Scottish girl at Fiorsen's concert:

> " And my heart reft of its own sun,
> Deep lies in death-torpor cold and gray."

Presently she crept into bed, and at last fell asleep.

She woke next morning with the joyful thought: 'It's Saturday; he'll be down soon after lunch!' And then she remembered. Ah, no! It was too much! At the pang of that remembrance, it was as if a devil entered into her—a devil of stubborn pride, which grew blacker with every hour of that morning. After lunch, that she might not be in when he came, she ordered her mare, and rode up on the downs alone. The rain had ceased, but the wind still blew strong from the sou'west, and the sky was torn and driven in swathes of white and grey to north, south, east, and west, and puffs of what looked like smoke scurried across the cloud banks and the glacier-blue rifts between. The mare had not been out the day before, and on the springy turf stretched herself in that thoroughbred gallop which bears a rider up, as it were, on air, till nothing but the thud of hoofs, the grass flying by, the beating of the wind in her face betrayed to Gyp that she was moving. For full two miles they went without a pull, only stopped at last by the finish of the level. From there, one could see far—away over to Wittenham Clumps across the Valley, and to the high woods above the river in the east—away, in the south and west, under that strange, torn sky, to a whole autumn land, of whitish grass, bare fields, woods of grey and gold and brown, fast being pillaged. But all that sweep of wind, and sky, freshness of rain, and distant colour could not drive out of Gyp's heart the hopeless aching and the devil begotten of it.

VIII

THERE are men who, however well-off—either in money or love—must gamble. Their affections may be deeply rooted, but they cannot repulse fate when it tantalizes them with a risk.

Summerhay, who loved Gyp, was not tired of her either physically or mentally, and even felt sure he would never tire, had yet dallied for months with this risk which yesterday had come to a head. And now, taking his seat in the train to return to her, he felt unquiet; and since he resented disquietude, he tried defiantly to think of other things, but he was very unsuccessful. Looking back, it was difficult for him to tell when the snapping of his defences had begun. A preference shown by one accustomed to exact preference is so insidious. The girl, his cousin, was herself a gambler. He did not respect her as he respected Gyp; she did not touch him as Gyp touched him, was not—no, not half—so deeply attractive; but she had—confound her! the power of turning his head at moments, a queer burning, skin-deep fascination, and, above all, that most dangerous quality in a woman—the lure of an imperious vitality. In love with life, she made him feel that he was letting things slip by. And since to drink deep of life was his nature, too—what chance had he of escape? Far-off cousinhood is a dangerous relationship. Its familiarity is not great enough to breed contempt, but sufficient to remove those outer defences to intimacy, the conquest of which, in other circumstances, demands the conscious effort which warns people whither they are going.

Summerhay had not realized the extent of the danger, but he had known that it existed, especially since Scotland. It would be interesting—as the historians say—to speculate on what he would have done, if he could have foretold what would happen. But he had certainly not foretold the crisis of yesterday evening. He had received a telegram from her at lunch-time, suggesting the fulfilment of a jesting promise, made in Scotland, that she should have tea with him and see his chambers—a small and harmless matter. Only, why had he dismissed his clerk so early? That is the worst of gamblers—they will put a polish on the risks they run. He had not reckoned, perhaps, that she would look so pretty, lying back in his big Oxford chair, with furs thrown open so that her white throat showed, her hair gleaming, a smile coming and going on her lips; her white hand, with polished nails, holding that cigarette; her brown eyes, so unlike Gyp's, fixed on him; her slim foot with high instep thrust forward in transparent stocking. Not reckoned that, when he bent to take her cup, she would put out her hands, draw his head down, press her lips to his, and say: "Now you know!" His head had gone round, still went round, thinking of it! That was all. A little matter—except that, in an hour, he would be meeting the eyes of one he loved much more. And yet—the poison was in his blood; a kiss so cut short—by what—what counter impulse?—leaving him gazing at her without a sound, inhaling that scent of hers—something like a pine wood's scent, only sweeter, while she gathered up her gloves, fastened her furs, as if it had been he, not she, who had snatched that kiss. But her hand had pressed his arm against her as they went down the stairs. And getting into her cab at the Temple Station, she had looked back at him with a little half-mocking smile of challenge and comradeship and promise. The link would be hard to break —even if he wanted to. And yet nothing would come of it! Heavens, no! He had never thought! Marriage! Impossible! Anything else—even more impossible! When he got back to his chambers, he had found in the box the letter, which her telegram had repeated, readdressed by Gyp from the Red House. And a faint uneasiness at its having gone down there passed through him. He spent a restless evening at the club, playing cards and losing; sat up late in his chambers over a case; had a hard morning's work, and only now that he was nearing Gyp, realized how utterly he had lost the straightforward simplicity of things.

When he reached the house and found that she had gone out riding alone, his uneasiness increased. Why had she not waited as usual for him to ride with her? And he paced up and down the garden, where the wind was melancholy in the boughs of the walnut-tree that had lost all its leaves. Little Gyp was out for her walk, and only poor old Ossy kept him company. Had she not expected him by the usual train? He would go and try to find out. He changed and went to the stables. Old Pettance was sitting on a corn-bin, examining an aged Ruff's Guide, which contained records of his long-past glory, scored under by a pencil: " June Stakes: Agility. E. Pettance 3rd." " Tidport Selling H'Cap: Dorothea, E. Pettance, o."

" Salisbury Cup: Also ran Plum Pudding, E. Pettance,"
with other triumphs. He got up, saying:

" Good-afternoon, sir; windy afternoon, sir. The
mistress has been gone out over two hours, sir. She
wouldn't take me with 'er."

" Hurry up, then, and saddle Hotspur."

" Yes, sir; very good, sir."

Over two hours! He went up on to the downs,
by the way they generally came home, and for an
hour he rode, keeping a sharp lookout for any sign of
her. No use; and he turned home, hot and uneasy.
On the hall table were her riding-whip and gloves.
His heart cleared, and he ran upstairs. She was doing
her hair and turned her head sharply as he entered.
Hurrying across the room he had the absurd feeling
that she was standing at bay. She drew back, bent
her face away from him, and said:

" No! Don't pretend! Anything's better than
pretence!"

He had never seen her look or speak like that—her
face so hard, her eyes so stabbing! And he recoiled
dumbfounded.

" What's the matter, Gyp?"

" Nothing. Only—don't pretend!" And, turning
to the glass, she went on twisting and coiling up her
hair.

She looked lovely, flushed from her ride in the wind,
and he had a longing to seize her in his arms. But
her face stopped him. With fear and a sort of anger,
he said:

" You might explain, I think."

An evil little smile crossed her face.

" *You* can do that. I am in the dark."

" I don't in the least understand what you mean."

" Don't you ?" There was something deadly in her utter disregard of him, while her fingers moved swiftly about her dark, shining hair—something so appallingly sudden in this hostility that Summerhay felt a peculiar sensation in his head, as if he must knock it against something. He sat down on the side of the bed. Was it that letter ? But how ? It had not been opened. He said:

" What on earth has happened, Gyp, since I went up yesterday ? Speak out, and don't keep me like this !"

She turned and looked at him.

" Don't pretend that you're upset because you can't kiss me ! Don't be false, Bryan ! You know it's been pretence for months."

Summerhay's voice grew high.

" I think you've gone mad. I don't know what you mean."

" Oh, yes, you do. Did you get a letter yesterday marked ' Immediate ' ?"

Ah ! So it *was* that ! To meet the definite, he hardened, and said stubbornly:

" Yes; from Diana Leyton. Do you object ?"

" No; only, how do you think it got back to you from here so quickly ?"

He said dully:

" I don't know. By post, I suppose."

" No; I put it in your letter-box myself—at half-past five."

Summerhay's mind was trained to quickness, and the full significance of those words came home to him at once. He stared at her fixedly.

" I suppose you saw us, then."

" Yes."

He got up, made a helpless movement, and said:

"Oh, Gyp, don't! Don't be so hard! I swear by——"

Gyp gave a little laugh, turned her back, and went on coiling at her hair. And again that horrid feeling that he must knock his head against something rose in Summerhay. He said helplessly:

"I only gave her tea. Why not? She's my cousin. It's nothing! Why should you think the worst of me? She asked to see my chambers. Why not? I couldn't refuse."

"Your *empty* chambers? Don't, Bryan—it's piti-ful! I can't bear to hear you."

At that lash of the whip, Summerhay turned and said:

"It pleases you to think the worst, then?"

Gyp stopped the movement of her fingers and looked round at him.

"I've always told you you were perfectly free. Do you think I haven't felt it going on for months? There comes a moment when pride revolts—that's all. Don't lie to me, *please!*"

"I am not in the habit of lying." But still he did not go. That awful feeling of encirclement, of a net round him, through which he could not break—a net which he dimly perceived even in his resentment to have been spun by himself, by that cursed intimacy, kept from her all to no purpose—beset him more closely every minute. Could he not make her see the truth, that it was only her he *really* loved? And he said:

"Gyp, I swear to you there's nothing but one kiss, and that was not——"

A shudder went through her from head to foot; she cried out:

" Oh, please go away !"

He went up to her, put his hands on her shoulders, and said:

" It's only you I really love. I swear it ! Why don't you believe me ? You must believe me. You can't be so wicked as not to. It's foolish—foolish ! Think of our life—think of our love—think of all——"

Her face was frozen; he loosened his grasp of her, and muttered: " Oh, your pride is awful !"

" Yes, it's all I've got. Lucky for you I have it. You can go to her when you like."

" Go to her ! It's absurd—I couldn't—— If you wish, I'll never see her again."

She turned away to the glass.

" Oh, don't ! What *is* the use ?"

Nothing is harder for one whom life has always spoiled than to find his best and deepest feelings disbelieved in. At that moment, Summerhay meant absolutely what he said. The girl was nothing to him ! If she was pursuing him, how could he help it ? And he could not make Gyp believe it ! How awful ! How truly terrible ! How unjust and unreasonable of her ! And why ? What had he done that she should be so unbelieving—should think him such a shallow scoundrel ? Could he help the girl's kissing him ? Help her being fond of him ? Help having a man's nature ? Unreasonable, unjust, ungenerous ! And giving her a furious look, he went out.

He went down to his study, flung himself on the sofa and turned his face to the wall. Devilish ! But he had not been there five minutes before his anger seemed childish and evaporated into the chill of deadly and insistent fear. He was perceiving himself up against much more than a mere incident, up against her nature—its pride and scepticism—yes—and the very depth and singleness of her love. While she wanted nothing but him, he wanted and took so much else. He perceived this but dimly, as part of that feeling that he could not break through, of the irritable longing to put his head down and butt his way out, no matter what the obstacles. What was coming? How long was this state of things to last? He got up and began to pace the room, his hands clasped behind him, his head thrown back; and every now and then he shook that head, trying to free it from this feeling of being held in chancery. And then Diana! He had said he would not see her again. But was that possible? After that kiss—after that last look back at him! How? What could he say—do? How break so suddenly? Then, at memory of Gyp's face, he shivered. Ah, how wretched it all was! There must be some way out—some way! Surely some way out! For when first, in the wood of life, fatality halts, turns her dim dark form among the trees, shows her pale cheek and those black eyes of hers, shows with awful swiftness her strange reality—men would be fools indeed who admitted that they saw her!

IX

GYP stayed in her room doing little things—as a woman will when she is particularly wretched—sewing pale ribbons into her garments, polishing her rings. And the devil that had entered into her when she woke that morning, having had his fling, slunk away, leaving the old bewildered misery. She had stabbed her lover with words and looks, felt pleasure in stabbing, and now was bitterly sad. What use—what satisfaction ? How by vengeful prickings cure the deep wound, disperse the canker in her life ? How heal herself by hurting him whom she loved so ? If he came up again now and made but a sign, she would throw herself into his arms. But hours passed, and he did not come, and she did not go down—too truly miserable. It grew dark, but she did not draw the curtains; the sight of the windy moonlit garden and the leaves driving across brought a melancholy distraction. Little Gyp came in and prattled. There was a tree blown down, and she had climbed on it; they had picked up two baskets of acorns, and the pigs had been so greedy; and she had been blown away, so that Betty had had to run after her. And Baryn was walking in the study; he was so busy he had only given her one kiss.

When she was gone, Gyp opened the window and let the wind full into her face. If only it would blow out of her heart this sickening sense that all was over, no matter how he might pretend to love her out of pity! In a nature like hers, so doubting and self-distrustful, confidence, once shaken to the roots, could never be restored. A proud nature that went all lengths in love could never be content with a half-love. She had been born too doubting, proud, and jealous, yet made to love too utterly. She—who had been afraid of love, and when it came had fought till it swept her away; who, since then, had lived for love and nothing else, who gave all, and wanted all—knew for certain and for ever that she could not have all.

It was " nothing," he had said! Nothing! That for months he had been thinking at least a little of another woman besides herself. She believed what he had told her, that there had been no more than a kiss—but was it nothing that they had reached that kiss? This girl—this cousin—who held all the cards, had everything on her side—the world, family influence, security of life; yes, and more, so terribly much more—a man's longing for the young and unawakened. This girl he could marry! It was this thought which haunted her. A mere momentary outbreak of man's natural wildness she could forgive and forget—oh, yes! It was the feeling that it was a girl, his own cousin, besieging him, dragging him away, that was so dreadful. Ah, how horrible it was—how horrible! How, in decent pride, keep him from her, fetter him?

She heard him come up to his dressing-room, and while he was still there, stole out and down. Life must go on, the servants be hoodwinked, and so forth. She went to the piano and played, turning the dagger in her heart, or hoping forlornly that music might work some miracle. He came in presently and stood by the fire, silent.

Dinner, with the talk needful to blinding the house-

hold—for what is more revolting than giving away the
sufferings of the heart?—was almost unendurable,
and directly it was over, they went, he to his study,
she back to the piano. There she sat, ready to strike
the notes if anyone came in; and tears fell on the
hands that rested in her lap. With all her soul she
longed to go and clasp him in her arms and cry: " I
don't care—I don't care ! Do what you like—go to
her—if only you'll love me a little !" And yet to
love—a *little !* Was it possible ? Not to her !

In sheer misery she went upstairs and to bed. She
heard him come up and go into his dressing-room—
and, at last, in the firelight saw him kneeling by her.

" Gyp !"

She raised herself and threw her arms round him.
Such an embrace a drowning woman might have
given. Pride and all were abandoned in an effort to
feel him close once more, to recover the irrecoverable
past. For a long time she listened to his pleading,
explanations, justifications, his protestations of un-
dying love—strange to her and painful, yet so boyish
and pathetic. She soothed him, clasping his head to
her breast, gazing out at the flickering fire. In that
hour, she rose to a height above herself. What
happened to her own heart did not matter so long as
he was happy, and had all that he wanted with her
and away from her—if need be, always away from
her.

But, when he had gone to sleep, a terrible time
began; for in the small hours, when things are at
their worst, she could not keep back her weeping,
though she smothered it into the pillow. It woke
him, and all began again; the burden of her cry:
" It's gone !" the burden of his: " It's *not*—can't you

see it isn't ?" Till, at last, that awful feeling that
he must knock his head against the wall made him leap
up and tramp up and down like a beast in a cage—
the cage of the impossible. For, as in all human
tragedies, both were right according to their natures.
She gave him all herself, wanted all in return, and
could not have it. He wanted her, the rest besides,
and no complaining, and could not have it. He did
not admit impossibility; she did.

At last came another of those pitying lulls till he
went to sleep in her arms. Long she lay awake,
staring at the darkness, admitting despair, trying to
find how to bear it, not succeeding. Impossible to
cut his other life away from him—impossible that,
while he lived it, this girl should not be tugging him
away from her. Impossible to watch and question
him. Impossible to live dumb and blind, accepting
the crumbs left over, showing nothing. Would it have
been better if they had been married ? But then it
would have been the same—reversed; perhaps worse !
The roots were so much deeper than that. He was
not single-hearted and she was. In spite of all that
he said, she knew he didn't really want to give up that
girl. How could he ? Even if the girl would let him
go ! And slowly there formed within her a gruesome
little plan to test him. Then, ever so gently withdrawing her arms, she turned over and slept, exhausted.

Next morning, remorselessly carrying out that plan,
she forced herself to smile and talk as if nothing had
happened, watching the relief in his face, his obvious
delight at the change, with a fearful aching in her
heart. She waited till he was ready to go down, and
then, still smiling, said:

" Forget all about yesterday, darling. Promise me

you won't let it make any difference. You must keep up your friendship; you mustn't lose anything. I shan't mind; I shall be quite happy." He knelt down and leaned his forehead against her waist. And, stroking his hair, she repeated: " I shall only be happy if you take everything that comes your way. I shan't mind a bit." And she watched his face that had lost its trouble.

" Do you really mean that ?"

" Yes; really !"

" Then you do see that it's nothing, never has been anything—compared with you—never !"

He had accepted her crucifixion. A black wave surged into her heart.

" It would be so difficult and awkward for you to give up that intimacy. It would hurt your cousin so."

She saw the relief deepen in his face and suddenly laughed. He got up from his knees and stared at her.

" Oh, Gyp, for God's sake don't begin again !"

But she went on laughing; then, with a sob, turned away and buried her face in her hands. To all his prayers and kisses she answered nothing, and breaking away from him, she rushed toward the door. A wild thought possessed her. Why go on ? If she were dead, it would be all right for him, quiet—peaceful, quiet—for them all ! But he had thrown himself in the way.

" Gyp, for heaven's sake ! I'll give her up—of course I'll give her up. Do—do—be reasonable ! I don't care a finger-snap for her compared with you !"

And presently there came another of those lulls that both were beginning to know were mere pauses of exhaustion. They were priceless all the same, for the heart cannot go on feeling at that rate.

It was Sunday morning, the church-bells ringing no wind, a lull in the sou'westerly gale—one of those calms that fall in the night and last, as a rule, twelve or fifteen hours, and the garden all strewn with leaves of every hue, from green spotted with yellow to deep copper.

Summerhay was afraid; he kept with her all the morning, making all sorts of little things to do in her company. But he gradually lost his fear, she seemed so calm now, and his was a nature that bore trouble badly, ever impatient to shake it off. And then, after lunch, the spirit-storm beat up again, with a swiftness that showed once more how deceptive were those lulls, how fearfully deep and lasting the wound. He had simply asked her whether he should try to match something for her when he went up, to-morrow. She was silent a moment, then answered:

" Oh, no, thanks; you'll have other things to do; people to see !"

The tone of her voice, the expression on her face showed him, with a fresh force of revelation, what paralysis had fallen on his life. If he could not re-convince her of his love, he would be in perpetual fear —that he might come back and find her gone, fear that she might even do something terrible to herself. He looked at her with a sort of horror, and, without a word, went out of the room. The feeling that he must hit his head against something was on him once more, and once more he sought to get rid of it by tramping up and down. Great God ! Such a little thing, such fearful consequences ! All her balance, her sanity almost, destroyed. Was what he had done so very dreadful ? He could not help Diana loving him !

In the night, Gyp had said: " You are cruel. Do you think there is any man in the world that I wouldn't hate the sight of if I knew that even to see him gave you a moment's pain ?" It was true—he felt it was true. But one couldn't hate a girl simply because she loved you; at least he couldn't—not even to save Gyp pain. That was not reasonable, not possible. But did that difference between a man and a woman necessarily mean that Gyp loved him so much more than he loved her ? Could she not see things in proportion ? See that a man might want, did want, other friendships, even passing moments of passion, and yet could love her just the same ? She thought him cruel, called him cruel—what for ? Because he had kissed a girl who had kissed him; because he liked talking to her, and—yes, might even lose his head with her. But cruel ! He was not ! Gyp would always be first with him. He must *make* her see—but how ? Give up everything ? Give up—Diana ? (Truth is so funny—it will out even in a man's thoughts !) Well, and he could ! His feeling was not deep—that was God's truth ! But it would be difficult, awkward, brutal to cut her suddenly, completely ! It could be done, though, sooner than that Gyp should think him cruel to her. It could be—should be done !

Only, would it be any use ? Would she believe ? Would she not always now be suspecting him when he was away from her, whatever he did ? Must he then sit down here in inactivity ? And a gust of anger with her swept him. Why should she treat him as if he were utterly unreliable ? Or—was he ? He stood still. When Diana had put her arms round his neck, he could no more have resisted answering her kiss than he could now fly through the window and over

those poplar trees. But he was not a blackguard, not
cruel, not a liar! How could he have helped it all?
The only way would have been never to have answered
the girl's first letter, nearly a year ago. How could
he foresee? And, since then, all so gradual, and
nothing, really, or almost nothing. Again the surge
of anger swelled his heart. She must have read the
letter which had been under that cursed bust of old
Voltaire all those months ago. The poison had been
working ever since! And in sudden fury at that
miserable mischance, he drove his fist into the bronze
face. The bust fell over, and Summerhay looked
stupidly at his bruised hand. A silly thing to do!
But it had quenched his anger. He only saw Gyp's
face now—so pitifully unhappy. Poor darling! What
could he do? If only she would believe! And again
he had the sickening conviction that whatever he did
would be of no avail. He could never get back, was
only at the beginning, of a trouble that had no end.
And, like a rat in a cage, his mind tried to rush out
of this entanglement now at one end, now at the other.
Ah, well! Why bruise your head against walls? If
it was hopeless—let it go! And, shrugging his
shoulders, he went out to the stables, and told old
Pettance to saddle Hotspur. While he stood there
waiting, he thought: 'Shall I ask her to come?' But
he could not stand another bout of misery—must
have rest! And mounting, he rode up towards the
downs.

Hotspur, the sixteen-hand brown horse, with not a
speck of white, that Gyp had ridden hunting the day
she first saw Summerhay, was nine years old now.
His master's two faults as a horseman—a habit of
thrusting, and not too light hands—had encouraged

his rather hard mouth, and something had happened
in the stables to-day to put him into a queer temper;
or perhaps he felt—as horses will—the disturbance
raging within his rider. At any rate, he gave an exhibition of his worst qualities, and Summerhay derived
perverse pleasure from that waywardness. He rode
a good hour up there; then, hot, with aching arms—
for the brute was pulling like the devil !—he made his
way back toward home and entered what little Gyp
called " the wild," those two rough sedgy fields with
the linhay in the corner where they joined. There
was a gap in the hedge-growth of the bank between
them, and at this he put Hotspur at speed. The horse
went over like a bird; and for the first time since
Diana's kiss Summerhay felt a moment's joy. He
turned him round and sent him at it again, and again
Hotspur cleared it beautifully. But the animal's
blood was up now. Summerhay could hardly hold
him. Muttering: " Oh, you *brute*, don't pull !" he
jagged the horse's mouth. There darted into his mind
Gyp's word: " Cruel !" And, viciously, in one of those
queer nerve-crises that beset us all, he struck the
pulling horse.

They were cantering toward the corner where the
fields joined, and suddenly he was aware that he
could no more hold the beast than if a steam-engine
had been under him. Straight at the linhay Hotspur
dashed, and Summerhay thought: ' My God ! He'll
kill himself !' Straight at the old stone linhay,
covered by the great ivy bush. Right at it—into it !
Summerhay ducked his head. Not low enough—the
ivy concealed a beam ! A sickening crash ! Torn
backward out of the saddle, he fell on his back in a

27

pool of leaves and mud. And the horse, slithering round the linhay walls, checked in his own length, unhurt, snorting, frightened, came out, turning his wild eyes on his master, who never stirred, then trotted back into the field, throwing up his head.

X

WHEN, at her words, Summerhay went out of the room, Gyp's heart sank. All the morning she had tried so hard to keep back her despairing jealousy, and now at the first reminder had broken down again. It was beyond her strength! To live day after day knowing that he, up in London, was either seeing that girl or painfully abstaining from seeing her! And then, when he returned, to be to him just what she had been, to show nothing—would it ever be possible? Hardest to bear was what seemed to her the falsity of his words, maintaining that he still really loved her. If he did, how could he hesitate one second? Would not the very thought of the girl be abhorrent to him? He would have shown that, not merely said it among other wild things. Words were no use when they contradicted action. She, who loved with every bit of her, could not grasp that a man can really love and want one woman and yet, at the same time, be attracted by another.

That sudden fearful impulse of the morning to make away with herself and end it for them both recurred so vaguely that it hardly counted in her struggles; the conflict centred now round the question whether life would be less utterly miserable if she withdrew from him and went back to Mildenham. Life without him? That was impossible! Life with him? Just as impossible, it seemed! There comes a point of mental anguish when the alternatives between which one swings, equally hopeless, become each so monstrous that the mind does not really work at all, but rushes helplessly from one to the other, no longer trying to decide, waiting on fate. So in Gyp that Sunday afternoon, doing little things all the time—mending a hole in one of his gloves, brushing and applying ointment to old Ossy, sorting bills and letters.

At five o'clock, knowing little Gyp must soon be back from her walk, and feeling unable to take part in gaiety, she went up and put on her hat. She turned from contemplation of her face with disgust. Since it was no longer the only face for him, what was the use of beauty? She slipped out by the side gate and went down toward the river. The lull was over; the south-west wind had begun sighing through the trees again, and gorgeous clouds were piled up from the horizon into the pale blue. She stood by the river watching its grey stream, edged by a scum of torn-off twigs and floating leaves, watched the wind shivering through the spoiled plume-branches of the willows. And, standing there, she had a sudden longing for her father; he alone could help her—just a little—by his quietness, and his love, by his mere presence.

She turned away and went up the lane again, avoiding the inn and the riverside houses, walking slowly, her head down. And a thought came, her first hopeful thought. Could they not travel—go round the world? Would he give up his work for that—that chance to break the spell? Dared she propose it? But would even that be anything more than a putting-off? If she was not enough for him now, would she not be still less, if his work were cut away? Still, it was a gleam, a gleam in the blackness. She came in at the far end of the fields they called "the wild."

A rose-leaf hue tinged the white cloud-banks, which towered away to the east beyond the river; and peeping over that mountain-top was the moon, fleecy and unsubstantial in the flax-blue sky. It was one of nature's moments of wild colour. The oak-trees above the hedgerows had not lost their leaves, and in the darting, rain-washed light from the setting sun, had a sheen of old gold with heart of ivy-green; the half-stripped beeches flamed with copper; the russet tufts of the ash-trees glowed. And past Gyp, a single leaf blown off, went soaring, turning over and over, going up on the rising wind, up—up, higher—higher into the sky, till it was lost—away.

The rain had drenched the long grass, and she turned back. At the gate beside the linhay, a horse was standing. It whinnied. Hotspur, saddled, bridled, with no rider ! Why ? Where—then ? Hastily she undid the latch, ran through, and saw Summerhay lying in the mud—on his back, with eyes wide-open, his forehead and hair all blood. Some leaves had dropped on him. God ! O God ! His eyes had no sight, his lips no breath; his heart did not beat; the leaves had dropped even on his face—in the blood on his poor head. Gyp raised him—stiffened, cold as ice ! She gave one cry, and fell, embracing his dead, stiffened body with all her strength, kissing his lips, his eyes, his broken forehead; clasping, warming him, trying to pass life into him; till, at last, she, too, lay still, her lips on his cold lips, her body on his cold body in the mud and the fallen leaves, while the wind crept and rustled in the ivy, and went over with the scent of rain. Close by, the horse, uneasy, put his head down and sniffed at her, then, backing away, neighed, and broke into a wild gallop round the field. . . .

Old Pettance, waiting for Summerhay's return to stable-up for the night, heard that distant neigh and went to the garden gate, screwing up his little eyes against the sunset. He could see a loose horse galloping down there in " the wild," where no horse should be, and thinking: ' There now; that artful devil's broke away from the guv'nor ! Now I'll 'ave to ketch 'im !' he went back, got some oats, and set forth at the best gait of his stiff-jointed feet. The old horseman characteristically did not think of accidents. The guv'nor had got off, no doubt, to unhitch that heavy gate—the one you had to lift. That 'orse—he was a masterpiece of mischief ! His difference with the animal still rankled in a mind that did not easily forgive.

Half an hour later, he entered the lighted kitchen shaking and gasping, tears rolling down his furrowed cheeks into the corners of his gargoyle's mouth, and panted out:

" O, my Gord ! Fetch the farmer—fetch an 'urdle ! O my Gord ! Betty, you and cook—I can't get 'er off him. She don't speak. I felt her—all cold. Come on, you sluts—quick ! O my Gord ! The poor guv'nor ! That 'orse must 'a' galloped into the linhay and killed him. I've see'd the marks on the devil's shoulder where he rubbed it scrapin' round the wall. Come on—come on ! Fetch an 'urdle or she'll die there on him in the mud. Put the child to bed and get the doctor, and send a wire to London, to the major, to come sharp. Oh, blarst you all—keep your 'eads ! What's the good o' howlin' and blubberin' !"

In the whispering corner of those fields, light from a lantern and the moon fell on the old stone linhay, on the ivy and the broken gate, on the mud, the golden leaves, and the two quiet bodies clasped together. Gyp's consciousness had flown; there seemed no difference between them. And presently, over the rushy grass, a procession moved back in the wind and the moonlight—two hurdles, two men carrying one, two women and a man the other, and, behind, old Pettance and the horse.

XI

WHEN Gyp recovered a consciousness, whose flight had been mercifully renewed with morphia, she was in her bed, and her first drowsy movement was toward her mate. With eyes still closed, she turned, as she was wont, and put out her hand to touch him before she dozed off again. There was no warmth, no substance; through her mind, still away in the mists of morphia, the thoughts passed vague and lonely: ' Ah, yes, in London !' And she turned on her back. London ! Something—something up there ! She opened her eyes. So the fire had kept in all night ! Someone was in a chair there, or—was she dreaming ! And suddenly, without knowing why, she began breathing hurriedly in little half-sobbing gasps. The figure moved, turned her face in the firelight. Betty ! Gyp closed her eyes. An icy sweat had broken out all over her. A dream ! In a whisper, she said:

" Betty !"

The muffled answer came.

" Yes, my darlin'."

" What is it ?"

No answer; then a half-choked, " Don't 'ee think—— —don't 'ee think ! Your Daddy'll be here directly, my sweetie !"

Gyp's eyes, wide open, passed from the firelight and that rocking figure to the little chink of light that was hardly light as yet, coming in at one corner of the curtain. She was remembering. Her tongue stole out and passed over her lips; beneath the bedclothes she folded both her hands tight across her heart. Then she was not dead with him—not dead! Not gone back with him into the ground—not—— And suddenly there flickered in her a flame of maniacal hatred. They were keeping her alive! A writhing smile forced its way up on to her parched lips.

"Betty, I'm so thirsty—so thirsty. Get me a cup of tea."

The stout form heaved itself from the chair and came toward the bed.

"Yes, my lovey, at once. It'll do you good. That's a brave girl."

"Yes."

The moment the door clicked to, Gyp sprang up. Her veins throbbed; her whole soul was alive with cunning. She ran to the wardrobe, seized her long fur coat, slipped her bare feet into her slippers, wound a piece of lace round her head, and opened the door. All dark and quiet! Holding her breath, stifling the sound of her feet, she glided down the stairs, slipped back the chain of the front door, opened it, and fled. Like a shadow she passed across the grass, out of the garden gate, down the road under the black dripping trees. The beginning of light was mixing its grey hue into the darkness; she could just see her feet among the puddles on the road. She heard the grinding and whirring of a motor-car on its top gear approaching up the hill, and cowered away against the hedge. Its light came searching along, picking out with a mysterious momentary brightness the bushes and tree-trunks, making the wet road gleam. Gyp saw the chauffeur turn his head back at her, then the car's body passed up into darkness, and its tail-light

was all that was left to see. Perhaps that car was
going to the Red House with her father, the doctor,
somebody, helping to keep her alive! The maniacal
hate flared up in her again; she flew on. The light
grew; a man with a dog came out of a gate she had
passed, and called "Hallo!" She did not turn her
head. She had lost her slippers, and ran with bare
feet, unconscious of stones, or the torn-off branches
strewing the road, making for the lane that ran right
down to the river, a little to the left of the inn, the
lane of yesterday, where the bank was free.

She turned into the lane; dimly, a hundred or more
yards away, she could see the willows, the width of
lighter grey that was the river. The river—"Away,
my rolling rivei!"—the river—and the happiest hours
of all her life! If he were anywhere, she would find
him there, where he had sung, and lain with his head
on her breast, and swum and splashed about her;
where she had dreamed, and seen beauty, and loved
him so! She reached the bank. Cold and grey and
silent, swifter than yesterday, the stream was flowing
by, its dim far shore brightening slowly in the first
break of dawn. And Gyp stood motionless, drawing
her breath in gasps after her long run; her knees
trembled; gave way. She sat down on the wet grass,
clasping her arms round her drawn-up legs, rocking
herself to and fro, and her loosened hair fell over her
face. The blood beat in her ears; her heart felt
suffocated; all her body seemed on fire, yet numb.
She sat, moving her head up and down—as the head
of one moves that is gasping her last—waiting for
breath—breath and strength to let go life, to slip
down into the grey water. And that queer apartness
from self, which is the property of fever, came on her,

so that she seemed to see herself sitting there, waiting, and thought: ' I shall see myself dead, floating among the reeds. I shall see the birds wondering above me !' And, suddenly, she broke into a storm of dry sobbing, and all things vanished from her, save just the rocking of her body, the gasping of her breath, and the sound of it in her ears. Her boy—her boy— and his poor hair ! " Away, my rolling river !" Swaying over, she lay face down, clasping at the wet grass and the earth.

The sun rose, laid a pale bright streak along the water, and hid himself again. A robin twittered in the willows; a leaf fell on her bare ankle.

Winton, who had been hunting on Saturday, had returned to town on Sunday by the evening train, and gone straight to his club for some supper. There, falling asleep over his cigar, he had to be awakened when they desired to close the club for the night. It was past two when he reached Bury Street and found a telegram.

" Something dreadful happened to Mr. Summerhay. Come quick.—BETTY."

Never had he so cursed the loss of his hand as during the time that followed, when Markey had to dress, help his master, pack bags, and fetch a taxi equipped for so long a journey. At half-past three they started. The whole way down, Winton, wrapped in his fur coat, sat a little forward on his seat, ready to put his head through the window and direct the driver. It was a wild night, and he would not let Markey, whose chest was not strong, go outside to act as guide. Twice that silent one, impelled by feelings too vehement even for his respectful taciturnity, had spoken.

" That'll be bad for Miss Gyp, sir."

" Bad, yes—terrible."

And later:

" D'you think it means he's dead, sir ?"

Winton answered sombrely:

" God knows, Markey ! We must hope for the best."

Dead ! Could Fate be cruel enough to deal one so soft and loving such a blow ? And he kept saying to himself: " Courage. Be ready for the worst. Be ready."

But the figures of Betty and a maid at the open garden gate, in the breaking darkness, standing there wringing their hands, were too much for his stoicism. Leaping out, he cried:

" What is it, woman ? Quick !"

" Oh, sir ! My dear's gone. I left her a moment to get her a cup of tea. And she's run out in the cold !"

Winton stood for two seconds as if turned to stone. Then, taking Betty by the shoulder, he asked quietly:

" What happened to *him ?*"

Betty could not answer, but the maid said:

" The horse killed him at that linhay, sir, down in ' the wild.' And the mistress was unconscious till quarter of an hour ago."

" Which way did she go ?"

" Out here, sir; the door and the gate was open— can't tell which way."

Through Winton flashed one dreadful thought: The river !

" Turn the cab round ! Stay in, Markey ! Betty and you, girl, go down to ' the wild,' and search there at once. Yes ? What is it ?"

The driver was leaning out.

" As we came up the hill, sir, I see a lady or something in a long dark coat with white on her head, against the hedge."

" Right ! Drive down again sharp, and use your eyes."

At such moments, thought is impossible, and a feverish use of every sense takes its place. But of thought there was no need, for the gardens of villas and the inn blocked the river at all but one spot. Winton stopped the car where the narrow lane branched down to the bank, and jumping out, ran. By instinct he ran silently on the grass edge, and Markey, imitating, ran behind. When he came in sight of a black shape lying on the bank, he suffered a moment of intense agony, for he thought it was just a dark garment thrown away. Then he saw it move, and, holding up his hand for Markey to stand still, walked on alone, tiptoeing in the grass, his heart swelling with a sort of rapture. Stealthily moving round between that prostrate figure and the water, he knelt down and said, as best he could, for the husk in his throat :

" My darling !"

Gyp raised her head and stared at him. Her white face, with eyes unnaturally dark and large, and hair falling all over it, was strange to him—the face of grief itself, stripped of the wrappings of form. And he knew not what to do, how to help or comfort, how to save. He could see so clearly in her eyes the look of a wild animal at the moment of its capture, and instinct made him say :

" I lost her just as cruelly, Gyp."

He saw the words reach her brain, and that wild look waver. Stretching out his arm, he drew her

close to him till her cheek was against his, her shaking
body against him and kept murmuring:

"For my sake, Gyp; for my sake!"

When, with Markey's aid, he had got her to the
cab, they took her, not back to the house, but to the
inn. She was in high fever, and soon delirious. By
noon, Aunt Rosamund and Mrs. Markey, summoned
by telegram, had arrived; and the whole inn was taken
lest there should be any noise to disturb her.

At five o'clock, Winton was summoned downstairs
to the little so-called reading-room. A tall woman
was standing at the window, shading her eyes with
the back of a gloved hand. Though they had lived
so long within ten miles of each other he only knew
Lady Summerhay by sight, and he waited for the
poor woman to speak first. She said in a low voice:

"There is nothing to say; only, I thought I must
see you. How is she?"

"Delirious."

They stood in silence a full minute, before she
whispered:

"My poor boy! Did you see him—his forehead?"
Her lips quivered. "I will take him back home."
And tears rolled, one after the other, slowly down her
flushed face under her veil. Poor woman! Poor
woman! She had turned to the window, passing her
handkerchief up under the veil, staring out at the
little strip of darkening lawn, and Winton, too, stared
out into that mournful daylight. At last, he said:

"I will send you all his things, except—except
anything that might help my poor girl."

She turned quickly.

"And so it's ended like this! Major Winton, is
there anything behind—were they really happy?"

Suddenly, she said, very low:

"And yet I wouldn't have been without it."

She was sitting, her hands clasped in her lap, two red spots high in her cheeks, her eyes shining strangely, the faint smile still on her lips. And Winton, staring with narrowed eyes, thought: 'Love! Beyond measure—beyond death—it nearly kills. But one wouldn't have been without it. Why?'

Three days later, leaving Gyp with his sister, he went back to Mildenham to start the necessary alterations in the cottages. He had told no one he was coming, and walked up from the station on a perfect June day, bright and hot. When he turned through the drive gate, into the beech-tree avenue, the leaf-shadows were thick on the ground, with golden gleams of the invincible sunlight thrusting their way through. The grey boles, the vivid green leaves, those glistening sun-shafts through the shade, entranced him, coming from the dusty road. Down in the very middle of the avenue, a small, white figure was standing, as if looking out for him. He heard a shrill shout.

"Oh, Grandy, you've come back—you've come back! What *fun!*"

Winton took her curls in his hand, and, looking into her face said:

"Well, my gipsy-bird, will you give me one of these?"

Little Gyp gazed at him with flying eyes, and, hugging his legs, answered furiously:

"Yes; because I love you. *Pull!*"

BILLING AND SONS, LTD. PRINTERS, GUILDFORD, ENGLAND

could make a sort of home at Mildenham where poor children could come to stay and get good air and food. There are such thousands of them."

Strangely moved by this, the first wish he had heard her express since the tragedy, Winton took her hand, and, looking at it as if for answer to his question, said:

" My dear, are you strong enough ?"

" Quite. There's nothing wrong with me now except here." She drew his hand to her and pressed it against her heart. " What's given, one can't get back. I can't help it; I would if I could. It's been so dreadful for you. I'm so sorry." Winton made an unintelligible sound, and she went on: " If I had them to see after, I shouldn't be able to think so much; the more I had to do the better. Good for our gipsy-bird, too, to have them there. I should like to begin it at once."

Winton nodded. Anything that she felt could do her good—anything !

" Yes, yes," he said; " I quite see—you could use the two old cottages to start with, and we can easily run up anything you want."

" Only let me do it all, won't you ?"

At that touch of her old self, Winton smiled. She should do everything, pay for everything, bring a whole street of children down, if it would give her any comfort !

" Rosamund 'll help you find 'em," he muttered. " She's first-rate at all that sort of thing." Then, looking at her fixedly, he added: " Courage, my soul; it'll all come back some day."

Gyp forced herself to smile. Watching her, he understood only too well the child's saying: " Mum lives away somewhere, I think."

proposed a visit to London. To his surprise, she acquiesced without hesitation. They went up in Whit-week. While they were passing Widrington, he forced himself to an unnatural spurt of talk; and it was not till fully quarter of an hour later that, glancing stealthily round his paper, he saw her sitting motionless, her face turned to the fields and tears rolling down it. And he dared not speak, dared not try to comfort her. She made no sound, her face no movement; only, those tears kept rolling down. And, behind his paper, Winton's eyes narrowed and retreated; his face hardened till the skin seemed tight drawn over the bones, and every inch of him quivered.

The usual route from the station to Bury Street was "up," and the cab went by narrow by-streets, town lanes where the misery of the world is on show, where ill-looking men, draggled and overdriven women, and the jaunty ghosts of little children in gutters and on doorsteps proclaim, by every feature of their clay-coloured faces and every movement of their underfed bodies, the post-datement of the millennium; where the lean and smutted houses have a look of dissolution indefinitely put off, and there is no more trace of beauty than in a sewer. Gyp, leaning forward, looked out, as one does after a long sea voyage; Winton felt her hand slip into his and squeeze it hard.

That evening after dinner—in the room he had furnished for her mother, where the satinwood chairs, the little Jacobean bureau, the old brass candelabra were still much as they had been just on thirty years ago—she said:

"Dad, I've been thinking. Would you mind if I

he had now and then glimpsed. Of the actual tragedy, her wandering spirit did not seem conscious; her lips were always telling the depth of her love, always repeating the dread of losing his; except when they would give a whispering laugh, uncanny and enchanting, as at some gleam of perfect happiness. Those little laughs were worst of all to hear; they never failed to bring tears into his eyes. But he drew a certain gruesome comfort from the conclusion slowly forced on him, that Summerhay's tragic death had cut short a situation which might have had an even more tragic issue. One night in the big chair at the side of her bed, he woke from a doze to see her eyes fixed on him. They were different; they saw, were her own eyes again. Her lips moved.

" Dad."

" Yes, my pet."

" I remember everything."

At that dreadful little saying, Winton leaned forward and put his lips to her hand, that lay outside the clothes.

" Where is he buried ?"

" At Widrington."

" Yes."

It was rather a sigh than a word and, raising his head, Winton saw her eyes closed again. Now that the fever had gone, the white transparency of her cheeks and forehead against the dark lashes and hair was too startling. Was it a living face, or was its beauty that of death ?

He bent over. She was breathing—asleep.

28

as he just that coherent thread of the familiar, by which the fevered, without knowing it, perhaps find their way a little in the dark mazes where they wander. And he would think of her as she used to be—well and happy—adopting unconsciously the methods of those mental and other scientists whom he looked upon as quacks.

He was astonished by the number of inquirers, even people whom he had considered enemies left cards or sent their servants, forcing him to the conclusion that people of position are obliged to reserve their human kindness for those as good as dead. But the small folk touched him daily by their genuine concern for her whose grace and softness had won their hearts. One morning he received a letter forwarded from Bury Street.

"DEAR MAJOR WINTON,

"I have read a paragraph in the paper about poor Mr. Summerhay's death. And, oh, I feel so sorry for her! She was so good to me; I do feel it most dreadfully. If you think she would like to know how we all feel for her, you would tell her, wouldn't you? I do think it's cruel.

"Very faithfully yours,

"DAPHNE WING."

So they knew Summerhay's name—he had not somehow expected that. He did not answer, not knowing what to say.

During those days of fever, the hardest thing to bear was the sound of her rapid whisperings and mutterings—incoherent phrases that said so little and told so much. Sometimes he would cover his ears, to avoid hearing of that long stress of mind at which

Winton looked straight at her and answered:

"Ah, too happy!"

Without a quiver, he met those tear-darkened, dilated eyes straining at his; with a heavy sigh, she once more turned away, and, brushing her handkerchief across her face, drew down her veil.

It was not true—he knew from the mutterings of Gyp's fever—but no one, not even Summerhay's mother, should hear a whisper if he could help it. At the door, he murmured:

"I don't know whether my girl will get through, or what she will do after. When Fate hits, she hits too hard. And you! Good-bye."

Lady Summerhay pressed his outstretched hand.

"Good-bye," she said, in a strangled voice. "I wish you—good-bye." Then, turning abruptly, she hastened away.

Winton went back to his guardianship upstairs.

In the days that followed, when Gyp, robbed of memory, hung between life and death, Winton hardly left her room, that low room with creepered windows whence the river could be seen, gliding down under the pale November sunshine or black beneath the stars. He would watch it, fascinated, as one sometimes watches the relentless sea. He had snatched her as by a miracle from that snaky river.

He had refused to have a nurse. Aunt Rosamund and Mrs. Markey were skilled in sickness, and he could not bear that a strange person should listen to those delirious mutterings. His own part of the nursing was just to sit there and keep her secrets from the others—if he could. And he grudged every minute away from his post. He would stay for hours, with eyes fixed on her face. No one could supply so well

THE
WORKS OF JOHN GALSWORTHY

NOVELS.

THE FREELANDS. **6s.**

" Whether as an enthralling story, a suggestive study in characterization, or a presentation of social and political controversies, it equally makes its appeal, and it will, no doubt, at once take its permanent place among the very best of recent novels."—*Bookseller*.

" No one ought to miss this book. People will be delighted with it even though their own views upon ' the land ' may not entirely coincide with Mr. Galsworthy's. It is, in fact, one of the most important and interesting novels of the year, and is certain to enjoy a deservedly wide popularity."—*Ladies' Field*.

" Irony of the subtlest, sensitive observation, and a fine craft of construction and development, will captivate any reader who knows what's what."—*Punch*.

THE DARK FLOWER. **6s.**

" The book has great beauty; its analysis of character and motive is as thorough and sure as all Mr. Galsworthy's work; his choice of words and imagery being exquisite the theme lifts his narrative to noble heights of style. There is nothing either forced or tame, but always a beautiful candour and justice of expression. This estimate of ' The Dark Flower ' takes account of French, Russian, as well as English masterpieces."—*Pall Mall Gazette*.

" With this novel Mr. Galsworthy has added another to his series of powerful, vivid, and sincere studies of human nature. Perhaps the chief triumph of his fiction is its portraiture. His characters stand out with the firmness of life."—*Daily Telegraph*.

" An extraordinarily acute and truthful analysis of the effect of passion upon character. Mr. Galsworthy has not done anything better than ' The Dark Flower.' He attains by simple and unstudied means a trenchant and extremely human disclosure of the betraying second self that nature has hidden away in mankind for her own purposes. . . . The book has the impressiveness which the sincere and earnest expression of an original and cultured mind conveys."—*Country Life*.

" Our space is gone, and we have no room to commend Mr. Galsworthy's wholly delightful and absorbing style, no room in which to appreciate his masterly little cameos of portraiture. All we can do is to commend ' The Dark Flower ' to the reader, to say that the intensity and pure passion with which it has been written will sound for him new depths in Mr. Galsworthy."—*Sheffield Daily Telegraph*.

Also a cheap edition, 1s. net.

THE WORKS OF JOHN GALSWORTHY

THE COUNTRY HOUSE. 6s.

" If there are any competitions going on for ' the finest novel of the year,' the ' best-drawn character in modern fiction,' the ' biggest dear in fiction,' or the ' coming novelist,' my votes unhesitatingly go to ' The Country House,' Mr. Barter, Mrs. Pendyce, and Mr. John Galsworthy."—*Punch*.

" The novel is a brilliant one, flexible and rich in style, and extremely suggestive in its broad background of class life in town and country. In Part III. the author reaches his highest level . . . and the scenes may be set beside many pages of ' Pendennis.' "—*Nation*.

" The brilliant satirist here dissects a class which he represents as animated by a spirit of conscious virtue, complete intellectual repose, and aloofness from suffering of any kind. His insight is keen and the portraiture in the author's gallery will reward all who love the mirror of truth."—*Athenæum*.

Also a cheap edition, 1s. net.

FRATERNITY. 6s.

" ' Fraternity ' is as stimulating a book as any Mr. Galsworthy has written, and those who have read ' A Man of Property ' and ' The Country House ' will realize that that is saying a great deal."—*Morning Post*.

" It is difficult to remember any novel in the English language in which London has been so poetically visioned. There are many things in this book that are unforgettable; there are whole chapters that are masterpieces of delicate and restrained workmanship. Mr. Galsworthy has never written such beautiful English prose before."—*Standard*.

" Its truth is as unquestionable as its art is supreme. It is worth whole libraries of ordinary novels."—*Pall Mall Gazette*.

Also a cheap edition, 1s. net.

THE ISLAND PHARISEES. 6s.

" ' The Island Pharisees,' in its mixture of strength, deliberation of purpose, perfection of detail, and transparent sincerity, is a book which stands distinct and clear as a work of conspicuous power."—*Nation*.

" It is a subtle and delicate analysis . . . an eloquent and valuable book."—R. A. Scott James in the *Daily News*.

" A masterly work, strong, vivid, observant, and stimulating . . . so vivid in its intensity that it seems to shine out above anything else that is being produced in contemporary fiction. Mr. Galsworthy has served a long apprenticeship and has reached the fulness of his powers. He is one of the few novelists who really count, and it is safe to prophesy for him an ever-increasing fame."—*Daily Mail*.

" There is no writer of our time in whose career and intellectual development a keener interest is felt than in that of Mr. Galsworthy. He is continually developing. . . . His is a fine and generous attitude, and we do not think that anyone who has carefully and impartially considered the matter will disagree with the conclusions he arrives at in his book. He is working towards a good end. . . . The book has a great deal of charm."—*Country Life*.

Also a cheap edition, 1s. net.

THE WORKS OF JOHN GALSWORTHY

THE MAN OF PROPERTY.   6s.

" The foundation of Mr. Galsworthy's talent, it seems to me, lies in a remarkable power of ironic insight combined with an extremely keen and faithful eye for all the phenomena on the surface of the life he observes. These are the purveyors of his imagination whose servant is a style clear, direct, sane, illumined by a perfectly unaffected sincerity. It is the style of a man whose sympathy with mankind is too genuine to allow him the smallest gratification of his vanity at the cost of his fellow-creatures . . . sufficiently pointed to carry deep his remorseless irony, and grave enough to be the dignified vehicle of his profound compassion. . . . From laboriously collected information, I am led to believe that most people read novels for amusement. . . . If they want amusement they shall find it between the covers of this book. They shall find amusement and perhaps something more lasting—if they care for it. . . . Mr. Galsworthy will never be found futile by anyone, and never uninteresting by the most exacting."—JOSEPH CONRAD in the *Outlook*.

Also a cheap edition, 1s. net.

THE PATRICIAN.   6s.

" It is a joy to read this book, to know that here is a true writer seeking the truth and the expression of it. ' The Patrician ' is like a beautiful frieze on marble. It marks the writer of it, with his ' Strife ' and certain short stories, as our first English writer."—*English Review*.

" Mr. Galsworthy's reputation as a novelist will be greatly enhanced by the publication of his latest work, ' The Patrician. . . . Its triumph is undoubted."—*Morning Post*.

" Certainly one would say that, if ever there was a work of pure art it was Mr. Galsworthy's novel ' The Patrician.' In its delicacy, its suavity, and its underlying incisiveness, a very Vandyke of literary portraiture."—WM. ARCHER in the *Morning Leader*.

POETRY.

MOODS, SONGS, AND DOGGERELS.   5s. net.

" Finely inspired work. . . . Mr. Galsworthy's first appearance as a poet is in every way a memorable literary event, and it gives his admirers an opportunity of seeing him and judging in a new and extremely fascinating light."—*Liverpool Post*.

" Mr. Galsworthy's work is delightful, admirably in hand, and much of it delightfully light and delicate. . . . Without splendour or tricks, pretension, or abandonment, it is strong and inspiriting work. With this volume Mr. Galsworthy comes to a place of some distinction in contemporary poetry."—*Manchester Guardian*.

" This rich and praise-compelling book is the studied speech of a man dowered with gifts, but no less dowered with proud sincerity."—*Pall Mall Gazette*.

" Very finely and gravely written . . . full of fine words and phrases."—*Evening News*.

STORIES AND ESSAYS.

A MOTLEY. 6s.

" The seriousness, the individuality, the technical skill of these sketches are enough to place their author among the writers of to-day who can justly claim consideration as artists."— *Spectator.*

" Undeniably it is a clever book. There are pages of a fine grimness, and others of a delicate tenderness. In some, triviality is brilliantly shown in its essential importance."—*Evening Standard.*

THE INN OF TRANQUILLITY : Studies and Essays. 6s.

" He voices the spirit of the age, the new spirit that has, as yet, ' no language but a cry.' Here is a man who has speech, and there is nothing that must abide his question, nothing but must come under the searching criticism of the new day; to all existing institutions he cries aloud his bold ' Why ?' and the forts of the past must be able to answer or prepare to fall. He stirs the mind from sluggish lethargy; he is mental oxygen; he interprets that vast questioning attitude that is the forerunner of change."—*Country Life.*

" It is a sober, restful, and gentle book. Through it shines with almost too intimate a sense of personality the sensitive, perplexed temperament of the fastidious and reflective weaver of exquisite words."—*Punch.*

THE LITTLE MAN AND OTHER SATIRES. 6s.

" No lover of Galsworthy would like to miss this volume, which should win new and wider appreciation of his great gifts and power."—*Literary World.*

" This book emphasizes all that the author stands for and all that has given him so indispensable a place in modern literature."—*Daily News.*

A SHEAF. 6s.

" Both as a pleader and a moralist Mr. Galsworthy is inspired by that bright persuasive influence which can only spring from self-evident and open-hearted sincerity. He is earnest and he is consistent. The spiritual assaults of the last two years have only served to strengthen in him that deep humane creed which he urged upon us in the days of nonchalance, when we dreamt that we were all at ease in our inns, and that life was going very well in a world of comfortable and comforting convenience."—*Outlook.*

" Mr. Galsworthy is always individual, always clear, and always consistent, and the book is helpful and stimulating."—*Daily Express.*

WILLIAM HEINEMANN, 21 BEDFORD STREET, LONDON, W.C. 2